BLUE WATER SCARLET TIDE

BLUE WATER SCARLET TIDE

BY

JOHN DANIELSKI

WWW.PENMOREPRESS.COM

ISBN-13: 978-1-942756-96-5(Paperback)
ISBN :-978-1-942756-97-2(e-book)

BISAC Subject Headings:
FIC014000FICTION / Historical
FIC032000FICTION / War & Military

Editing: Chris Wozney

Cover Illustration by Christine Horner

Address all correspondence to:

                    Penmore Press LLC
                    920 N Javelina Pl
                    Tucson AZ 85748

DEDICATION

This book is dedicated to Calvin Comfort, a good friend who departed this life far too soon.

Chesapeake Bay: 24 July, 1814

CHAPTER ONE

The salt water churned past Thomas Pennywhistle's naked body as his muscled arms and legs propelled him forward. Bear grease covered his skin in a thick, slick layer, giving it the matte black color of an eel's hide. The coating absorbed the reflected glare from the bright moonlight and rendered him nearly invisible to unfriendly eyes, as well as preventing the water from leeching the warmth from his blood. Even in summer, the Chesapeake was veined with cold undercurrents.

The tide rose and a slight current pushed him forward. A night breeze rippled the surface of the Bay and stirred the hot, humid Maryland air. The approach to the mouth of the Patuxent River looked clear. Pennywhistle focused on his breaths and the rhythmic movement of the water sluicing past his scissoring legs. He shuttered his mind against random thoughts and poured his energy into the goal of reaching the distant shore. He was towing a heavily tarred bag that slowed his passage, but it could not be helped: the bag contained the tools for the night's work. The cutlass and scabbard on a cross-belt strapped to his back increased the drag as well. He hoped swordplay would not be necessary, but it was as well to be prepared.

He had swum a mile and a half and had another quarter mile to go. No one would be expecting an approach of this sort. Plenty of alert eyes watched for boats, but none for a single man whose head did not even show above the chop of the small waves.

His muscles performed admirably, as he had schooled them to do. Rather than growing fatigued, he was sustained by surges of energy which made him feel powerfully alive. He had felt fear and excitement in the first minutes of his swim: normal enough; but they had been replaced by a calm, meditative state as his senses stretched to their farthest boundaries of awareness. He adjusted his stroke rhythm to the rolling motion of the waves.

He had first paddled in the Tweed River in Scotland when he was three, and he'd loved the water ever since. It puzzled him that a considerable number of officers in the Royal Navy had never learned to swim.

Pennywhistle caught sight of a large dorsal fin several yards away on his port side. Its owner circled three times, each circle closer and slower than the last. On the final pass, the shark's pectoral fin glided by within a foot of his face. In awed fascination, he gaped into the obsidian abyss of its right eye. He sensed no intelligence, only a relentless hunger. Rows of triangular upper teeth and pointed lower teeth made its mouth a series of giant hunting knives with serrated blades, useful for tearing large prey into digestible chunks.

This leviathan was a Great Hammerhead, an aggressive subspecies uncommon in the Chesapeake. Its head was wider across than he was tall, and there was a good twenty feet between its snout and tail. He wondered what had drawn the monster to visit these waters. Did it sense, in some incomprehensible way, the advent of carnage?

He was being appraised. Icy tendrils of fear slithered up his back. The creature conjured ancient memories of mankind's most primal terror: being naked and defenseless before a gigantic, ravenous animal. He knew his best defense was an even, uniform motion through the water. He did not deviate from his chosen course—only prey flee a predator—and he overrode his fear with an even deeper attention to his breathing.

Sharks were not particularly interested in humans. They wanted an easy kill and sought the weak and injured of any species. They looked for odd, uncoordinated motions, what you'd expect from a wounded animal or a panicked man. His steady strokes and disciplined kicks sent the message that he was a strong, powerful creature who would be a poor choice for a meal.

The shark paralleled his course for two minutes, during which he aged two years, then it suddenly veered off. Its presence had reminded him that he, too, was a predator. He hoped to cause as little death as possible, but one way or another, he would bring his man out alive. The Americans intended to hang Lieutenant Marcus Chalmers tomorrow morning because he had infiltrated their lines foolishly wearing civilian clothes instead of his uniform.

The Americans were within their rights to proclaim him a spy, but they knew full well he was a British serving officer and entitled, by moral if not legal right, to treatment as a prisoner of war. Formal efforts to secure his release through a prisoner exchange cartel had been rebuffed.

The Americans had been just as bull-headed in the War of Independence and had hanged Major John Andre for the same thing; Washington had ungallantly refused him the firing squad due an officer. The Americans were touchy about honor, and their normally civilized sense of disposition was seriously out of joint just now. They were smarting from the impact of Admiral George Cockburn's frequent and destructive raids along the Chesapeake. The prisoner had been an exploring officer, a Royal Marine just like himself, trained in covert reconnaissance. The Americans wanted to make an example of him, to send Cockburn a message that their coastline could not be penetrated with impunity.

Pennywhistle had only met the lieutenant twice, but quite liked him. Chalmers was a cheerful, solid, reliable officer. But his character was not the point; it was about principle. There were but five exploring officers, and they operated alone for extended periods behind enemy lines. They had pledged to never leave any of their brethren behind.

Pennywhistle swam determinedly for another twenty minutes, entering a cove on the south shore of the Patuxent. He noted the presence of pickleweed, jumea, and cordgrass, common markers of tidal flats. He was getting close.

A rotting scent of decaying plants pricked his nose. The unpleasant aroma was commonly referred to by sailors as the scent of land. Something slender and three feet long glided past him. Moonlight glinted off its mottled reddish skin, marking it as a copperhead; venomous, but its bite was seldom fatal. Bull frogs and cicadas, momentarily silenced, resumed their chorus after he, and the snake, passed. He could see the spit of land ahead and the tall cliff above. He expected to find it unguarded; any guards would be posted near the dock, half a mile away.

He hoped his contact was ready. Pennywhistle was doing something many deemed unthinkable, risking his life on a black man's word. He did not think he had misread the man. He knew character when he saw it, even if many Americans viewed slaves as less than human. He had treated Jed with the dignity he accorded any new acquaintance, and Jed had responded by giving him the particulars of Chalmers' confinement.

Pennywhistle knew from official communications that Chalmers was being held at the White Oak Plantation House. Mr. Edward Randolph, the owner, was a local militia chieftain as well as one of the most virulent Anglophobes in Congress. His estate encompassed 10,000 acres and more than 100 slaves. Jed was one of them. He had told Pennywhistle where the British prisoner was detained—a bedroom on the second floor—and the disposition of the guards: two within the house and six more near the dock. He'd warned Pennywhistle that the Americans anticipated a rescue attempt, but they expected it to be as forthright and showy as an advancing line of Redcoats: cutters and launches blazing straight up the main channel, packed to the teeth with armed men shouting at the tops of their lungs. That was Cockburn's flamboyant style. The militia regiment was camped a quarter mile away from the estate, ready to mount a spirited defense against a landing party. The house guards were in place to prevent any escape attempt by the prisoner, and to fire signal rockets to summon the militia in the unlikely event of trouble at White Oak.

Pennywhistle swam a few hundred feet more until it grew shallow enough for him to stand. He slogged ashore through an outcrop of tall reeds and sat down on the beach to compose himself and review his plans. This tiny backwater, guarded by steep cliffs, was too cramped to accommodate even a small landing force. But one determined man could penetrate where a show of numbers could not.

The marine walked five hundred yards along the beach and found the jolly boat that had been left for him, concealed beneath some recently cut brush and swamp grass. He cleared the brush and checked the small storage locker: plenty of provisions. It also contained a pair of nankeen trousers and a shirt. He smiled. He was eager to wipe off the layer of slime and get some real clothing on, but for now he still needed the grease for concealment from the bright moonlight.

Jed had done a fine job of stocking the boat. It had oars, as well as a stowed mast and sail. The breeze blew from the northwest, perfect for escaping into the Bay. Pennywhistle had no idea how Jed had procured the boat and transported it; but then, slaves performed many tasks on the plantation under minimal supervision and often knew more about the disposition of the property than the Master himself. Jed undoubtedly had had help. Slaves would do almost anything to help one of their own secure freedom. Knowing that Jed would quickly be identified as the inside man and flogged within an inch of his life, if not killed outright should he remain behind, Pennywhistle had told him, "Say your good-byes quietly today. You will be coming with us when we depart." The British rewarded those who assisted them. Jed would be a free man once he crossed British lines. Several hundred blacks had already fled bondage, to the intense chagrin of their American owners.

Pennywhistle rubbed his hands on reeds to cleanse them, then unsheathed his cutlass and flourished it a few times to make sure his hands were dry enough for a secure grip. Next he inventoried the contents of the waterproof bag, satisfied himself everything was undamaged, and tugged a pair of dark cutoff seaman's slops over his greasy hips. Swimming nude was efficient, but he had no wish to startle Jed or Lieutenant Chalmers.

He looked up at the chalk cliff towering a hundred feet above. Jeb had been correct: it would be a dangerous, laborious climb for a man unassisted, and Pennywhistle had no time to spare. He took out the modified pump pneumatic air gun from the tarred bag. The Austrian design dated to the 17th century, but he had altered it for reconnaissance missions. He checked the large reservoir of heavily compressed air in its oddly shaped butt and was relieved to see the psi level was where it should be. He had only enough air for one shot. *This had better work.*

He inserted the grappling hook and coiled rope into the large bore of the gun. The muzzle was a wide brass cup, similar to those found on weapons designed to launch grenades. He assessed the land beyond the cliff's edge, looking for indications of rocky or heavy ground cover, calculating angles and trajectories, then sighted the piece toward the top of the bluff, held his breath, and gently squeezed the trigger. There was no explosion, no smoke, no noise save a *pfft* that even he could barely hear over the sounds of the shore. The hook and rope shot silently through the night air and disappeared over the edge of the bluff. The grapnel head landed with a barely audible thump, and he tugged the rope carefully until resistance indicated the flukes had bitten strongly, possibly into the roots of an oak tree stump. The long rope tail snaked back down the cliff and dangled in front of him.

He hauled back and pulled the rope taut with all his might, then twined his hands and feet around the rope and began the climb up the cliff face. The narrow hempen rope was rough against his palms, but his hands were hardened by years of frequent soaking in pickle brine, a trick he had learned from an old boatswain's mate. It made his hands deadly in fights, and now his palms and fingers did not break or bleed as he pulled himself upwards, bunching and extending in the manner of a caterpillar.

He dropped into the tall grass at the top a few minutes later and wormed his way forward until he could peer through the foliage for a view of the plantation house. The moon and stars blazed brightly and gave more ambient light than was strictly good for a stealth approach. Insects chirped and clicked around him, and rustling noises heralded the movements of small animals. He was about to rise and proceed when he heard footfalls—faint, but coming closer. He stayed perfectly still and waited. It was a soldier, damn it, short, narrow-shouldered, and bow-legged.

The disheveled soldier lurched unsteadily forward, his musket slung carelessly over his left shoulder. He had an open bottle in one hand, from which he periodically took a huge gulp. He staggered and belched loudly, then he bent forward, laughed drunkenly, and expelled a long fart.

The small man was clearly militia on detached duty, not regular army. Evidently he had determined a good bender would brighten his spirits and make him forget his boredom. He was probably no threat, but it was foolish to take chances. Pennywhistle debated whether to kill him; that was surest, but from the man's unsteady gait he was probably not too far from passing out. The alcohol just needed a little assistance.

The marine waited until the soldier reeled past, then ghosted up behind him. His left arm retracted, then his hand flashed forward like a serpent striking. The heel of his palm

*

8

connected smartly with the base of the soldier's neck. He flailed briefly, dropping the bottle, then collapsed to the ground, unconscious.

Pennywhistle sprinted the hundred yards to the plantation kitchen. As was the case with most Maryland plantations, the kitchen was separate from the main house because of all of the heat it generated. Summers were sultry here, and the gentry wanted the main house kept as cool as possible.

Jed was waiting for him. In a low whisper, he informed Pennywhistle that the house was quiet now, all in it asleep, except for the guards.

"You go in the back way and use the servants' stairs. No guard there. Lieutenant Chalmers weren't real hungry when I laid out his last supper. Made sense, I guess, but he were real pleasant and polite. He going to die tomorrow morning, but he still got the grace to thank me for fetching him a meal. The guards in the entrance hall laughed when I brought his supper. 'Why waste good food on a dead man?' the ornery big one said." He handed Pennywhistle the key to a box lock. "I took this off the rack after I brought supper. Them no account guards didn't notice."

Pennywhistle heard a snuffling noise and noted a large bull mastiff sleeping in the corner, its legs twitching slightly as it pursued some quarry across the dreamscape. It looked a nasty beast; he was glad that it would not be prowling the halls tonight.

"Thanks, Jed, I am grateful. I could never have made it even this far without your help. Now, are you sure about the ambergris?"

"I am. Mistah Randolf invests a heap o' money in Nantucket whalers, and he be selling their ambergris to

Baltimore merchants. He got two big jars of it in the warehouse by the dock."

Ambergris was a greasy substance ejected from the intestines of sperm whales, and it was extremely valuable as a perfume additive. It also was an ingredient in the scented spermaceti candles favored by aristocrats; they burned long and bright, yet gave virtually no smoke. But to Pennywhistle, the only important consideration was that sizeable quantities of it would make an exciting and expensive fire that would divert attention away from the rescue.

"You mentioned there is a back way into the warehouse?"

"Yes, Cap'n. I checked earlier tonight. The guards be lookin' at the Bay in front of them, not the House behind. But Mistah Randolf got lots of stuff in the warehouse. Got half a dozen barrels of powder stored there for the militia, too."

"Excellent! Meet me at the cliff in twenty minutes. Be clear: the mission comes first. I cannot wait for you. If you do not make the rendezvous, I must leave without you." His words were hard, but he tempered them with a look of genuine compassion. "I have my duty. You understand that, don't you?"

"Yes, Cap'n, I do. I am right grateful for a chance to leave all this. My wife be dead and my children sold down the river; ain't nothing for me here."

Pennywhistle extended his hand. Jed looked blank for a second, then his eyes welled. He took Pennywhistle's hand tentatively at first, then shook it vigorously. A white American gentleman never offered his hand in fellowship to a slave.

"I'll see you at the rendezvous." Pennywhistle turned and loped towards the warehouse, four hundred yards distant.

"Godspeed, Cap'n."

The ground was open and he was fully exposed, so Pennywhistle put on a burst of speed. When he reached the southwest corner of the long, weather-beaten warehouse, he stopped and crouched low. The full moon gave good illumination; he examined the clapboards carefully until he found a large X marked with chalk. He pressed his fingers against the boards beneath, and they felt soft and spongy. He positioned himself on his back and kicked the boards as hard as he could, wishing he had his heavy hessian boots instead of bare feet. There was no splintering nose, just a mushy thud as the rotten wood gave way. He sat up and widened the breach with his hands. It was small, barely wide enough to crawl through, but it would serve. The grease on his skin made squirming through easier.

Once inside, he crawled a few feet to the left and found the lantern Jed had left. He drew a flint and striker from his tarred bag, lit the lantern, held it high, and panned it in a semi-circle. The warehouse contained a variety of items, all valuable, most of them also combustible: everything from bales of cotton to bolts of fine wool. Mr. Randolph had eclectic tastes. He was one of the most vocal War Hawks in Congress, a man who rattled on about teaching the British a lesson. He was about to get a taste of his own medicine.

Pennywhistle discovered the ambergris easily, guided to it by a pungent aroma that was distinctive. There were probably ten pounds of it in two large blobs—a small fortune. Then he spied the ninety-pound barrels of powder. They were ten yards from the two glass preserve jars containing the waxy, dark grey substance. The powder would provide the ignition, but the ambergris would be a splendid accelerant and give the fire force and staying power.

He extracted two long waterproof fuses from his sack, color-coded red to indicate a ten-minute burn time. One fuse was usually sufficient, but he liked to add a second for insurance. Ten minutes was cutting it short, but the longer the burn time, the greater the risk of a misfire. He unfurled the fuses' long tails carefully to make sure there were no constrictions or humps that could interfere with a clean burn. He laid the fuses under two powder barrels five yards apart. Next he extracted his Blancpain watch from the tarred bag and checked the time. The fireworks would start at midnight. He lit both fuses, and they flared evilly into life. He dove to the floor and wiggled his way through the tight opening into the muggy night air. He leaped to his feet and raced across the grounds toward the plantation house.

He was congratulating himself on his cleverness and mentally calculating the progress of the fuses when he slammed headlong into a sentry listlessly walking his post who'd just turned a corner. Pennywhistle staggered and the other man went down with a surprised yelp. Pennywhistle smelled rum on the American's breath. Did all militia men drink like Cossacks? As the sentry rose unsteadily to his feet, Pennywhistle's fist smashed into his chin and he went down again, thrashing about like a beached fish. Pennywhistle kicked him hard at the base of the skull and he stopped moving. The marine continued on his way.

Soon he was mounting the short stairs of the back veranda, silent as a cat. He stopped, checked every direction, and listened intently at the door, his cutlass held in readiness for any eventuality. Hearing only silence on the other side, he opened the door and stepped through. The back hall was dark, quiet, and deserted. He located the cramped servants' staircase and walked up stealthily, cutlass advanced. At the top of the stairs he reconnoitered. No guards present; likely the lazy yokels had removed themselves to the entrance hall instead of maintaining a dedicated surveillance outside the prisoner's room. A light shone under a single door. Chalmers was awake; good. He'd probably figured there was no point to squandering his few remaining hours of life in sleep.

Pennywhistle thrust the large key into the heavy box lock and turned it quickly. He heard a distinctive *click* and pushed the door hard. It flew open to reveal the very startled face of Chalmers, a book held open in his hands. The flickering candle gave uncertain light, but Pennywhistle could make out it was Gibbon's *The Decline and Fall of the Roman Empire*. A strange literary choice for a final night of life, but then exactly what was appropriate? Chalmers clapped the book shut and shot to his feet, a broad smile on his face. He advanced quickly and extended his hand, which Pennywhistle shook vigorously.

"By God, Tom, you are a sight! I'd swear you were Beelzebub's right hand man! Can't say I am mad about your tailor. I knew if they sent anyone, it would be you. I assume you have a plan."

"I do indeed, Mark. You may not know it, but you have a real friend among the slaves here."

"Jed? He's displayed more kindness toward me then the two arrogant Yank guards in the hall. They have deviled me for the past two days. They are low, cowardly whelps who can't stand the sight of a gentleman with the King's Commission. I am sick to death of their ballyragging. I know not all the Jonathans are like that, but they have left a bad taste in my mouth. I'd love to have a go at both those sorry-arsed blockheads with a gun or a sword, although I'd settle for fists."

Pennywhistle smiled in understanding. Nothing galled seasoned professionals more than arrogant amateurs acting as their wardens.

13

"Wish I could oblige you, Mark, but we only have a few minutes until the Jonathans figure things out. Jed's coming with us. I have a boat on the beach and the wind is fair for Tangier." Tangier Island was the main British base in the Chesapeake and a day's sail if the wind held.

Boom! The window panes vibrated and lurid lances of flame shot into the night sky.

"What the devil is that?" exclaimed Chalmers.

"Diversion. Give the Yanks something to do. Come, we haven't much time."

Chalmers threw on his round hat and scarlet coat, then he and Pennywhistle moved into the hall. Pennywhistle caught the dull thud of boots clomping up the stairs and stopped short. He made a quick two-fingered motion to Chalmers, who nodded agreement. The bored guards had apparently heard the explosion and were headed to the second floor for a better view out the great bow window. Chalmers was about to have his wish granted.

The two marine officers crouched low on either side of the head of the staircase and exchanged hand signals: Chalmers would take the first soldier, Pennywhistle the second.

The guards held their weapons carelessly, oblivious to the danger. Chalmers lay on his side and waited until the first man had advanced onto the landing, then the marine's boots lashed out. One foot locked the first guard's ankle firmly in place while the other booted heel kicked the man's right knee. The crushing hold caused him to cry out and crash heavily to the floor. Chalmers grabbed the rude guard's head, yanked the neck taut and twisted violently to the right. There was a sharp *snap* and darkness blanked the American's eyes.

Pennywhistle had silently drawn his cutlass. The second guard saw and heard nothing as the razor sharp blade impaled his heart from behind. He gasped once, dropped to his knees, and sank to the floor.

Pennywhistle wiped and sheathed his sword, and the two marines ran down the back stairs and out into the night. Silhouettes dashed by in the darkness, shouting, cursing, and gesticulating in the moonlight. A fire bell sounded its dread knell in the distance.

Blue rockets flashed into the sky, summoning the militia. A regiment of thinly trained, part-time soldiers would probably only add to the confusion. Still, if an enterprising officer had the wit to conduct a systematic sweep of the grounds, it would make things hot for him and Chalmers.

The dock area was a chaotic whirlpool, sucking in soldiers and civilians. They dashed about, grabbing fire buckets and running off towards the warehouse, sloshing most of the water out of the buckets as they ran. Someone was trying to organize a line to pass buckets from the well to the fire, but he did not appear to be succeeding. The shooting flames weirdly outlined the mob against the night sky, and the fact that the fire was powerful enough to do so indicated the disorganized fire brigade was already too late. Pennywhistle estimated the goods going up in smoke were worth a quarter of a million dollars and would take a serious bite out of the local economy, certainly a boon to the British war effort. Mr. Randolph and a lot of Baltimore merchants would be very upset, and they would lay the blame squarely on Cockburn's doorstep. The British admiral was already the most hated man in America; a little more vitriol directed his way would trouble him not at all.

The two marines jogged to the edge of the cliff to find the grapnel and rope intact, but no sign of Jed. They turned round, moved a few yards forward, and flopped down on their bellies beside a small, dry, stream bed. Chalmers looked anxiously at Pennywhistle. "Let's give him a while longer. I'm willing to chance it," he said.

"I am too, but no more than ten minutes," Pennywhistle replied.

Five minutes later, however, a mounted militia officer cantered into view, followed by at least four companies of infantry. It was a prompt response and the men marched in good order. The column halted and a man ran up to a tall officer. Pennywhistle could not hear the words, but from the vigorous gesticulating it was clear they knew Chalmers had slipped the noose. The officer shouted some orders, and troops spread themselves out in a loose skirmish line. They began a slow, steady advance toward the marines' position. They were out of time.

Just then, Jed raced out of the darkness, heading directly for their position. He ran with the energy of a man grasping for a bright new life just out of reach. Two soldiers were in hot pursuit, twenty yards behind. Pennywhistle swore under his breath. A jolt of adrenaline shot through him and it took every ounce of his self-control to restrain himself from rising and dashing forward. One of the soldiers stopped and raised his weapon. He fired, and Jed pitched violently forward.

Pennywhistle looked at Chalmers and saw the same expression of anger and frustration he knew must be on his own face. They very badly wanted those two soldiers dead. But they were both professionals and made the hard choice, consonant with duty although strongly opposed to personal feelings. Even had they been armed and fired, they would have given away their position to the militia. Jed was gone, and nothing could change that. The hardest test for men of action was to know when not to act.

Pennywhistle jerked his head towards the cliff. They slithered the last few yards to the grappling hook as the light infantry continued to advance slowly on their position, like beaters on a Scots grouse hunt. Chalmers grabbed the rope and began his descent. Pennywhistle followed quickly. Pennywhistle's feet had just touched the ground when he felt puffs of air zip past his face. He looked up and saw the outlines of men with guns at the top of the cliff. Popping noises followed, and bits of sand flew up on either side of him. "Don't let the spies get away!" someone yelled. "They must have a boat!" shouted another. Two men started down the rope, and more looked eager to follow.

As Chalmers turned to the boat, Pennywhistle scraped some of the grease off his body and swabbed it onto the rope; grease atop the dry hempen rope would make it burn very quickly. He set it alight with flint and striker, and the fire sped up the rope like a long finger reaching toward the two descending militia men. The top one was able to scramble back over the edge of the cliff, but his mate was not so lucky. Flames engulfed his body and he relinquished his grip with a cry, then he screamed as he fell. He landed with a dull *whump!* a yard from Pennywhistle and did not move.

His companions began firing ragged volleys from the cliff's edge amidst a chorus of curses and shouts. Bullets flew through the night air and pock-marked the beach sand just astern of Pennywhistle's racing feet. Despite the full moon and short range, militia marksmanship was poor and operated on the principle that if enough men fired into a small area someone was bound to get hit. Pennywhistle felt something pluck at his hair as he dove into shallow water.

Chalmers had already manhandled the boat into the water; Pennywhistle slithered aboard and together they hoisted the mast and ran up the large driver as a hail of bullets, mercifully depleted of force by the distance, pattered around them. Pennywhistle manned the helm while Chalmers adjusted the sail. A steady six-knot breeze coming over the port quarter filled the sail and shoved them forward. The boat surged through the water, leaving behind a wake of twinkling phosphorescence. Within five minutes they had cleared the Patuxent and were standing out into the Bay. The full moon brilliantly illuminated a clear, sparkling path upon the water. With a little luck, they would be in Tangier by evening on the morrow.

The mission was a success, but all Pennywhistle felt was overwhelming sadness and regret. He saw the downcast expression on Chalmers face and knew it mirrored his own. A good man had died, and he had been unable to avenge his death. Jed had trusted him, and the only reward he got was an eternal one.

Both marines ate quietly and did not speak much. Neither was a stranger to death, but sometimes a particularly sad ending like Jed's shoved Bellona, Goddess of War, naked on to the stage. Stripped of her cloak of patriotic respectability, she was a shriveled old whore; skeletal, sunken eyed, and sickening to behold.

CHAPTER TWO

Two weeks after the rescue of Chalmers, Pennywhistle was in the field again, as were the other three exploring officers. Taken together, their reports would give Admiral Cockburn a reckoning of possible sites for a major landing.

Pennywhistle landed in a secluded spot while the upper curve of the sun was barely peeking above the horizon. Shapes were a soft blur in the humid, misty air, which provided good cover for a scout.

Two cardinals were singing a duet in a tree ahead. The local Piscataway Indians believed them harbingers of romance; if one crossed the path of single man, a good woman would soon make an appearance. *Would that legends were true,* he mused.

He'd allowed himself plenty of time to make the rendezvous with his intelligence source. The early hour, the shrouding mist, and the tranquility of the woods soothed him into carelessness. He had advanced fifty yards up the heavily forested trail from the Patuxent when a tall form materialized in front of him. The American leveled his musket and snarled, "No tricks, Englishman. Unbuckle your sword belt and lay down the cutlass. Do as I say and live, disobey me and die. My colonel will want to speak to you."

The Maryland Militia private held his Springfield musket uncertainly and his voice quivered slightly. Nevertheless, he had his finger on the trigger and could discharge his piece faster than Pennywhistle could close and bat it aside. The marine unclasped the fastener of his hunting frock and the garment dropped to the ground. His scarlet coat left no doubt about his allegiance; he was no Chalmers. He did as ordered, then put his hands up.

The American's homely face wore an expression of determination that did not match the voice. "This way, Englishman," he said, more sternly. He gestured with the bayonet on the end of his musket, "Up that trail. You go first; I will be right behind."

Blast! He didn't have time for some damn fool rustic determined to play the hero. At least the militiaman had not bothered to shout an alarm—he probably wanted to claim all the credit for the capture himself. The area was heavily wooded, with plenty of places to dump a body. Even if the American's corpse were discovered, the lack of bullet holes would proclaim him a victim of foul play or drunken quarrel, not military action. Just so: he wanted no trace of an English presence.

He regarded the militia private closely. Callow; he couldn't be more than eighteen. No doubt he wanted to impress his superiors. Presenting a trophy capture would demonstrate that he was a fire-eater, a man on the rise. But even though his prisoner was obviously an officer, the soldier had not addressed Pennywhistle as sir. The courtesies of war were clearly not part of his limited training, or perhaps it was just a reflection of the egalitarian attitude of this young republic. His captor contemptuously squirted a jet of tobacco juice that barely missed Pennywhistle's boots. Pennywhistle wrinkled his nose in distaste, glad he had never acquired the evil habit.

Pennywhistle assessed the private's clothing. The blue uniform coat was homespun, thin, and inexpensively dyed. The dirty white trousers looked to be of very cheap linen. His heavy brogans were old and battered; a left toe protruded. The man, no, the boy impersonating a man, had a day's growth of stubble on his cheeks and, young as he was, his tobacco-stained teeth were missing an upper right incisor. His wide chest, powerful arms, and deeply tanned hands suggested he was accustomed to heavy manual work outdoors—probably an agricultural laborer. He belonged behind a plough with a long life ahead, not playing soldier.

The boy was six feet of lean muscle, two inches shorter than Pennywhistle, but strong enough to put up quite a struggle if given half a chance, and his unit was probably close by. The thing had to be done quietly. Pennywhistle thought back to the Edinburgh anatomy theatre. *Ears, throat, clavicle.* Quick and clean; *savate* applied decisively.

He pasted a resigned look onto his face and sighed, as if accepting his fate. "You have the advantage of me, Private. I am unarmed, as you see. I charge you, on your honor, to escort me to your colonel without offering violence." The Englishman raised his hands even higher above his head to show he would cause no trouble. Even as he spoke, he was calculating how quickly he could reach the dirk hidden in the top of his right boot, if the inexperienced private proved so obliging as not to search him.

"I would love to smash your face in, you English bastard," growled the private. "I hate the fancy airs you people give yourselves. I wish I could return a little of the pain that devil Cockburn's dished out to my country, but the Colonel would be angry with me. My name is Private Carstairs, but I am pretty sure it will be Corporal Carstairs after I bring you in." He grinned now, with cocksure arrogance. "You got a name, Redcoat?"

"It's Captain Pennywhistle to you, Private." He spoke in a quietly firm schoolmaster's voice, as if instructing a dim child.

"That's sure an odd name, but I guess it don't matter none. It's what you know that counts, and I bet you know a heap. Let's get moving. Fall in ahead of me, Englishman." He snarled the words, enjoying his dominance of the enemy officer. "Do as I say." He poked his bayonet into the English officer's back. "Now move, and do it damned quick!"

Pennywhistle walked slowly, his step resigned and deliberate, the steel at his back prodding him along. "My arms grow tired. Might I put them down for just a bit, Private?"

"Go ahead," said the private contemptuously. "All you English officers are lazy hounds."

He dropped his arms listlessly to his sides in a show of fatigue and despair. The bayonet jabbing his spine hurt, yet was just what he needed to calculate relative positions. In a blur of motion, his right arm stiffened and shot out behind him, knocking the musket barrel clear of his body as he simultaneously pivoted. The spin brought him face to face with his captor as his right arm continued to sweep the gun clear. He slammed the flat of his left hand hard against the Springfield, propelling the barrel away. It happened in a fraction of a second. Even an experienced soldier would have had trouble countering the move. The novice stood paralyzed with confusion.

Time slowed to a crawl, every detail frozen and outlined in clear focus.

Disorient. The marine's wide open hands swung upwards and he clapped them hard against Carstairs' ears. Such a blow not only killed the hearing but caused severe balance and depth perception problems.

Disarm. Pennywhistle stiffened his hands into vertical blades. Swiftly he raised them high above his head and struck down at the points where the left and right clavicles joined the neck. These bones were surprisingly fragile and snapped easily. The weapon clattered to the ground.

Disable. He shaped his left hand into a C and smashed hard with the palm heel at the Adam's apple. Carstairs croaked and staggered, unable to breathe, let alone shout.

Carstairs was defenseless. Time to be merciful and quick.

Pennywhistle whipped the dirk out of his boot, brought it round the back of the man's neck and stabbed at the base of the third cervical vertebra, severing the spinal column. There was little blood. Carstairs eyes went wide with shock as he crashed to the ground.

The marine steadied himself, and willed his racing heart to slow down. He looked at the American's unlined face; ordinary, naïve, wearing a frozen look of bewilderment. It was a sad waste, but war devoured lives like the locusts of Egypt devoured grain. He himself had been on the path to become a physician a thousand years ago. A foolish duel had changed everything. Knowledge of anatomy had proven useful on numerous occasions; it facilitated efficient killing just as much as it informed healing. The irony was poignant.

He reclaimed his hunting frock, refastened his sword belt, and then slung Carstairs' musket over his own left shoulder. He maneuvered the body and hoisted it over his right shoulder, then staggered a few hundred feet into deep woods and dumped the man unceremoniously among three rotten logs in a small ravine. He thought about retaining the musket but found its touch-hole so enlarged that most of the force of the main charge would vent through it and give the piece little hitting power. He clambered down and placed the weapon next to the private. He checked the man's canteen and his nose crinkled in disapproval. It reeked of frighteningly vile, potent whiskey. He poured the contents over the corpse, then covered it with branches and leaves. Unless you were standing directly over the site, nothing was visible. The smell might alert people eventually; the summer was sultry, but the forest creatures would inaugurate their own disposal program.

What was a private doing out alone several hundred yards from the main camp? Scouting? Foraging for food? The militia was notoriously ill supplied. There were also many small stills in the area. Likely Carstairs had just come from refilling his canteen.

He would put it all in his report. Information about militia readiness and training were of vital interest, since British regulars were invariably outnumbered.

Pennywhistle checked his watch. He could still make the rendezvous with Gabriel. He began walking, briskly now and belatedly alert, as his brain commenced an orderly review of landing site requirements.

He'd taken ten widely spaced soundings of the Patuxent River and drawn charcoal sketches of corresponding shorelines. Skilled draftsmanship was required of every exploring officer. The Chesapeake had an average depth of only 26 feet and was littered with shoals and sand bars that posed hazards to navigation; careful reconnaissance was required before any major movement of ships.

The Patuxent's mouth was 23 feet deep at high tide, 21 feet at low; deep enough for ships-of-the-line to pass, but the sites he had in mind were eight miles upriver. The frigates, sloops, smaller vessels, and troop transports could approach close in. Deeper draught ships-of-the-line, including Cockburn's flagship *Albion*, would have to anchor four miles downstream.

He had paid special attention to high and low tide variation, as well as wind direction, constancy, and strength —vital concerns for sailing ships. He had identified several wide, defensible beaches capable of accommodating numerous ships' boats, locations with mild currents and reasonable depths close to shore, so that the Fleet's frigates could provide covering fire for the landing. He wanted hard bottoms devoid of shoals, sand bars, or oyster beds that could ground boats. He'd also looked for serviceable roads that offered quick advance into the interior, and blocking points to frustrate counter attacks. He'd verified there were no garrisons of regular soldiers nearby. Other exploring officers had recommended landing sites farther north, but each had lacked at least one essential that Cockburn demanded, whereas the area around Benedict met every particular.

Benedict, Maryland was an old tobacco port of perhaps a thousand souls. Once a major shipping center, it was now merely a prosperous town. The flat Tidewater country was heavily forested in spots, laced with creeks, rivers, and inlets, providing plenty of opportunities for maritime invaders. The area was rich with a variety of seafood and livestock, as well as fields and farms fat with grains and produce: more than enough to supply a small army. Orchards dotted the area; he'd pilfered a small supply of tart Newtown Pippin apples. Their delicious flavor made the long hours of observation pass more enjoyably. There was plenty of potable water, and he'd identified numerous clearings in which to pitch tents.

The only possible naval opposition was Commodore Joshua Barney's flotilla of gunboats, eighteen miles up river near Nottingham. The river narrowed and grew shallow there; the Fleet's larger vessels would not be able to penetrate. Barney had launched a few raids against the British over the last month, playing cat-and-mouse and boosting American morale, but they were pinpricks of only nuisance value. Informants reported that Barney had made plans to defend his current position but had no intention of assuming the offensive. If a rumor could be circulated that the main target of the landing was the indefatigable Barney, it might provide cover for more important strategic considerations.

He had slept in a forest hide for the past three nights. The diverse scents and animal noises delighted his senses; so different from the tang of salt air, the moaning of ship's timbers, and the whistling of wind swaying rope on *Albion*. His bed of reeds was actually quite comfortable, shielded from all but the closest inspection by artfully arranged leaves, weeds, and brambles.

He'd brought ship's biscuit and salt pork, but had dispensed with them when his deadfall trap produced a deer. Dressing and carving the carcass gave him something to focus on, as well as fresh meat for the next several days. He stored the extra meat under rocks in a fast, cold, freshwater stream and thoroughly scoured the area before risking a camp fire. The venison steak provided a delicious conclusion to a day spent lying in patient concealment. The forest also furnished plenty of edible berries.

Despite America's reputation as a land of great woodsmen, he was far better adapted to the forest than most of the locals. They were prosperous, sedentary townsmen, with little interest in poking about heavy woods. His grandfather's estate in Scotland was different terrain, but the summers he'd spent there in the company of the chief ghillie had furnished him an intimate knowledge of woodcraft. He'd had to spend some time acquainting himself with the mixture of familiar and unknown trees and undergrowth, but the essential skills had served him well.

Pennywhistle was an anomaly, half scientific soldier and half wilderness long hunter. He could hold his own in learned conversation, but plunked down alone and weaponless in any forest, he would never starve. Conventional thinkers were bothered by their inability to properly place him, in an age in which every man was expected to have an exact societal niche. His education, speech, and polished manners proclaimed him a gentleman, but the more perceptive sensed it was but a veneer covering something frighteningly raw and deeply primal, a tiger amused to play the role of a house cat.

His cold rationality sometimes chaffed against a deeply hot, emotional inner self. The love of detached intellectual scholarship was a gift from his Scots mother. She had been raised by a wealthy father who was a good friend of the philosopher David Hume. James Murray had no son and hired a stable of tutors to furnish his daughter a rigorously cerebral education that properly belonged to the province of men. She grew into a frigidly analytical being who was a stranger to maternal feelings. She viewed her son not so much as a person but as a scientific experiment to be conducted with logic rather than love. She took great pains to make sure her son's education reflected the ideals of the Scottish Enlightenment: reason, empiricism, and skepticism directed toward bettering the lot of the individual as well as elevating the collective virtue of society. He had pledged those ideals to the military service of King and Country, but had lately begun to wonder if long-lasting war created its own peculiar agenda that served no society well.

His warm-hearted English father had bequeathed him a love of the vigorous life spent outdoors: hunting, fishing, and reveling in nature. "A good mind is a wonderful thing," he'd told his son, "but the body craves a close acquaintance with the earth which gives it life. *Mens sana in corpore sano.*"

Now the burnt-out cabin chosen for the rendezvous loomed a hundred yards ahead. He stopped and checked his Blancpain; 6 a.m. Gabriel was usually prompt.

Gabriel Prosser was his best intelligence asset. Trustworthy intelligence nearly always flowed from heartfelt belief and commitment; bribes or blackmail usually tainted a source. Gabriel was smart and perceptive; other slaves liked him and looked up to him. When he asked questions, they did their best to supply an answer, even if it involved prying into dangerous corners. He drank little, did not use tobacco, and had asked nothing in return for his help; he knew the British had freed many slaves, so he viewed them as liberators, not invaders. Privately, Pennywhistle had resolved he'd make certain Gabriel never spent another day in bondage once the mission was completed; he would not let this man suffer Jed's fate.

Gabriel walked up the trail five minutes later, a smile on his face. He was an affable man of perhaps twice the Englishman's years, his optimism a survival mechanism against the burdens of slavery, yet there was not a hint of servility about him. An innate sense of dignity shone through.

"Mornin, Cap'n. Another fine day on God's green earth. I got news for you 'bout those things you asked. Been talking to folk, specially Isaac."

"Excellent, Gabriel. Pray sit and be comfortable. I have narrowed the six locations we discussed at our last meeting to three possibilities. I need your expert opinion to make a final choice. Oh, I know it's early, but I thought a small wet might be in order: Scotland's finest export."

He always watched the alcohol consumption of his contacts to make sure they did not have too great an affinity for drink. It was a character test. Heavy drinkers were supremely cooperative, but often the information they brought was the product of imagination rather than solid investigation. Gabriel was always content with one small, sociable drink.

"Just one little one, Cap'n. Put some fire in the belly for the day to come."

Pennywhistle poured a small shot of Glen Garioch from an elegant silver flask into an inelegant tin cup. He handed it to Gabriel.

Gabriel sipped it slowly and smiled appreciatively. "I bet this be better than what the folk on the plantation drink. I'm lucky to have made your acquaintance, Cap'n."

Pennywhistle smiled back. "And I yours." Meeting Gabriel had been a matter of patience and asking the right questions. Pennywhistle had stayed hidden and observed the comings and goings at Calvert's Fortune, the largest plantation in the area. He'd watched for careless overseers, then picked out isolated slaves on the edges of fields. His stone jug full of very old, very smooth Scots Whiskey lured men by its scent alone. His accent and a flash of scarlet convinced slaves he meant them no harm. Most slaves hated their lot, despite America's blather about their great contentment, and would talk to a plain-dealing British gentleman who listened with understanding and treated them with respect. He'd repeatedly inquired, "Who do you trust the most? I require the assistance of a man whose character, conduct, and knowledge are beyond reproach."

"Gabriel Prosser" was the nearly unanimous reply. Gabriel had been taught to read and write—a sign he had been singled out for his intelligence and reliability. Gabriel would have access to high level information, for Calvert fielded the best pack of foxhounds in Maryland and only the rich and powerful were allowed to participate in his hunts. Nonetheless, Gabriel's loyalty was superficial, since Calvert was notorious for capriciousness and casual cruelty.

A field hand named Sharper had told Pennywhistle he would convey a message to Gabriel and arrange a meeting. As Sharper described the secure channels by which the message would be passed, Pennywhistle realized that slaves had developed clandestine methods, sources, and lines of communication that amounted to a disciplined underground intelligence network that went wholly unnoticed by men schooled to believe that blacks never reasoned beyond the level of children. It was similar to networks established by French and American POW's at Dartmoor Prison to fox their British captors, but more elaborate and effective. When they needed real privacy, slaves spoke in a patois derived from African roots. That patois was as incomprehensible to whites as if it had been encoded into the most advanced European intelligence ciphers.

Pennywhistle unfurled a map and showed it to Gabriel. "The three best possibilities for a landing are Bartram's Cove hard by Glebe Gut, Aubrey's Inlet, and Bailey's Point. Which do you think best? I scouted them all and drew sketches, but I lack a local's experience and it's easy to miss things: unexpected riptides, sinkholes, and drop-offs, as well as hidden underwater obstacles. Old unmarked shipwrecks can be a particular problem."

Gabriel examined the map and pointed to one of three x's. "I'd say Bartram's Cove be best, Cap'n. I fished it lots o' times with Mastah Calvert's son. It's got a nice sandy bottom with an easy grade; no drop-offs or sinkholes, and a meek current. No wrecks. It's three feet deep close to shore for nigh on two miles, so boats can approach real close, and the sand near to shore is firm, it won't sink feet. Course, I ain't sure just how many boats you be bringing."

The marine shook his head. "I cannot tell you that, for I do not know; let's just say it will be more than two."

"I heard talk when company was over. They say your people will strike at Baltimore. Me, I think it be Washington."

"Think what you will, Gabriel. I am not privy to Admiral Cockburn's plans, but he does need every scrap of information so he may have the widest possible range of options."

Gabriel suddenly jerked his head toward the woods. He cupped his hand to his ear and put a finger to his lips.

Pennywhistle heard it then, very faint: voices and the tread of feet coming up the narrow trail. He put his ear to the ground and listened. It sounded like four or five men. Not a good omen at this early hour. He gestured to the field of tall reeds behind the cabin. Gabriel acknowledged with a quick nod. They took cover among the reeds, lay flat on their bellies, and waited.

Four middle-aged men approached, all well dressed and carefully groomed. They looked relaxed and happy, like little children about to be handed new toys. They obviously had not been trailing Gabriel. What business did they have coming to an old burnt out cabin at six in the morning?

"We should move everything to my warehouse in Alexandria," a tall man, elegantly dressed in blue velvet, was saying. Pennywhistle wondered what sort of man would wear such heavy stuff in the present heat. Probably a man whose need to proclaim his status outweighed comfort. "I worry that someone might stumble on our treasure by accident; all sorts of wanderers are about in the woods. It is imperative we move the gold."

Gold? Four prosperous gentlemen moving gold in the early morning made no sense at all. They looked to be merchants, not prospectors. There were a few small gold mines in North Carolina, but none anywhere near the Chesapeake. Gold coins were much prized in America for the simple reason they were hard to come by. Gold fever explained their expressions. He had seen it before—men bewitched by what he regarded as merely a useful heavy metal.

Perhaps some sort of treasure was hidden nearby. Pirates? He laughed inwardly. Pirates were not dashing corsairs but foolish brigands who squandered their money quickly; they never buried it. No, whatever gold was out there had a much more prosaic source.

"Robert is right," said a shorter, bald man in a bright red waistcoat. "We should move the gold today. It's been two months since *Surly,* and most folks have forgotten. No one has made the connection with us. Right now, everyone is worried about the British, and I doubt anyone is going to care *how* we laid our hands on the gold." The man beamed when he said the word *gold* with a nearly lascivious leer.

"What happened with *Surly* wasn't our fault anyway," said a thin one in a bottle-green frock coat. "We just hired the wrong captain. He didn't rein in the men. So he killed some British tars, so what? That ogre Cockburn has a few less shellbacks; that's hardly a bad thing. The British do not know what happened, that is the significant point. The captain's kept his mouth shut; he wants his cut." The third man's contempt was obvious. He spat out tobacco juice.

"But their captain had surrendered!" observed a portly one in a tall top hat. "He took twenty of our men down but lost half his crew. He did not deserve to be murdered! The sailors were drunk when they took *Surly*, that's why they got out of hand. They have big mouths when they drink, too. It's just a matter of time before one goes on a spree and starts talking." The worry in his voice was plain. "My reputation as a man of honor must never be impugned!" he added indignantly.

"The captain took care of that," said the tall man in blue velvet. "Bought 'em all plenty of rum one night, then dropped 'em aboard a whaler. They will be gone at least two years." He laughed. "We have covered our tracks just fine. It's safe to start spending some of the money."

Pennywhistle's face flooded with blood to a deep crimson and a blazing surge of anger shot through him; his emerald eyes burned with the fury of Alecto. Everything was suddenly as clear as the conclusion was dark. HMS *Surly* had been carrying an army payroll, golden guineas, and was thought to have foundered in a gale. She had been a single-masted cutter of 137 tons armed with ten small four-pounders and a crew of fifty. A slow, somewhat clumsy sailor, she could have easily been run down by a sleek Baltimore privateer with twice her crew and twice her armament.

He had met her commander, Lieutenant Lucas, upon his arrival in America. Lucas had seemed a stalwart enough fellow and had evidently put up a stiff fight. Instead of the traditional honorable captivity, he and his men had been butchered by an ill-disciplined prize crew. It was an outrageous violation of the laws of war.

These four men were what the Prince Regent called pinks; fastidiously dressed and groomed members of the local *bon ton* who were greatly concerned with appearances. They were the owners of the privateer and did not want to look like anything less than solid moral pillars of society. Now that their reputations were safe, the coins could be melted down and recast. They could spend their blood money freely. They had not committed murder themselves, but they had directly financed it and planned to profit from it.

It was not his job to play the part of Tisiphone and administer blood justice, but it was certainly part of his duty to recover any portion of the gold he could. The loss of the payroll had understandably upset the army, and its recovery would be treated as a gift from heaven. He would let these pinks lead him to the payroll.

The four walked purposefully around the rear of the cabin, not more than ten feet from where the two men lay. With some effort, they slid aside an uprooted tree stump, kicked dirt away, and opened a trap door. They descended some steps and vanished from sight.

A dark part of Pennywhistle demanded these men to pay for Lucas and his crew, but his better angel murmured the harshest punishment would not be blood but deprivation. They had gold fever, the Midas madness; he would ensure their lust remained painfully unrequited. It would be like batting away an opium addict's pipe at the last second. They all carried swords, but he judged they'd have much less skill than he did. Gentlemen practiced, but their goal was usually to score and satisfy honor, not to kill outright. None of them looked to be very fit, and one was quite portly. Genuine swordsmen were usually lithe and spry like panthers, or muscled like tigers.

He had only his cutlass. His Ferguson Rifle would have made things much easier, but he had anticipated only a short, secretive mission and had left it concealed in the jolly boat. He considered the factors, and the odds. A sudden appearance, absolute confidence, and the threat of bloodshed —theirs—might serve to overawe them.

The four emerged from the hide a while later, chortling and laughing in discordant keys that made them sound like a chorus of the damned. Each carried a heavy canvas sack emblazoned with the letters *GR* with a crown above. Their eyes glittered with avarice and their lips curled in rictus smiles—common symptoms of gold fever.

Pennywhistle rose silently from the tall grass, drew his sword, and strutted forward with every ounce of arrogance he could summon. He halted directly in front of the startled pinks. He unfastened the neck clasp and cast off the hunting frock to reveal his lustrous scarlet coat and gleaming gold epaulettes. The four men turned white as sheets and froze. They looked as if they were seeing the devil himself, and in a way, perhaps they were.

"Good morning, gentlemen." He smiled and spoke in friendly, cheerful tones. "It was very kind of you to recover King George's gold for me. You have saved me a great deal of time and effort. If you will please deposit the bags on the ground and retire whence you came, there need be no unpleasantness. We British value *detente* and concord and disdain unnecessary bloodshed."

The man in blue velvet recovered first. "I think perhaps you misread the situation, sir," he drawled. "There are four of us and one of you. We are all armed. We have all read Angelo's treatise and practice his evolutions with our fencing master weekly. I would say it is you who should retire." He flashed a cocky smile and seemed well pleased with his bravado; his colleagues were clearly impressed. He touched the hilt of his sword, his intention clear.

Pennywhistle shook his head and laughed loudly at the misplaced confidence of un-blooded amateurs. Gold fever often overpowered common sense. The four men looked at each other in puzzlement.

Training was useful but there was no substitute for experience. The training salon bore the same relation to the battlefield as a riding a hobby horse did to riding a real one. Intricate, beautifully choreographed evolutions usually failed in the face of simple, practical maneuvers pressed home with determination. With no practice fighting at the hazard of their lives, the pinks might as well have been taking lessons from a dancing master.

Pennywhistle sighed in gentle exasperation. "I am doing you a great kindness. I will allow you to walk out of here with your lives if you will but see reason. Far more generous then what your hirelings allowed Lieutenant Lucas on *Surly*." His emerald eyes flashed, hard and grim; his voice dropped an octave. "Lay the gold and your weapons on the ground, and back away slowly."

The four pinks saw the steel in his expression. Three of them dropped their bags in front of them and began to unbuckle their sword belts, but "No!" Robert, the leader in blue velvet, shouted at his fellows. He put down his bag of gold, but straddled it. It was a possession to be defended, not an offering. He drew his sword and advanced it belligerently, glaring at Pennywhistle. "We have come too far to lose it all to this damn interloper. He's only an errand boy, a pedigreed pansy in a fancy uniform. We can handle him!" The other three hesitated, then drew their swords and moved closer to their comrade.

Gabriel rose from his concealment, brandishing a stout tree branch as a club. He walked purposefully over to Pennywhistle and stared angrily at the four men. "Can I help, Cap'n?"

"No," said Pennywhistle firmly. "Thanks, but they are my problem."

Robert sneered. "See boys, he's just a no account, nigger-lovin' swell."

The expression on Pennywhistle's face hardened to something implacable. With a swift motion he consulted his timepiece, marking the position of the second hand before returning it to his pocket. "Time's up, gentlemen," Pennywhistle stated coolly. "This is your final warning to put your swords away and enjoy what remains of your contemptible lives." His voice deepened in anger as he spoke and he spat the last two words.

The four stepped forward, swords advanced, safety in numbers, by way of an answer. He grinned fiercely. He was going to enjoy this. Justice would be served. These despicable blackguards had less than a minute left to live.

The pinks expected preliminaries: artful steps in the service of a chess-like opening gambit. Instead, they got a quick, direct attack. Without any *en garde* of warning, Pennywhistle took two swift steps forward and lunged. The calf muscles of his extended left leg supplied raw power and his bent right knee provided guidance; the force of his thrust propelled the razor sharp cutlass tip under the leader's sternum. The marine saw the beating heart in his mind's eye and jabbed upwards toward its center. The man's blade jerked as his hand spasmed, then it fell from his suddenly nerveless grasp. His face bore a stunned expression as his knees buckled and he dropped to the ground.

The marine yanked his blade free even before the man collapsed. The leader was eliminated; the others would either flee or attempt to exact revenge. But Pennywhistle was determined that none of the pinks ever see another sunrise. The man in the red waistcoat was turning to confront the marine directly when the edge of Pennywhistle's sword ripped across the side of his neck. Blood jetted in spray and the man's head drooped in an unnatural angle as he gasped, and red froth bubbled from his mouth. Pennywhistle elbowed the falling corpse aside and parried a badly aimed cut to his head from the third man. He riposted with a thrust to the stomach—an abundant target. He twisted the blade to gore the man's insides and jerked it free. The astonished man howled, dropped his sword and fell to the ground, rolling in agony.

The thin man in the bottle green frock coat came at him from behind, but Pennywhistle had anticipated the move and pivoted to the side. He felt a rush of air, but the blade missed him and slashed only space, leaving the man over balanced and exposed. Pennywhistle whirled the rest of the way around, raised his blade high and amputated the man's sword hand with a ferocious downward stroke. The last pink stared in stupid disbelief at the blood spurting from the stump as Pennywhistle rammed the tip of his cutlass through the base of his throat.

Pennywhistle turned to the writhing man on the ground. He moaned horribly, as foul rivers of blood and feces flowed from his intestines. Left alone, he would suffer hours of living perdition before death claimed him. Pennywhistle mercifully thrust his cutlass through the man's temple and the noise ended. He braced his boot on the man's head and wrenched the blade clear.

He wiped the gore from his blade and sheathed his sword, then opened his watch case. One minute and fifty-one seconds. He frowned. Far too slow; he resolved to practice more. The four had been little more than armed parlor maids. He contemptuously shook his head and kicked each body carefully to make certain there was no movement.

Their deaths would occasion a great deal of outcry. The authorities would investigate; robbery would be ruled out as a motive since the corpses all retained their valuables. In the end, their deaths would remain a mystery. If the men had enemies, they might come under scrutiny; but authorities would probably find a way to blame their deaths on renegade slaves. Never mind that most black men had no acquaintance with swords. Americans seemed to see no contradiction in regarding blacks simultaneously as docile children and murderous savages. Black bogymen made convenient scapegoats for almost any crime and served to stoke the fear of poor whites who owned no slaves. Such fear sometimes conjured forth angry rabble who lynched blacks. Irrational terror of "The Other" was a time-honored method by which those with wealth and power controlled the lower orders of their society by focusing resentment away from themselves. A line from Voltaire sprang into Pennywhistle's mind: "Those who can make you believe absurdities can make you commit atrocities."

Gabriel walked up to him, a look of awe on his face. "I never seen anyone use a sword so fine, Cap'n, and I seen Mastah Calvert fight plenty o' duels, seeing slights where their ain't none and looking to make the other fellow pay with his life. He say a true gentleman fight with a blade, not barking irons. There's always black folk called to be ready to spirit the dead body away. He had a powerful expensive fencing instructor from Philadelphia, but I'm thinkin' he wouldn't last a minute 'gainst you. How you get so good?"

"Practice," said Pennywhistle, pleased that someone had asked about his efficiency. "Constant practice under the reproachful eye of a demanding master. Only a chap who has actually slain men in war is a teacher of any worth. The dueling your master favors has fair moves and foul, but on the battlefield, only survival matters. Gentlemen such as I just killed play at swords; they do not work at them. Such men often believe they train best under the influence of John Barleycorn and do not grasp that as you train, so you fight."

"I am guessin' you had a most particular teacher, Cap'n."

A sigh escaped Pennywhistle's lips. "I did, Gabriel. I miss him greatly. Major Justin du Motier fled The Terror and taught me to fight, on battlefields as well as in dark alleys. Swordsmanship and *savate* were drummed into me with equal vigor. "

What be *savate*, cap'n? I ain't never heard such a term."

Pennywhistle's brows knitted in frustration at to how to render a complex fighting art into a few simple words. "It's sometimes called *boxe française*. It's an amalgam of Paris street-fighting techniques practiced by the lower orders: plenty of kicks, slaps, and back-handed strikes as well as punches. Not pretty, not elegant, but effective and practical. I doubt most English pugilists would approve, but it's designed for survival, not for the awe of the crowd. I would not stand a chance fighting Gentleman Jackson with English boxing rules, but using *savate*, I would have a fair prospect of prevailing."

He pulled himself up short. He had been on the verge of boasting and that simply wasn't done. He pasted a determined expression on his face and looked Gabriel in the eye. "Now, Gabriel, please help me carry the sacks to the boat. This gold is going to make a lot of British soldiers very happy."

It took them half an hour to lug the heavy canvas bags to the sixteen-foot boat. As they slogged along, the tension drained out of Pennywhistle gradually and he noticed it was a lovely day. Gabriel furnished him a wealth of information on Bartram's Cove, including the location of two militia caches of arms and four of food. Gabriel had accompanied Calvert when he supervised their placement.

When they reached the boat and stowed the gold, Gabriel took a pocket ledger from his jacket. He read off units, numbers, and locations of the militia in the area and told Pennywhistle that no regulars were present. He had compiled almost the complete American order of battle for the area. Pennywhistle committed the lot to memory and thought that, in a better world, Gabriel would be a fine candidate for a university education.

Gabriel had done a lot of talking to local slaves who served as man-servants to officers who conversed carelessly in front of people they regarded as incapable of comprehension. He related juicy bits of gossip on the peccadilloes of many of the militia commanders. Some drank, some chased women, and some enriched themselves from the public coffers. Some were brave, some cowardly, some weak, and some plain stupid. Each bit alone was of no military value, but taken together, it gave a very revealing picture of the local command structure.

Before he shoved off, Pennywhistle shook Gabriel's hand vigorously. "I cannot thank you enough. You have proven invaluable. I regret I cannot take you with me today, but upon my honor, I shall come back for you in a week's time. Bring your friend Isaac along, too. Tell everyone you trust that when the British come, it will be... how did you put it earlier? Ah, yes, your day of jubilee. Your friends no longer need endure bondage. They will receive sanctuary behind our lines."

Promises of freedom, such as he had just made, had placed a severe strain on the British commissariat to feed the legions of runaways that had appeared, but those refugees were providing detailed and valuable information, acting as local guides, and helping with the inevitable chores of camp life. The runaways were also causing great disruption to an economy based on slave labor. Pennywhistle was no great admirer of William Wilberforce, the evangelical MP who'd succeeded in abolishing slavery in Britain; he deemed him a dreary, sanctimonious extremist, but he agreed that slavery degraded everyone involved.

Gabriel's eyes shone, and he spoke as carefully as his education allowed. "I thank you, Cap'n. I always expected to die a slave. The idea of freedom will take some getting used to, but I will enjoy the prospect until you come. I've been lied to by a heap a white men, all who called themselves gentlemen. You be the first gentleman I have met who behaves like one should. I am right proud to know you."

"Thank you, Gabriel, you are a man of honor as well. Remember: one week, at the place of our first meeting."

Gabriel helped him fasten the oars to the locks and push the boat into the river. Pennywhistle waved to Gabriel, then rowed out into the main channel of the Patuxent. Despite the stiff breeze, the humid morning air made his wool uniform oppressive and he sweated heavily. He scanned the channel with his spyglass. Clear, in every direction. He shipped oars, hoisted the small mast, and ran up the sail. No need for stealth; speed was more important. The sail filled and the vessel began to move forward. He would be back on Tangier Island by evening the following day if the wind held fair. The gold would occasion a lot of celebrating, although Cockburn would be livid when he learned of the fate of Lucas and his crew.

Gabriel's information on Bartram's Cove had clinched matters in Pennywhistle's mind. He would recommend Benedict as the landing site. Four of Wellington's best infantry regiments were scheduled to arrive from France via Bermuda within the week; with Fleet marines, the British would have a strike force of 5,000 men, and it was devoutly hoped their actions would be decisive. This dim-witted little war no longer made sense.

The British seizure of American sailors to man Royal Navy ships had ceased a month before the war began. Sadly, word of the new policy had only reached Washington two weeks *after* the Americans had decided on war by the closest of Congressional votes. The recent defeat of Napoleon placed the American War Hawks in an untenable position. They had sought to capture Canada while the British were distracted, but they now were receiving the Crown's undivided attention. Bad, bad timing all around.

Rear Admiral George Cockburn would grill him relentlessly. He reviewed his information and began to anticipate likely questions. He opened the circular red dispatch case one last time to make sure the charcoal drawings he had done were secure.

Pennywhistle had worked with Cockburn for nearly a year and appreciated his attention to even the most obscure detail. He liked Cockburn, a lordly, imperious figure who nevertheless possessed "The Nelson Touch" with common sailors. He enjoyed the man's wry, rather mordant sense of humor. The Admiral was fair, good to his men, but he also had a deserved reputation for ruthlessness. His highly effective raids up and down the Chesapeake had destroyed tons of valuable stores and stirred feelings of dread and uncertainty. The British appeared without warning, seemingly able to strike anywhere, anytime.

Cockburn had boasted he would make the Yankees howl, and he was proving as good as his word. He had short patience with civilians who offered resistance. As he burned the town of Harve de Grace after civilian snipers fired on his men, he had cheekily asked a local, "How do you like the war now?" The war was becoming unpopular with the Jonathans.

The American military considered Cockburn a formidable and cunning antagonist. *The National Intelligencer* trumpeted his alleged misdeeds in lurid headlines and transformed him into Satan in a naval uniform. He was regularly referred to in its pages as a devil, monster, ogre, and bandit. *The Intelligencer* encouraged the derisive pronunciation of his name as cock burn, rather than co burn, as was proper. The Americans offered a $500 reward for his ears and $1000 for his head.

The continuance of Cockburn's successful raiding strategy on a large scale would divert American attention from the Canadian frontier. The Americans had torched York, the capital of Upper Canada. Cockburn was angry about that, and *Surly's* story would not improve his disposition. Benedict was only sixty miles from Washington, D.C. Washington might well suffer York's fate by way of retaliation.

He would lay the groundwork with his report, but he was quite sure the name of Captain Thomas Pennywhistle would never find its way into the history books.

CHAPTER THREE

Gabriel and Isaac ran on. Two days of running through tidal marshes had given them the beginnings of trench foot. Every step was painful. They had consumed their small supply of cornbread and water and were hungry and thirsty. Their scratched legs were beginning to sting and swell from a passage through a sea of nettles. They were soaked in sweat; the day had been boiling, close to one hundred degrees Fahrenheit and dripping with humidity. The tidal swamp was fetid and unwelcoming, but the tall reeds provided temporary sanctuary from their pursuers. They waded through brackish water until they found a small island that was mostly dry, where they hunkered down and gasped for breath.

Isaac Gates was angry and scared. He was a runaway, risking everything on the word of his friend, Gabriel, and right now he wondered why he had done such a crazy thing. He hated being a hunted creature. His life as a field hand had been miserable, but at least it was predictable and unlikely to result in an early death. Recapture meant flogging at the very least, possibly execution as a warning to other slaves.

Gabriel saw the fear and doubt in his friend's eyes. "Isaac; look at me." Isaac looked anxiously at Gabriel. "We had to do this, Isaac. Had to! Mastah Tom found out I was gone when those four gents were killed. He was grilling everyone for answers, you saw that yourself. And one of the house slaves said you'd been asking a lot of odd questions lately. How long do you think it'll be before you and me be accused of murder?"

Isaac bobbed his head and sighed. Gabriel was right. They really had no choice.

Gabriel put his hand on Isaac's shoulder in reassurance. "We can have a better life. The Cap'n says he will find a place for us in their Colonial Marines, give us a chance to strike back at those who hurt us. That's a heap better than living a life under a whip hand."

Gabriel heard a trumpet blast, similar to the tally-ho sounded by fox hunters. A minute later he heard the dread, unmistakable yelping of bloodhounds locking their noses onto the scent of a quarry. Then he saw the riders, fifteen men, all local gentry: a typical runaway slave patrol, armed with short, double-barreled shotguns. Filled with buck and ball, shotguns were easily discharged from horseback into the backs of fleeing targets.

He recognized the distinctive, ugly silhouette of one man framed against the setting sun. The riders were too far away for him to discern facial expressions, but he guessed they were all smiling. Slaves were valuable property, but every man in the local patrol was a keen hunter, and there was nothing more challenging than hunting human quarry. Sometimes the *hunter* got the better of the *landowner* as the thrill of the chase took hold. A slave might die, but such deaths discouraged others bent on a similar course. Dead slaves cost them dollars, but all of them could afford it. Local authorities would make no inquires because they *were* the local authorities.

Fate was cruel. They were almost there! The meeting place was just ahead, but there was no sign of any British officer. And even the best swordsman alive would be no match for horsemen with guns.

Gabriel told Isaac to lie down and stay still. The muddy water might conceal their trail temporarily from the bloodhounds noses, but any movement of the tall reeds would likely be detected by their human masters, some of whom undoubtedly had their spyglasses unfurled. Gabriel was trying to be strong to put hope into Isaac, but now he shivered with fear and prayed.

The hoof-beats grew louder, as did the baying of the hounds.

Gabriel didn't know it, but the local Baptist preacher had been ordered to preach sermons that would make slaves more docile, more accepting of their lot. The preacher certainly had a way with words. Gabriel liked the message of the man from Nazareth. The verses about the meek inheriting the earth and the difficulty of rich men entering heaven gave him hope. He remembered the 23rd Psalm and murmured it aloud. Maybe it was hopeless now, but he would meet death with confidence, knowing a better life lay ahead. He might be a slave in the eyes of the men pursuing him, but he would die a man in the eyes of God.

The baying was savage, insistent, almost upon him. The pounding of horse's hooves rose to an awful crescendo, then stopped. Gabriel summoned the courage to look up, only to see the hard face of Tom Calvert looking down on him from atop his favorite stallion, the gigantic grey, Scipio. He heard the loud click as both triggers were thumbed to full cock.

"We have the damned murderers!"

Gabriel closed his eyes, prepared to yield up his life. But then he heard something else, a loud rustling in the reeds, and an English voice that caused his heart to jump. He opened his eyes, looked up, and saw astonishment in the eyes of the horseman.

"Marines, up and make ready!"

It was Pennywhistle! The Englishman had been as good as his word. Framed against the dying sun, the rangy marine stood tall. A second later, 28 shapes in brick-red rose menacingly out of the reeds, all armed and pointing their weapons toward the riders. They had been there all the time. The patrol had ridden into a trap.

Pennywhistle had more than one source of information, and he had been alerted just that morning that Gabriel Prosser was "in for it" and had turned runaway. Haunted by the memory of what had happened to Jed, he had set out with a force of marines, hoping that, against the odds, he would be able to redeem his word to Gabriel Prosser.

The tall Englishman advanced. He held a rifle against his shoulder which he kept aimed at the big man on the lead horse. "Put down your weapons and withdraw, sir. These two men are under my protection. They are no murderers. No murders were committed; it was merely the administration of justice."

Calvert replied dismissively, "And just how would a British officer know that?"

Pennywhistle's eyes glinted. He despised bullies and those eager to blame anything bad on the powerless. "*I* slew those four dishonorable gentlemen with my own hand." His voice took on a hard edge. "They stole a British Army payroll. I offered them their lives if they would see reason and simply walk away. They choose poorly. I am now making you the same offer. I trust you will profit from their example and choose wisely." He called over his shoulder, never once removing his gaze from his target. "Sarn't Dale!" A solidly built man in his early forties appeared as his side. "Take out my watch and open it."

"Aye, aye, sir!" Dale did as ordered.

"You have precisely one minute to depart." Pennywhistle leveled his piece to aim directly at the rider's throat. The big man's florid face turned pale.

"Leave in peace and rejoice that I am no disciple of unnecessary violence," the Englishman continued. He full cocked the rifle, his resolve clear.

But then the man on the snorting horse retorted. "These men may not be murderers, but they *are* property, Captain, and have run away from their lawful owners. This is a legally constituted posse authorized to reclaim what is ours under Common Law." The leader shrugged his shoulders to reassert his dignity. "You may wish to war against our government, but surely you do not wish to war against the sacred right of property which both of our countries hold dear."

As Calvert spoke, the sound of his own voice restored his confidence. He extracted an expensive silver flask from his saddle bag, took a long, contemptuous swig from it, and continued. "I and my men represent the law in these parts. I cannot believe *your* masters in London would wish you to support a breakdown of civilization by encouraging slaves to violate the social contract that is the bedrock of order. Anarchy would be the calamitous result!"

There was an odd, sadistic gleam in Calvert's eye, as if he believed conventional morality applied only to lesser beings. The last time Pennywhistle had seen that look was on the face of a highwayman, nicknamed Jack of the Sixteen Strings, marched to the Newgate Gallows for the brutal murder and evisceration of four women. The man's eyes had danced with a chillingly merry twinkle; he'd leered at the women in the crowd as if he could see them with their skins flayed off.

The entire patrol lapsed into a tense stillness. Pennywhistle glanced at the watch when no one made a move. "You have twenty seconds left. My patience grows thin."

Dale raised two fingers in a V as a silent signal to the marines, and every man menacingly attached a razor sharp sword bayonet to his Baker Rifle. Dale knew most untrained men had a greater terror of cold steel than bullets. Bullets could be extracted and wounds sewn up, but deep gouges often presented irremediable problems to even the best surgeons.

A low murmur rippled among the riders; the fear in their faces showed Dale had not misread them.

Calvert was incensed. The appearance of the British in the Chesapeake had provoked an epidemic of runaways. "Is your hypocrisy studied, or accidental, Captain? It is the height of obscene hubris that you dare obstruct the execution of justice, sir! Would you tolerate mutiny at sea, among your marines, *Captain*?" he demanded, mockingly.

Pennywhistle's emerald-green eyes narrowed, ignited, and his face flushed a hot crimson. He saw his men stiffen. They knew his battle face. The line had been crossed.

Dale flashed three fingers. Every marine lined up an individual member of the patrol in his sights and moved his index finger to rest on his weapon's trigger. Marine faces turned hard; those of the patrol turned pale.

"Every Royal Marine is a volunteer, sir," said Pennywhistle with asperity. "They are proudly here by choice —free men, not slaves. The only hubris lies in thinking the actions of your hateful patrol have anything to do with true justice. It is hardly mutinous when a brave man does the sensible thing and flees a thief who would steal his basic humanity." He sighed in exasperation. "But I have no interest in your remonstrations, sir, nor will I debate subjects best left to Parliaments and Congresses. For the last time, holster your weapons and depart. Leave these men to me. Tell those of your kind that you met death in the form of Thomas Pennywhistle, but he mercifully spared you for the sake of your wives." The voice was steady, measured; but the face was grim and indomitable. A reasonable man would have backed away as fast as possible.

But Calvert made no motion to withdraw. He took another swig from his flask, steadied himself in the saddle, sneered, then laughed. The Dutch courage was having an effect. This, Pennywhistle realized, might turn ugly fast.

"Captain, Captain, you British were so eager to argue legal points when you were impressing our sailors on the high seas! Yet you now dance carefully away from any discussion. Why should I allow you to impress our slaves upon our very own soil?" From his smug look he was sure he had made a wily legal argument.

Slave patrols had no practice with armed opposition. That induced collective stupidity, rather than caution. Stupid men often did dangerous things.

"Times up," Pennywhistle snapped. Dale shut the watch case with an echoing snap.

Calvert snarled an obscenity and swung his shotgun toward Pennywhistle. His left hand raised the short barrel while his right braced the stock against his stomach. His fingers fumbled at the long, twin triggers. The men in his patrol mirrored their leader's action because they were used to following his lead as members of his Hunt.

Pennywhistle had survived a dozen years of war by always anticipating the worst. He saw Calvert's intention in his blazing eyes and rippling neck veins long before the man's finger touched the triggers.

"Fire!" yelled Pennywhistle. A thunderclap cracked the humid air. Marine discipline and marksmanship were impeccable; the simultaneous reports blended together to sound a mass volley. A cloud of grey-white smoke blossomed and the reek of brimstone choked the air. At a range of ten yards, few bullets did not find a mark.

Southern grandees shouted in pain, surprise, and terror as bullets ripped through torsos, smashing ribs, exposing intestines, and shattering skulls. War suddenly became shockingly real to these pampered gentry bred on romantic, bloodless fairy tales of battle. Blood gushed from wounds and crimson stains bloomed on expensive frock coats. Not a few riders experienced a searing agony before slumping forward in their saddles. Others writhed in pain, clutching frantically at gaping stomach holes as pink blood bubbled from their mouths. Eyes widened in terror as they realized Death hunted them. Half of them died from that volley.

Some few managed to fire back, but their horses were shieing and the haze of gunpowder obscured their targets.

Pennywhistle had offered them an honorable exit; now there would be no quarter. He did not have the luxury of accommodations for prisoners. At his signal, the marines quickly reloaded and discharged a second volley at the men who still sat upright in their saddles.

Horses whinnied, snorted, and chuffed as they bucked and reared in fear and confusion. The Marines had to dodge and dance away from flailing, angry hooves for several minutes, but finally they got the horses under restraint, save for one unruly tan stallion. They yanked the two remaining Yankees left alive from their saddles. Both were badly hurt.

Once on the ground, marines quickly ended their agonies with efficient applications of the bayonet. In a way, they performed acts of mercy. They did not relish their duties but felt the Jonathans needed to be reminded that war was not the jolly hunting party for which these men were dressed and provisioned; arrogant foolishness brought consequences.

But the marines had missed one man—the one on the unruly horse. The gentleman in the blue coat had only feigned death; suddenly he came alive and put the spurs to his tan stallion in a mad dash for freedom. The horse, sensing his master's urgency and already wild from the efforts of men to catch him, put on an extra burst of speed.

"We have a loose end that needs tying up, Sarn't," said Pennywhistle matter-of-factly, pointing toward the galloping horse.

"Consider it done, sir.'

"Very good, Sarn't."

Dale raised his Baker and lined up the sights on the blue coated man's back. The man had made it convenient for him by pursuing a straight line course instead of zigzagging. Frightened men tended to seek the most direct route to safety. At one hundred and fifty yards, it was an easy shot for an experienced marksman such as Dale. The .61 caliber ball penetrated between the man's shoulder blades and he pitched forward onto his horse's mane. The horse continued toward home on pure instinct. The man's family would get a nasty surprise.

Pennywhistle nodded approval to Dale. Not an American remained alive. He felt no remorse; that was reserved for the innocent. The gentlemen in the patrol may not have been bad men in their everyday lives, but they had been on a despicable errand. From their attire and bearing, nearly all of the posse members probably enjoyed high rank in the local militia, so they would have been called out directly the British landed. He had in all likelihood just decapitated the local command structure.

Pennywhistle walked over to Calvert's corpse, the body's arms and legs splayed haphazardly on the grass; his elegant clothing in stark contrast to the gross indignity of his posture of death. The dead man's final expression was one of disbelief that he had not triumphed. Pennywhistle would ask Gabriel for the man's full name later. He did not care personally. He had no interest in dead poltroons, but he needed it for his report.

He had acquired some fine mounts, all thoroughbred hunters. But more than that, he had acquired a way for his men to hide in plain sight.

Isaac and Gabriel came forward now, and Gabriel introduced Isaac, who smiled for a brief second, but then his face assumed an anxious cast, as if he wanted nothing more than to put as much distance as possible between himself and the corpse of the man he had been forced to call Master. His eyebrows knitted together. "I wa... waa... wanna... he... he... hep... ya." He stuttered badly as he spoke, a common affliction of slaves, often noted in wanted posters for runaways; a product of stress born of oppression. Isaac balled his fists, thrust his arms downward in frustration, and shook his head twice. His face showed angry resolve. "I won't go back! I'll fight them for what they done to me!" He blinked in surprise. It was the first time in his adult life he had uttered a sentence with perfect clarity.

"You shall have your chance," Pennywhistle said, then he turned toward the older man. "Gabriel, I need your help. You told me before you could guide me to Commodore Barney's flotilla. I accept that offer, then I will see you and your friend back to our base. You are free men now, but I need both of you to obey my orders without hesitation, so I can get everyone to safety."

Gabriel and Isaac looked at each other, and Gabriel nodded.

"Sarn't Dale!" Pennywhistle called. Dale left the horses and came to parade ground attention. Well, not quite. His posture was impeccable, but his teeth were bared in a huge grin . He was delighted to have dealt the arrogant Jonathans a smart jab. "How can I help, sir?"

"We need to dispose of the bodies and organize the horses. Get the men on it. Find Gabriel and Isaac some weapons and shoes. Rustle them up some food as well, they look famished. The late members of the slave patrol will provide. I think we have two fine recruits here!"

Dale was nonplussed. He was a good man, but conventional. "Sir, well, I mean... these men are... well, negroes! They run fast enough and they look strong, but I'm not sure they have the stomach for real soldiering."

Pennywhistle laughed. "That's just what the Americans want you to believe, Sarn't! If blacks are so weak and cowardly, why are the locals so terrified of slave insurrections? They have plenty of black sailors in their navy. Why can't we have black infantry? I've seen you work miracles and make the oddest ragamuffins stand and fight. In Spain you got ordinary peasants to fight like tigers. These two fine fellows have every reason to want to strike back at their oppressors. We just need to give them training and the means, then point them in the right direction."

"Aye, aye, sir!" Dale saluted smartly. He slowly and thoughtfully looked the two black men up and down, and his expression changed to one of firm resolve. If his captain said that runaway black men could be made into proper soldiers, it was obviously possible, and he would do his utmost to make it so.

Pennywhistle made his calculations. A night ride lay ahead, but his men could be in position by dawn. He checked the map. Overland would be more direct than by boat. If the grandees clothes were cleaned up a bit, half of the men would have a disguise, one that should work fine as long as no one approached too close. Getting out would be more problematic than getting in, but he had the germ of an idea. They were supposed to observe and report, but they might be able to cause a little mischief as well.

CHAPTER FOUR

The mission continued on a disagreeable note. The pack of bloodhounds and beagles accompanying the slave patrol had to be eliminated lest they return home and raise an alarm. Englishmen have a great fondness for dogs and the marines hesitated in a way they never would have with men.

The dogs were easy enough to round up, milling about in confusion but staying close to the corpses of their recently deceased masters. Two howled in mourning, but most yipped and yelped in expectancy of a new task. A few cocked their heads slowly from side to side, as if in deep understanding of the marines speaking to them. The majority wore expressions of confused amiability, looking to please but not quite certain how. Tails wagged, some vigorously, some uncertainly. These red jacketed fellows seemed to be members of a pack and dogs were pack animals. None apprehended that the men were angels of death.

Marine faces turned grim and they muttered uncharacteristically. "Bloody Hell! Damn War! Stinking orders!" Many a man felt bile in rise in his throat as he pulled the trigger and blew his victim's head apart. A second later, all of the dogs lay dead. All but one.

Private Michael O'Laughlin, nicknamed "Gramps" because of his advanced age of 35, simply could not do it. He tried three times to pull the trigger but his finger would not obey. He had never violated a direct order but the sad faced bloodhound in front of him was so pathetically trusting that he touched a sentimental streak O'Laughlin had thought long dead. Tears dribbled down his ruddy cheeks.

Dale saw the pain in his face and walked over. "Is there a problem with your weapon, Gramps? " Dale asked with solicitude. O'Laughlin was one of his most reliable men and well respected by the rest of the company. He was not prone to act impulsively.

"Can't do it, Sarn't, can't kill him. It's a waste and a violation of the Almighty's canon to murder such a fine and noble animal."

Dale raised his eyebrows in surprise. O'Laughlin winced; he had just committed rank insubordination. But O'Laughlin squared his shoulders and spoke earnestly, in the manner of a lawyer pleading clemency for a client condemned to hang.

"I used to be in charge of Lord Cavanaugh's kennels. I know dogs, Sarn't Dale, and I know breeds. This here beast is a purebred bloodhound, from a line that goes way back to the time o' knights! You might think him a no account brute because he has a face like a waterfall of old dough, but he be bred special for tracking: deer, boar, but best for tracking people. Bloodhounds be real docile animals, but stubborn too. Once they scent out what they be looking for, they don't never give up on it until they run it down. I reckon his nose could sniff out a fox under a hay rick at a mile."

O'Laughlin warmed to his subject and his expression changed to a smile, as an inspiration struck him. "He could be of real use to us, Sarn't, as a tracker. If he can track slaves for the Yanks, why can't he track Yanks for us? Didn't you tell me once you once owned a dog named Mercury that scouted for you?"

Dale sighed with sadness. Mercury had died saving his life. "He was a treasure. I miss him." Dale looked the bloodhound over carefully. It was not a handsome animal like his mastiff, yet if what O'Laughlin said were true, he might have an even more acute nose.

O'Laughlin saw the wistful expression on Dale's face and knew he had an opening. "Can we keep him, Sarn't, can we, can we?" he burbled, like an enthusiastic child trying to persuade a dubious parent. O'Laughlin's normally subdued brogue grew more pronounced as his excitement peaked. "I have a feeling about him! He be a lucky beast, too, Sarn't, luckier than a basket of four leaf clovers! That luck is bound to rub off on every man jack here. We can never have too much luck!"

Dale looked at him skeptically. Irishmen had poetical hearts and vivid imaginations that frequently carried them away on flights of fancy unrelated to the hard logic Dale prized. Coupled to their silver tongues, those flights frequently enraptured unwary bystanders. Still, many marines were superstitious and accounted oddments such as rabbit's feet, playing cards, and St. Christopher medallions as good luck talismans. O'Laughlin's enthusiasm could well persuade the men that this hound be numbered among them. Dale noted other marines listening eagerly to the conversation. They no longer looked downcast. The animal might at least have a temporary value as a morale booster.

Pennywhistle saw that one dog remained alive, and it annoyed him. His order had not been executed completely. He understood why it was so, but sentiment had no place here; the Service depended on unquestioning obedience to lawfully given orders, no matter how personally distasteful they might be. Time to be hard.

He strode menacingly over to Dale and the Irishman, put his hands on his hips in challenge and stared down his nose at them, meaning to intimidate. He spoke harshly. "Well? Explain yourselves!" He let his words hang in the air. O'Laughlin flinched, but not Dale. He had been with Pennywhistle too long to be fooled by his considerable gifts as an actor. His commander simply wanted honest answers, and sometimes those were best obtained by sowing a little fear.

Dale answered calmly. "Well, sir, O'Laughlin here maybe onto something. His says this dog has a superior nose and might be useful to us as a tracker. With all of the rough country here in America, I think we could use one."

As if in understanding, the bloodhound panted and gave a doggy grin. O'Laughlin spoke out of turn and added, "He will bring us good fortune, sir!'

Pennywhistle eyed the beast. He certainly was a homely animal; yet function, not form, was what counted. His anger evaporated as he considered possibilities. He stroked his chin and noticed the men looking at him anxiously. They wanted the animal's life spared. He gathered Dale had reached the same conclusion. Whatever the dog's actual talents, it had become a sentimental favorite. Sparing it would help assuage the pain the marines felt over the deaths of its mates. It might be of use as a mascot; symbols were important in war. At moments like this a small gesture could pay big dividends. He did not want to encourage disobedience, but the case seemed exceptional, and he trusted his men would not regard it as a precedent.

"O'Laughlin," he said sternly, "you are sure about this beast's nose?" His unforgiving green eyes bored into the Irishman's determined blue ones.

O'Laughlin refused to be intimidated. "Yes, sir, I am. Grew up with dogs and there ain't no finer breed on the planet for tracking."

Pennywhistle liked the private's confidence. "Very well then, bring him along," he said brusquely. He pointed a finger accusingly at O'Laughlin's heart. "I shall hold *you* wholly responsible for his feeding and care, since you are so keen on his abilities."

O'Laughlin knuckled his round hat in salute. "Yes, sir! I won't let you down." He patted the dog gently on the head, and the dog favored him with another grin. "Neither will he! But one thing, sir. The beast needs a name."

Pennywhistle realized the men's emotions were in flux and if he used this moment wisely, he could bind the men more strongly together as a unit. He looked at the faces of his men, who had formed a semi-circle around him. "Marines, will you help name this beast?"

"Aye, aye, sir," they chorused with enthusiasm. He knew how to work a crowd.

"I will give you all a minute to consider suitable names. Then I will ask each man in turn for his best suggestion."

It was a trivial matter, but the marines' faces grew as thoughtful as if they were considering a question of life or death. Much better to focus on something positive than regret what they had just done.

The choices the men made were predictable. Fido, Rex, Bowser, and Spot were suggested. Some favored mythical names: Zeus, Mars, Odin, and Thor.

"The name should be fierce, sir, just like we are," one private proclaimed. "I like Cerberus, sir; the hound that guards hell."

Two men referenced qualities about the dog itself: Snooper, Nosey. One marine favored Penmore, after his hometown in Scotland.

The last offering—well, non-offering really—came from Private Crouchback, a Cockney sourpuss who conspicuously lacked the breezy optimism associated with those London men. "I don't have no particular choice, sir. Personally, I think this is all a load of blarney."

The men laughed. Pennywhistle laughed too. "Blarney," Pennywhistle said loudly." I think that might work rather well as a name! The politicians who started this war are certainly well acquainted with it! What say you, Marines?"

"Aye, aye sir!" The marines shouted merrily. Several tossed their hats in the air, glad for the emotional release. The spell of grief was broken.

Time to move out, and see if Blarney's nose worked as advertised.

Sundown cooled the temperature only a little. The moisture-saturated air made Pennywhistle's men feel as if they were riding through a steam bath. The night came alive with the sound of cicadas, frogs, and owls. The agreeable smells of Black-Eyed Susans, blazing star blossoms, and cardinal flowers mixed uncertainly with the unpleasant rotting smell of tidal flats. Pennywhistle, as a former medical student, was fascinated by the way that the local Piscataway Indians employed extract of cardinal flower as a highly effective treatment for cramps. He wondered why no one from Europe had bothered to make a detailed study of Indian botanical medicine.

Gabriel had said that the Commodore had 18 vessels in his flotilla, and while Gabriel knew little about boats and ships, he had an excellent memory. Careful questioning about general appearance, number of cannon, oars, and sails gave Pennywhistle some idea of the configuration of the vessels. Most of the vessels were coastal craft, glorified barges, unsuited to the open sea. Gabriel had seen their hulls at low tide and the marine was able to make educated guesses as to their tonnage. Pennywhistle asked particularly how low the vessels rode in the water at high tide. Vessels rode low when fully provisioned and ready for sea, high when stripped of everything but the basics. Gabriel's observations confirmed earlier reports that the vessels rode high and were there to block, not attack.

Gabriel knew plenty about supplies: the quantity, quality, and kinds of food delivered. For all of his alleged patriotism, Calvert had been a purse proud, profit-minded man who sold Barney second-rate food at premium prices. The food was brought to a camp of huts and tents onshore, rather than hoisted aboard, further evidence of a defensive posture. From the amount of food delivered and the sailors and marines Gabriel had seen working purposefully, Pennywhistle estimated the Commodore commanded about 400 men. These were not un-blooded rookies like the militia, but experienced veterans who had seen combat.

Joshua Barney had made himself a household name by his brilliant capture of the privateer *General Monk* in the Revolutionary War. He had recently completed a cruise as the captain of the Baltimore privateer *Rossie*, taking 18 prizes valued at one and a half million dollars. Pennywhistle had complete respect for his fighting abilities and his determination. He would approach with caution.

Barney was undoubtedly expecting some kind of British attack and would have posted sentries and taken precautions; adequate against standard troops. Yet it was unlikely he was prepared for a small contingent of 28 marines skilled at stealth, speed, and the use of cover.

The big British effort would come the day after tomorrow. Depending on the caprices of the wind, Pennywhistle figured he had forty hours to do his business and report back. He would push his men hard to make every minute count.

All of the marines carried "housewives"—small portable sewing kits in deer horn containers, useful for temporarily stitching either clothes or wounds. Before setting out, they had done a creditable job of mending the bullet holes in the clothing they'd taken off the dead men. The frock coats and headgear of the extinct slave patrol made convincing silhouettes if viewed from a distance, but there were only enough to costume half of Pennywhistle's men. The rest of the marines retained their hunting frocks but removed their distinctive round hats. Calvert's clothes fitted Pennywhistle reasonably well. The blue coat and buff trousers had been expertly tailored. The pink-flowered waistcoat looked garish, but then, Americans had never been noted for subtlety in clothing.

A wagon was needed to transport the unmounted marines and the "runaways"—Gabriel and Isaac, prominently on display. One was found, thanks to Gabriel and his underground network of slave contacts. The slaves at Fall Creek plantation provided one wagon and two old horses, which would not be missed because their master had been part of the slave posse. Pennywhistle had attached a large, red-lettered sign to the wagon's side: *The fate of runaways*. He placed a small lantern alongside to illuminate those letters; this was no time to be subtle. Several of the marines in the wagon were given a set of slave chains taken from Fall Creek to rattle loudly should anyone approach too close. The sound was distinctive and ominous.

Pennywhistle detached two men, Privates McCarthy and Blandon, to sail the yawl that had brought them upriver. The yawl was a large, wide, double-ended craft designed by Captain Edward Brenton, expressly for coastal raids. The thirty-foot vessel contained a nasty brass surprise on twin wooden rails which ran the length of the boat; it could do its business from either bow or stern. It was now stowed deep in the center boards to increase the yawl's stability.

The rising twilight breeze coming off the cooling land was fair and they would be in position by late morning. Gabriel had drawn several maps of Barney's position, so the men had a good idea of their final destination. Once his command had stirred things up enough to be pursued, Barney's men would look for them to flee the way they had come—by land. They would instead head downriver by boat. Even people in tidewater country tended to forget the efficiency of sea-borne transport.

Most people operated on a dawn-to-dark routine and turned in when the sun went down, yet Pennywhistle encountered plenty of people on the road, mostly bang straws—farm hands on the walk home from distant fields. He also noted itinerant merchants on their way to the next town, some washerwomen, and a group of loudly laughing gentlemen on horseback somewhat the worse for drink. Two ruffians in black slouch hats passed Pennywhistle's men a few minutes later. He guessed they were shadowing the intoxicated gentlemen with a view to relieving them of the valuables when an opportunity presented itself.

People do not like to be reminded of that which they consider unpleasant, and slave patrols certainly fell under that heading. Passersby noted their presence, but none talked to them. Poor whites were only supposed to speak when spoken to by gentlemen. Most looked quickly away, just as they would if seeing men afflicted with leprosy or scrofula.

A little while later, the marines passed a caravan of four fire-red Conestoga wagons bearing what Pennywhistle judged to be a traveling novelty and variety show. Such shows were common in America, traveling from county fair to county fair during the summer months. Illuminated by lanterns, "Wigsby's World of Wonderments" was boldly emblazoned in tall gold letters across the back of each vehicle.

Unlike ordinary folk on the road, the show people in the wagons waved cheerfully at his men. Show people were always eager to spread the news of upcoming performances, even if it involved getting the attention of men about unpleasant business. They were stolidly ignored.

A sign on the side of the lead wagon, illuminated by two swinging lanterns, proclaimed, "You won't believe your eyes! See Jo-Jo, the dog-faced boy! Bepo, the three-legged dancer! Crespo, conjurer for kings!" A small band in the rear wagon played "The Minstrel Boy". These people truly craved attention!

A crazy, cruel thought struck Pennywhistle. He needed a diversion in the day ahead. Paid with gold, Wigsby's entertainers would probably be right glad to stage an impromptu show. Soldiers loved shows and entertainment, no matter how amateurishly they might be performed.

Wigsby's show probably used a well-tested, crowd-pleasing formula: music, magic, pretty singers, jugglers, acrobats, dancers, a few freaks, a patriotic orator, and a past-his-prime actor hamming up Shakespeare. They were headed in the same direction as his men, if proceeding far more slowly.

Pennywhistle's mind began to work through permutations of a performance that would literally bring down the house. Wigsby's arrival in the American camp needed to be as showy as possible, to distract the Americans from Pennywhistle's advance. The band could handle that. He would need to keep track of their progress. Blarney's nose should do the job nicely, justifying O'Laughlin's prediction.

He checked his purse of golden guineas. He had more than enough to make this happen. Cockburn had allotted him some of the funds he had recovered from the lost payroll. The Admiral understood that useful intelligence sometimes required substantial payments to unusual persons.

Pennywhistle turned his horse around and rode back to the lead wagon in the theatrical caravan. He pulled alongside and smiled at the man who held the reins: a wide-faced, heavily freckled, jack sprat of a man, dressed in a silver-buttoned tailcoat of purple with a matching cravat and a top hat of yellow. He had carrot-colored, curly hair and sported a single gold earring. He put Pennywhistle in mind of a leprechaun.

"Good evening, sir, wither are you bound?" Pennywhistle spoke in his breeziest voice.

The small man looked Pennywhistle up and down. The long-shanked stranger looked a bit of a stiff-rump, but his dress proclaimed him a prosperous gentleman. Gentlemen meant money, and their patronage could lead to new bookings. His mouth quickly blossomed into the oily smile of the professional huckster. The eyes did not match; they belonged to an accountant. He answered in the cheerfully booming voice of a carnival barker.

"Why, sir, we are bound for the Prince George's County Fair in Nottingham, which commences the day after tomorrow. I am Mortimer Wigsby, your servant, sir, and the proprietor of this splendid show. We are no ordinary show, mind you, but an emporium of entertainments, a massing of marvelous muses. Members of my troupe have played the best stages in New York and Philadelphia. You would have a most diverting evening if your journey takes you to Nottingham. Might I know to whom I the great pleasure of speaking?"

This leprechaun spoke not with a brogue, but with the nasal vowels of a New Englander. They had a reputation for sharp practice. *He's a tongue pad*, thought Pennywhistle, *a glib-tongued, insinuating fellow ready to promote his show at a moment's notice.* But the road to Nottingham would take his caravan past the entrance to Barney's camp. "My name's Tom Calvert, Mr. Wigsby. You passed my plantation a few miles back." Plantation ownership would square perfectly with his attire taken from the real man. "I am sure you are an extraordinary troupe. I should like to make arrangements for a private performance for some friends of mine. If you could pull your wagon over to the side, we can discuss schedules and compensation."

Wigsby's smile was genuine this time. "Of course, sir, of course. Always delighted to arrange a performance for a gentleman of refinement and discrimination. I assure you, it will be a night to remember!"

It took Pennywhistle twenty minutes and four golden guineas to arrange the performance. He knew he was overpaying Wigsby, but he wanted to impress him that he was a gentleman of plump purse, unconcerned with anything as trifling as a few gold coins. He implied that if the show went over well he might be willing to fund others.

Wigsby did not complain that he was being paid with English coin, nor that the gentleman's mannerisms were British. After all, many of the wealthiest men in the country were scions of noble English, Scottish, even Irish families—although not always on the right side of the blanket. Gold of any minting was real currency, and when someone gave itinerant performers hard coin up front, it was imprudent to ask questions.

Pennywhistle explained the performance was a thank-you for Joshua Barney's sailors and marines, who several days before had assisted his patrol in rounding up runaways. He wanted the whole thing to be a grand surprise to "those noble saviors of the republic." Wigsby was merely to tell Barney the gift was from "a patriotic gentleman who greatly respected the service his men had given fighting that devil Cockburn." Pennywhistle explained that, as a deeply private man, he wished to remain anonymous; he lived quietly and did not choose to be upset by unwelcome visitors coming to sing his praises. He wanted the focus of acclaim firmly kept on Barney and his men, where it belonged. Did Wigsby understand? Wigsby assured his patron that he understood perfectly.

Pennywhistle, who had memorized the contents already, gave his copy of Gabriel's map to Wigsby and marked the location of Barney's camp. He pointed to an open area at the front of the camp where he thought they could set up their stage.

Wigsby estimated he could reach the camp and have his performers ready to go by 4 o'clock the following afternoon if he did not stop for the night. He said a performance typically took about two hours. Pennywhistle calculated his marines could be in position before four.

He asked Wigsby for a précis of his show. Wigsby showed him his playbill and declaimed the highlights of each performer's genius. It was the sort of mélange of acts Pennywhistle had guessed at. He estimated which act would be the loudest—useful to know when launching an attack.

"I was wondering if your band could strike up some patriotic airs when you are a mile or so from camp, Mr. Wigsby? Sailors and Marines love music, and it would be a fine way to proclaim your arrival. 'Hail, Columbia', 'Jefferson and Liberty', 'Yankee Doodle', that sort of thing." He rightly assumed Wigsby loved a splashy entrance; more importantly, it would alert Pennywhistle that his diversion approached.

"It would be our pleasure, sir! We have the finest bandsman in the world, sir, and they have a truly astounding repertoire of tunes, marches, and airs to fire and inspire fighting men the world over!"

"Ah, one more thing, Mr. Wigsby. I have a fondness for cravats and collect them. I love the princely color purple and have never seen one in that shade until a few minutes ago, when I first observed yours." Pennywhistle pretended to admire the huckster's neckwear. "I wonder, might I persuade you to part with it? The gift would be a fine way to seal our bargain, and it would assure that I remember you without fail, and with gratitude, every time I behold it." Pennywhistle had no interest in the garish confection, but it would be impregnated with Wigsby's scent, a way for Blarney to track the progress of the caravan.

Wigsby thought the request odd, but then, gentlemen collected all manner of objects. This man disdained the public recognition Wigsby lived for; no doubt this was just one more component of an unusual personality he would never understand. Besides, for four guineas, he was prepared to indulge almost any eccentric request. He unbound the cravat and handed it to Pennywhistle.

"I thank you again, Mr. Wigsby, for being so willing to interrupt your schedule on short notice," said Pennywhistle, after he mounted his horse.

"I consider it my great good fortune in having met you, Mr. Calvert. There is nothing more important than showing our gallant troops how much we value their exemplary conduct. We are lucky to have them, and they are blessed to have such a chivalrous gentleman as yourself as their benefactor."

Pennywhistle waved a condescending acknowledgment and resumed his ride. He pulled alongside O'Laughlin, handed him the cravat, and explained its purpose. Blarney padded alongside O'Laughlin's horse and seemed quite content with his new master. O'Laughlin really did seem to have an affinity for canines. He halted his horse, dismounted, and made sure Blarney sniffed the cravat thoroughly. The hound gave a short bark, indicating he had the scent.

Pennywhistle refined his plan as he rode. He wished he knew more about horses. He tried to remember what Boomer Vandeleur had told him in Spain about cavalry charges. At the same time, he found himself automatically trying to identify the creatures making the various calls, clicking, and cooing noises common to the heavily wooded areas on either side of the road.

He smiled at the memory of one captured militia man who had earnestly tried to convince him a creature called a jackalope might be found in the deep forest: a beast with the head and body of a rabbit but bearing gigantic antlers and often attaining the height of a horse. Yankees loved tall tales and playing tricks on gullible foreigners. He was about to return the favor by playing a highly destructive trick on them.

Pennywhistle felt he was generally successful in matching noises to their owners, but one sound was utterly strange to him. His guess was that it was made by a wolverine. He had seen one up close only once. They were supremely reclusive, and fought fiercely when cornered, which struck him as an apt totem for the local American forces.

The marines rode quietly, too well trained for talking or murmuring. They ate as they rode, having helped themselves to the generous and luxurious provisions found in the dead men's saddlebags. The slave patrol had been on a terrible errand, but it clearly had some of the air of a holiday outing. Smithfield ham, roast beef, meat pies, apples, pears, peaches, and fresh bread, as well as apple, cherry, and rhubarb pies, were all consumed with silent gusto. Good food in time of war assumed an exaggerated importance and the marines had never been so well fed. It buoyed their spirits; pleasantly full stomachs helped fade from memory the sad business with the dogs.

Prodigious drinking was common among gentlemen. The slave patrol and its leader were no exceptions and had come well prepared. Gabriel had explained that Calvert's round the clock guzzling began with ale for breakfast, a glass of hock and soda shortly after to banish the hangover and get the morning moving, followed by a glass of sherry around 11. A flask of brandy sustained him through the afternoon and dinner included clarets followed by port, Madeira, and bourbon. Supper featured champagne, with brandy served afterwards. No wonder Calvert had been so foolishly combative.

Most of the slaver's saddles bore large flasks containing high quality, high potency brandy, and there were two large barrels of local beer each carried by a pack horse. Foolish conceits in time of war, but they had only been riding after defenseless runaways. Pennywhistle instructed his men to dump nearly all the alcohol. They were reluctant to destroy such fine liquor, but understood they would need their wits about them in the night and day ahead. Alcohol also increased dehydration in hot, humid weather. Pennywhistle did, however, allow each man one shot of spirits and one draught of brew; let them appreciate in small quantities what would be detrimental as an indulgence. Gabriel guided them to a spring where they filled their canteens.

Pennywhistle called a halt at 2 a.m. and posted a sentry. They were close to Barney's camp, but his men needed rest, and he could spare them two hours. The men were experienced soldiers and used to grabbing sleep where they could. Most were sound asleep a minute after their heads touched the ground.

After the stop, they continued on their way and reached their destination as the pink fingers of dawn caressed the eastern sky. He halted the men near a stand of exceptionally tall pines. He'd noticed a deep ravine to the rear, which would conceal the horses. Perfect for what he had in mind for later. Pennywhistle could see Barney's flotilla clearly through his glass; it was a quarter mile upstream, on the same side of the river. It was time to mobilize his men. Gabriel and Isaac had experience as farriers and agreed to act as horse holders and keep the beasts quiet. Both seemed knowledgeable about creatures Pennywhistle regarded with suspicion. He had met only one horse he liked and who liked him, but Lightning had died a sad death in Spain.

The marines quietly dismounted and assembled in front of him. He spent fifteen minutes explaining his plans to them in a voice barely above a whisper. He said he would give them the final details after he and Dale had conducted a proper reconnoiter. The more complex the design, the more important it was for each individual to understand exactly the part he would play. Pennywhistle had chosen these men for their intelligence, independence, and resourcefulness; only men with those qualities could execute his unusual plan. Eyebrows arched in surprise as he laid out his expectations, but the unbroken string of victories he had delivered gave them confidence in him and in themselves.

He had them post sentries, then instructed them to lie down under the shade of the pines and snatch a few hours' rest. They still had plenty of food left when it came time to eat. It was important to conserve energy, since the day ahead promised to be a scorcher. Fresh, well-fed troops had a marked advantage over opponents who had spent the day laboring under an unforgiving sun.

As the sun glowered just above the horizon, he turned command over to Corporal Withers, then he and Dale made a series of stooping, weaving dashes forward, taking every advantage of cover. He finally plopped down on a small hillock and unfurled his Ramsden spyglass. Dale did the same two hundred yards to the right. Dale had an inferior telescope taken from one of the dead slavers, but it would have to do. They would survey the area, then assemble back at the pine grove and compare impressions.

He made a thorough examination of the 18 vessels he could now see clearly. Gabriel had been right about the numbers. Only one merited the designation ship and had a name: *Scorpion* flew a Commodore's broad pennant. The rest were gunboats varying in length from forty to seventy-five feet, mounting from two to four guns each. They would be easy enough to deal with out in the Bay, but in the close confines of a river they could cause real trouble. He would give an exact accounting to his superiors, but planned to leave a destructive calling card before departing.

He needed to get an idea of patrols and routines so he could discover some sort of opening in their defenses. Waiting for an assault that might never come was dull, boring duty that sapped the morale of even the best-led troops. The blast-furnace heat added to their problem. It was easy to become careless and slipshod in small, nearly imperceptible ways. Such behaviors would go unmarked by civilian eyes, but Pennywhistle knew every dodge, shortcut, and cheap evasion favored by soldiers, and he could spot them. He just needed a little time.

He calculated Wigsby's people would appear sometime in the early afternoon. He had sent O'Laughlin and Blarney two miles down the road to wait for their arrival, relying on Blarney's nose to detect the caravan before it could be seen. He wanted as much advance notice as possible. He was betting a lot on innocent entertainers. It was cruel, turning them into unwitting pawns in a violent game they neither anticipated nor understood, but war had little regard for the innocent.

Pennywhistle had what he needed after a three-hour reconnoiter. The American camp covered several acres, was well guarded, and the sentries were intelligently positioned. One sentry was stationed at each of the four corners of the camp, two at its entrance, and one was assigned to the large supply dump, its contents hidden under a number of large tarpaulins. Marine sentries walked their posts smartly and with vigilance; he could detect no slackness despite the heat. He could see their faces clearly through the Ramsden. They were neither fierce nor bored. He saw them as calmly observant; the hallmark of professionals.

A full company of just over a hundred marines, not in the shirtsleeves, waist coats, and forage caps he was accustomed to seeing on Americans in the field, but wearing blue-coated battledress and sporting tall shakos, practiced drill on the parade ground. Their commander apparently conceded nothing to the terrible heat. Their evolutions were precise, their wheeling movements especially crisp. How a company performed drill under adverse conditions often gave a good indication of how they would fight in actual battle.

The camp bustled with activity. Sailors and marines were unloading boxes and barrels from four recently arrived wagons and moving them to the supply dump. They looked to contain foodstuffs; Barney was not breaking camp anytime soon. The men were directed very competently by two tall Marine Lieutenants. Everyone moved with a purpose; these were no stupid militia. Shot and barrels of gunpowder were also being hoisted onto the gunboats.

A Marine section of fifteen entered the camp from the east two hours after daybreak, having likely returned from an all-night patrol. An hour later, Pennywhistle observed a second patrol headed out into the woods to the west. Barney was more security conscious than he had anticipated.

Patrols usually followed an extended perimeter search pattern: throw the net out very wide, then gradually draw it inwards. The last place patrols would reach would be dead center, just where Pennywhistle was now. If the patrol returned in the early evening, as he guessed, he had enough time. If they returned any sooner, he was in deep trouble. His men were masters of concealment, but sooner or later US Marine searchers would find them.

He considered immediate withdrawal. He faced more than 400 seasoned professionals and was badly outgunned. He had all the information he needed about the flotilla. Withdrawal was the safe move, the sure bet. But much as he disdained cards and wagering for money, he was a born gambler when it came to fighting. Yet he was far from reckless; he calculated odds and capabilities with the cold, detached precision of a mathematician—Leibniz's lessons employed to create algorithms of battlefield probabilities.

He decided to stay and administer some swift kicks to American backsides. He also wanted to pilfer a few documents from the command tent to supplement and confirm the intelligence he had gathered visually. He held a questionable hand, but if he played things carefully, he could prevail.

He thought Wigsby's people probably possessed enough talent to beguile the Americans for a spell. Military camps were tedious places when the men were off duty; men sometimes got into mischief because of the sheer boredom of it all. Anything that broke that monotony was welcomed. Variety shows usually played fairs and cities, not military encampments, so the appearance of a troupe of players would be regarded as an unexpected and great gift.

He and Dale rendezvoused back at the pine grove, right on schedule. Dale's impressions squared with his own: the odds were daunting; nevertheless, Dale backed his officer's decision to proceed. Pennywhistle would use half the men as an advanced picket line to watch, observe, and report. He would keep the other half in reserve, allowing them to eat and rest. The two would change places at noon. The picket line would withdraw when Wigsby's people arrived.

Privates McCarthy and Blandon reported in. They had followed their copy of Gabriel's map carefully on their journey upriver and had arrived early, due to a fair wind. They had concealed the yawl inside some tall swamp grass and walked cautiously through the woods, making their Bob White calls every few minutes until they were answered by one of Pennywhistle's men. The method of egress was secure.

Half of the marines moved quietly forward, in short rushes, crouched low, and spread themselves out in a wide skirmish line. They operated in pairs, each man covering the other. At one hundred yards from the American camp they got on their bellies, then crawled and slithered the last few yards until they found suitable hides at the camp's edge. The grass was high and luxurious, which suited splendidly. No one on the American side had thought to cut the reeds to give clear fields for observation and fire—a mistake he would not have made. It was quite odd; all of their other security measures were excellent.

Pennywhistle noticed four large piles of boxes and barrels at each corner of the supply dump, all covered in tarpaulins. He hoped one or more contained what he sought. He had told his men to keep an eye out for stores of powder. If they saw anything, they were to signal him with a Bob White call.

American boatswains' mates checked breeching ropes on the gunboat cannons and carronades. Sailors began loading canister aboard the several vessels. The Jonathans meant to fight if attacked; canister would be very effective in a close quarter battle against British longboats. Cockburn would have a hot contest on his hands should he use conventional cutting out tactics. Pennywhistle would give him an assist.

Pennywhistle's force was too small to destroy or capture the ships, but if the cannon lacked powder to fire, the ships would be of little account. Besides, explosions had a way of spreading fire randomly, and fire found congenial the tarred ropes so prominent on ships and boats.

His men were disciplined and patient. Hours passed; their hunting frocks grew sodden on the marshy ground, but canvas covers fastened over the lock-plates and touch holes kept their weapons free of damp and fully functional. This was the sort of patient observation for which they were perfectly suited. Anyone could be taught to shoot, but not many had the discipline to wait for precisely the right moment to do it. Pennywhistle took great pride in his men, and he thought specialized scouting units had an important future in the Royal Marines.

He had made one important adjustment in the armament of his men. They all carried Baker Rifles rather than standard issue Sea Service Brown Bess muskets. The 1806 Pattern Baker was sturdy and reliable, with hitting power like a meteor through a bottle-glass window. It had been the favored weapon of British Army rifle regiments in the Peninsular War. More than a few commanding officers of line regiments had armed their light companies with it at their own expense. Admiral Cockburn was a forward-thinking commander receptive to the idea of specially armed and trained units; he had provided much of the cash for the Bakers' purchase from his own prize money.

The .65 caliber pieces were precise instruments with more than double the range of smoothbores. They were slower to load than muskets, a drawback in conventional fighting, but that was of less moment in scouting missions where one usually fired from concealment. The short, 30-inch barrel made the piece easily reloadable from kneeling or prone positions.

Unlike civilian rifles, the Baker took a bayonet, making cold steel a fall back option. But it was not the conventional 17-inch socket bayonet used on muskets; it was a true, stirrup-hilted sword of 24 inches that attached to the side of the barrel rather than encircling the muzzle and could be used separately from the rifle—a superb gutting weapon similar to the *gladius* favored by Roman legionnaires. The marines carried theirs in black leather scabbards suspended from a white leather belt worn diagonally across the chest.

Today, the marines would use the bayonets for a purpose no one had ever considered. They were a little short for Pennywhistle's design; yet no plan was perfect, and war was nothing if not a showcase for fast improvisation.

Pennywhistle himself carried a unique .65 caliber Ferguson Rifle, a gift from his father, who had been a friend of the original inventor. The four-foot Ferguson was a breech loader years ahead of its time. It needed no ramrod and could be reloaded from any position. Even in the confusion of combat, he could squeeze off six shots a minute; much better than the three you could expect from a Brown Bess, or the two from a Baker. It was a lovely weapon and he had used it with deadly accuracy on three continents.

He kept a lookout for Barney. The Commodore's death would be a severe blow to the flotilla and American morale in general. He had a good description of the man, and the uniform would be distinctive. But he could discover no officer matching his expectations. Barney did not appear to be present.

He passed the time by lining up and rehearsing shots—only the challenging ones; the kill interested him far less than the artistry in setting up the shot, and only officers; he would never waste time on ordinary soldiers. They only followed orders.

One marine officer attracted his attention. He was a captain, apparently the highest ranking officer in the camp today. His height seemed to be almost the same as his own—six feet, two inches—and few in either army were over six feet. The man's platinum blond hair was also distinctive. His back was turned; Pennywhistle willed the man to turn round so he could glimpse the face, but he had no psychic powers and his curiosity went unrewarded. The officer issued a lot of orders and was the center of a great deal of activity. He wrote notes frequently in a large ledger. Pennywhistle deduced the man was checking supplies: the epitome of a good officer, meticulous and thorough. He would die first, if it were up to Pennywhistle.

The hours passed slowly and the day grew hotter and hotter. It would probably hit one hundred degrees Fahrenheit again. He continued to scan the area with his spyglass, compiling a mental ledger of guard movements and troop routines. Some of the tarpaulin covers were pulled back as new supplies arrived—barrels of beef, pork, and flour mostly, clear indicators Barney had no plans to break camp. Each hour furnished him more and more information.

The movements of the Americans became slower and slower as the day dragged on. About one, when the landscape positively boiled, many took impromptu American versions of the siesta he had observed in Spain. They lay in no particular order under the pine trees, desperately hoping for some relief from the shade, if not a passing breeze.

The blond officer had been diligent and strict with his marines, ensuring that all the caches were closely covered as soon as the new supplies had been lugged over by unhappy looking soldiers. There were always unpopular duties to perform—latrine duty came to mind, as Pennywhistle reflected—and camps usually evolved a pecking order to pass these jobs off to the least popular, or the lowest ranking soldiers. Ah, yes, human nature at its less than angelic best. As men were called to join small groups sharing provender, two marines neglected to fully replace one of the tarpaulins before they moved off.

It was just as had Pennywhistle hoped. He faced good men, but even good men got careless and slipshod in blistering heat.

Pennywhistle slithered forward and managed to get a good look at what was underneath, reading the print on the barrels with his spyglass. "*E. I. du Pont de Numours.*" He smiled. They produced only one product in their mill on the Brandywine. It looked to be at least fifty barrels of the slow burning, coarsely grained powder required for naval ordinance. It might not be the only cache, but it was enough. The distance was perhaps fifty yards from the nearest gunboat, so it might well take a gunboat or two with it when it blew. The trick would be to light it off without getting spotted or killed in the process. He had no extra powder, but Dale had four waterproof fuses in his haversack that could be spliced.

He heard a Bob White call to his rear, trilled three times in quick succession—a prearranged signal that O'Laughlin had arrived. Thank God! He stealthily withdrew from his position and made a stooped dash back to the pine grove.

O'Laughlin smiled broadly and patted Blarney on the head. The dog gave his trademark lop-sided grin. Pennywhistle said calmly, "Report, Private."

"I told you, sir, we was right to spare this dog and trust him. Wigsby's comin', sir! Blarney scented him and I stayed round until the wagons came in sight. Then I ran here just as fast as I could. My guess is Wigsby will be here in about an hour."

Wigsby had moved faster than expected. Pennywhistle smiled briefly in relief. His timetable could be advanced. Perhaps the prospect of more gold and future shows had speeded Wigsby's progress.

Every minute he stayed in place increased the risk. The US Marine perimeter patrol might be closing on his position this very minute. A stray marine or sailor might stumble on his hide by accident; even the best laid plan might be undone by random chance. But there was another problem.

The men of the slave patrol would have been missed as early as the previous evening. His men had hidden the bodies, but the day was torrid and the smell would soon disclose their location, even if hunting dogs were not enlisted in the search. Fourteen dead local notables would rouse the countryside because the nature of the wounds would lead to only one possible conclusion: Cold-blooded murder! Massacre! British perfidy! He could almost hear town criers shouting to stunned crowds round local courthouses. The militia would be called out, then it would simply be a matter of following the hoof prints to their present location.

It was entirely possible a large group of militia might arrive at any moment. Unlike the foot-sloggers in the North, Southern militia were usually mounted on good horses and could move quickly. Militia might be inept opponents alone, but acting in conjunction with professionals, such as the US Marines, they could spell disaster. It was now a race between the gaily-caparisoned troupe of entertainers and the hell-bent militia, and he had no way of reckoning which group would arrive first.

After making arrangements with Dale based on their new information, Pennywhistle returned to his previous position to continue his observations of the supply dump. Less than an hour remained to wait, but the minutes lumbered by at the stately pace of a drugged turtle. He grew impatient and wondered if the supply dump guard would be missed if he took the man out. He was tempted to take the risk and have Dale lay the fuses under the powder barrels early, so they'd be ready to light off the minute Wigsby's show began. But these Yanks displayed no slackness; the guard would be missed. He was being hasty; far better to see if the guard would be decoyed by the performers. It would spare him having to dispose of a body.

Patience was needed. Impetuosity was easy in war, but it was the mark of amateurs. He would watch and wait. If worst came to worst and the militia descended upon them, they would have a shooting war on their hands in two directions; quite possibly the last action any of them would see. The lucky ones might be taken prisoner and exchanged later, but anger was running high, and if he managed to do as much damage as he intended, clemency might be in very short supply.

"What you doing, Mister?" said a thin, piping voice.

Pennywhistle almost jumped out of his skin. He swiveled his head toward the voice. It was a camp follower, a blonde waif of a girl no more than seven and her mongrel puppy, happily wagging its tail. There was no fear in her face, merely curiosity. He had outfoxed professionals but been caught by an innocent amateur and her dog.

He would have quietly silenced a soldier permanently, but children were off limits. He did not know much about these odd little creatures; they puzzled him quite as much as horses did. He needed her silence, but perhaps if he could persuade her he required her help, he could obtain that silence. He could tell her she would be rewarded for that help. What did children want that he had? Thank goodness his hunting frock concealed his scarlet coat.

He fastened on his most pleasant smile and spoke in a quiet, welcoming voice. "Good day, little one. My name is Tom. What's yours?"

"My name is Molly. My ma does the camp laundry and I help sometimes." Her tone was friendly; she truly was an innocent. "Why are you down in the reeds like that, Mr. Tom?" She did not seem bothered he had a weapon.

He noticed a ladybug crawling up his sleeve. Nature had come to his rescue. He fabricated a charade in an instant. "Well, Molly, I am a person who collects things. I collect bugs, you see, so I can study them. The reeds around here are their home, so that is where I must look. I preserve them and then mount them on a board. It's like what hunters sometimes do with bear and deer heads. I work for the College of New Jersey, a big place where lots of people come to learn about the bugs I bring back. Do you like to learn things, Molly?

The little girl smiled brightly. "I sure do, Mister Tom. Right now, I am learning my letters on a hornbook. I can already read a bit. Hope to learn ciphering next year. My ma thinks I am real smart." She said the last with pride.

"I bet you are smart, Molly! I could use the help of a smart person right now. Would you help me collect more of these?" He beckoned for her to sit down next to him, then he plucked the ladybug off his sleeve and held it up to her eyes. She looked at it closely.

"Take a good look at him, Molly. In Italy, these creatures are considered to be bringers of good luck. This one is a true beauty, Molly, but I need a lot more of them." He kept repeating her name because it was the best way to command the attention of a new acquaintance.

He reached into his pocket and extracted a silver half crown. The sun glinted off it and she looked at it in amazement. She and her mother probably saw very little hard coin, and it was doubtful she would know one currency form another—only the value of the metal. "I will give you this and another just like it, if you can bring me a box of these ladybugs before sundown."

She looked at him in surprise. "You ain't funnin' me, are you, Mister Tom? These critters are easy to find. I don't want to be stealing your money. Ma raised me to fear God and be honest with folk."

Far more principled than most of the adults I meet, thought Pennywhistle. "Don't worry about taking my money, Molly. I am sure you will bring me wonderful specimens, and as many as possible! That will take all the afternoon; you will earn your pay." He did not want her reappearing anytime soon. "One thing, though; do not tell anyone. If you do, lots of people will be asking to help and I do not have funds enough to pay them all. One helper is enough, and all I can afford. Besides, some people might not want to help but steal. These bugs have great value for scholars. That's why I keep this rifle handy. If you ma asks you where you are going, show her the coin and tell her another one is on the way. What's the name of the man in charge here today, Molly?"

"It be Captain Tracy." She smiled. "He's always polite and courteous to Ma and me; a lot of officers look down their noses at Followers like us'uns. Ma calls him Captain Johnny in private because she has a big crush on him. He's seen lots o' fighting and is powerful strict with his men. Funny, he looks kind of like you."

"Well, if your Ma asks what you are about, explain that you are doing something important for Captain Tracy. Can you do that, Molly?"

"Ma don't like me to lie." She frowned. She looked upward in thought, and then directly at him when she had reached a conclusion. "But this is a kind of a game, isn't it? Kind of hide and seek with bugs. I reckon it don't signify if you fib a little when you are playing a game."

Thank God for the rationalizations of children, thought Pennywhistle. "Yes, it is all a game, Molly. Games make life fun." War certainly was a game of sorts, albeit one a sensible person would avoid playing. He got through its brutality with rationalizations as childlike as the one the waif had just uttered. "I would like you to get started immediately." He handed her the coin. "I trust you, Molly. Please do not let me down."

"I trust you too, Mr. Tom, and I aim to please!"

"Excellent!" He smiled broadly but felt hollow inside. The lies had come fast and easy; war had reduced him to duping children. "Now, be off with you, Molly, and do not come back until you have lots of bugs!"

She nodded several times, smiled, and sprang to her feet. She bounded off in the ignorance that is nature's gift to children, the puppy barking happily and chasing her heels. He guessed she felt she had made a new friend, but he was the kind of friend no child should have.

He sighed in relief. He was wound far too tight. He breathed deeply and tried to calm down. He was not a religious man, but he sent God a silent supplication that she never wander into his world again. He wanted an heir someday, but wondered if war had so damaged his soul that he would be incapable of not tainting any child's innocence with his corruption.

This was turning into a very odd outing.

He checked his Blancpain. Forty minutes to go until Wigsby made his appearance. His men would be sharpening their sword bayonets on whetstones, but he had nothing to do. He reviewed his plans in detail to pass the time. A lot could go wrong, but he had reduced the odds against him to a minimum.

He focused his glass on the Marine he guessed was the Captain Tracy of whom Molly had spoken. He was the same blond officer he had observed earlier writing orders. He and an aide walked the camp, stopping now and then to converse with individual marines. He looked to be a man after his own heart, someone concerned that underlings appreciate that performing their duties with precision and grace increased not only their self worth but their value to the unit as a whole. That was the foundation of true *Espirit d'Corps*. Tracy took one private's musket and gave him a quick demonstration of the manual of arms. The private bobbed his head in understanding then perfectly repeated the motions. The private had just become a better soldier.

Poorly trained men reminded Pennywhistle of Molly's mongrel puppy: bundles of noisy energy that frolicked about mindlessly, enjoying themselves yet looking for guidance to fulfill some better purpose. Dogs and soldiers lacking training broke some things, chewed apart others, and choked the ground with their wastage. Men, like dogs, formed packs, but could be counted on for nothing, save unpredictability, until officers had established dominance as pack leaders. Tracy had very clearly established that dominance, yet he appeared to have done so via respect, not fear.

Rather than one grand gesture, good training centered on the unrelenting and constant attention to hundreds of little details that established dominance through discipline. Those little details were usually neglected or wholly ignored by militia officers, which was why militia were often undependable in battle.

Tracy was clearly an officer who paid attention to the little things in a highly personal way. Judging from the smart appearance of the marines in camp, he probably did as Pennywhistle did, taking blunt, callow boys and shaping them into razors. He made them disciplined fighting men who were better than mere soldiers—in a word, Marines. Pennywhistle surmised that morale among the US Marines here would be high.

Tracy radiated energy and moved about briskly. Pennywhistle only got fleeting looks at his face through the Ramsden, but there was something oddly familiar about it, something he could not quite place. What was it that Molly had said? But his looks were unimportant. What was important was he would be a formidable antagonist.

Pennywhistle impatiently checked his timepiece; thirty more minutes gone. Even the smallest movements in the camp had ceased. An old black hound lay splayed out under a pine tree and moved not a hair, dead to the world. The air was completely still and saturated with humidity.

Pennywhistle heard the faintest hint of music drifting through the air. Some US Marines in the camp heard it too, stood up, and cocked their ears towards it source. As the minutes passed the noise grew in volume and resolved itself into a very sprightly version of "Yankee Doodle." Finally! Wigsby was almost here.

Pennywhistle gave the two Bob White calls that indicated the picket line should retire back to the pine grove. The men stealthily did as ordered. Pennywhistle remained where he was, and Dale slithered forward slightly, moving closer to the powder barrels at the southwest edge of the supply dump. As soon as the guard was decoyed, he would lay the fuses, then light them off when Pennywhistle gave the final signal.

Back at the pine grove, Gabriel spoke to the assembled Royal Marines about what to expect from galloping horses. Hunters were fast animals, nothing like the plow horses that the marines from rural backgrounds had encountered in their boyhoods. Some of the Marines found it odd being given instructions by a runaway black man, but the Captain trusted him, and he certainly seemed to know his stuff.

The riders would first use the 12-gauge shotguns they'd taken from the slave patrol rather than their Bakers. The short, smoothbore shotguns were easier to fire from horseback than the longer rifles. Then they would switch weapons. No one had ever thought to use a Baker bayonet as a cavalry saber, but the Captain liked to try new things. "After you discharge your shot guns, chuck them. You will want to draw the sword—bayonet...." He stopped. "No, today think of it as a real sword; draw it straight upward from the strap on your back, then let its weight bring it down and to a point. Slash with your sword, don't thrust. A thrust is usually fatal, but you may not be able to extract your blade. Keep moving at all costs; this is a charge, not a pitched battle. Slashing is faster and you can hit a lot more men, plus you will recover easily and quickly. You will wound rather than kill, but all that is important is to put the most men possible out of action. Remember to stiffen your legs and stand high in your stirrups when you slash to increase force. Angle your wrist slightly for steadiness. Those high collars on the bluecoats will deflect your blows, so ride past your man and give him a backstroke to the face. Don't stop for anything, and once through the camp ride hard for the yawl."

The marines would give the engagement their best efforts, but no one had ever employed them as improvised cavalry before. They all harbored doubts, but if their captain believed it possible, then it could be made so. Pennywhistle had told them they did not have to be good cavalry, merely cavalry that charged hard and fast. They could manage that. Their opponents had fought well on shipboard, but had probably never faced a cavalry charge. Even the best men hesitated when confronted with something thunderously loud and terrifyingly new. Fourteen shouting men on horseback might not be the Mongol Horde, but they could still do plenty of damage. The un-mounted marines would fire two aimed shots each to precede the charge; officers and NCOs would be the targets.

Pennywhistle decided to give the Yankees a taste of their own medicine in an unexpected way. He had once seen a local woodsman frighten off a charging bear with an awful, high-pitched cry. He'd captured the man but was so intrigued with the deed he'd agreed to release him if he would teach him the yell. He'd had his marines rehearse it during the night ride, to their vast amusement. Howling under orders was a marvelous tension release. The yell was pure, primal noise: a high-pitched, keening sound that sounded like a pack of feral cats being strangled crossed with a banshee scream. The men termed it "Pennywhistle's Screech", but in a later conflict, it would be called "The Rebel Yell". Sound was a hugely effective weapon in war.

"The Girl I Left Behind Me", a jaunty, popular tune, swelled to a thunderous climax with tubas booming, bassoons shouting, and symbols clanging as Wigsby's Caravan pulled to a halt in front of the camp entrance. Two stern Marines guarding the camp's main entrance walked up to the lead wagon. With a merry grin backed by an air of great theatricality, Wigsby stepped down from the buckboard and strolled over to them.

"Good afternoon, gentlemen."

The higher ranking sentry, wearing corporal's stripes and the grizzled face of experience, advanced his bayonet and spoke the conventional challenge. "Halt! Who goes there?"

Wigsby spoke in the pleasantly booming voice of the showman. "Ah! I know what you are thinking, dear fellow. Who am I, why have I come, and who are the people in the wagons following me? I am Mortimer Wigsby, and I have brought you all... a surprise!" He laughed in what appeared to be sheer delight in life. It was infectious. Against good order and discipline the two Marine sentries smiled; this man radiated likeability.

With his ruby-red trousers, blue-checked weskit, purple tailcoat and yellow hat, Wigsby's colors attracted attention and made him look every inch the extravagant showman. He took off his top hat and executed a deep and excellent bow only experienced courtiers could manage.

"I am here to entertain, sir!" he said to the corporal. "I not only guarantee no harm, I promise several hours of delight and diversion. Magical sights you will see! Wonders never dreamed of, acts that make the fantastic real! Songs, beautiful women, and a man whose magnificent oratory will make you proud to be an American! My troupe is a present, a gift sent to you by an extraordinary patriot who is enamored of your martial valour. Could you please take me to your commanding officer that I might explain fully and find a place to set up my stage?"

Wigsby's show sounded wonderful to the Marine corporal, whose blue wool uniform was plastered to his skin from long hours in the sun. "Why of course, sir. Just follow me." As he and Wigsby walked through the camp, sailors and marines glanced up from their torpor, and looks of curiosity bloomed on their faces. Small groups of them got up and began walking toward the wagons, reading the signs on them and wondering if the troupe were here to perform a show or had merely made a short stop to ask for directions.

Sound carried well in the humid air and Pennywhistle could hear most of Wigsby's patter as he and the corporal sought out Captain Tracy. He was selling himself and his show well; the question was, would a worldly officer buy it?

Wigsby moved out of earshot, but Pennywhistle watched him through the Ramsden in animated conversation with Tracy. The showman acted friendly and ebullient, but Tracy wore a skeptical countenance that stopped just short of disapproval. Molly had called Tracy strict. He probably did everything according to regulations. Wigsby's troupe represented undisciplined frivolity. Wigsby gestured a lot as

94

he spoke and kept his smile glued on. Tracy bowed his head in deliberation. When he raised it, his face bore just the hint of a smile. He said a few sentences to Wigsby, who laughed and pumped his hand vigorously. The show would go on. Pennywhistle exhaled a quiet sigh of relief.

Wigsby's people were efficient. It only took them half an hour to set up their stage and get their props ready. As they labored, Pennywhistle divided his attention between monitoring the camp and casting glances back along the road, dreading that at any moment militia might arrive, riled up and ready to kill any British they encountered. The worst part was that, with his scouts recalled, there would be almost no warning. But the troupe completed their preparations without any interruption, and a crowd of sailors and marines quickly gathered and they took seats on the grass in front of the stage area.

Wigsby welcomed and lured more with his booming voice. "Hurry, Hurry, Hurry! Step right up, gents, gather round and see the show that has delighted princes and potentates, presidents and pro-counsels!" The man certainly had a vivid imagination and glib tongue.

By the time the show started, most of the camp had assembled in front of the stage. Tracy had evidently decided the boost to morale warranted a temporary slackening of routine and discipline. Unfortunately, the guard remained in place at the supply dump, as did the guards at the camp's perimeter. Still, they had all surreptitiously moved away from their original positions by a few yards, trying to cage a better view of the stage. Given time and a good show to draw them ever closer, they might leave an opening for Dale to infiltrate and lay fuses to the powder barrels.

95

The show opened with a statuesque older woman marching boldly onto the stage amidst a short musical fanfare from the small band. Pennywhistle figured she had once been a great beauty, now gone to seed and slightly blowzy, but the sailors and marines cheered and whistled approval. She was outfitted in a long, diaphanous dress in the style of Classical Greece. From the high waist down, the dress featured the red and white stripes of the American flag. Above the waist, it displayed the white stars on a blue field of the National Ensign's upper left quarter. Her head was covered by a flame-red Liberty Cap of the sort by worn by both American and French revolutionaries. She was Columbia, the mythical incarnation of America. Naturally, when she began to sing, the song she belted out was "Hail, Columbia".

Pennywhistle found such overblown patriotic displays laughable, but the men in audience clearly did not. The woman had a fine soprano voice and put a lot of emotion into her singing. He saw hard-boiled marines and sailors tear up. She ended with a suitably grand flourish and took several deep bows to thunderous applause.

Pennywhistle noticed the guard at the supply dump had strayed several more yards from his position. From the look on his face, he liked her singing but liked her appearance even more. Female camp followers tended to be drab; the men in camp had probably not seen any approximation of a comely looking woman for a long time. Pennywhistle remembered from Wigsby's playbill that a much younger woman would be performing some slightly risqué songs. That might be the time to make his move.

The next performer was more serious. An actor grandly styled "The Magnificent Marko" performed Hamlet's "To be or not to be" soliloquy. He had a deep, sonorous voice, a fine sense of timing, and spoke the words devoid of the bombast Pennywhistle expected from a road show performer. He wore a dark costume of doublet and hose straight out of Elizabethan England. But what fascinated his audience was less his voice than his height. He was a dwarf, perhaps four feet tall. People associated a lack of height with a lack of intelligence, but this man projected intense intelligence. He received a big round of applause when he concluded.

The supply dump guard had now strayed quite far from his original position. Three more acts and Dale would probably have the opening he needed. Then it would be time for Pennywhistle to set his own show in motion.

Crespo the Conjurer came next on the bill. He performed several card tricks. He captured the crowd's allegiance when he asked a marine to select any card at random from the deck, show it to the audience, then put it back in the deck. The marine did as asked. Crespo shuffled the deck fast and expertly, then plucked a card from it and showed it to the marine. It was the same card the marine had held earlier. Crespo then performed a series of tricks with rings and handkerchiefs and managed to make coins disappear and reappear. The crowd went wild with applause.

The supply dump guard had nearly abandoned his post and his eyes were riveted on the stage. Pennywhistle dashed and slithered his way over to Dale, who already had the fuses spliced together. Dale had also brought a marine with him to act as a runner. The man departed to the rear. The attack would begin directly the explosion went off. Pennywhistle returned to his position.

The Fireproof Lady came next. Madame Renaldi was a tall, thin woman with an ascetic face wearing an outlandish red turban. Her costume of flowing purple blouse, baggy yellow pantaloons, and pointed gold slippers looked to be a cross between that of a harem girl and a gypsy fortune teller.

Several assistants brought props out. Over the next ten minutes, Madame Renaldi dipped her limbs in boiling oil, boiling lead, and nitric acid. She then chewed on melted lead and touched a red hot poker to various parts of her body, all without any ill effect. The crowd gasped in astonishment after each trick.

Likely the substances were not what they appeared, yet the illusion was convincing. Tricking a crowd was of a piece with tricking your opponent in battle. Both were predicated on the assumption you should give your audience what they expected and make them believe theatre was reality.

There was a short appearance by a non-human performer who practiced an entirely different form of illusion. Through grunts, squeals, and foot stomping in response to his handler's questions, "Toby the Learned Pig" appeared to be able to do simple arithmetic, give his age, and tell time. Whispers of *How does he do that?* rippled through the crowd. This troupe really did seem to have something for everybody and would have been right at home at the Bartholomew Fair in London.

Pennywhistle felt the tension building inside him. It was always thus before action. His nerves calmed somewhat as he watched the next act. The performance was so peculiar, so *outré*, that Pennywhistle found it bizarrely compelling. He had never seen a three-legged man before. More than that, he had never seen a three-legged man dance a sailor's hornpipe and then an Irish jig. Bepo was actually quite a good dancer, but that third leg's motions beggared the marine's powers of description. The audience turned utterly silent: awed, repulsed, fascinated. Bepo gave a sweeping bow at the end to a smattering of applause. *At least the man probably makes a living this way*, thought Pennywhistle, *better than the begging that is usually the lot of the freakish.*

Pennywhistle turned his Ramsden on the supply dump guard, who had completely abandoned his post. Almost time. Pennywhistle signaled Dale with a sound mimicking a whippoorwill.

The young woman who came on stage next was every bit what Pennywhistle had hoped. She was introduced as Miss Angela, and she certainly did have the appearance of an angel. She was greeted with loud clapping, whistles, and cheers from the audience. She had a pretty, heart-shaped face and curves in all the right places. Her dress had a scooped neckline that nicely showcased what his marines called "cupid's kettledrums". Pennywhistle felt a wave of lust ripple through the crowd. Even if she were the worst performer in the world, she had their hearts in her hands. She curtsied to the audience and gave them a coquettish smile. More cheers followed. She then burst into a rousing version of "Oyster Nan", an amusing, risqué song that was not really about clams. Pennywhistle looked around—at the posted guards especially—and saw that every man's attention was riveted. Truth be told, he found it an effort to look away from the charms on display.

It was time to move. Miss Angela had the crowd where he wanted them. The supply dump guard had actually joined the crowd, his duty completely forgotten. The guards at the camp perimeter had done the same. *Cherchez la femme!* Amazing how men's lust could corrupt discipline. He cast off his hunting frock and let his scarlet uniform show proudly. He made on last bird song to Dale, and Dale lit the fuse. Now He had two minutes to make one last call. Dale ran toward a gully from which he could provide covering fire.

Pennywhistle dashed for the command tent of Captain Tracy. He would grab whatever documents he could and bring them to Cockburn's flag captain for evaluation. Tracy had exited the tent a few minutes before and was impatiently watching Miss Angela. He alone of the crowd appeared unsmitten by her charms.

Miss Angela was now warbling a bawdy ballad called "The Lusty John Smith". She actually had a sweet, innocent voice, which made her choice of lewd songs all the more amusing. Her singing was punctuated at intervals by cheers and whistling from men completely off guard, oblivious to what was about to happen.

Pennywhistle entered the command tent. It was quite Spartan. A folding chair was placed before a table, which was covered with documents. He had no time to examine the papers; he grabbed the lot and began stuffing them into his haversack.

"Put your hands in the air, Redcoat. Turn around slowly," said a low, ominous voice from behind. Pennywhistle heard the distinctive sound of a pistol being full cocked. Damn! He had no choice but to comply. He turned slowly—and blinked twice in surprise when he saw the other man. The other man blinked also—a mirroring action.

John Tracy had china blue eyes and platinum blond hair. Pennywhistle had emerald green eyes and sandy red hair. Other than those details, the men might have been twins. Pennywhistle pushed his shock down and replied with courtliness. Just a minute left until the chaos started. *Delay, delay.* "John Tracy, I presume. I did not expect to cross your path."

Tracy looked startled, then rallied. He nodded. His right hand did not waver and his pistol pointed directly at

Pennywhistle's heart. He said in a thick, languid Virginia drawl, "I'm guessing you are the Captain Pennywhistle who snatched that British spy from the White Oak plantation. Word gets around. Commodore Barney will have questions for you."

Again Pennywhistle blinked. The accent was different, but the resonance and inflection in Tracy's voice were close to his own. How could that be?

"I must felicitate you on your marines, Captain Tracy." *Keep talking until the blast.* "I have observed them closely today, and they are a credit to good order and discipline."

"We United States Marines are good at everything we do," retorted Tracy with a confidence bordering on arrogance. "That's an unusual weapon you have slung over your shoulder. I would like to discuss it at length later. For now, I must ask you if you came alone or brought—"

A huge flash outside was accompanied by an ear-splitting boom. The ground shook and the tents canvas walls rippled violently. Men screamed and shouted. Pennywhistle was ready; Tracy was not.

The Briton put his head down and made a mad rush at Tracy. His left shoulder slammed into Tracy's chest, knocking the pistol from his grip. Tracy went down as Pennywhistle's blow forced the air from his chest. Pennywhistle did not stop but dashed out into the madness.

A thick cloud of grey-white smoke swirled up from the southwest corner of the supply dump. Smoldering pieces of barrels, boxes, and canvas littered the ground. Arms, legs, heads, and viscera shot a hundred feet into the air plunged back toward earth. *Plop, plop, plop!* A smoking torso, a head with no face, and a pair of boots with feet still in them landed at Pennywhistle's feet. Someone's index finger had landed squarely on the toe of his right boot. He looked closer and realized the bit of flesh was not a finger.

A score of sailors and marines lay dead, and an equal number moaned from wounds; those alive appeared frozen in shocked indecision. But the survivors were professionals; they would recover quickly.

Several glowing orange spots bloomed and expanded on the masts of two gunboats. The fire was spreading.

A sailor reeled past, almost blundering into him. He moaned piteously, "For the love of Jesus, shoot me! Shoot me!" His clothes were gone and his body had been burnt to a crisp. His eyes had been fried and his ears scorched off; a white kneecap protruded through charred flesh. Pennywhistle wished he had the time to oblige the poor man.

Pennywhistle spun away from the stumbling corpse, then froze. "Oh dear God, no." He felt close to vomiting. A little blonde rag doll lay not ten yards from the tent. A splinter of wood three inches long protruded from its bloodied forehead; ladybugs crawled over its chest. It was Molly. She must have finished her task early and had been taking a short cut through the camp to find him. His eyes misted over. He had killed her, just as surely as if he had put a pistol to her head.

Snap out of it! A stern inner voice shouted. *You can cry later. Remember your duty. Think of your men. You can't help her but you can help them.*

A sooty-faced US Marine subaltern was already rallying dazed survivors and marshaling them into line. The marines might have been enraptured by the show, but each had kept his musket close. Despite the ringing in their ears, their dulled hearing, and the smoky confusion, they remembered their training and instinctively responded to the voice of an officer. Give these men a few minutes and they would be formidable foes. Pennywhistle had to make sure they did not get those few minutes. He wiped the tears from his eyes, ran to a small gully that gave some concealment, and unslung his Ferguson. He pointed his weapon at a nearby sergeant who had rallied a file of men. He squeezed the trigger and the NCO collapsed.

Then he heard the sharp report of rifles, different from the *spat spat* sound of muskets. Royal Marines were firing. US Marines began to fall.

He heard the crack of a Baker, twenty yards to his left. Dale! Another US Marine sergeant fell.

The ground commenced to shake with the pounding of hooves. A loud voice bellowed, "Charge!" Then he heard shrill screams that seemed to issue from Hell itself.

Tracy stumbled from his tent, shook his head, and recovered himself. He looked quickly in every direction to assess the damage. Then he saw the tiny body of Molly. He clutched his stomach with one hand and clapped the other over his mouth in an effort to fight down a surge of nausea. His face turned red with anger. She had been a fine, gentle soul. That damned Pennywhistle had killed her! The Englishman had just made this very personal. He would make that Limey pay if it was the last thing he ever did.

He had to rally the men. Lieutenant Graves had already begun the task. He looked to have fifty or so men formed into line. Good! But then Tracy heard the sharp report of rifles and saw some US Marines fall.

"Fire!" Graves' line fired a volley in the direction of the Royal Marines. But the Royal Marines were firing from prone positions, and the bullets passed over their heads. "Reload in quick time!" Graves bellowed.

The blood drained quickly from Tracy's face when he saw the horses. They had just appeared from over the brow of a ravine at the camp's edge and thundered full speed toward Grave's line. The riders held shotguns and shouted a yell that would unman Satan himself. Graves' parade ground straight line was a perfect defense against infantry but exactly the wrong defense against cavalry.

Most of the marines had not finished reloading their muskets. They also had not fixed bayonets.

The red-jacketed horseman fired their shotguns. Because of the bouncing motion and their inexperience with horses, most shots missed. However, the noisy blasts had shock value and unsettled Graves' line. One round of buck and ball did connect solidly with a US Marine's face and reduced it to a smoking crater oozing unsavory black pudding.

From their red jackets and distinctive round hats Tracy knew them to be Royal Marines. Royal marine cavalry? That made no sense!

The horses went from gallop to charge. The riders drew their swords and continued to shout like demons. They smashed the formation of US Marines like a sledgehammer striking glass.

Tracy frantically ran toward Graves' line, shouting for him to have the men scatter and lie down, but he was too late. The horsemen were already among them, cutting, slashing, and gutting with fierce abandon if limited skill. One US Marine clasped his hands to his neck, trying to stanch the flow of blood and air hissing through a gaping sword cut. A corporal who'd been back-slashed across the bridge of the nose wondered about aimlessly, continuing to blink even though both eyes were gone. Blood squirted from the empty sockets. A private stared mindlessly at a left shoulder now lacking an arm. The artery had been severed and blood soared high into the air over his head.

The marines broke and ran, and the horsemen galloped off.

Pennywhistle ran out of his gully and signaled to one horseman, who stopped and helped Pennywhistle up. A second horseman picked up Dale. Time to make for the yawl and safety.

Mortimer Wigsby's ears rang. He realized he was lucky the explosion had not damaged his performers, nor had shards of flaming wood and canvas ignited his wagons. He had never seen a battle before, and he watched, awestruck. It was all quite exciting, and as a showman he appreciated the drama. He was dismayed by the rout of the Americans, but at least he had already gotten paid. He turned his mind to the troupe's next performance in Nottingham.

Miss Angela pouted. She had had all those nice young men worshipping her. She had been giving the best performance of her career and this stupid war had to come along and ruin it! There was no justice in the world!

A jet of flame had turned Toby the Learned Pig into a large slab of sizzling bacon.

Madame Renaldi gasped in horror. These men were certainly not fireproof. Tears came to her eyes, but they could do nothing to restore the dead to life. She did have the presence of mind to realize water could help the survivors. She filled a bucket from the horse trough and splashed it on two burning marines, putting out the fires on their chests.

She refilled the bucket and commenced giving the wounded water in small tin cups.

Bepo and Marko brought willow leaves to the wounded, telling the men to chew to relieve the pain. The men were grateful for the kindness. The leaves contained salicylic acid, which years later would become the active ingredient in aspirin.

Tracy waved to them in acknowledgement as he organized first aid efforts. He found it ironic that a freak and a dwarf were ministering to people who likely would have ridiculed them had they not been part of a theatre troupe. Perhaps because such people had endured so much pain, they felt an instinctive need to relieve it in others.

Jo-Jo the Dog-Faced Boy rushed forward to help, but he was concerned about only one person. He had been in love with Miss Angela from afar ever since he could remember. She was the loveliest thing he had ever seen. He wrote sonnets to that beauty which he never had the nerve to deliver. With his face and head encased in an unruly mass of hair, a pug nose, long floppy ears, and vestigial tail, he was a beast, albeit one with a poetical soul. It was ridiculous to hope Beauty would ever consider the Beast.

Now Miss Angela wandered past him aimlessly: intact, but dazed by the violence that had spoiled her best performance.

"Are you alright?" Jo-Jo asked earnestly.

"Yes, yes, I suppose I am," she answered uncertainly. She looked at the ugly brute and smiled slightly. At least *someone* was paying attention to her!

That smile possessed the brightness of a thousand suns to Jo-Jo. Standing in the midst of carnage and destruction, all he saw was that smile. This was the best day ever!

The Royal Marines on foot quick-marched through the woods back to the yawl. Corporal Withers reminded them to spread themselves out on the trail and not bunch up; bunched up men made easier targets for volleys. Even as he admonished the men, a mass of bullets whistled through the pines, and two marines fell dead.

Withers looked in the direction the bullets had come from. Fifteen men in blue formed a line in a small clearing, twenty yards ahead. They were poised to deliver a second volley. "Shit!" he muttered. He had run headlong into a US Marine patrol.

Normally, Withers would have ordered a charge; it was safer to advance against bullets than to stay fixed in one spot. But these Red Jackets were trained to wring the maximum advantage from the use of cover, and on his word they scattered. Moments later, from behind rocks and trees they were firing back at the line of standing US Marines. Three US Marines buckled and folded. This was an odd reversal of the War of Independence, when US militia had fired from cover at Redcoats who stood out in the open. But the US Marines were not stupid, nor wedded to formality. They soon took cover and began blazing away.

Withers trusted his men to use their training and woodsmanship. He passed the word to scatter and make their best speed to the yawl. He would remain behind as a one-man rearguard.

Pennywhistle's riders reached the yawl and dismounted. To Pennywhistle's surprise and dismay, his men on foot were not there. Had they run into trouble?

"Sir, sir!" Private Blandon shouted as he ran toward Pennywhistle. He had been detailed to guard the yawl, but had posted himself a few hundred yards away on the Nottingham Road, sensibly figuring if enemy came it would along that road.

In his anxiousness to convey his news, he forgot to watch out. He tripped over a clump of weeds, cursed, stumbled to a halt in front of Pennywhistle, came to attention, and snapped a salute. "Sir, a passel of men is comin' up the road, sir. I'd say fifty or sixty, all armed, and all on horseback. I think it's Yankee militia, sir."

Pennywhistle groaned inwardly. He needed to buy time to allow the rest of his marines to assemble. He did not want a firefight with the Yanks, even if they were mere militia.

Horses! That was it. His men had been riding thoroughbred hunters. They were all valuable, and Yankees appeared to prize good horses even over good wives.

He quickly explained his plan to his men. They nodded their heads in silent approval, glad their officer was blessed with ingenuity.

The marines fixed bayonets, shouted their dread yell, and ran at the horses. The thoroughly panicked beasts shied, then galloped. Horses were herd animals, and each instinctively tried to outpace the others. The 14 horses raced headlong into the Yankee militia.

The Yankees recognized a few of the horses as belonging to the dead slave patrol and realized they must be getting close to the men who'd killed their owners. But the murderers could wait a few minutes; the horses had to be rounded up.

For nearly thirty minutes men dashed about, trying to recapture the alarmed thoroughbreds. But these animals had

had the fear of the Lord put into them and proved difficult to calm down and capture.

In the meantime, ten Royal Marines slogged in; tired, bedraggled, but still full of fight. Their trusted corporal was not with them. O'Laughlin told Pennywhistle of the fight in the woods; he had seen three privates fall. "What about Withers?" Pennywhistle inquired sadly, already guessing the obvious.

"He stayed behind as a rearguard, Cap'n." Tears welled in O'Laughlin's eyes. "I don't think he is comin'. He saved us all."

"He was a good man," said Dale. The marines nodded. Those few words were high praise from a man who seldom complimented anyone.

Pennywhistle knew O'Laughlin was right. No point in waiting further. Every minute his men remained on shore increased the risk. It was time to go.

The men boarded the yawl in an orderly fashion. Their faces were grim. Gabriel and Isaac were the only ones wearing smiles. Natural enough: they were finally going to be free! As Pennywhistle shoved off from shore, it hit him that he might just be able to deliver a parting shot. He had never quite realized the depth of his contempt for slave-holders. The boat glided into the channel. He had the men lie down, and let the current move the yawl.

The militia riders on the road were a hundred and fifty yards away, fully exposed. The range was too far for muskets, but just fine for Bakers. The militiamen were focused on the horses, oblivious to the vessel traversing the middle of the river.

The marines lined up their shots carefully; they kneeled and balanced their pieces on the bulwarks of the boat. Each marine held his breath, let it out slowly, and lightly applied pressure to his trigger, as Pennywhistle had drilled into them. *Clack, woosh, bang!* The flintlocks discharged and a blanket of smoke cloaked the cutter from view.

The smoke did not so much dissipate as hang in the air while the boat floated downstream, allowing Pennywhistle to see the results through his spyglass. Ten horses now lacked riders. Men spun their horses around in close circles, puzzled as to the sources of the shots. One man yelled imprecations and orders. No one listened.

Molly's face flashed in Pennywhistle's mind and it triggered an irrational surge of anger. He had seen scores of innocents die in his career, but her death was that one too many. He compared the purity of her heart to the dark hearts of those milling about on shore. He had not done enough. Not nearly enough.

"Sarn't Dale, run out the carronade by the stern. Stand by to fire." Dale looked at him in surprise. The militia were not a threat; it was unnecessary to fire on them again. His commander had always been brutally efficient, but he had never shown himself bloodthirsty. Dale saw a thundercloud on Pennywhistle's brow and hatred in his eyes. It was not the calm face of the Enlightenment Galahad he trusted, but the bitter countenance of a zealot Roundhead about to yell, "Sack the town!" His captain meant to wipe out every last one of the Yanks on the road.

Dale pasted his usual poker face back on. " Aye, aye, sir." He and another marine pushed the stubby carronade up out of its well in the boat's center and along the rails until its muzzle protruded from the stern. The sunlight glinted off its short brass barrel. It was already charged with canister, two hundred musket balls in a tin; the 12-pounder carronade was essentially a wide-mouth shotgun. Dale attached the gunlock and stood ready to jerk the lanyard.

Pennywhistle carefully adjusted the tiller and the stern swung toward the militia men. Almost time. Wait! This was an occasion for some poetic justice. "Sarn't Dale! Let Gabriel have the honor of firing."

"Aye, aye, sir!" Dale motioned for Gabriel to come forward. The black man looked solemn. He knew the Good Book inveighed against revenge, but right now it seemed awfully sweet.

The range was just over 180 yards, about the outside limit of the carronade's effectiveness. The stern continued to swing round. The carronade pointed straight at the center of the confused mass of men and horses. Pennywhistle smiled coldly. He had them dead to rights. Fire!" he snarled.

Gabriel jerked the lanyard with all of his strength.

The carronade boomed and shot back on its wooden slide. Sans breeching ropes, the slide traveled nearly the entire length of the boat's rails.

A cloud of smoke billowed up. Balls zipped through the air with an odd chirping sound, as if from the throats of angry birds. Pennywhistle saw nothing, but heard shouts, screams, and curses. Equine shrieks of pain rose above the human ones.

When the smoke cleared, he unfurled his glass. Slain men and horses littered the road. One horse dashed crazily in circles, then violently butted his head against a tree. He sank down into an odd squatting position and moved no more. After that, the only movements were small twitches from dying men and horses. Ten minutes from now there would be nothing left alive on the Nottingham Road.

He snapped his glass shut. He felt cold and empty, at the bottom of a dark, arid abyss where tears could not rise. It was sad about the horses, though. The men stared at him in shock. He glowered fiercely back at them. They quickly averted their eyes and wondered what was wrong with their officer.

He put up the boat's mast and ran the sail up the halyard. The wind caught it and the boat began to pick up speed. In five minutes, they left the deathscape far behind.

The expedition had been a military success. He'd damaged the enemy, kept the butcher's bill low, accumulated some valuable intelligence, and was spiriting two men to freedom. He had wiped out a militia detachment. He carried a sheaf of documents which likely would prove valuable.

Morally, the expedition had been an epic personal failure. He had killed Molly, just like he had killed Jed, and annihilating the militia men did not bring any surcease of guilt. At least Jed had lived some kind of life; Molly had had all of hers ahead. He saw their faces in his mind's eye and knew they would reappear in deeply troubled dreams in the nights and years ahead. And it was probably of small cosmic moment that he had slaughtered some horses and dogs, but he liked animals and it bothered him greatly. He heard a short woof and saw that Blarney was in the boat, enjoying the attention as O'Laughlin lovingly stroked his head. Pennywhistle was glad he had listened to O'Laughlin.

He had also been stupid and careless. Why had he not killed Captain Tracy after he knocked him down? He'd had the perfect opportunity and had never left loose ends before. He knew in his bones Tracy would be back to devil him and his cause. Was it because the man had his face? He

JOHN DANIELSKI

wondered what that meant, but was too tired to consider it deeply.

He saw with horror a slight twitching of his right index finger and quickly clamped his left hand over it lest the men notice. Was he getting soft? Was he losing his edge? He had seen it happen to good men who had served too long.

Collapse usually came gradually, in three stages: "I CANNOT BE killed; I am simply too valuable to the cosmos. I CAN BE killed; I had better be more careful. I WILL BE killed; I should avoid battle whenever I can."

Collapse could also happen suddenly, without warning. One day a man wrote a large draft on the bank account of the soul, only to find his subconscious had not been keeping a good ledger of the account's balance over the years. That single overdraft immediately closed out the account and turned a weapon into a useless bundle of gibbering flesh.

He had been at this for twelve years. He had promised himself he would leave the Service when Bonaparte was beaten and return to university, yet here he was. Part of him worried he had become addicted to the thrill of battle, but another, more rational part assured him it was sheer fatigue talking. Fatigue had enveloped not just his body but his soul as well.

"Take the tiller, Sarn't Dale. Keep her straight and steady. Wake me in two hours."

"Aye, aye, sir," Dale replied with great sympathy in his voice. His officer badly needed a good rest.

Pennywhistle braced himself against the stern sheets. He idly wondered what Jo-Jo the Dog-Faced Boy looked like. He pulled his hat over his eyes and fell fast asleep. The nightmares began.

CHAPTER FIVE

Captain John Tracy seethed with anger and struggled to keep it out of the written report he was penning. He had spent yesterday afternoon and most of night reorganizing the camp after the British attack. He looked at his watch and was startled to see it was five am; sure enough, the morning sun's rays were visible around the edges of the tent flap. He had been trying to complete this report for three hours. He was failing miserably.

He slammed the quill down in disgust. He needed to calm down. This anger was unproductive and getting him nowhere. *You were roundly beaten*, he told himself, *there is no way to disguise it*. He would make no attempt to do so. He prized honor above all things and would not besmirch it by seeking to shift blame to underlings, circumstances beyond his control, or bad luck. A commander had to be held to account for the lives of his men; only a cur would seek to wiggle out of that responsibility. He had been caught off guard and good men had died because of it.

Barney would want a straightforward analysis of the British attack and the resultant damage stated in plain, unequivocal language. Barney was a bluff-spoken man who hated florid phrases and soaring rhetoric designed to make excuses and put an optimistic face on bad news.

Barney valued him and would forgive his stupidity. He was not sure he could forgive himself. He had never been beaten before, and it stung badly.

His stupidity had caused the death of twenty good men and the wounding of twenty others. But worst of all, it had killed Molly. Dear sweet, gentle, kind Molly, the uncorrupted little thing who had daily brought him bundles of wildflowers for no other reason than she thought he needed cheering up. She said he sometimes looked so grim that she wanted to make him smile. She reminded him that in the midst of bloody war, innocence still lived: a daisy amidst a field of thistles and briars. Her short visits brought welcome respite from the burdens of command. He had to be stern with his men, but he could be silly and playful with her. She had brought simple joy into his life. He had no living relatives, and she had been the closest thing he had to family. Now she was gone forever. He brushed a tear from his eye. It was illogical, but the death of one often hit a man far harder than the death of thousands.

Militarily, things could have been much worse. One gunboat destroyed, one badly damaged, a quarter of the powder gone, but most of the flotilla was still intact. It could perform its function, just not for as long with so much powder gone. Far more men would have died had they not been watching the show. The ones who perished were at the rearmost row of the audience, closest to the supply dump. The men were angry but undaunted. If anything, his marines were more eager than ever to have a good bash at the British.

It surprised him the men still reposed trust in his command ability.

He had organized a pursuit force of forty men after the explosion, but it had taken fifty critical minutes to get them moving. They had found the carnage on the Nottingham road an hour later, but not a militia man remained left alive to tell them what had happened. Flies crawled over everything. He'd walked the road slowly and tried to reconstruct the action. Rummaging through some saddle bags, he'd discovered a bloody notebook which contained details of the mission the militia had been on. He'd winced; an entire slave patrol wiped out!

Examining the weapons that were still intact revealed that none of them had been fired. The militia must have ridden into an ambush. Most of the human and animal corpses looked as if they had been fed into a cheese shredder; the jagged strips of flesh evidence they had been blasted apart by canister. How the blazes had the British obtained artillery?

He wished he'd had time to give the bodies a decent burial, but he needed his men to search out the British escape route. The corpses had already begun to reek from the obscene heat, and flies swarmed and crawled over everything. He would send a detail back in the evening composed of hardcore defaulters. Such details were hated by the men; they made latrine duty seem almost glamorous. Slaves usually performed such onerous duties, but he had almost none in camp. Of course, the hardcore among the defaulters included more than a few thieves; no doubt they would loot the bodies of valuables. It was one of the cruel ironies of war that bad men often contrived to make their fortunes flourish as other, usually better, men died.

There could be no individual burials, since it was hard to figure out which body part belonged to which body. The burial party would stuff green leaves up their nostrils and wear cloths over their mouths and noses to block the stench. They would simply dig a long deep trench. They would use bayonets bent into hooks on the ends of long wooden poles to spear and push the more intact bodies into the ditch. The smaller remains would be shoveled in and hastily covered with ten inches of dirt. Old Pudding Sleeves, the largely worthless camp chaplain, would read a few words from the Bible in his nasal, sing-song voice.

Twenty minutes after exiting the road, his men had found the mashed swamp reeds by the river where the British had stowed their escape craft; the way the reeds were parted indicated the shape and length of the boat. Could the boat have mounted a carronade? If so, Pennywhistle had probably fired from the river; not a place horsemen would be likely to look. Very foresighted; the Redcoat seemed to have planned for every eventuality.

The Englishman would likely reappear to cause more disruption. It was his military duty to bring the man down. But more than that, he bitterly wanted Molly's killer dead. He cordoned off his heart and commanded his mind to take over. This was a military problem to be solved rationally.

Major Leander Jones had been in technical command of the Marines in camp and would probably receive the official censure. Jones was absent just now, his absence not officially authorized, but not unusual: he was off in Washington pleading for more troops. Jones was the sort of fellow who always claimed he could not do the job unless he was allowed more men. No doubt he also preferred the comforts and pleasures that abounded in the capital city over the rough life of field camp, Tracy reflected sourly.

Tracy had recommended that Jones increase both the size and the range of marine patrols from the camp, but Jones had refused. Instead, he had entrusted most of the patrolling to the militia and focused on placating an annoying, three-hundred-pound Washington insider, a militia colonel named Septimus Pritchett. His body resembled a giant cannonball with arms and legs attached, but he had a penchant for beautiful, superbly tailored uniforms which concealed his bulk. His squat, melon-shaped head was dominated by pendulous jowls that overpowered a thin, cruel mouth and watery grey eyes. He possessed a loud, booming voice and a honey tongue which persuaded many in Washington that he was an expert on all things military. When asked his opinion of the man, Tracy had politely told Barney that Pritchett was "a confident incompetent." He'd overheard one marine private express it better: "The man is a pig-eyed sack o' shit."

Washington had stressed the need to maintain cooperation with the militia. Tracy knew it was a bad mistake to entrust an important task to a rich fool and a parcel of untrained, braying amateurs, but Jones had followed orders. Colonel Pritchett had been tasked with clearing fields of fire on all of the camp approaches. He had done nothing. Well, not quite nothing. Pritchett had strutted a lot and his untrained men took their cue from their commander. Pritchett proclaimed loudly how he would thrash the British when he met them in battle. His men made similar boasts. If boastfulness could have won a war, Septimus Pritchett would have been a perfect supreme commander. But success in war depended on truth and efficiency and Pritchett was a stranger to both.

Pritchett had been off drinking and prating at a local tavern when the explosion hit. It would have been a boost to the cause if Pritchett had died instead of veterans, but no such luck. War was like that: the stalwarts died and the boasters survived to steal credit for other men's brave deeds.

The real problem was that the British knew exactly where they were. They would come for the flotilla; it was only a question of how soon. Whatever his personal animus toward the British captain, professionally speaking, the Englishman had been careful, observant, and methodical, so it could be assumed he would have noted numbers, guns, and capabilities. Tracy had to conclude the dreaded Cockburn was now in possession of all of that information.

Why was a British unit like that in the area at all? It was too small to be a raiding force—he had fought several of those—yet larger than needed for a scouting party. They had used stealth and deception very effectively. What if it prefigured a very, very large raid? Reports had been filtering in that the British were to receive substantial reinforcements, and the annoying Barney would be a natural target.

Tracy needed to find out for himself what the enemy intended, carrying out a proper reconnaissance with real marines, not the damn fools from the militia. Barney had 120 marines left, he only needed to borrow a few. All had seen combat, including fifty who had served on the *Constitution* when she had destroyed the *Guerriere*. Every man was a hardened stalwart who had seen the worst carnage imaginable, and enjoyed a wonderful confidence he would prevail in any future engagements.

The Royal Marines had fled downriver. There was a good possibility the British would land in a place where most of their ships could approach close-in. How soon? Probably, he mused, within a day, two at the outside, if yesterday had been the final reconnoiter before the big event.

The leadership in Washington disgusted him. It had been consummate folly to declare war in the first place, opposing mighty Britain with a standing army of only 10,000 men and a navy of 20 ships. It was the equivalent of bringing a butter knife to a sword fight.

War was a horrid business, one that should never be entered into for reasons of bad temper and posturing. Congress had done exactly that. The final tally of lives wasted and treasure lost always exceeded any gains. It was far wiser to exercise patience; justifications for a war where usually long forgotten before its bitter, weary conclusion. The people of America no longer talked of sailors' rights, which had been this war's *causus belli*. The feather-pated politicians in Washington City had metaphorical blood on their hands, but it was only soldiers like himself who saw actual blood spilled.

He remembered Shakespeare's *Henry V*: "But if the cause be not good, the king hath a heavy reckoning to make when all those legs and arms and heads chopp'd off in battle shall join together at a latter day and cry all 'We died at such a place'—some swearing, some crying for a surgeon, some upon their wives left poor behind them, some upon the debts they owe, and some upon their children rawly left." That heavy reckoning had already begun; the economy was a shambles, inflation was soaring, and the New England states spoke darkly of secession.

The war was being conducted with breathtaking stupidity. President "Little Jemmy" Madison and dithering politicians had placed indecisive Brigadier General William H. Winder in charge of the newly created Tenth Military district, which included Washington City, Maryland, and Northern Virginia. Winder was a civilian who had been made an instant Lieutenant Colonel by Madison several years back; he had fought ineptly on the Canadian frontier and been taken prisoner. Upon his return after exchange, he had been promoted to brigadier general, thanks to his cousin being the governor of Maryland. It was hoped such an appointment would encourage the turnout of the Maryland Militia. The unpopular war made many militia men reluctant to report unless it was an absolute emergency. By then, it was usually too late. It may have been good politics appointing Winder, but it had been a terrible military decision.

Winder had 9,000 militia at his disposal to bear the brunt of the defense. They were widely scattered, the biggest concentration being 3,000 near Baltimore. Most were thinly trained, ill supplied, and led by officers of almost no experience. Chain of command was confused, poorly defined, and top heavy with know-it-all meddlers from Washington. Amateurs led by amateurs. Tracy shuddered to think of them facing British regulars.

The only reliable defenders the capital had were 350 regulars, 125 dragoons, and 150 marines. There were another 220 regulars in Baltimore, but they were tied down garrisoning Ft. McHenry. Barney had 120 marines and 350 sailors, but no one had even talked to him about his men being used to defend the capital.

The capital had no field works, no place where inexperienced troops might gain extra courage from extra protection. No one had even thought to begin construction. One man behind well constructed fortifications was worth five in the open. Washington would have to depend entirely on field forces. The politicians talked, debated, and vacillated. Members of the president's cabinet offered up all sorts of foolish opinions. Professional soldiers like himself were in short supply and their advice unsought.

He might be wrong. The target could be Baltimore. It was a nest of privateers which truly vexed the British. But after yesterday's explosion, he did not think so. A landing in the Patuxent made sense. Baltimore would eventually be a target, but Washington would be first.

He felt that destiny had somehow linked his fate to that of the red-coated Royal Marine. Silly superstition, perhaps, but he felt it in his bones. He could not apprehend the exact circumstances of their next encounter, but likely it would take place on the field of battle.

He had seen the ruthlessness in the Englishman's face; he'd wondered why the man had not shot him when he had the perfect opportunity. He certainly would have. Misplaced chivalry? Regard for a fellow professional? Nonsense! He had wiped out an entire slave patrol and sixty militia men after rescuing two escaped slaves. Perhaps he was one of those damned abolitionists. Those people were hard to figure. Slavery bothered him, but radical action was hardly the answer.

Something else troubled him on a deeper level. He picked up the looking glass on his desk and brought it to his face. He contemplated his visage briefly and with a touch of vanity; most women reckoned him handsome. He scowled because he could no longer ignore a truth that was literally staring him in the face. With a few changes in color and the absence of the deep crow's feet around the eyes, he was looking at his opponent's face. Same inverted triangle shape, straight nose, and deep set, brooding eyes. Same full lipped wide mouth, strong teeth, and unyielding jaw.

The odds the resemblance was due to pure coincidence were slight, no matter how much he wanted to subscribe to that interpretation. Resemblance was actually too weak a word; the faces were copies of each other. Chance had nothing to do with it; this was a matter of bloodline. They had to be related in some way. That distressed him greatly, but it was the only conclusion that made sense.

Even more unsettling, the Englishman's conduct reflected what he himself might well have done had their positions been reversed. The Royal Marine appeared gifted with attributes similar to his own: a disciplined imagination tempered with common sense and an astute perception of exactly the right moment to launch the decisive stroke.

Corporal Ryan, his orderly, poked his head through the tent flap. "Sorry to bother you, sir, but you told me to come by and wake you before Reveille. Brought your morning tea, with fresh cream, just the way you like it."

Ryan smiled, hoping to cheer up his commander. The captain bore the dour expression of a man who had just bitten into a lemon.

Tracy recollected he had indeed instructed Ryan to call early, worried he would be so tired from his exertions that his internal clock would not wake him as it usually did. But his precaution had proven unnecessary; he had gotten no sleep at all. Hot tea sounded wonderful. The aroma alone was already boosting his spirits.

"Come in, come in, Corporal. Set the tray down on the desk." He tried to return Ryan's hearty smile but all he could muster was a slight upturn at the corners of his mouth. There was no point to spreading his gloom to the men.

Ryan did not want to intrude on his commander's concentration. He quietly set the tray down. "Is there anything else I can get you, sir?"

"No, corporal, that will be all for now." Ryan was discretion itself, but he knew the man well enough to see by his eyes something was troubling him, something he needed to get off his chest.

Tracy's voice came out more gruffly than he intended. He really was weary. "All right, Corporal. Spit it out. Something is on your mind. What is it?"

Ryan hesitated. "Well sir, it's like this, uh, uh..."

"Out with it man! Speak plainly. I won't bite!"

"That British officer, sir, the one who led the attack, some of the men got a good look at him. They've been talking. He... he looked like you, sir."

So the men had noticed. Under the stress of battle some men's powers of observation increased tenfold. Ryan would swiftly convey whatever explanation he supplied back to the men. He had to tell him something. Best to be honest; at least to a point.

"I have no idea who the Briton was, Ryan. I had never seen him before yesterday. He certainly did look like me. It's a mystery. I don't like mysteries; they give me a bellyache." Tracy realized he needed to add something to boost morale. "What I do know for certain is that he is a very dangerous man. He needs to be stopped. I plan to do just that."

Ryan grinned. "The men are all behind you, sir; they will give their all without hesitation. They are all vexed at those British bas—uh... raiders, and want to take the fight to them. We all want to show them limeys the wrath of the United States Marines is a great and a terrible thing."

"I am most gratified to hear that, Corporal. Now I must attend to this blasted report. You are dismissed."

Ryan snapped a crisp salute, spun on his heel, and exited the tent. He was heartened to know his commander intended to strike back at those damned Lobsters. He would spread the word.

Tracy did indeed have a mystery on his hands. He knew nothing about his paternal family. He had been orphaned early and raised by an aunt and an uncle on his mother's side. His adoptive parents had been kind people, but they had refused to say anything about his father. Whenever he had raised the subject, they had ignored him as if they were trying to protect him from a hard truth. Tracy feared that he was the by-blow of a bad man.

He put aside his riled emotions, but cold analysis continued to hammer the point that he and the Englishmen must share some family ties. The Englishman's exceptional height, his lean build, even the decisiveness and authority of his carriage were, he had to admit, the mirror image of his own.

Tracy idly fingered the lapels on his uniform. It was made of finest blue broadcloth, expertly tailored by the same man who made President Madison's clothes. He could have gotten by with something far less expensive, but he had a touch of the dandy about him. Because of his uncertainty about his father, appearances were especially important. He had to look every inch the proper gentleman.

His English opponent seemed to share his penchant for fine clothes. His scarlet jacket was superbly cut and flattered the Englishman's form every bit as well as his blue coat complimented his own trim physique.

What truly unnerved him was the voice. The British officer's was deep and cultured with the kind of well-modulated resonance which orators coveted. It rippled with the short, clipped vowels of the British upper classes. He said "puhth" instead of "paath" and " car" instead of care." Tracy's own speech was easy-going, slow and relaxed, and favored the long, expansively drawled vowels of the South. Yet the timbre of the two voices was eerily similar.

He put his speculations aside and went back to finishing his report. Barney would be returning from Washington by 9 a.m. A plan began to form in his mind.

Yes. He would present Barney his report, then suggest an expedition that would help set things right and finally bring in some actionable intelligence The Commodore would see things his way. The Commodore would not risk the whole flotilla, but could certainly spare a single vessel. The British landing party that Tracy suspected was even now preparing to strike their supplies would undoubtedly be defended by frigates and smaller craft, but one vessel stood a chance of slipping in, wreaking havoc, then darting to safety. He would, in effect, be returning the compliment the Royal Marine had paid him in kind. Viciously he wondered how the Englishman would like being dosed with his own medicine.

Gunboat Number 11 had no official name, but the men had christened her *The Charming Nancy* after the wife of one their petty officers. *The Charming Nancy* mounted an 18-pound long gun in the bow, a 32-pound carronade in the stern, and could carry forty men. One solid shot from the bow gun, scoring a good hit, could destroy a landing craft filled to the gunwales with men. The carronade was a short range weapon, but loaded with a double dose of canister, over four hundred musket balls, it was deadly against closely packed bodies of men.

He would probably only get one round off from each weapon, but he would have one priceless advantage: surprise. The British had mainly fought militia recently, had a justifiably low opinion of them, and believed the Americans thoroughly cowed where they weren't inept.

The Royal Navy would not be expecting professionals. Grimly smiling, Tracy resolved to make the Limeys laugh out of the other sides of their arrogant mouths. He would reserve the last laugh for himself as his men punched out a few British teeth.

Minnows attacking whales; maybe not the best-advised course, but somebody had to do something. No one expected anything from minnows.

No, that was defeatist, entirely the wrong analogy. He remembered a conversation with a newly arrived marine who had served on board USS *Hornet* during its stunning victory over HMS *Peacock*. His men would be hornets, hornets attacking the British lion. Hornets could not bring down a lion, but their stings could certainly make him howl.

Only the British had shown any initiative lately. It was high time to show what well-led United States Marines could do. At the very least, it would be a boost to sagging American morale. He wished he could take all the marines with him in multiple boats and mount a big effort, but realized Barney would need them to defend the American flotilla, and later, the capital itself.

It would require a night voyage, but if he started preparations immediately, he could be in Benedict by dawn tomorrow. He smiled. The prospect of action made finishing the vexatious report suddenly seem child's play. Once it was done, he strode from the tent and hailed Gunnery Sergeant Griggs, the senior NCO.

"Gunny, I want every marine assembled on the parade ground in thirty minutes. Tell them..." he pondered just how to put it, "... an extremely hazardous undertaking lies ahead and I shall need some stout hearts to carry it out. I want only volunteers. There is a good possibility that many will not return. I shall attach no opprobrium to those sensible enough to demur."

Griggs grinned. "Hazardous you say sir? Some may not return? Count me in, Captain! You will only have one problem with the men, sir."

"What's that?" asked Tracy, puzzled.

"Holding 'em back!"

CHAPTER SIX

Rivulets of perspiration rolled down Pennywhistle's back, his sleeves clung damply to his arms, and parts of his anatomy that preferred to be cool and comfortable were too hot, too moist, and itchy, yet his watch said it was only 6 a.m. Another scorcher lay ahead. The Royal Marines had landed at Bartram's Cove at 4 am, just before the first wave of boats, and his men had spread themselves out in a wide skirmish line. The landing had been delayed a day because contrary winds had kept ships out of the Patuxent's mouth.

The marine had a full company with him, just over a hundred men. Several hundred soldiers of the 85th Foot were already ashore. It would take the remainder of the day to land the rest, but the site Gabriel had shown him was indeed ideal for their uses.

The men of the four army regiments had been at sea for three months since departing Bordeaux, with only a short pause in Bermuda. Typhus had broken out on the voyage; men who had been fit on departure were now much less so. The heat made things worse. Wellington's veterans had endured the dry heat of the Iberian Peninsula, but the tidewater air dripped with an obscene humidity that rapidly enervated anyone not used to it. Still, they were resolved, and that was what really mattered. They would march just as fast and hard as they had in Spain and France. Everything depended on speed.

The Fleet marines were much fitter, having been in the area longer, with time to adapt to the abominable climate and plenty of landings, cutting-out expeditions, and miscellaneous small raids to maintain their constitutions. All of the men had been allowed to discard their hated stocks, the leather collars worn round the neck to keep the head erect. In this climate, they caused painful neck welts.

Each of the four ships of the line and seven frigates of the British Fleet contributed a portion of their marines to a separate 700-man brigade; it constituted the closest thing the expedition had to an elite strike force.

Cockburn had arranged diversions to mystify the Americans. Captain Sir Peter Parker and his frigate *Menelaus* had been making very active demonstrations and landings in the Baltimore area. Cockburn had proclaimed the city "a nest of pirates" and had convinced many that he was softening things up for a main push there. Washington was a more logical target, but Cockburn's incessant raiding kept the Yankees in a state of angry bewilderment, off-balance and unable to distinguish feints from major attacks.

Commodore James Alexander Gordon was working his way up the Potomac toward Washington with two frigates and three mortar vessels, or bombs, as well as several smaller craft. His presence was intended to distract attention from the main thrust delivered by land. Pennywhistle had served with Gordon on *HMS Active* in the Adriatic. Gordon was a cousin on his mother's side, but more than that, a firm and trusted friend.

The lesser ships of the 46 vessel fleet, mostly sloops and brigs, patrolled the coves and inlets of the Bay.

Pennywhistle had been up since midnight. Officers and men were rising earlier, changing their routines, getting important things done before the fire of the day began. He and his men had come four miles in their cutters as the sky gradually brightened in the east, rowing the last two when the breeze dropped.

Now he and Dale advanced to the top of a small hill known as Reed's Knob, which gave an excellent view both of the landing site and the surrounding area. It was a stirring and inspiring prospect: waves of boats glided toward the shore, and empty craft sped back toward the transports. The movements were practiced, coordinated: a nautical *quadrille*. This amphibious capability enabled the British to move and land troops much faster than overland messengers could carry word of their landing.

The artist in Pennywhistle would not be denied. Drawing calmed the mind, as well as focusing it to remember important details. Since his scouts had reported the Yankees did not seem to be up to any tricks, he took out his sketchpad and pencil, and over the next thirty minutes drew the waves of landing craft from two different perspectives. No artistic triumphs these, more akin to the technical drawings of a military engineer; nevertheless, he hoped they would eventually serve as the basis for an oil painting. Satisfied, he put away his supplies and returned to where the troops were gathered.

Pennywhistle organized a formal defense point atop the Knob and requested some grasshoppers—small, mobile field pieces—be sent forward. He would have a clear view of any Yankee militia headed this way. He doubted they would put in an appearance, and so far he had been right, but Yankees were nothing if not unpredictable. He valued unpredictability as a weapon and had used it successfully on numerous occasions. But his unpredictability had been planned, meticulously thought through. Yankee unpredictability was more on the order of a pack of squabbling children arguing about a course of action and only at the last second deciding what to do. Still, that kind of capriciousness could catch you off guard.

Ten members of the Royal Marine Rocket Troop accompanied him. He mistrusted their Congreves, as they were wildly inaccurate, but they were portable and useful as terror weapons. You could see a cannon ball or mortar shell coming; their flight paths were predictable enough to give you a good idea if you would be hit. The Congreves flight patterns were erratic; they hissed like loud snakes as they zigzagged crazily and sometimes even reversed direction. No man knew if he was safe. Congreves worked particularly well against inexperienced troops, but they could frighten even veterans. A British rocket troop at the Battle of Leipzig had managed to stampede a regiment of Napoleon's best cavalry and had greatly impressed Czar Alexander.

Once the expedition began to move inland and away from Fleet support, they would be almost the only artillery available. That worried him. The Americans would undoubtedly have field pieces, and not just six-pounders; probably some heavy ordinance too, 12-pounders. He had an idea, however, about the Congreves that he had been toying with for weeks. He wondered why the ingenious Mr. Congreve had not thought of it. If it worked, it might change engagements in the future.

So far, the only Americans about were those with black skins, and these were allies. Several runaways had materialized only thirty minutes after he had waded ashore, their faces glowing with the light of new-found freedom, and they not only brought strategically important information, they had managed to smuggle supplies. On their word, a squad of the 85th headed out to secure one hundred new muskets hidden in a hay loft. Another squad departed to retrieve powder barrels hidden in a wine cellar.

The best find, to Pennywhistle's way of thinking, was a twenty-pound sack of Brazilian coffee beans. O'Laughlin crushed and ground a handful with his rifle butt and roasted them in a tin pot, then presented his officer with a steaming mug of coffee that was pure heaven. "Sure and you should have the whole sack, sir. A reward, direct from Almighty, I'm thinkin', seein' how in your great wisdom and mercy you spared this noble beast's life." O'Laughlin patted Blarney on the head. The dog panted and gave an approving snuffle.

The Irishman was laying it on pretty thick. He probably hoped the chicken claw protruding from under his jacket would go unnoticed if he talked fast and hearty; undoubtedly the fowl was his and the dog's next meal. Pennywhistle had spotted it immediately, but decided in the interests of morale he would ignore it. One-eyed Lord Nelson had it right: "A man has the right to be blind sometimes."

"Thank you, private," he said simply. He would accept the gift. The sack would keep him supplied for months, and he would happily share his bounty with two fellow officers who shared his belief that while good wine was silver, good coffee was gold.

He needed to find a new manservant to keep track of the coffee. His previous one had died a month ago, a victim of malaria. The pestilential climate of the tidewater played havoc with men not inured to its rigors from childhood.

Chagrinned, Pennywhistle watched groups of hungry soldiers break away from the main forces and bound for nearby peach and apple orchards. The officers were not restraining them. Indeed, some appeared about to join in the fun. He disapproved, but soldiers were human, after all. It was also hypocritical to condemn them as he sipped coffee for which no Yankee would ever receive payment. Three months of stale ship's fare: rotten beef, salt pork, dry peas, and weevily, rock-hard biscuit would drive any man to slip the bonds of discipline. The lure of fresh fruit was particularly strong. He guessed the next targets of the soldiers would be the hog pens.

He saw several soldiers in succession milk a cow, or at least try to. The men laughed at each other; they were no farmers, but judging by the pail one lugged away, they had been at least partly successful. Fresh milk was a great luxury, and they were welcomed as heroes by their mates when they returned.

The British had paid for provender in Spain and France, for Wellington had been harsh with looters, but things were different here in America. Cockburn had allowed towns along the Chesapeake to buy their way out of looting by paying indemnities, but this being a surprise landing, Benedict had had no such opportunity. The men would take what they wanted and eat their fill, but they would not be allowed to engage in wanton, mindless destruction. They had a job to do, and once their bellies were filled, they would return to it, or answer to Cockburn.

Pennywhistle's wool uniform was already glued to his skin from the heat, nevertheless he continued to scan the horizon, not sure why he bothered, or what he expected to see. It was just years of methodical habits asserting themselves—or maybe it was something subtler. He was just about to furl his glass when something caught his eye; a flash of blue below the distant tree line. It was gone a second later, but he continued to look; one minute, two, then three. Nothing. Maybe it had just been a pair of Maryland grosbeaks. The bold blue colors of these large birds could easily distract an eye too eager to see something anomalous. Maybe he was just too keyed up, looking for a fight when none was likely. Maybe the heat was making him see mirages.

Then he saw it again. This time it was visible for ten seconds and he got a good look. It was only one man, but he moved with the stealth of a warrior, and he undoubtedly brought friends. He wore his hair clubbed and powdered. Only one branch of the American military wore their hair in that old fashion: The United States Marine Corps. His uniform confirmed Pennywhistle's assessment: navy blue tunic with scarlet collar and cuffs, white trousers with black gaiters, and black, red-plumed shakos with *Fortitudine* emblazoned on a brass plate. The entire Corps numbered only about 500, small in relation to the Royal Marines 30,000, but they had developed a reputation for consummate professionalism.

With most of the US Navy's ships bottled up in harbor by the British blockade, a large portion of that 500 was stationed on land and deployed in the Washington area; if the Americans had the wit to send a good sized contingent to dispute the landing, they could give his 100 a very hot contest indeed. Major Malcolm and the other 600 men of the Royal Marine Brigade would not be landing for another two hours.

He frowned, then smiled wryly. No, the Yankee leadership in Washington knew nothing of this landing. Even had they been in possession of that information, they were too pusillanimous to launch a major effort to dispute it. This was a much smaller effort, and it was led by someone local. Tracy! He must have survived the cavalry attack!

The man's good fortune almost persuaded Pennywhistle's sternly rational mind that luck was an actual lady, one who could be flirted with and courted. Bonaparte believed thus: for all of his genius his superstitious streak always shone through. He habitually inquired of advisors before promoting a man to Marshal, "Yes, yes, I know he is skilled. But is he lucky?"

The man with his face would be earnestly trying to kill him and his marines in the minutes ahead. He remembered the look on Tracy's face when he had knocked him to the ground. It had burned with anger. Yet in his short conversation with the American Marine, he'd gained the impression the man had a thoughtful cast of mind, not unlike it his own. The attack would be no impulsive thing.

He shivered briefly; an eerie feeling sent a queer tingling sensation through his limbs that made the hairs on his forearm stand on end. Was he facing some kind of Yankee doppelganger? He loathed admitting it, but Tracy had to be some blood relation; he hoped it was from a long forgotten, cadet branch of the family. He seemed to recall a younger son of Nicholas Pennywhistle in the 17th century had become a Quaker, fled the family home, and simply disappeared; perhaps he had gone to America. What was of immediate concern was that his opponent was willing to challenge a large force with just a few men. That took a powerful amount of guts and audacity.

Perhaps Tracy was just scouting, gathering information—sensible, logical conduct. No, that was too tepid for the man. He had not misread him. The man would want to cause trouble, and it would all be coldly calculated; none of the gallant, hot blooded stupidity at which the Yankees excelled. The attack would be aimed at a weak point determined by logical analysis. What was it? He searched his mind, asked himself what he would do in a similar situation. A small part of his brain noted: *We do think alike. Perhaps it is in the blood.* The answer struck him in a flash. Make the enemy look one way, but smash him from the opposite direction. Attack by land, but go for the boats! Damn! This was about to get interesting!

CHAPTER SEVEN

The Charming Nancy rocked gently at her moorings in Glebe Gut, a small tidal inlet a hundred yards from the main channel of the Patuxent. Even at high tide, the Gut was only suitable for shallow draft vessels, but that was one advantage a gunboat had over a ship. She was bound, fore and aft, to two large overhanging trees and was covered in reeds, bushes, and leaves. With her twin masts stowed, she presented a very low, almost indiscernible silhouette. She would be very easy to miss unless you were looking for her.

Tracy and his marines had arrived an hour before dawn the previous day. To his surprise and chagrin, the rising sun disclosed absolutely nothing out the ordinary. Bees, birds, and beasts went about their business; no signs whatsoever of a hostile military presence. The river and surrounding landscape looked as peaceable as if they had been lifted straight from a Constable painting.

After all the excitement, bustle, and high purpose generated in assembling the mission, his marines felt let down and disappointed. He could not blame them. He had made it all sound an urgent, desperate, dangerous enterprise, but now it was looking as if this sortie was just a pointless training exercise lead by an overzealous officer.

Yet he knew his instincts were right. What had he missed? A fierce gust of wind nearly removed his hat. Wind! Of course! Nature was the wild card. The same wind that blew fair for them and sped their arrival would be blowing in a contrary direction for a British Fleet trying to approach from the Bay. They would be blocked from entering the Patuxent until the wind changed. Nature had actually done him a favor and given him an extra day to prepare.

He also had an extra day to fret. Pennywhistle had taken a letter Tracy should have burned immediately upon receipt. It was a private correspondence from a prominent New Englander who represented a shadowy organization grandly self-styled "The Knights of the Golden Horseshoe". Since it was not an official missive, perhaps it would be ignored. No, the odd phrases in it likely would rouse curiosity in an intelligent officer like Pennywhistle. The letter writer employed euphemisms and code words to cloak what amounted to treason, but his efforts were crude and ineffectual, the work of an amateur in the game of intrigue. The Briton could figure them out given time. Tracy wanted no part of an absurd conspiracy doomed to failure, but should any part of it leak it would be damaging to the United States.

He'd suppressed his private worries and the demons pitchforking his stomach and put on his public, optimistic mask of command. He'd assembled the men and told them that Nature had gifted them with an extra day, one that he would use to prepare for them a very pleasant surprise. "The British will come. I am as sure of that as I am certain that no one here is a teetotaler. You shall have your revenge, and much more. We shall singe the tails off those British lions and show that devil Cockburn how real devils fight. We shall give that damned scoundrel a hell of a whipping, and one of you just may be able to claim that $1,000 reward for his head."

The men had cheered. They were itching to fight and they were willing to wait patiently for an opportunity to do it. But they would not be waiting idly.

Just before departing Barney's camp, a special consignment of weapons had arrived from the Harper's Ferry Arsenal. He had requested them months before and had finally despaired of Secretary of War Armstrong ever approving his proposal. He had never been more pleased to be proved wrong. He had brought the boxes along, as well as plenty of spare ammunition, and issued the short, sturdy weapons just after breakfast. The men acted like giddy children given presents at Christmas. Then he'd found a low sandy ridge not far from the Gut and spent the entire day instructing the marines in their use. Each man fired fifteen rounds at a life size target. A short training regimen, to be sure, but his men were all battle-tested veterans who learned quickly.

His marines were tired and their faces black with powder stains by evening, but were very, very pleased with their new toys, eager to arrange a play session with the Lobsterbacks. Morale was sky high.

The next day, Tracy rose just before 4 a.m. and settled in to wait and watch. The wind had finally shifted. His men spent the time quietly eating salt pork and biscuit and cleaning their new weapons. A thick, humid mist swirled above the water as the first cherry shafts of light emerged above the horizon. Blast, he couldn't see a thing. He drummed the fingers of his left hand on the gunwale in frustration and absentmindedly hummed the opening bars of Beethoven's Fifth. The British were out there, he knew it! The wind began to pick up; first a slight breeze, then a brisk one, and finally respectable zephyr.

The mist suddenly vanished. He gasped. The armada was just there; as if conjured from thin air by a wizard's wand. He had been right; a little too right. The sight both heartened and alarmed him. Ships blotted out the horizon, many more than he'd anticipated: three frigates, numerous sloops, brigs, transports, and landing craft. He stopped counting after forty.

Red-coated soldiers choked the decks of the ships and transports and prepared to transfer to smaller craft. It was an army readying to land! This was a major effort, no mere raid, feint, or diversion. His superiors would need to know as soon as possible. The other two British operations commanded Washington's attention, but he now saw them for the distractions they were. Still, the advance of the vessels up the Potomac made sense if British planned to march by land for Washington; the army would need nautical support, including evacuation routes.

His most sensible course of action, no doubt, was to depart with his men as quickly and quietly as possible; withdraw and report immediately, but it galled him to retreat without inflicting some damage. A lot of the British military dismissed the Americans as bold in word only, like yapping mongrel dogs of no moment. One captured British private had said Yankees were "all mouth and trousers." Tracy wanted to show them the Americans were the eagles of their Great Seal, with keen eyes and sharp talons.

Tracy watched the first waves of cutters, barges, and launches head toward shore, packed with troops. Even the smallest carried at least 25 soldiers. Many of the boats normally mounted carronades for protection, but those had been stripped out to carry more troops. They would not be able to return fire, although they were theoretically covered by the guns of the frigates. A solid wind was blowing and they were going in under sail rather than oars. The river was three quarters of a mile wide at the landing site, so it was not a long journey.

The Charming Nancy did not look like any specific landing craft, but she also did not look wildly different from the smaller configurations present. A few of the craft were not military, but local rigs, probably captured. *Charming Nancy's* blue and white paint scheme mirrored that of several cutters. The deception would only buy him a few minutes, half an hour at the outside, but that would be sufficient as long as the wind held.

He only needed ten men to work the boat and guns if he used the sail, rather than oars. The rest of the men could be a land-based nuisance and get the landing craft looking toward shore while danger approached from behind. His men on shore only had to keep things active for twenty minutes or so. They could withdraw through the woods and head back toward Nottingham. One of the marines was local and knew the roads well. Meanwhile, he would do what every good hunter did—look for outliers. He would seek boats on the fringes that had fallen behind. He would be the wolf who takes down the straying sheep all unobserved.

His men loaded the cannon and carronade with great care. They were all experienced gunners. They, too, smiled with wolfish eagerness.

It could work very nicely. It could also fail disastrously. But good plan or bad, there was no one else. At this moment, the honor of the United States rested on his shoulders.

Pennywhistle debated whether to send a runner to the beach to warn Lieutenant Colonel Thornton, the commander of the 85th and the senior officer present, that American scouts were afoot. He had no solid evidence of any specific threat, and he did not want to be thought an alarmist. He sent the runner anyway, with orders to inform the colonel that the Americans were about some mischief and that he was commencing a reconnaissance in force.

He formed the company into a loose skirmish order and moved slowly down the hill toward the tree line two hundred yards distant. Most of the men had short range Brown Besses, and he positioned them in the center. He divided his riflemen to form the two flanks. The rocket men followed behind, holding the long shafts of their Congreves over their shoulders, almost like pike-men of old.

Rather than the straight line advance favored by regular infantry, the men moved forward in low, stooping dashes, zigzagging, and stopping to take advantage of natural cover. Standard light infantry practice was to operate in pairs, each man protecting his partner. Those pairs were usually close friends off the battlefield as well. When slower loading rifles were employed, two pair often worked together in what was known as chain order. One man would fire, quickly fall back to reload, then his mate would dash forward and discharge his piece. The first man from the second pair would advance and fire, followed immediately by his partner. By the time the fourth man had fired, the first was ready to shoot again. Their practiced movements displayed a definite rhythm and resembled a dance; Shorncliffe choreography courtesy of Sir John Moore.

Pennywhistle loaded his Ferguson as he walked, something very hard to do with a conventional muzzle loader that required a ramrod. He was supremely comfortable with the piece; it was almost a third arm. Most officers led from the front, exposing themselves heroically, flourishing their swords and shouting brave commands and exhortations. It was a risky position, of course, but it gave the men confidence in their officer and his orders—he was so clearly putting his own life on the line, they could do no less. However, many officers avoided actual killing as beneath their dignity and left that to the men. They might carry a sword or a pistol for last ditch defense, but disdain to personally wield an effective offensive weapon.

Such aloofness made little sense to Pennywhistle. The business of war, no matter how dressed up in rhetoric and patriotic appeals, was the calculated and efficient infliction of death. As a leader, it was his job not to avoid it, but to do it better, faster, and more skillfully than any of his men. Richard Lionheart would have understood; he slew 29 men in personal combat.

His musings were cut short as five shots erupted from the tree line. It was not the *pop, pop, pop* of muskets, but the sharp crack of rifle fire. Two of his forward men fell dead, and the others sought cover as they had been trained to do. They lay on their bellies to present small targets while they assessed the situation.

The range was at least 150 yards; the enemy riflemen had skill. American Marines using rifles? Extraordinary! Clearly, he held no monopoly on innovation. If he had thought of it, there was no reason Captain Tracy might not have reached the same conclusion. The Americans were probably using the 1803 Harper's Ferry Rifle; the caliber, weight, and barrel length were nearly the same as the British Baker. Both were deadly weapons in experienced hands.

He wondered how many lay in wait for him. He had heard five distinct cracks, but others were probably holding their fire. The first shots had been ranging shots and good ones too. Placement: the shots had struck men in the center of the line, not the flanks, so the enemy line was probably shorter than his.

He lay down, unfurled his glass, and carefully began to survey the tree line. He saw blue movement behind some logs sandwiched between two tall pine trees. It was good cover and perfect for sniping. He saw two blue dots posted high in oak trees just beyond the right flank of the line; probably their best marksmen, seeking enemy officers. The Americans had all the advantage of ground and cover, offsetting his advantage of numbers. He thought about using the Congreve's, but their flight pattern was so erratic they might well miss the Americans' nest completely.

His men held their fire and waited. The minutes dragged by slowly as he surveyed the American position and the terrain with his glass, panning back and forth; searching for something off, something anomalous, something he could use to advantage.

Shots erupted from the American position at irregular intervals, hitting no one, but calculated to keep heads down. They seemed quite content with stalemate: keep the British occupied while important things happened elsewhere. If he sent his men against them with an objective of flanking and over-running them, it would be costly. Thinking furiously, he scanned the terrain for something that might give his men an edge. When he saw it, he actually laughed out loud. He knew exactly what he was looking at. Nature had come to his rescue. Thank God for all the time he'd spent in the forest as a boy.

He passed word to runners, who relayed it down the line: general assault in two minutes. Fix bayonets, do it at the run, close the distance quickly. He would give the order himself, and lead in the expected fashion with all the heroic posturing he could manage. Ridiculously melodramatic, but it never failed to inspire the men. But first, he needed to set the stage.

He decided on the distance shooting position favored by the 95th. Rifleman Plunkett of that regiment had used it to knock a French general from his charging horse at five hundred yards—a shot without parallel in any army of the time. The range to his target was 150 yards; the light was bright, his object in a fixed position, and the wind was negligible. All good; but his target was far smaller than a man—only slightly greater than the size of a shilling.

The shot challenged every skill he had as a marksman. Distance shooting was his gift, his art, his craft. Unlike most gentlemen of his class, he treated every undertaking as something to be pursued with an almost religious fervor; everything done full bore, yet with great care and attention to detail. He practiced marksmanship as often and intentionally as a Jesuit stroked his rosary beads. Mayfair bucks and beaus had coined a disdainful new term for what he was: expert.

It had taken years to refine his gift to the point where a shot like this was even possible.

He placed the folding rear sight in the full upright position. It was an improvement he had designed himself, and the carefully measured tick marks set up shots over a range of distances. However, to use the sight effectively one needed to have a fine intuitive sense of the correct range to the target.

He reclined comfortably on his back, right leg folded over the left, one boot on top of the other. He balanced the piece on the toe of his right boot and wrapped the fore-end of the weapons sling around his right toe and the back-end around his right hand to further brace it. He placed his left hand on the butt to lend additional steadiness. The position was nearly as stable as a firing stand. He estimated the range one final time, allowing for a wind of 1 knot, then elevated the piece to factor in the arc of the bullet. The target hung high enough above the American position that the fall should smash it wide open. It inhabitants would seek vengeance on the nearest living things.

He slowed his breathing and pulse, blanking everything from his consciousness except the target. He was completely relaxed and absolutely focused. He held his breath, let it out slowly, and squeezed the trigger.

Smoke puffed in front of his face and cleared slowly. When he checked his work, the branch was gone, but there was no stirring below. Then, thirty seconds later, he saw what he'd hoped for: movement, violent movement, followed by shouts of surprise, pain, and anger. Lots of blue-uniformed men in severe agitation. Men abandoned all pretense of concealment, rose to their full heights and began slapping and beating wildly at unseen enemies. The hornet's nest had dropped directly on the American position and a large cloud of angry insects had enveloped the marines as thoroughly as any general could wish from his troops. Hornets offered no quarter, could sting multiple times, and were considerably more venomous than ordinary bees.

He estimated thirty Americans in the main position and five more deployed in echelon slightly to the rear of each flank. Most of them had dropped their weapons the better to bat away their tormentors. Not logical; the British posed a deadly danger, but pain was a harsh mistress. The discipline that would have held them firm in battle against men was no defense against offended Nature.

Now. Pennywhistle jumped to his full height, flourished his cutlass three times, and bellowed, "Charge!"

The Marines rose up like dragon's teeth from the earth, shouted a long, rolling "Huzzah!" and dashed forward, prepared to carry the day with zeal and bayonets. They covered the distance quickly, a blood and thunder charge, ready to commit murder, but by the time they reached the tree line, all but one of the Americans had fled. They heard shouts and cries in the woods to the north. The hornets' thirst for vengeance was not yet slaked.

The one American had recovered sufficiently to loose off a shot at the last minute, but his eyes were nearly swollen shut by stings and it went wild. He had made his choice to stand his ground instead of flee; soon he was surrounded, disarmed and subdued. The Royal Marines were laughing heartily at the discomfiture of the Americans. They thought their captain very clever: he had spared their lives and ammunition and driven the enemy from their position. Yet two marines were still dead, and Pennywhistle found nothing funny about that.

The men were eager to pursue, but Pennywhistle reined them in. They were needed at the beach. The main event was there. He had lost precious time on this sideshow. He wondered how bad things were.

CHAPTER EIGHT

The Charming Nancy sailed slowly out of Glebe Gut. Her cannon and carronade were concealed and protected by tarpaulins, as was the supply of powder and shot. At a distance, she might well be mistaken for some sort of transport craft landing provisions. The Red British Naval Ensign she sported at her stern was genuine. It had been captured in a small engagement some months before.

Tracy had had his men remove their shakos, uniform jackets, and hated leather stocks. Since the day was as hot as the heels of the Earl of Hell's boots, they appreciated this order, and now casual viewers would see men in white shirts, sleeves rolled up—sailors. Each man donned a tarred round hat, favored by ordinary seamen of both navies, to further their camouflage.

"Remember, don't be stiff and precise; that marks you as marines," Tracy admonished. "Move in a slouching, unmilitary way. No smart salutes. Don't start shouting until I give you the word, then make it loud and convincing. Pretend the Gunny caught you sleeping on guard duty and you are proclaiming your innocence. You all know your jobs. We aim to make it out of here alive; remember the rally point ashore. We can't stop the limeys, but we can sure send a few to the bottom of the river. We have one advantage over our opponents—all of you can swim. To your posts! Remember *Fortitudine!*"

The Corps motto, *Have courage,* made a good rallying cry. He had formally requested the motto be changed to *Semper Fidelis,* but Jones, the Secretary of the Navy, had denied his submission on the grounds that the motto was already in use by the British 11th Regiment of Foot.

His marines raised the twin masts and unfurled the sails. The vessel gathered way and the rudder began to bite. Unobtrusively the craft entered the main channel, attracting no notice at all. They looked like a vessel of the flotilla returning from a detour to replenish their stocks of water from one of the small streams nearby. Landing troops was a thirsty business on such a sultry day.

The Charming Nancy moved smartly toward the rear rank of landing craft. Most of the boats carried sails, but those closest to shore had stowed them and were backing oars to slow the boats for a smooth landfall. Tracy realized he was in a dangerous position, not one any sane saboteur would choose: their gunboat was well within range of the 18-pound main battery of the nearest frigate, *HMS Severn,* 36 guns. One broadside would reduce *The Charming Nancy* to kindling and his men to corpses.

Tracy scrutinized the landing craft through his spyglass, looking for targets. He saw a cutter packed with men on right flank of the line, a hundred yards ahead. Next to it was a longer vessel, a launch, also crammed with Redcoats. They would serve. The better to protect his men and *The*

Charming Nancy, Tracy shifted their position so that other boats rode between them and *Severn's* guns. Now the frigate could not open fire on the intruder without smashing British boats.

Sounds of musket fire ashore attracted the attention of the men in the boats. Puffs of smoke erupted from the woods. Soon a line of Redcoats moving down the hill toward the shots was clearly visible. A few petty officers unshipped their spyglasses for a better view. It had an oddly theatrical element to it, as if a compelling stage play was unfolding and the men in the boats were the audience.

The attack should have provoked increased vigilance on the part of the Royal Navy, but it did not, due to simple arrogance. While it was indeed surprising to the British that the Yankees had managed to stage any kind of land-based attack, it never occurred to them that Jonathans had either the resources or audacity to launch a simultaneous one by sea. No European naval power would be foolish enough to contest a Royal Navy landing from the sea, given the amount of firepower covering those landings.

Perfect! While the British were gazing to shore, Tracy had his marines prepare the cannon that would deal with the cutter. The handiest sailors were directed to wear the gunboat quickly, as soon as the cannon fired, to bring the carronade to bear on the launch. They would likely sink the cutter, but the launch would survive. Many of her passengers, however, would not.

After that.... He had the men check the fuses one more time. *The Charming Nancy* was rigged to blow, with fuses set for thirty seconds. Her career had been short and dull, but her demise promised a spectacular display of fireworks and death.

The men also checked their muskets. Tracy had decided not to use the rifles, since the range would be very short and the increased accuracy would be unnecessary. The muskets would then be dumped over the side when the men swam for it. He had sent the precious rifles ahead to the rally point at the Fox and Grapes Inn.

Seventy-five yards now. He could see the British in the cutter clearly; they looked very fit. Their faces were determined, expectant, superficially fearless to those untrained to observe deeper signs. Tracy, however, noted tightened lips, furrowed brows, and how their heavily tanned skins were stretched taut across some of the sailors' cheek bones. They were probably in their early twenties, but their wariness indicated hard service. War aged people quickly and experience left its marks. He had more than a few grey hairs on his own head, and he was only thirty-five. The Redcoat with his face was probably five years younger, judging by the lack of deep crow's feet around the eyes.

The rank and file of both sides was young because war was a young man's game. Bellona was a jealous mistress and fools, the unwary, and the unlucky died quickly; a twenty-eight-year-old veteran might be nicknamed "Daddy". The young were full of the fire, optimism, and zeal that cynical old men on both sides of the Atlantic loved to exploit. Old men controlled the chessboard and young men were the pawns sacrificed.

Tracy deemed it foolish to demonize the enemy, far more profitable to understand them as young men with swelling pride who wanted to make a difference. He guessed Royal Marines joined for the same motives as United States Marines: poverty, unemployment, bounties, and love gone wrong, as well as genuine patriotism and a zest for adventure. While a few had suffered brushes with the law and had been offered a cruel choice of imprisonment or enlistment, the canard about soldiers on both sides being mostly jailbirds was insulting nonsense. Nearly all were decent, honest young men seeking a worthy cause that would give their lives meaning.

He treated his duty to shape his men correctly as a sacred trust; the honor of the Marine Corps needed constant burnishing so that it would be a bright beacon to stalwart hearts and an inspiration to others. British officers and NCOs surely took a similar pride in evolving their men. The British were arrogant bastards, yet he had to admit it was with some justification. The tough, indomitable Lobsterbacks had beaten the best of Napoleon's marshals in Spain and France.

His men could all mouth patriotic slogans, but few understood the complex causes of the war. Most of his men thought little about President Madison, and he guessed the Redcoats thought little about King George. For them it was about fighting for their mates, for their units, for the success of the current enterprise, whatever that might be, and for survival. Tracy took no joy in killing veterans. Ordinary soldiers understood the horror of real war far better than the comfortable, bloodthirsty civilians who caused them. And yet, here he was, about to unleash terrible death.

Fifty yards now. The cannon and carronade crews had not unmasked their pieces but stood at action stations. Tracy nodded to a private at the stern of the boat, who lit the small pile of rags with a slow match. The private fanned the incipient flames and a column of smoke began to rise. Tracy waited a full minute before giving his men the order.

"Fire, fire, fire!" shouted ten seemingly affrighted marines. Sailors in wooden boats had a primal terror of that one simple word. Fire was ravenous for wood, rope, and heavily tarred rigging.

The lusty yelling of the marines attracted the attention of nearby sailors, and the iron law of the sea took immediate effect. All nearby vessels were obligated to render assistance. Four boats swung their bows toward the gunboat, including the cutter and the launch.

The rowers in the British boats responded with urgency and put their backs fully into their strokes. The four boats surged toward *The Charming Nancy.* Marines in the boats signaled and shouted that help was on the way.

Twenty-five yards. The cutter was bows on to *The Charming Nancy.* The range was perfect. The marine at the tiller ripped down the Union Flag and ran up a small jack-staff featuring the Stars and Stripes.

"Now!" shouted Tracy. Two marines in the bow ripped the camouflage off the cannon at the same moment the British realized their mistake. It happened in an eye-blink, no time for the British to sheer off. Lookouts on the frigate saw it at the same moment, their eyes drawn by the rising smoke.

Gunny Griggs sighted the piece expertly in just a few seconds. He adjusted the elevating quoin ever so slightly, then nodded quickly to Private Martin, who brought the glowing portfire down on the touch-hole quill covered in powder.

Boom! Nine feet and three thousand pounds of metal and wood tore violently backwards on its wooden slide. The breaching ropes screamed with the strain. The ball shot forward at five hundred miles an hour.

The iron missile slammed into the stem of the cutter and ploughed down the length of the keel. It was like shooting out the backbone of a person; with nothing to bind the ribs together, the cutter disintegrated. A bloom of red mist appeared and there were a few shouts, but the boat and its inhabitants vanished from the surface five seconds after first impact. Most of the soldiers in the boats could not swim, and even if they could have, sixty pounds of equipment would have made that difficult. Thirty lives ended in choking water.

Tracy made his decision. The game was up. To pivot the gunboat to bring the stern carronade to bear would be difficult and invite pursuit. The breeze had increased and the sails were drawing nicely. He would not retreat; far better to keep the course steady and true, directly into the heart of the invasion boats. But there was no reason his men had to stay and risk their lives on a suicide mission; he could do this alone. Greater rank carried greater responsibility.

The bow of the launch grew larger. *The Charming Nancy* was closing the distance quickly. For a gunboat, she had a surprising turn of speed. Officers on the frigate targeted the gunboat but realized they could not fire until they had a clear shot. Soldiers in the launch reached for their muskets, hoping to do something. Marines on the American vessel fired first, with deadly accuracy. Eight Redcoats fell back or slumped forward into the arms of Death.

Each marine put down his spent piece and quickly grabbed another, already loaded. A second volley crashed out and six more Redcoats died. The Americans cheered, then tossed their muskets overboard.

"Jump for it! See you at the rally point!" bellowed Tracy. His men did not hesitate; they leaped or slithered overboard. He knew they cared about him, but they respected him even more, and an order was an order. They had no truck with false heroics. He had always told them a live marine was better than a dead hero. It looked like he was about to become the dead hero. It was several hundred yards to shore, but they were strong swimmers and swimming men were hard to hit at distance with muskets through the chop of water.

Something buzzed past his ear. He saw short, red flashes from the launch. No point in making himself a target. He threw himself down in the rear of the gunboat, his hand on the tiller. The bow of *The Charming Nancy* was only five yards from that of the launch. The breeze increased and the gunboat's sails swelled. The burst of speed should see him clear in under a minute. Once the launch was directly astern, he would fire the carronade. Fifty yards was a good range for 400 musket balls.

The seconds crawled by as if they were millennia. He heard shouts and curses from the launch, but these faded quickly as he sailed past. He popped his head up for quick look. His timing was just about right. The launch was forty yards astern; another enemy boat lay fifty yards ahead. Good enough!

He touched the portfire to the carronade. It made a tinier boom than the cannon, then canisters disintegrated and the balls flared out in a lethal cone. The discharge cloaked the boat in smoke and he coughed hard. As the reverberations faded, he heard piteous lamentations from the launch, and as the breeze blew the smoke clear he assessed the damage. The interior of the launch was a red and black gumbo of body parts, uniforms, and smashed equipment. The cries indicated at least a few had survived. He fought down the urge to retch and focused on the next task: lighting the fuses to the two tons of powder. Last of all, he rose to his full height to thrust the red-hot portfire to the masts and sails. The sails blazed brightly and the masts began to glow. *The*

Charming Nancy was now a fire ship. Standing among the burning shrouds, he felt puffs of air ruffle his hair. They had his range.

He dove over the port gunwale, getting as much distance from the fireboat as his long, muscled legs could generate, and began to swim with all his might. He estimated twenty seconds until the big fireworks. The water felt warm and languid. An insane part of him wanted to enjoy its embrace and hang about to see the results of his handiwork. He mentally spat at the idea and focused on making his low-breasting stroke strong and efficient and keeping his head down. Years of tidewater swimming paid real dividends.

He'd timed it well. Just before detonation, he dove beneath the waves for extra protection. Even so, the shock wave pummeled him. He stayed under for a full minute before surfacing.

Nothing remained of the gunboat save a few pieces of wood. The explosion had vaporized most of it. There was shouting and confusion among the British; two of their landing craft had vanished with *The Charming Nancy*.

He felt satisfaction, but no pleasure. He had done his job: four craft gone and at least eighty dead. It was a fair exchange for a gun boat that would have had limited usefulness as a defensive weapon.

He wondered how many were left alive from the land diversion. No good in worrying; he would find out at the rally point soon enough.

With the smoke swirling low over the water and the efforts underway to rescue those who could be rescued from among the wreckage, no one noticed a lone swimmer; Tracy continued swimming toward shore as fast as he could. He would organize his men at the rally point, then head back to

Barney with his report. The American command, beset with unfounded rumors and speculation, would finally have some detailed, first hand intelligence. He hoped he would be believed that the landing party at Bartram's Cove was no mere raiding force.

The real problem America faced was leadership. American men-of-arms needed experienced, sensible, decisive command at the highest levels. They required someone with a plan and the will to execute it. Barney had fought the British well and cleverly, but no one in authority was disposed to advance him because he was devoid of political connections, unlike the knuckle-headed Winder. The two generals with promise, Jacob Brown and Winfield Scott, were tied up on the Niagara frontier.

The Marines and Navy had first class small unit leadership, of which he was proud to count himself a part. The Army was developing it, but sadly, most of it was happening far from Washington. Men fought only as well as they were trained, and behaved only as well as they were led. His men had fought well today because he had given them thorough instruction in the school of the soldier. Real training was wanting in the majority of those under Winder's command, and Winder had neither the time nor inclination to remedy the deficit.

The British had excellent leadership at all levels of command, from NCOs to commodores. Their men were trained, coordinated, and highly experienced—the opposite of most American soldiers. Captain Pennywhistle and his men had painfully schooled him in the excellence of British small unit cohesion and tactics. He told himself speculation on what lay ahead was dangerous and unproductive. There was nothing he could do about the higher ups, but plenty he could do with his command.

He reached the shore and drew up himself up on some reeds to rest.

He wished he could be certain that the British knew that the author of their misery had been the United States Marine Corps, but that might not happen. His men had pretended to be sailors, and the British had no reason to believe otherwise. Still, the forces below the hill were definitely marines, and someone would have taken note. It was a point of pride. He wanted to shout at them, the way Ulysses had contemptuously yelled out his name when Polyphemeus begged to know who had put his eye out. He reined in his hubris and told himself that what really mattered was that Americans had shown their teeth to be sharp and nasty. The British would be more cautious in the future.

His pride turned gradually to discouragement as he watched the continuing waves of British boats for a few minutes. They seemed to have an endless supply. Enough! He pulled himself up hard and moved up the trail into the woods. It was high time to focus on the future. He wondered if Captain Pennywhistle would deduce the author of the attack. He guessed he would. He badly wanted the man dead, yet somehow it pleased him that the Englishman might know the author of his misery. He had no idea why.

Pennywhistle had nearly made his way to the shoreline when the explosion went off. He was furious with himself: he had let himself be diverted back on the hill, and this was the consequence; had he arrived earlier, he might have been in position to prevent the sabotage. He mastered his breathing to calm and discipline his rampaging emotions, focusing on the cold logic of the situation. No, he could not have done any differently than he had. There had been a threat, and he had countered it. Even if he had arrived earlier, what would he have told the Navy? It was unlikely he would have discerned the American attack, which, he had to admit, had been well designed and clever—an excellent use of limited resources.

He hoped he would encounter Captain Tracy again; no, he corrected himself, he knew with absolute certainty they would meet again. He disdained superstition, but nonetheless he felt their blood connection was pulling them together like iron filings drawn toward some common magnetic source. Tracy had earned his grudging admiration.

His mind devised all manner of military reasons why Tracy needed to be sought out, but in the end, personal curiosity overmastered professionalism. Tracy was a mystery; he wanted to know exactly who and what the man was. Such curiosity could prove a dangerous flame that seduced good sense by its brilliance, yet sometimes the fire to know burned so intensely that it could not be quenched by cool reason alone.

CHAPTER NINE

"My men need rest, Admiral; rest and plenty of fresh food. They have been busy foraging all day in this murderous heat. They are far from recovered from the voyage here. Tomorrow midday is the earliest I can advance. Anything before that will reduce half of my force to stragglers." Brigadier General Robert Ross did not have to explain himself to Rear Admiral Cockburn, but he had developed a good working relationship with the Navy. Explaining was the reasonable, gentlemanly thing to do, and he was the epitome of the reasonable gentleman: a man uninterested in personal glory, but very concerned for the welfare of his troops.

He was worried, but kept his face calm. The truth was, he was in a dangerous spot: outnumbered more than three-to-one in the heart of enemy country. A fast moving campaign was the safest course when numbers were against you. Seize the initiative and never let go; use feints, spoiling attacks, and hard marching to keep the enemy off balance, guessing, reacting to your moves. Keep a good screen between your forces and the enemy, travel light, and above all, ensure a secure supply line back to the Navy. He had learned the right lessons from the Duke of Wellington.

But even experienced soldiers were prisoners of their physical forms and could be pushed only so hard. His men deserved a few extra hours to prepare for the arduous days ahead. It was not just the right thing to do, it was the smart thing to do.

He understood his men perfectly. They expected strict discipline and they got it, but they also received fair treatment and, most importantly, they had enjoyed an unbroken string of victories. His ear had caught an old sergeant quietly reassuring a baby-faced private new to his command: "Old Rossie, he don't know how to lose a battle."

Ross had sweated, toiled, and bled alongside his Redcoats and had shared their worst hardships and darkest moments of battle. He knew them capable of magnificent feats of arms, endurance, and self-sacrifice. The long Iberian campaign had taught him to read their moods and judge exactly the times to push and the times to relent—intuitive knowledge recorded in no manual and only acquired through years of hard field service.

Ross, like most Army officers, had purchased his first commission, an ensigncy in the 25th Foot back in 1789. He was a gentleman by birth, from a long line of them. But even had he not been, the signature of the King on the parchment document conferred the status of a gentleman upon the purchaser. It did not confer the respect of the men, however. Respect was never for sale and had to be earned through courage, sacrifice, and steadfast conduct.

Battle made no deference to rank, which sometimes came as a surprise to nobility, and plenty of well-heeled gentlemen and aristocrats found they could not stand her hard pounding. Some froze, some ran, some babbled incoherent orders, and some were simply nowhere to be found when bullets began to fly. Weak, feckless, or cowardly officers were quietly encouraged to sell their commissions. They were a terrible detriment to the military, which was usually of no concern at all to men who cared only for their own skins and their own ease, but they did care about their reputations back home. A warning that their good name would be jeopardized if they stayed in uniform was sometimes enough to persuade them to retire "honorably", then tell what lies they would about personal triumphs in the heat of battle.

Much was expected of the remaining officers who had passed the vetting of fire. Battle showed their gallantry no special consideration; rather the reverse. They typically had a casualty rate nearly double that of the rank and file. Ross himself suffered intermittent pain from a neck wound that refused to completely heal.

At sea and on the transports, it was a Navy show and overall command belonged to Admiral Cockburn. Once ashore, it became an Army operation and command was his. Ross's orders were to conduct raids and harass the enemy. The capture of Washington was Cockburn's brainchild and *idée fixe,* and Ross had allowed himself to be swept along by Cockburn's enthusiasm and powerful personality. Cockburn had repeatedly assured him the thing could be done, waxing lyrical on its effect on the war; but it was Ross's job to make it happen, and his responsibility to call it off if things became too risky.

Once he started moving north he was committed and there could be no turning back. He had prepared plans for almost every contingency, but some circumstances simply could not be foreseen. The plans were also predicated on his opponent reacting predictably, always an unwise assumption when dealing with Americans.

Cockburn appeared to understand his concerns. The Army needed the Navy to protect its flank and secure their supply line as they advanced up the Patuxent. Barney was a threat to that supply line, and Ross wanted him eliminated.

The most dangerous part of the campaign would be when the army struck inland, away from naval support. Ross had very few mounted scouts, because he had few horses and fewer wagons. He had virtually eliminated the large baggage train and its attendant coterie of camp followers, which greatly slowed most armies. Almost everything would have to be carried. His artillery consisted of a trio of three-pounders and four very light grasshoppers. His only other ordinance were the unreliable Congreve rockets.

The Navy would have to keep making active demonstrations to draw American attention away from the British Army. A strike at Washington necessitated hard marching, at least fifteen miles a day in scorching heat with heavy packs; fast in, fast out. Ross wanted the Naval transports ready to take his men off when the job was done, although he had a sketchy emergency plan to march them out should the navigation hazards on the Potomac slow the Navy. Speed was of the essence to prevent the Yankees rallying and mounting a counterattack. One serious mistake and his men could be cut off from supplies and surrounded. Even the best army could be overwhelmed by sheer numbers, as had happened to Burgoyne at Saratoga.

He intended only a military attack, but he got the feeling Cockburn wanted something more. Cockburn had never explicitly said he wanted wholesale destruction, but he was angry about the Americans burning York and he had mentioned something about torching the offices of the *National Intelligencer,* which regularly printed horror stories about him. Cockburn was an outsize personality invulnerable to intimidation, yet surprisingly thin-skinned when it came to his reputation. The expedition had assumed the character of a vendetta for him.

Cockburn spoke swiftly, confidently. "Tomorrow is perfectly satisfactory to me, General. The landing went well. Our men are champing at the bit. They realize they have a splendid opportunity to do Brother Jonathan real hurt. The success of this operation has implications far beyond this campaign; seizing the enemy capital will be a remarkable achievement that will strengthen our hand in the peace negotiations now languishing in Ghent. It will play well in the press back home and add luster to the high reputation of British arms in the world in general.

"Consider the effect on American morale. Imagine their consternation! Their own capital, the gem so carefully and artfully designed to proclaim a brave new republic to the world, in the hands of the enemy! I am most pleased that the Army has given this plan its full and unstinting support. You will not be disappointed.

"Except for this blasted heat, I believe we are in an enviable position. I regret the disagreeable incursion of the American gunboat, but the flotilla from which it came will be dealt with tomorrow. My officer, Captain Pennywhistle, has furnished me exact information on its position and components. I am dispatching a strong force upriver, and I think it likely the Americans will choose to destroy Barney's flotilla lest it fall into our hands; but the Yankees are contrarians and may chose to slug it out. Captain Pennywhistle and a company of marines will march before dawn to assess the situation and prepare the way for an attack, if that should prove necessary."

Ross was pleased to hear this and nodded approvingly. The risk was still great, but it was one less obstacle for the army to worry out. He still wondered how Vice Admiral Sir Alexander Cochrane, Cockburn's boss and the chief of the North American Station, had come to approve this hazardous operation. Cochrane had a reputation as a cautious commander, one who did not exceed the letter of his orders. He speculated that Cockburn had very calculatedly withheld key details in the briefings he had advanced.

"I have twenty-three vessels," Cockburn continued, "ready to protect your flank when you advance tomorrow. Success cannot fail to attend us!" Admiral Cockburn's voice was tinged with a touch of glee. His hooded, cobra-like eyes glowed with anticipation. He had all the certainty Ross lacked. Ross had the impression that Cockburn respected him but also deemed he lacked ruthlessness. Cockburn constantly prodded him in subtle ways. For his part, Ross respected Cockburn greatly, but felt Cockburn's attitude toward the Americans was tainted by too much personal animus.

Cockburn's voice and conviction were like drugs, seductive and full of promise. They changed nothing about the dangerous reality of the situation but bolstered his spirits. Other than the gunboat episode and minor skirmishing, the Americans had offered no opposition. He had excellent intelligence on them, thanks to the runaways. Today had proven they knew he was there, but they probably had no idea how few troops he really had. Reports made by beaten troops would inflate his numbers—if only to justify their own failures.

Ross parted pleasantly with Cockburn and agreed to meet with him again at dawn the next day. Cockburn would sleep aboard the frigate *Severn* tonight, probably the last time he would do so for several days. He invited Ross to join him in the interests of hospitality and safety, but Ross politely declined, since he wanted to stay close to his men. He decided to make a very informal inspection of the army encampment before heading back to the whitewashed farmhouse where he had established his headquarters.

The heat abated slightly as the sun dipped below the horizon and an evening breeze moved through the tall pines that marked the edge of the British camp. The camp lay atop a small, easily defended plateau twenty feet above the surrounding coastal plain. It had been efficiently laid out in a rectangular pattern according to the classic rules of castrametation that dated from Roman times . Each mess of six slept in a canvas bell tent, the men's feet arrayed in a circle around the center pole. Officers favored much larger, square marquee tents.

His officers had made sure routines were followed carefully; sentries had been posted, patrols sent out, and the brigade majors had distributed details of the next day's march to the regimental adjutants. Some men were playing cards or musical instruments to relax, but most soldiers were cooking their meals—improved by apples and peaches—with their messmates and talking around camp fires. It might be several days before the next hot meal.

Ross liked music, and it seemed to him the army was like an orchestra of war: every player master of his instrument, familiar with his part of the melody, and attuned to the commands of the conductor. The parts would blend into the dread symphony of battle. His opponents, he reflected, were more like a poorly trained town band.

He walked about the encampment informally, unobtrusively checking little things easily missed and occasionally stopping to talk to officers and men. He asked the officers if they understood their objectives and the men if they had everything they needed. He also personally verified that soldiers were carrying sixty rounds and four days' worth of rations.

The sixty rounds weighed ten pounds and the four days rations even more. The baking heat made every ounce carried feel especially oppressive. Soldiers did not like the weight of full loads during hard marching, and more often than Ross liked to admit some new recruits would lighten their packs of the items most necessary for their survival and success: food and ammunition. You could easily track the progress and assess the morale of a poorly officered army by the wake it left of discarded items.

The men loved him for his concern, and it was quite genuine. They were particularly grateful that he had allowed them to dispense with their stocks. Those hated leather collars, symbolic of obedience and pride, were pure hell in this obscenely hot weather. Sometimes symbols were best dispensed with.

Ross felt it was important not to get so caught up in the sweep of grand strategy that the details that made strategy possible went unattended. He had every confidence in his staff officers, but it was even better to make last minute checks with his own eyes. He was far more personable than the aloof Wellington, but he shared Wellington's passion for widespread and careful personal observation.

He satisfied himself that everything was in order before returning to headquarters. The Arabian he had brought from France had split a hoof, so his officers introduced him to the horse he would ride tomorrow. It was a large white stallion named Tamino whose previous owner had been a great fan of *The Magic Flute*. He would be one of the few officers who would be mounted. The horse was handsome enough and agreeable, but not up to the quality of animals he rode at the family estate of Rosstrevor.

He consumed a delicious supper of cold chicken, Maryland crab, and local cider with three of his officers, then retired to the upstairs garret where he slept to write a long letter to Lys, his wife. He missed her greatly. She had traveled from Ireland to France to nurse him through his neck wound; without her tender care, he would not have survived. From the depressed tone of her last letter, it was clear she too was suffering pain: the pain of her beloved's extended absence. War demanded sacrifice not just of the men who fought it, but of their families as well.

He finished writing at about ten and snuffed the candle. At three the next morning, he was awake. He generally dispatched most of his routine correspondence before six am.

Eight miles to the north and several hours after sundown, an exhausted Captain John Tracy staggered through the doors of the *Fox and Grapes Inn*, the spot designated as the rally point for his men. The flames in the large stone fireplace reminded him he needed to dry his clothes. He was at the point of falling asleep on his feet, but a jolt of adrenaline revived him when he spied twenty of his men seated on benches, talking quietly. They looked even more fatigued than he. They saw him at the same moment and started to rise, but he smiled slightly and motioned with his hands to stay seated. They raised their tankards of beer in tribute and relief. A beer would be really splendid about now. He smelled cooking meat and his stomach growled. He was famished. He noticed that several of the marines had faces covered with large red blotches that looked like... hornet stings? How had that happened? It was particularly odd because he had seen his men as metaphorical hornets just before the attack.

"Come in, come in, Captain, I was beginning to despair of your ever arriving," said the innkeeper, a portly, cheerful man who looked like he regularly sampled the food and drink for which the inn was famous. "Your men told me you would come no matter what, said you were hard to kill and too ornery for the devil to take you. Sit down and let me get you something. You look like a man who appreciates a fine steak and a strong beer. And it's on the house; my contribution to the war effort. Your men have been entertaining me with tales of your exploits. Glad to see someone take real action to stop the British! I am sick of prating politicians and prancing militia colonels."

The steak was just what he needed, and the locally brewed beer had a mellow, slightly buttery taste. He relaxed over the next hour and listened to various marines relate their parts in the day's events. He managed to keep a straight face as they explained, with gesticulations and much anger, about the hornets' nest that had descended upon them like a devil's trick. Tracy could not help but respect a commander who used finesse to get the job done and spare men's lives.

The men brightened when he told them he had destroyed four British boats. Their efforts, and their sacrifices, had made a difference.

Two more men wandered in during the conversation. Twenty-two men out of fifty—not good. But he was getting ahead of himself; more might put in appearances before morning. Those that were here were being fed, and fed well, and rest was in order. Since most of the locals had fled at the approach of the British, there were rooms available, so the marines could sleep indoors for a change. A few lucky ones would actually have a bed, even if they had to share it with one or two others.

He was about to plod upstairs and seek out deep sleep on what the Innkeeper had dubbed "the softest featherbed in creation" when an expensively dressed traveler in buff and brown stormed through the Inn's main door. The man was tall, raw-boned, and red-headed and looked to be in his mid-fifties. His clothes were mud-stained, indicating recent travel, and he was accompanied by a servant carrying a heavy portmanteau. He seemed in great haste and full of energetic self importance. He snapped his fingers at the innkeeper.

"Innkeeper, I shall need a room for the night, your best. I also require supper immediately. Mutton chops well done will do, and a decent bottle of claret to accompany them." The man radiated aristocratic hauteur and disdain. Clearly, he was used to being obeyed.

The innkeeper was startled, but gratified he would have at least one paying guest for the night. "Very good, sir, would you please sign the register." The man briskly did as asked, acting as if it were an imposition on his extremely valuable time. The innkeeper looked at the register in surprise and became instantly deferential. "Let me show your man our finest room, sir." It would actually be his second-best room, since he had just given Tracy his best, but he knew what the man wanted to hear. "Why don't you make yourself comfortable at that table nearest the fireplace. My wife will prepare your supper directly."

The gentleman looked the innkeeper up and down, as if appraising his character, nodded curtly, then strode over to a table and seated himself with great dignity. He opened his leather valise and extracted some documents which he scanned quickly, then produced a small inkpot and quill and began making annotations. He appeared lost in weighty thoughts.

Tracy was puzzled. The man looked vaguely familiar. What gentleman would arrive at midnight in a war zone deserted by most of the residents? He was no refugee. He radiated confidence, not panic. Almost as if to answer his question, the gentleman looked up and smiled at him. The smile carried no warmth. It seemed a reflex triggered by noticing a resource that might prove useful.

"Captain, please come here. I would speak with you." The voice was preemptory with a heavy overlay of condescension. Tracy didn't care to be addressed in that fashion and felt an immediate dislike for the man. Still, he was curious, and it would not hurt to discover what the fellow wanted.

He walked slowly over to the gentleman, a fixed look on his face proclaiming he was not intimidated. He stood over the man and waited for him to speak.

"Please, Captain, sit down, and make yourself comfortable. You look to have had a very busy day, just as I have." Tracy frowned. He doubted very much this gentleman's day had been much like his. The man caught the look and sighed, then smiled again, this time with a hint of real warmth.

"Forgive me, Captain, I forget my manners. I have ridden so much today, I have barely had time to collect my thoughts. Allow me to introduce myself. I am James Monroe, Secretary of State."

Tracy was completely taken aback and his features betrayed it. What the blazes was the Secretary doing here, instead of attending to affairs in Washington? The Department of State had nothing to do with military matters. He hoped he was wrong about the suspicion that sprang full blown to mind; was another meddling amateur trying to insert himself into this misbegotten war? He was sick of them. He composed himself and tried to assume a modest, courtly manner.

"John Tracy, Captain, United States Marine Corps, at your service... sir." He had to force himself to add the *sir* at the end. "How might I be of assistance?" It seemed reasonable to ask, although a part of him was tired and peevish and did not want to.

The Secretary was surprisingly direct, for a politician. "I have been out all day making a personal reconnaissance, Captain, recording my observations of the British. It was the most unexpected good luck that I happened to be visiting a friend's home in the area the same day they made their incursion. You look to have seen some hard service, and I should like to know how your observations square with mine. If you could give me a summation of your activities, I should be most grateful."

Oh lord, that was the last thing he needed. He just wanted to sleep. He would make the report as brief as possible. This man certainly was not in anyone's chain of command, but it was definitely unwise to vex anyone with the ear of the President.

He gave a spare summary of his deeds in fifteen minutes. Monroe smiled from time to time, nodded, and his eyes grew wide and wistful. Tracy recognized the look: an old soldier relieving glory days through the deeds of another. He knew

Monroe had been an officer in the Revolution. He might have been a good officer then, but to Tracy he was a used up old prune who had spent too long as a diplomat to remember anything useful about soldiering.

Monroe spoke with real admiration when he concluded. "That is remarkable tale, Captain, very brave and ingenious conduct. You have done yourself, the Corps, and your country proud today."

Tracy pasted a smile on his tired face. He knew he had done his duty well and did not need a courtier to tell him so and spice it with patriotic fervor.

"Your report has been most useful, most useful. However, I believe your estimate of 5,000 is far too low. I would reckon the British have double that number." He spoke with complete certainty.

What arrogant, insulting condescension! 10,000 men! That would frighten the wits out of a pusillanimous blockhead like Winder. What the hell did Monroe know about making a proper reconnaissance and estimating numbers? Tracy struggled to bridle his tongue and keep a look of contempt out of his eyes. Instead, he spoke in his most disarmingly cordial manner. "Mr. Secretary, might you favor me with a description of just how you made your observations?"

"I shadowed their movements for some hours today on horseback, Captain, and took careful notes."

Tracy nodded pleasantly. "How close did you approach, sir? I hope you did not put yourself in any danger." Somehow, he strongly doubted it.

"A mile and a half was the closest."

A mile and a half? Incredible! To the naked eye at that distance, a very large block of men with muskets and bayonets glistening in the sun could be discerned, but little else. Infantry could be distinguished from cavalry at 1,300 yards, and you could make a rough estimate of numbers by the size of each block of men. Something as small as a regiment could be recognized at 1,000 yards, and individual movements and uniform colors discerned at 600. You could pick out unit markings and distinguish line infantry from grenadiers and light troops at 300 yards.

"You watched through a spyglass I presume, sir?" A mounted man with a mediocre telescope could double those viewing distances; one equipped with a superb instrument, like a British Ramsden, could triple them.

"Actually, no, Captain, I departed in haste from Washington and my man forgot to pack one."

It was with effort that Tracy stopped his mouth from falling open in astonishment. Any marine officer under him who produced such a reconnaissance report would have been greeted by derisive laughter—followed immediately by summary relief of his command.

He tried to be tactful. "Mr. Secretary, I would hope you would make a few more observations before you return to the capital. I should be happy to lend you my own spyglass. It gives excellent views at distance."

"Thank you very much, young man, but that will be unnecessary. I have seen everything I came to see and will convey my information to the President. I shall also relate your gallant conduct to him."

There was no point in arguing; the man's mind was made up. And it certainly would not hurt if the President heard of what he had done. "Very kind of you, sir. Now I will take my leave. I have men to command and we leave at first light. I wish you well in your journey back to Washington." He bowed graciously.

"I bid you a pleasant good evening, Captain. Get some rest; you have earned it."

True enough, and he hardly needed an aging politician to tell him, but he was too agitated now for sleep. The worst possible misinformation was being swiftly communicated to the highest possible authority. No wonder the war was such a mess. Very bad times lay ahead if anyone acted on that information. Tomorrow he would talk to Barney. He, at least, would listen and understand. What a pity Barney was not in charge.

CHAPTER TEN

The gaudy apparition popped above the tree line without warning, backlit by the rising sun. It rose quickly to around 1,000 feet, stopped abruptly as its tether line jerked taut, and floated like a dwarf moon. The startled marines in the three boats speeding up the Patuxent let out a loud, spontaneous "Ahhhh": part admiration, part worry. The thing was a work of art, a tool of exploration, and a military weapon all in one package; a 30-foot-high cloud in a silk bag. The material was a patchwork of uneven squares, triangle, and trapezoids of blues, reds, greens, whites, and pinks, as if it had been constructed from pieces of women's dresses. A rectangular wicker basket suspended by eight ropes dangled beneath what Pennywhistle recognized as a venting valve.

Pennywhistle smiled. Balloons were beautiful things that furnished an opportunity to break the earthly chains that shackled body and imagination and soar heavenward, to see the land and life itself from an entirely new perspective. He was fascinated by them and had flown with the great balloonist Jacques-Andre Garnerin when the Frenchman visited London during the Peace of Amiens in 1802. It had cost him two guineas to persuade the Frenchman to take him aloft, but never had money been so well spent. He had felt a boundless exhilaration and joy he had not known since childhood when the balloon parted from the ground and a sprightly wind caused it to rise rapidly. It was not just an emotional delight; it was almost a physical rapture. It was as if he were soaring into a magical realm, away from all of the Earth's torments and troubles.

They had launched from Chelsea Gardens, flown along the line of the Thames, from West End to East End over the City, and then landed in the Essex marshes. The sprawling, seething mass of London had dwindled beneath them and all of the cacophonous noises below had vanished. Between his boots and the distant earth there was nothing but a thin layer of wicker. It was an incredible feeling of freedom. He was truly walking on air!

When they landed, he had bought Garnerin dinner. The man had expensive tastes, and two bottles of champagne rendered him very talkative about the technical details of ballooning.

Inspired by this flight, Pennywhistle had purchased General John Money's *A Short Treatise on the Use of Balloons in Military Operations*. The French had flown the first balloon in 1783, crossed the channel in 1785, and formed first balloon regiment, the *Corps d'Aerostiers,* in 1794. They had used them for spying out enemy movements at the Battle of Fleurus that same year.

All of that knowledge flooded back into Pennywhistle's head. He pushed aside the artist in him, and regarded the balloon from a technical, military standpoint.

From its size, the balloon soaring above him had to be fueled with hydrogen, not air. Likely the gas had been obtained through the process of burning sulphur and zinc. He remembered from Lavosier's *Traité Élementaire de Chimie* that 1,000 cubic feet of hydrogen weighed five pounds and 1,000 cubic feet of air weighed 75 pounds. A hot air balloon would be closer to eighty feet tall rather than the thirty feet he was looking at.

He estimated the balloon contained approximately 20,000 cubic feet of hydrogen. Its lifting capacity would be in the neighborhood of 800 pounds.

Who had constructed the balloon? Had it been built in America or brought here from Europe? The only balloon flight in America had been made in Philadelphia in 1793 by the Frenchman Jean-Pierre Blanchard. The flight had impressed President Washington, yet ballooning had never caught on in America as it had in Europe. Was a French émigré responsible for this one? Since the balloon was tethered by a long thick rope, today's effort might be some sort of test, or it might be sightseers going aloft—maybe a military reconnaissance and a threat to today's expedition!

He made his decision quickly and ordered the three boats to furl sail and heave to. Oars were inserted into oar locks and quickly dipped into the river. The men pulled hard toward shore.

He and his men were supposed to carry out on final reconnoiter on Barney's flotilla to see if the Commodore planned to withdraw, fight, or torch the vessels lest the British capture them. Cockburn had a strong force of boats packed to the gunwales with sailors following five miles astern of his men; Pennywhistle's report would determine its action. Cockburn had heard that a number of small merchant vessels had taken shelter under Barney's guns. Their capture would mean substantial prize money.

Barney's camp and its attached flotilla buzzed with the frenzied yet purposeful activity of scuttling ships. The men were on a timetable; the British were coming, lots of them. Numerous details of three and four men moved about the camp, each detail charged with a very specific task. Orchestrated demolition itself was noisy chaos, but the process of bringing it about was quiet, orderly, and systematic. Barney wanted nothing left behind for the British to commandeer.

The men were surly and muttered curses under their breath as they spliced fuses, hoisted barrels of powder onto the gunboats, and blocked all the cannon muzzles with heavy tampions. Each cannon had been crammed with triple charges of power and would be blown into unsalvageable pieces once the ships exploded. The British would dredge no intact cannons from the river. The men would do their duty and obey orders, but they hated the business they were about. They could appreciate the logic behind the orders, but they still wanted to collectively smash John Bull in the face with a giant Yankee fist.

The few wagons available were being packed with supplies that could be moved. All supplies that could not be fitted in the wagons or were too heavy to move were being disposed of or destroyed. Sailors had started dumping excess shot into the Patuxent just after dawn. Surplus powder barrels had holes punched in the tops and water poured in. Once powder came in contact with moisture, it was rendered inert. Hundreds of barrels of flour, pickled peas, salt pork, and salt beef were being stove in by sailors vigorously swinging boarding axes. Their contents spewed onto the soil, and birds and small animals came to feed as soon as the men moved away.

"Mining the flotilla is throwing away everything we worked so hard to build; doesn't make any sense, sir. It's almost as if we are giving the British everything they want without putting up a proper fight. The Commodore's a scrapper. How come he's decided to withdraw?" Marine Corporal Obadiah Thomas asked in genuine puzzlement.

"Corporal, you are a good fighter, but you'd never make a good general," replied Marine Lieutenant Solomon Frazier, the maestro orchestrating the destruction. "A good general fights only when he has a reasonable chance of success. Barney does not, and he knows that. We got word this morning the British have landed at Benedict in force. They know we are here; that damned Englishman who slaughtered the Militia will have informed them. That Devil Cockburn will come for us with everything he's got. He doesn't know the meaning of mercy and plays for keeps. My bet is he will come today, certainly no later than tomorrow. Therefore, haste is of the essence, Corporal.

"We could fight them, but it would not change the outcome, just slow it down a bit. They have far more men and guns then we do, and a fight would just create a large butcher's bill. The Limeys would likely capture many of our gunboats and use our own cannon against us later on. Barney is betting the British objective is Washington City; he needs every experienced fighter there. That's why he took most of the Marines and sailors with him when he departed this morning, leaving you, me and a few other shellbacks to blow this lot"—Frazier pointed toward the flotilla—"to Kingdom Come. Barney is putting a lot of trust in us,

Corporal; you should be proud. Our job is critical. The flotilla cannot be allowed to fall into enemy hands."

"But sir," protested Thomas, "what about the militia who arrived this morning? There are almost three hundred of them, and they have detachments covering all of the camp approaches. I was talking to a few of them earlier, and they say they have been training hard. They say their commander Major Taney is a good man. They say--"

Frazier cut him off in irritation. "Stop! They're long-winded braggarts who know less about war than a virgin does about fornicating. You're a trained United States Marine, Thomas; why do you listen to such silly-arsed yammering? I can only imagine that you are so eager to stop the British that your mind has become unbalanced and attached itself to any fantasy in which the United States prevails.

"You know the truth, Thomas. The militia are just for show, to keep up morale; no one in Washington expects them to really fight. They are here to make civilians in these parts think that Washington is doing *something*. People are sick of this damn war and rapidly losing faith in the government. Militia who have never seen a fight always think they are tough enough to lick a regiment of ten-foot giants faster than one of them can spit a quid of tobacco. If it came to a fight, the militia presence *might* give the British a few moments of pause before they launch an attack. If we are very, very lucky, the militia might even squeeze off a couple of rounds before they turn and high-tail it like so many scared deer." He shrugged contemptuously.

"Our job is to make sure none of that happens. We all need to be long gone before the British arrive. That includes the militia. I want the British to find nothing but a smoking hole where the camp was and a few smoldering sticks of wood floating in the Patuxent."

Thomas looked chagrined. "Sorry, sir. You are right, sir. But it galls me no end."

Frazier sighed and shook his head. "Most of your comrades share your frustration, Corporal. I appreciate your fighting spirit. I ask you to have faith. You will get your chance to fight. Our forces will make a stand very soon. For now, do you job, remember your training, and things will work out. Don't forget to put some extra powder barrels into the hold of *Scorpion*; I want her vaporized. It would be an enormous propaganda coup if the Commodore's flagship fell into the hands of the British Navy.

"Now I have to deal with those damn merchant skippers. I'd rather pull teeth from an angry bear. I can't order them— civilians, you see. I can merely make entreaties. I strongly suggested they sail away last night with lanterns doused, and trust their speed to slip past the British in darkness. They were not willing to take the risk; I think they thought we were bluffing about blowing the flotilla. Ten ships are still riding at anchor this morning, just begging to be made British prizes. You don't realize how blessed you are, Corporal, not to be cursed with the responsibilities of a commission. Damn those bloody fool captains!"

Frazier then bowed his head as if walking into a hailstorm and stalked off to confront the merchant ship captains, one at a time. His day just kept getting worse and worse.

"Such calm! Such immensity! Such astonishing prospects!" murmured an entranced Pennywhistle. His day just kept getting better and better. This was even more intense than his first ride. His habitual cynicism had dissolved and he could not help but feel a sense of wonderment viewing the world from a balloon 1,000 feet above the surrounding countryside. To see as if from an eagle's eye was a transcendent experience vouchsafed few men. For a brief interval, he forgot the war and his mission.

Other than the soughing of the rising wind, everything was quiet. The cool air was a very pleasant contrast to the baking heat below. From this height, the world looked neat, ordered, and well tended.

He realized with pleasure that his arms remained relaxed; there were no pestiferous insects to slap away at this altitude. America had legions of them; they were far more potent defenders of the United States than her armed forces. His men's faces bore souvenirs of their assaults. Flies of various kinds swarmed everywhere, some species large and biting. You could not bring a biscuit or piece of salt pork to your mouth without having to first brush away flies which covered it. Mosquitoes bred prodigiously in tidal marshes, and clouds of them attacked marching columns. Hordes of gnats seemed to act as their advance scouts. Tiny beasts called chiggers bored into sleeping men and left tiny, itchy red spots which were sheer agony when your uniform and boots prevented you from scratching them. Each morning men made a ritual of removing wood ticks from their bodies; these unwelcome guests generally sought out accommodation in moist areas such as groins and armpits.

Nature looked benign from above, but much of the Tidewater was extremely unhealthy. Malodorous and miasmic winds blew between the rivers and creeks, carrying with them malaria from the many swamps. Fever and ague seemed to love the area. Thirsty soldiers on the march sometimes incautiously plundered brackish streams for water, resulting in widespread diarrhea and dysentery. At any given time, probably thirty percent of His Majesty's land based forces were on the sick list.

He shook his head and once again became the calculating soldier. He panned his glass slowly and methodically over Barney's camp, studying it as a scientist would study the microorganisms in a droplet of swamp water under a microscope. There was a lot of activity going on, rather like insects scurrying across the top of a hot stove lid. He saw wagons being loaded, powder barrels being hoisted aboard gunboats, but no signs whatsoever that any of the flotilla vessels were being made ready for sea. No shot was being loaded aboard the vessels. They weren't going to fight. They were going to blow everything.

He shifted his glass downstream on the Patuxent and could see Cockburn's forces steadily plowing upstream with the wind at their backs. His marines waited by their beached boats half a mile away from the balloon's launch area. He reached for the signal flags stored in the basket.

A gust of wind slammed into the basket, knocking him off his feet. The basket vibrated violently and spun three quarters of a circle until it punched the tether line. At the same time, the change in the temperature and humidity was causing the hydrogen to contract, shrinking the balloon's surface area and reducing lift.

The balloon began to lose altitude rapidly. It surged laterally as it plunged downward, nearly spilling him from the basket. He pulled himself to his knees and frantically waved a signal flag to the men below manning the winch. They acknowledged with hand gestures and began turning the hand cranks to reel in the balloon as fast as they could.

The wind dropped slightly and the balloon steadied as it was pulled downward. He had what he needed, if he were content with a conventional attack.

The man who owned the balloon had indeed been a French émigré. Rene du Lac had come to the United States three years before with the intent of persuading the US government to form a balloon corps similar to the one employed by Napoleon. He had been persistent, but the US government had expressed no interest whatsoever—until a few weeks ago. He had been reduced to giving rides to locals at county fairs. "I have been turned from a serious explorer of the air into a cheap carnival barker!" he'd complained angrily to a solicitous Pennywhistle.

Monsieur du Lac had no love for Englishmen, but his attitude had changed when Pennywhistle mentioned he had flown with Garnerin, adding that it had been "a magnificent experience."

"*Quelle surprise!* I was once Garnerin's apprentice!" Du Lac had thrown his arms around Pennywhistle in Gallic exuberance. After years of pleading with American dolts who could not begin to understand, he was finally meeting someone who fully appreciated the joys of flight. It also pleased du Lac that he was able to converse in his native language with a gentleman who appreciated its lilting beauty. Most Americans were disdainful of languages other than English. Ungrateful louts; they'd still be singing, "God Save The King" if it weren't for the aid they'd received from the French during their Revolution—help they had refused to return in kind during France's bid for liberty. This Redcoat's French was refined and courtly, with the accent of Versailles.

Pennywhistle's inquiries as how the balloon operated had opened a floodgate; the Frenchman had talked energetically and with gesticulations, delighted he finally had an audience who could appreciate the genius of his creation. Pennywhistle's interest was quite genuine. Even in wartime, fascination with the unknown bonded men of scientific bent, regardless of international boundaries.

Because the British naval blockade had caused a shortage of silk, du Lac had constructed its skin out of ladies' dresses purchased locally. Du Lac had explained the special refinements he had incorporated into the balloon and its accoutrements. The balloon's duplex venting valve was ingenious, and the addition of a rip panel positively brilliant. The escape parachute was modeled after the one used by French Aeronaut Sophie Blanchard. She had been the first woman to make a parachute jump in 1799, and she'd made regular jumps during her Paris aerial shows.

Du Lac seemed to take no notice of the war and, enchanted by the camaraderie of a fellow enthusiast, actually begged the marine take the balloon aloft, saying with pride, *"Monsieur le capitaine*, its perfection must be experienced to be fully appreciated."

One hundred feet above the ground, a very unwelcome sight caught the marine's eye. A troop of United States Dragoons riding ahead of several wagons was cantering down the Nottingham Road a mile away. He guessed they meant to treat Monsieur du Lac to a display of the *force majeure* reserved for non-citizens. The US government had expressed interest in the balloon weeks ago, but no contract had been offered, nor had terms of payment had been discussed.

They were simply going to seize the balloon. Washington was low on funds but desperate for any advantage. Someone, perhaps Barney, had probably decided that in war possession truly was nine-tenths of the law.

He could hardly fault the Americans. He had been willing to do the same thing himself. Now he guessed that if the Frenchman had to lose his pride and joy, he would rather lose it to someone who appreciated it than to a skinflint government who had short-sightedly rebuffed his overtures for three years.

He made his decision; time to banish caution, throw the dice, and give his invention a real test. He pulled a pencil and notebook from his pocket and began madly scribbling orders for Dale. He also dashed off a quick summation of his reconnaissance for Cockburn. He knew the Admiral would plot the boldest possible course based on his information. He was betting his life on that.

He rolled each set of instructions into a ball and tossed each one into a small canvas drawstring pouch weighted with a small amount of shot. He marked a large "A" on Dale's pouch, a "B" on Cockburn's.

When he was fifty feet above the ground he grabbed the speaking trumpet. "Du Lac! Point your glass up the road. The Americans are coming to seize you and your balloon!"

"*Sacre bleu!*" shouted du Lac. He studied the road for a minute, then threw his glass to the ground in disgust. You didn't send a sizeable party of armed men if you intended to pay for something. "*C'est des conneries!*" He capered in rage and cursed the Yankees as Philistines, scoundrels, and whoresons.

The two men at the winch cranked as they had never cranked before, and the balloon soon hovered even with Du Lac, standing at the edge of the six-foot tall launching platform. Pennywhistle quickly composed his pitch.

"Monsieur, those Yankees approaching are your enemies as well as mine. They will take what they want and offer you nothing, save indignity; I offer you a better choice. I will pay for your balloon with the twenty gold guineas I have on my person. I know it is but a fraction of what the balloon is worth, but I will make history with your balloon in a way I cannot explain just now. If my idea works, your balloon will be famous. I need the tether line cut."

Three expressions flashed across du Lac's face in rapid succession: anger, surprise, and calculation. Du Lac hated the idea of losing his balloon, but liked the idea of fame.

Pennywhistle glanced at the cavalry coming up the road. The troop commander, sporting an oversize, plumed *chapeau de bras*, halted the column and unfurled his spyglass. He could undoubtedly see the hovering balloon clearly. As if to confirm Pennywhistle's worst fears, the man snapped his glass shut and bellowed some instructions. The cavalry quickly formed into line. A trumpet sounded. Thirty men drew sabers and charged.

"You must decide now, monsieur!" yelled Pennywhistle, the urgency in his voice plain. The cavalry would reach their location in less than a minute. "Sarn't Dale, bring the rocket and prepare to receive new orders."

Dale and O'Laughlin began manhandling the 24-pound Congreve on its long pole up the wooden ramp to the launch platform.

The look in du Lac's eye grew speculative, then he said, "Very well, *Capitaine* Pennywhistle. I accept your terms."

"Here is your payment, Monsieur!" Pennywhistle tossed a leather pouch full of coins to du Lac. The Frenchmen snatched it out of the air, opened it, and began examining the coins.

"Monsieur, count them later! I need the tether line cut! But I must first instruct my men." He turned toward the two marines with the Congreve. "Dale! Get that rocket into the basket!"

Dale and O'Laughlin shoved the rocket into the six-foot-square wicker basket. Its nose touched the basket floor and its long tail pointed up at the sky. Pennywhistle secured the nose to a lantern hook with a quickly tied sailor's knot.

He turned and tossed the two canvas pouches to Dale. "*A* contains amendments to your orders; *B* is for Cockburn. Make sure he gets it. I'll see you at the rendezvous in the reeds. Now get out of here and make for the boats."

"Aye, aye, sir!" Dale kept his face neutral, but he was worried. He had no idea how Pennywhistle could make the rendezvous. It was crazy to hazard your life on an uncontrollable balloon, but his captain specialized in making unusual actions succeed. The drumming of approaching cavalry hooves made him spin round; he saw the thundering cavalry was closing rapidly. Dale jumped off the platform, followed quickly by O'Laughlin. They rolled into balls when they hit the ground to absorb the impact, then rose and broke into a mad dash toward the tree line, forty yards distant.

Ten cavalrymen veered off from the main line, swords at the point, and rode after them. The backs of running, red-coated foot soldiers were targets too tempting to ignore.

Pennywhistle frantically sawed at the thick tether rope with his cutlass. Du Lac chopped energetically at the rope from the opposite side with a woodsman's axe. The rope was heavy and tough, designed to stoutly resist the tug of strong winds. It was yielding far more slowly than Pennywhistle expected. The screams and shouts of the cavalry rose to a crescendo. They were only twenty yards away, roaring forward at full gallop.

Dale, running toward the long stand of pines, could smell a pursuing horse's breath. The cavalryman riding him could not be more than a few yards behind. He and O'Laughlin would not make the tree line. "Down!" He shouted at O'Laughlin. They both pitched forward onto the long grass. Horses tried to avoid trampling large objects, and the horsemen blew right past them.

Bang! Bang! Ten Bakers barked, fired by marines Dale had thoughtfully posted as a rearguard. The blue-coated horseman saw nothing of the men concealed beneath the trees, but five of them clutched their chests or shoulders in agony as rapidly spreading blood purpled their splendid uniforms. Three toppled slowly from their saddles and writhed in agony on the ground. Two others remained in their saddles but were out of action. Cavalry had no way to deal with infantryman concealed behind logs in deep forest, so the unwounded five quickly turned their horses round and put the spurs to them, followed more slowly by their wounded brothers in arms.

Dale and O'Laughlin picked themselves up, smiling with relief that all their body parts were intact, and ran for the tree line. Within a minute, Dale had the rearguard marines formed up and quick marching for the boats a quarter mile away. He read Pennywhistle's orders as he marched; he would see to it they were carried out.

The last fibers of the heavy hempen rope parted reluctantly just as the first cavalrymen reached the inclined ramp at the base of the launch platform, but the rise was painfully slow. Pennywhistle threw out two sacks of sand that served as ballast in an effort to speed things along, and the balloon lifted off the platform. The two lead cavalrymen did not stop their charge but bounded their horses up the ramp. Du Lac fled in terror, covering his head with his hands in anticipation of saber blows.

The balloon was six feet above the platform. Pennywhistle tossed out a third bag of ballast. The balloon started to ascend more rapidly. If only he could pick up a low altitude thermal!

What happened next earned Pennywhistle's admiration quite as much as his surprise. The two cavalrymen did not rein in their horses as they neared the platform's edge but put the spurs to their beasts. Just as Pennywhistle chucked the last ballast bag over the side, they leaped from their saddles, flew through the air, and slammed into the side of the basket, their hands clutching the wicker frame, their booted feet scrabbling for purchase. One black-haired man clung to the starboard corner of the basket, and a blond one to port. The horses shot over the edge of the platform and plunged six feet to the ground.

Suddenly, despite the weight of the clinging cavalry men, the balloon began rising rapidly: fifty feet, eighty feet, one hundred feet. Pennywhistle's luck was in; the balloon had hit a thermal. Pennywhistle felt a heavy hand of air trying to compress him into a ball and his stomach fluttered. The dangling Americans hung on for dear life. As the altitude indicator read eight hundred feet, the black-haired one managed to get a leg over the edge of the basket. His blond mate looked ready to make the same attempt.

Pennywhistle's peripheral vision caught a flash of blue. The black-haired cavalry man had slithered over the side and sprung to his feet. The marine turned swiftly round and shot a right jab to the man's jaw. His fist connected and the man slumped against the side of the four-foot high basket. Pennywhistle grabbed him by his collar and sword belt and hoisted him to his feet. With a mighty heave and the strength born of desperation, he hurled him over the top and into space.

"YAAAAAAAHHHHH!" The man squealed like a gutted pig as gravity sucked him downwards. The body spun as it plunged, making it seem a pin-wheeling scarecrow rather than anything human, and bounced three feet into the air after it slammed into the ground.

The balloon continued to shoot upwards, so fast it was hard to stand up. The altitude indicator registered fifteen hundred feet.

A fist slammed hard into Pennywhistle's kidneys from behind; the blond cavalryman had made it aboard. The pain made him rear backwards as another savage jab followed. Pennywhistle spun around to confront his assailant and got a punch to the cheek for his trouble. Stars flashed darkly behind his eyes and he staggered, but he saw the cavalryman's left hook coming and batted it away with his right arm, then drove the hard fingers of his right hand into the man's eyes, gouging so deeply he scooped out one of the eyeballs; it dangled below the man's right cheekbone. He screamed in pain and his hands flew to his face. Pennywhistle drove his fist into the man's stomach, causing him to double over.

Pennywhistle put one hand behind the man's neck and locked the other onto his elbow. He threw the man against the side of the basket, expecting him to go over the top. The man's upper torso went over the edge, but his legs reminded inside, two inches above the basket floor, his weight balanced on a narrow fulcrum, needing only a small amount of force to sending him plunging to oblivion. Pennywhistle applied that force vigorously, scooping up his legs with a sweep from one of his own.

Then he collapsed into a sitting position, rubbing the sore side of his face and wincing. Slowly his breathing returned to normal and the pain in his back subsided. The basket rocked gently, and gradually Pennywhistle recovered, taking a moment to marvel again at the utter quiet. It was so peaceful aloft that it seemed as if the fight with the cavalry men must have been a dream—until he tried to move and his back spasmed.

Moving gingerly, he squatted to examine the row of instruments bolted to a low corner shelf. The equipment was as modern as anything he had observed when he toured Sir Humphrey Davies' laboratory. The barometer was falling rapidly, indicating that bad weather was on the way. The hydrometer's hand was pushed far to the right, but he didn't need that to tell him the air was saturated with humidity. The spinning wind gage indicated a breeze out of the Southeast with a speed of 10 knots. The compass showed a course heading of 320 degrees. The altitude gauge read 2,200 feet, and the vertical speed indicator showed the balloon was gaining height.

All this information did not enable him to control the balloon's journey. He was exceedingly lucky the prevailing wind was pushing him toward Barney's camp, but he was at the mercy of Mother Nature. Things would turn critical if he were still aloft when the storm hit. The sky above was clear, but a line of glowering thunderheads was beginning to build over the Bay.

He needed to think, but it felt pleasant to ignore responsibility, to rest and relax; simply drift and embrace the dream of a world where he was the sole inhabitant. The scenery below of vibrant greens, browns, and blues captivated the artist in him. Harried officers wished for quiet beaches to walk on away from the burdens of command, but it was so much better floating high and free, literally soaring above mere human concerns. It was if he had entered the Land of the Lotus Eaters in *The Odyssey*, that place of easy repose where men forgot their duty.

The balloon's rise began to slow and the breeze started to slacken.

That episode had not ended well for Ulysses' men; the thought jerked him back to his duty. He glanced at his watch. My God! He had been daydreaming for fully half an hour! He was a soldier, not a sybarite; a fire-eater, not a lotus eater. He unfurled his glass and scanned the land below. There was plenty of movement.

He could see the remains of Barney's camp and a mass of red moving steadily up the Patuxent: Dale leading his Marines. Two miles behind Dale there was a large blob of blue, also steadily advancing up the Patuxent—Cockburn's Strike Force.

Far to the right of the Patuxent on the Nottingham Road, dust clouds rose as mounted men in blue cantered briskly toward Barney's camp: the US Dragoons he had encountered earlier, determined to give Barney warning.

Aeolus, God of Winds, suddenly decided to pout; the wind dropped and his balloon hung limply 5,500 feet above the ground.

The boats on the river were still moving, which meant the wind was still blowing several thousand feet lower. His balloon had evidently risen above the thermal and was mired in a level of dead air. He needed to lose some altitude.

He went to the release valve, planning to vent enough hydrogen to dump several thousand feet of altitude. Then he looked at the rectangular panel next to the valve. He remembered du Lac's words of warning.

"You see this red square, *monsieur le capitaine*? Whatever you do, don't touch it!"

"Why not?"

"Because pulling it down releases this section of the balloon and activates the emergency gas release. It will vent all of the gas rapidly and cause a very, very fast descent. That is not what it is for! Balloons are inclined to bounce along for hundreds of meters once they hit the ground, causing all manner of injuries. I designed the rip panel to prevent that, to make it stay on the ground when it touches the ground. Once you pull the rip panel, there is no going back."

Pennywhistle decided to wait on any venting and again trained his glass on the ground below. He was suspended almost directly over Barney's camp. The exceedingly colorful balloon must be visible to the Americans.

Indeed it was. Men were looking skywards, shouting and pointing. It was entirely possible the men below thought the aerial reconnaissance was for their benefit, if Barney knew of the cavalry sent to commandeer the balloon. If so, they were in for a rude surprise—if Pennywhistle's modification worked. But if Barney had not been informed, his troops were more likely to be discomfited and demoralized by the strange sight. Anything overhead and out of reach betokens menace to the animal part of the brain, and like rabbits when a hawk circles overhead, men felt instinctive alarm. It was as if the enemy general had his eyes stationed directly above their camp. How could soldiers hope to keep anything secret from an all-seeing eye in the sky? Every soldier felt that he had been personally singled out for close observation. Indeed, many became apprehensive that their very thoughts were naked to the enemy. Movements slowed and coordinated actions broke down as men stopped to gaze upward with looks of consternation, dismay, and fear on their faces. A few stared curiously.

Pennywhistle panned his glass along the river and made some guesses. Dale and his men would likely be in position in an hour. Cockburn's force would arrive an hour after that. He wanted to act immediately, but the prudent course was to simply wait: wait and do nothing until all the pieces of the puzzle were in place for final assembly. He had already given the British an advantage; the longer his balloon hung there the more dread and curiosity it would arouse. It would be the colorful conjurer's object for men to fasten their eyes upon while unseen forces prepared to carry out the real magic.

He decided to use the two hours to calculate the best launch altitude and optimum angle of trajectory for the Congreve. He would also make one last set of adjustments. He had one chance to get things right, both to damage the enemy and prove his postulations correct. He decided against venting some gas and lowering the altitude. It was a scorching hot day and it was easier to think at a cool 5,000 feet than at sea level.

Aiming his weapon would be difficult; he debated whether he should fire it kneeling, from the shoulder, or stand and balance the warhead on the rim of the basket. If his engineering was sound, its flight path should be straight and steady to target, but he no idea where the balloon would finally land when he pulled the rip panel. He might well end up a prisoner of war, or dead.

One night, reminiscing about his medical studies in Edinburgh, a thought had hit him. The Congreves had serious guidance problems. Why not treat them as a medical condition? He'd studied the anatomy of the device and made several alterations, like giving a cane to a limping man. Physics applied equally to mechanical contrivances as to human bodies.

Ships' rudders and Bernoulli's Law had furnished the basis for his idea. Rudders moved through a sea of water and controlled the course of a ship. Air was a sea of a kind, and the Congreve moved through that sea. A rudder-like contrivance attached to a Congreve should provide guidance and eliminate the unpredictability that had rendered the Congreve chiefly useful as a weapon of terror rather than destruction.

Bernoulli's Law stated that as the speed of moving water increased, the pressure within that water decreased. Bernoulli had forced water through a tube that resembled an hour glass turned on its side. High-pressure, low-velocity water changed to low-pressure, high-velocity water as it constricted at the narrow belt of the tube. Passing out of the waist into the top half of the tube, the velocity slowed and pressure rose to drive out the low. Any object placed between the high-pressure ridge pushing up to confront the low would be lifted. If you substituted air for water, a fin-like projection could give both lift and guidance.

He had carefully crafted three small, triangular-shaped fins and bolted them to the base of the rocket, equidistant from each other and three inches above the exhaust. He borrowed the shape from sharks' fins he had seen at sea; the best man-made contrivances took their inspirations from designs that had already proven their worth in nature. The tin fabric was solid enough without adding much weight to the rocket. If his guess was correct, the fins would stop the chronic zigzagging of the weapon and might actually increase its range.

"That balloon's just been hanging up there for two hours, Lieutenant. Everyone is watching it; they don't like a spy in the sky. What do you think it means?" asked an alarmed Corporal Thomas. He had heard about balloons capable of carrying passengers, but had never seen one. This one seemed both awesome and sinister.

"I am not sure," replied Lieutenant Frazier. "It looks too garish to be anything military. I would expect a military balloon to be decked in colors that blended in with the sky that it might be harder to see. The variegated colors of the one above seem designed to call attention to its presence. It looks more like something a showman would put up. I have heard about air shows where such balloons are featured, but I have never heard of a show being staged here. I know they are sometimes used to advertise an event, but I know of no local event. I understand there is a very eccentric Frenchman in the area who constructs them; I think he is the likely owner of the one above." He looked upward appraisingly.

"However, I find it ominous that the balloon has suddenly appeared on this particular day when something of critical importance is in the offing. I mistrust coincidence, Corporal."

"The men are edgy, sir, they think the balloon a bad omen," said Thomas. "It's definitely unsettling them. Maybe if you spoke a few words to them sir, it would help quiet their fears."

"I will do that, Corporal, but I can only appeal to their common sense. I have no clever explanations or inspirational thoughts to offer. They will take greater comfort from my actions. I want the patrols outside the camp doubled in size and frequency. I will instruct the militia commander, Major Taney, to deploy his men to the East and South of the camp. I think it likely any attack will come from that direction. Furthermore, I want his men to use their time digging trenches for defense. They will howl; militia men are lazy and do not understand the spade is sometimes just as effective as a musket. Nevertheless, I will make sure it gets done, even if I have to flog a few to persuade the rest. We may be attacked today, but we will not be surprised."

"We have to do something to help him, Sarn't. We can't just leave him there... hanging like... well, like bait!" O'Laughlin, like all the other marines, had his eyes glued to the balloon overhead, knowing Pennywhistle was inside.

Dale looked O'Laughlin in the eye and smiled gently. "What do you want me to do, throw him a rope and haul him down, all under the eyes of the Americans?"

O'Laughlin shrugged his shoulders. "Guess'n that wouldn't be very practical, Sarn't."

"He'll shout when he needs us," said Dale patiently, "or send us a signal. Believe me, you will know when the time is right for us to move. Just be patient and don't fret. Now get back to your post and stick to the plan the Captain has given us."

Dale had posted 50 men behind tall reeds, a hundred yards north of Barney's camp. They lay on their bellies and awaited the blue rockets that would signal Cockburn's attack. Cockburn would assault the camp by water from the south. The marine line was long and loose, taking advantage of every cover. The US patrols this afternoon were proving quite aggressive and several squads had had to shift positions to evade detection.

Fifty other marines, the strongest swimmers among the fleet, lay concealed behind six-foot tall stalks of Big Blue Stem grass in three feet of brackish water. The river here was narrow, shallow, and sluggish, and it was but a two-hundred yard swim to the flotilla.

The marines wore only their underclothes and were armed solely with cutlasses they wore in scabbards on leather straps, leaving their hands free for the climbs. Each pair of men had been assigned a specific gunboat.

Admiral Cockburn was fascinated by the balloon overhead. If it survived the upcoming encounter, he might go aloft himself. He thought Pennywhistle's idea ingenious, if risky; but even if it did not work, the balloon had already provided a diversion for his attack. It was certainly a morale booster for his own men.

The men in his small fleet of launches, cutters, and yawls dashing up the Patuxent were hot to wipe out Barney and eager to obtain prize money. Their eyes reflected fierce determination, and the joyful fire of upcoming battle caused many to smile. He felt honored to command such men. He checked his watch. He would fire the blue rockets in ten minutes.

Pennywhistle heard a crackling noise overhead and realized the hydrogen was contracting again. The balloon was slowly losing lift and altitude: 5,000 feet; 4,900; 4,800. For all of his planning, Nature was making the final decision on altitude. He made one last survey of Barney's camp. No regulars had arrived at the last minute to bolster its defense; it was defended entirely by militia. Excellent! Dale's marines were settled and Cockburn's sailors were moving into position. Now was as good a time as any to set things moving and find out if his tin confections proved him a visionary or a fool.

He strapped on the parachute. Hurling oneself into space was a terrifying prospect, but he might not have any choice if things went badly. He understood the physics of the device and knew Madam Blanchard had repeatedly proven that aerofoils worked, but he nonetheless judged the idea of jumping from a perfectly safe platform into nothingness as completely insane. Of course, if he needed to jump it would be because the platform had become less than safe.

He tightened the straps across his back and chest, then made sure the twin red silk cords which opened the chute hung free and clear, within easy reach. If the contraption failed to open fully, he would become a plunging red brick. At least his death would be quick.

He tried to remember everything du Lac had told him. The problem was that du Lac had explained the chute as Blanchard had used it, and she usually jumped from 8,000 feet. The altitude indicator in the balloon now registered only 3,000 feet. If he jumped, the time between exiting the balloon and pulling the cords would have to be greatly shortened, but he had no idea by just how much. He'd have to guess. He hated guessing but had no choice.

He laid out his flint and striker. He ignited the five-foot long portfire and its end glowed with life. He glanced up with some trepidation. Hydrogen gas was highly flammable. One false move and the balloon would become a fireball.

He got on his knees and hoisted the heavy Congreve atop his shoulder. The thing was unwieldy at the best of times and not meant to be fired from a man's shoulder. The rocking of the basket was not helping. He struggled to steady the six-foot shaft so that it pointed down at a forty-five degree angle.

The altitude indicator now showed 2,500 feet. He had a clear view of Barney's flagship, the *Scorpion*. He aligned the warhead with a spot on the quarterdeck, just in front of the ship's wheel. The expanding blast of canister from the warhead should sweep the deck clear of men, assuming everything worked as planned. Then Dale would open fire, the swimmers would use that covering fire to gain the ships and kill the fuses, and Cockburn would hear the spit spat of musketry and launch his own attack.

He saw the dragoon in the elaborately plumed *chapeau de bras* gallop into the camp along with his men. But the rider had lost the race; his warning would come seconds too late.

Pennywhistle took a deep breath, grabbed an old slouch hat du Lac had left behind, and pulled it down low to shield his face. The men in front of the wheel looked like blue ants. He zeroed in on a spot just in front of them, swaying slightly to compensate for the basket's movement. He needed to factor in Newton's Third Law, that for each action there was an equal and opposite reaction, and fire as the basket swung forward so that the recoil would not coincide with the backwards motion. He braced himself and bent his knees to lower his center of gravity, lest the blast recoil dump him from the basket. He had the rhythm. Not quite yet. Wait. Wait. Now! He reached up with the portfire and touched its burning end to the tip of the Congreve's tail. The Congreve sparked and hissed, then shot from Pennywhistle's shoulder. The fiery tail burned off one of his epaulettes and left a smoking gash on his collar; the air blast knocked him into the basket's side, which mashed a purple bruise on his right check.

He was dazed, but the adrenaline of excitement and the siren's lure of curiosity powered him back to his knees. Time slowed oddly, as if each tenth of a second were an hour. He had just poked his head over the side of the basket when it happened.

BOOM! The explosion made thunder sound like whispers. Bits of flaming wood, canvas and human flesh shot skyward. The rocket had flown straight and true. His invention worked. But the result was beyond anything he had calculated.

A spiral cloud of smoke and a mist of dust, dirt, and swirling woodchips was all that remained of *Scorpion*. The canister warhead was supposed to merely clear the quarterdeck, but the blast of impact had ignited all of the powder barrels used to mine her, and the ship had vanished in one immense explosion.

The dramatic end of *Scorpion* was only the beginning. Boom! Boom! Boom! Blasts rippled down the line of gunboats as burning bits of wood, canvas, and metal shot in every direction and ignited a chain reaction on the heavily mined ships. One ship after another disintegrated in gouts of orange flame and ear-killing noise. The air grew so thick with smoke, debris, and wood chips that it was hard to see or breathe. A terrible smell of roast meat hung in the air.

The law of unintended consequences was in operation. Pennywhistle had inadvertently done Barney's job for him; the British would acquire no new military vessels, nor any cannon. Yet he had also accomplished Cockburn's goal of removing the flotilla as a threat to British navigation of the Patuxent.

The ten un-mined merchant ships anchored upstream were unscathed. Those aboard gasped in amazement that the gunboat flotilla they had counted on for protection had suddenly, horribly ceased to exist. They were defenseless.

Something was burning! Pennywhistle's nose apprehended the danger before his brain could catalog it. A small glowing wad of canvas blown upwards from the *Scorpion* had attached itself to the balloon's rip panel. An explosion was seconds away, as was the end of his life.

He did not hesitate, even though the action felt completely opposed to self preservation. He leaped over the basket edge with his arms extended as if in a swan dive from a ship. He was flying! His soul experienced a wonderful feeling of liberation for that brief second, even though his mind realized he was in grave danger.

The ground below was racing up to meet him. He gave up trying to guess correct timing and jerked the two silken cords. For the blink of an eye, nothing happened and his stomach lurched with dread. Then he heard a loud "pop" and felt as if a Titan's hands had grasped his shoulders and yanked him skyward. He was suddenly floating, slowly and gently drifting towards earth with a god's eye view of all the events beneath.

Boom! The balloon's hydrogen exploded above him. Wisps of flaming silk and basket shards showered around him, some of them bouncing and sliding off his parachute. For a terrible instant, he feared they would ignite the aerofoil, but the contacts were too brief.

Most of the Americans in the camp had been knocked off their feet by the blast waves, the rest had thrown themselves on the ground for protection. When they struggled to their feet, they milled in confusion or stood frozen in shock. Their ears rang from the explosions, their eyes burned from the gritty mist, and dust in their throats occasioned much coughing. They were not quite sure what had happened, but something horrific had issued from the balloon. The evil javelin with a bright orange tail had served notice the perfidious British could launch attacks from the sky.

Pennywhistle had seen fanciful drawings of Napoleon's men invading Britain from the air: whole regiments on huge platforms suspended from gigantic balloons floating over a terrified and cowed populace. Fantastical nonsense, of course, but it was just possible some of the Americans below might have seen similar drawings and were beginning to believe that such things were indeed possible. At the very least, the balloon might be only the first of a wave to come.

Militia men at the camp's edge fell as Dale's fire started to tell. Many Americans were shot in the back, since they were all mesmerized: looking skyward, expecting the imminent arrival of more missiles and paying no attention to their duty. Two of Cockburn's long nine-pounders boomed, giving cover for a large force of sailors armed with cutlasses and boarding pikes debarking from the boats. The 50 marine swimmers with no ships to board swam back to their starting point, eager to recover uniforms and weapons and join Cockburn's attack. But these threats went unnoticed by many of the surviving Americans, their attention riveted elsewhere.

Dust-covered American sailors and militia, professionals and amateurs alike, were staring at the tall figure in scarlet slowly descending from the sky. He was not a god, but he had just thrown Zeus's own thunderbolt, causing damage worthy of a wrathful deity.

Pennywhistle blinked in surprise as the upraised faces on the ground became clearer; not a one was contorted in anger. The Americans seemed transfixed, as if viewing some unearthly messenger gifted with special power and arcane knowledge. As he sank lower and lower, he became a perfect target for rifles and muskets. He was absolutely defenseless, imprisoned in the air by his chute. He assumed it was just a matter of seconds before some enterprising individual opened fire. He wished he had left a will.

But no one fired. What happened next was bizarre; he had never seen anything like it. American resistance simply collapsed as surrender fever raced through the camp like a virulent outbreak of Yellow Jack. Men threw down their weapons and threw up their hands in capitulation. They were being attacked by land, sea, and air; it was just too much. These Americans weren't cowards, just stunned animals submissively showing their bellies to forestall any more bloodletting. They had been trained to fight a conventional enemy, but resistance was futile against one armed with a super weapon.

Pennywhistle's boots hit the ground more gently than he'd expected, but he remembered du Lac's advice and rolled into a ball to absorb the impact. He quickly pushed himself to his feet. The Americans gazed at him in wonder and stunned silence, almost as if he were not human but a trickster God like Loki, just itching to spring one more deadly prank.

Pennywhistle thought men in their normal minds would just shoot him; he was ridiculously vulnerable. But there was nothing normal about the situation. He would take advantage of that.

He undid the parachute harness. He took a small brush from his pocket and meticulously chased away some canvas fragments that had attached themselves to his jacket. He very deliberately smoothed the wrinkles from his uniform and adjusted his sword belt as if about to be presented to

King George. His leisurely movements conveyed the impression he had all the time in the world and his nonchalance sent the message that dropping from the sky was an everyday occurrence for him.

He summoned up every ounce of brashness he could muster and walked boldly up to the man who looked to be the highest ranking officer. He wore the uniform of a major of a Maryland Militia regiment.

"Are you in command, sir? I am here to demand the surrender of this camp and I do not wish to waste time with an underling. I have had a long and unusual journey"-- an understatement of epic proportions—"and wish to conclude the surrender obsequies at the earliest possible moment." His tone was pleasant, although the purport of his words was anything but. He acted as if the surrender was a foregone conclusion not subject to debate.

The major did not hesitate and immediately offered Pennywhistle his sword. The Redcoat's face was bruised, his shoulder singed and his collar ripped, but that in no way detracted from the impeccable dignity and power the man projected. Rather the reverse; it made him seem a true warrior blessed with *sang froid,* not a headquarters' pencil jockey.

"I am indeed the ranking officer present upon the field, sir. Lieutenant Frazier, the ranking regular officer, was killed in the blast. The fortunes of war have gone against us; we have no defense against infernal devices from the sky. My men are your prisoners and I trust you will accord them proper treatment."

Pennywhistle looked the man up and down. He saw resignation in the man's face, and dignity; not a hint of craven capitulation. He was probably not a bad fellow, and there was no point in adding to his humiliation. This war had plenty of the elements of a family squabble. The Americans were cousins metaphorically, and in some cases literally.

"This is no disgrace to you, sir. Surrender is the only reasonable course. In the interest of future amity between our warring peoples, retain your sword and remember the British are gracious victors."

The major looked puzzled. Pennywhistle guessed he did not expect chivalric behavior from followers of that devil Cockburn. "Thank you very kindly, Captain..."

"Pennywhistle," he replied matter-of-factly. "And you are?"

"Major Richard Taney, Fourth Maryland Volunteers, at your service." He looked stunned when the Englishman offered his hand and smiled.

"Your men will be treated in accordance with the rules of war, Major; have no fear on that account. I will post guards over them and we will see to their disposition later. I trust I have your parole for your men, that they will attempt no escape?"

"You do indeed, sir! We value honor as much as you do. We Americans are not as uncivilized as you British seem to think. I have an excellent sherry in my tent; may I offer you a glass?"

"I should be delighted, Major, although I should be even more delighted if you had some decent coffee."

Taney laughed outright. "It just so happens I have a cache of beans from Curaçao that slipped through your blockade. But I thought all Englishman preferred tea!"

"I consider tea a dull drink fit only for old men, dainty ladies, and insipid fops, Major. Coffee is a splendid beverage which stimulates the mind, sharpens the perceptions, and lightens every burden. You Americans were quite right to stage that Tea Party in Boston."

Dale and O'Laughlin watched the proceedings from fifty yards away. O'Laughlin shook his head. "That is the most amazing thing I have ever seen, Sarn't. I would not have believed it if I had not been here. If any man told me such a tale, I would call him a bald-faced liar."

Dale sighed, "I told you to have faith. For a Popish Irishman, you seem to have little of it. The Captain always thinks things through. His mind never rests. Our minds are slow, like mules, O'Laughlin; his is quick, like a thoroughbred. Come on, Gramps; looks like the Captain will be needing us and the rest of the company to disarm and corral all of this militia."

"Right, Sarn't." O'Laughlin trailed after Dale, murmuring under his breath. "I ain't never seen

the like, ain't never seen the like."

Pennywhistle felt the weight of the usual post battle fatigue and adrenaline hangover, but summoned forth enough energy to accomplish the routine tasks occasioned by the end of combat. He coordinated with naval officers to see that paroles were taken properly, billeted his men in the shade of the trees, and inspected the camp for useful supplies. The camp still contained plenty of food—dull military fare, but comparatively fresh and a pleasant change from food that had been packed in barrels or crates for months. The militia's salt pork was supple, instead of being so hard it could actually be sculpted into snuff boxes.

He sat with his back comfortably braced against a tall pine, waved off the usual regiment of mosquitoes, and plucked a Newtown Pippin from his haversack. He replenished his supply of apples whenever he passed an orchard. He took a large and satisfying bite. Despite the heat, insect pests, and roads that turned into quagmires after any rain, America was a wonderful land for agriculture. The fruits here seemed larger and tastier than their European counterparts.

He spied a figure clad in a sinister black uniform of unique design. It was Cockburn, who on days of battle wore an outfit which he rightly believed added to his fearsome reputation. The man understood theatricality! Pennywhistle finished his apple quickly, rose, and walked over to make his report.

"Good afternoon, Admiral. Very good to see you, sir." He snapped to attention and favored Cockburn with a crisp salute.

"A handsome performance, Mr. Pennywhistle! A good day's work, I would say; the gunboats destroyed and ten fine prizes. You performed your role admirably, if in an unusual fashion. Always a pleasure to see these American rascals fold up like cheap camp chairs. But much remains to be done. We need to keep moving."

"Sir, I know of your fondness for fruits, and I think you will find the local apples delicious. They're very firm and have just the right impudent spark of tartness." He extracted another Pippin from his haversack and handed it to a startled Cockburn.

"Very kind of you, Mr. Pennywhistle. The Americans do produce fine apples. The same cannot be said of their government or their fighting men, however. America is a country of great bounty. The trouble is, it's inhabited by Americans!" He let out a short bark of a laugh and bit a large chunk out of the apple. Flies swarmed and settled on the new cavity.

"Very good indeed, Mr. Pennywhistle. A pleasant relief after battle. Now if we could just get some relief from this cursed heat, these damned flies, and the wretched mosquitoes. They talk about a sickly season here. After reviewing our long sick list, I am beginning to understand exactly what that means."

"I quite agree with you about the heat, sir. I am taking special care to make sure we stop regularly to fill canteens. The area has plenty of local springs, and I plan on taking full advantage of them." Perhaps it was the heat affecting him, but he suddenly felt very bold and impertinent. "Sir, have you decided to forego attacking Baltimore?"

Cockburn respected boldness, hated toadies, and responded forthrightly. "No, Mr. Pennywhistle, I am determined we will take that damned nest of pirates, but first we shall attend to Washington. Subsequent action will be predicated on the weather, how our men bear up, and how badly the Yankees are fuddled. If they become as disorganized as I expect, I will recommend an immediate strike at Baltimore before they have a chance to firm up their defenses. I have written Lord Bathurst for reinforcements; it would certainly make things easier of we had more soldiers. Victory might make him amenable to parting with more of Wellington's men. With 15,000, it would be child's play to secure the entire Chesapeake and end this damned war once and for all." His eyes glowed.

"Walk with me, Mr. Pennywhistle. I should like to hear your account of what just happened, particularly with regard to the temper and morale of the enemy. I have a few ideas for your men I should like to discuss. Now that this Barney fellow is out of the way and our flank is secure, I want to join up with General Ross and the main advance. He is a good man and a fine soldier. He just needs a bit of extra encouragement sometimes." Cockburn smiled, brushed away the flies, and took another bite of his apple.

"I would like that extra encouragement to take the form of Naval and Marine reinforcements. I propose to give him 100 gunners and 200 sailors, and also assign him all of the Fleet Marines brigaded together. That will increase his force by close to 1,000. Major Malcolm would command the marine brigade, as he is most senior, but I would like you to be his second. I know you two have worked together in the past. Meet with Malcolm and proceed north at dawn tomorrow. Tonight I want your men to get plenty of rest; much hard marching lies ahead."

"Aye, aye, sir. I shall begin making my preparations directly I finish this very pleasant conversation. If you will permit me, sir, I should like to furnish you more information on the modifications I made to the Congreve used today. I am most pleased with the results of the test, and I think if similar improvements are made to the rest of our rockets, it will greatly improve our chances of success in this campaign."

"I should be most interested to hear details of that which you alluded to in your brief note, Mr. Pennywhistle. I value independent thinking and new ideas."

Over the next half hour Pennywhistle explained the physics and the possibilities opened up by accurate guidance and predictability of performance. Cockburn nodded at several points, and occasionally interjected very perceptive questions.

"And so, Admiral," Pennywhistle concluded, "with your leave, I should like to modify enough Congreves to arm the Marine Brigade. Success may persuade the Army to adopt the same changes. With enough men working on the project,

I believe the modifications could be made in an afternoon. I should be happy to furnish you a demonstration when preparations are complete."

"You shall have everything you need, sir. I am most impressed with your initiative. Now, if I might trouble you for another apple." Cockburn laughed heartily, something Pennywhistle seldom heard him do. The Admiral idly scratched some small red spots above his stiff collar; chiggers were no respecters of rank. "I shall be setting up temporary headquarters in that plantation house yonder. I should be pleased if you would join me for supper. You can let me know how your exertions are proceeding."

"Very good, sir!" It pleased him to be serving under an officer who valued unconventional thinking; many senior officers preferred simple obedience. Cockburn was a true fire-eater, and the enemy near him always got burned.

Captain Tracy had not gotten burned during the attack. He was not among the dead or wounded, and his name was not on the parole list. Pennywhistle wondered if the outcome might have been different had he been in command. It surprised Pennywhistle that Tracy had not been placed in charge of the demolition; but perhaps higher command had saved his abilities for a task of greater moment. Now what might that be?

Fifteen miles away, Captain John Tracy heard a tremendous explosion and smiled. He assumed it meant that Barney had successfully scuttled the flotilla. Barney had instructed Tracy to march his marines to the Woodyard, the designated assembly point of American forces twelve miles southeast of the capital. Their experience and his leadership would put backbone into the militia there.

His hundred-and-twenty marines marched well. The day was blisteringly hot and the mosquitoes were as active as ever, but the men never complained and plodded stolidly forward. All they would be doing today was marching, not fighting. They did not need his supervision. Lieutenant Runyon could handle the business just as well as he.

The militia scouting reports filtering in to Washington from various locations on Chesapeake Bay were confused and contradictory, only slightly better than the harebrained summation he had heard from the esteemed Secretary of State. Barney had told him his judgment was sorely needed at the Woodyard; that was certainly true. Tracy had no false humility about his gifts. Still, all the judgment in the world was useless without up-to-date and accurate information. He needed to carry out a proper reconnaissance: see things with his own eyes, draw his own conclusions, and return with a report that was based on direct observation, not third-, fourth-, fifth-hand accounts that were little better than surmise.

He only took four men with him, chosen for their observational skills and reliability, as well as their exceptional eyesight. He would play hide and seek with the British, only the British would not know the game was in progress.

For their observation point Tracy and his marines chose one of the few small hills in the area of the flat tidewater. They had been in position only an hour when they heard the sound of thousands of tramping feet transmitted through the humid air.

Five minutes later, the first soldiers appeared round the curve in the road. The marching men wore swallow-tailed red tunics, cinched at the waist, blue-grey trousers, and tall black shakos that vaguely resembled stovepipes. Two broad white leather straps crossed diagonally on each man's chest, one supporting the cartridge box, the other the bayonet scabbard. A brass plate emblazoned with the regimental number marked where the belts intersected.

Tracy extended his best spyglass to its full foot length. He could see the skirmishers in advance of the main column and light infantry probing the woods on either side of the road. Six men rode at the front of the column. Ross was easy to spot, a handsome, spare man in his late forties in a very well-tailored uniform. His thoughtful and judicious face matched his military reputation. He talked animatedly to a staff officer and pointed up the road toward the hill from which Tracy observed him. It was almost as if Ross could sense him.

The infantry marched quickly, faster than American troops, although both reckoned the standard pace as thirty inches. It had to be "the Moore quickstep", named after General Sir John Moore, who'd originated it in Spain. American Marines marched at roughly two miles an hour; the quickstep appeared closer to four. It would be punishing on a day like this. The soldiers were tired, to judge by their faces, but no murmurs of complaint or lamentation drifted up from the column. They steadfastly ignored the gnats and mosquitoes pursuing the column with vigor. Morale looked to be excellent, exactly what you'd expect from well-led professionals. Would that the American militia could march like that!

A single battalion of the British Army regiment theoretically numbered a thousand souls split equally among ten companies, but actual field numbers were often considerably less. These looked to be in the neighborhood of

700-800 men. Lieutenant colonels usually commanded regiments, and captains led companies.

The British marched by column of companies at the half distance. The grenadier company, composed of the tallest men, led each battalion. Like the line companies, it marched with a sixty-foot front of men. The nine companies that followed stretched back three hundred feet. Thirty feet separated each company from those fore and aft. It was an excellent marching arrangement for fast movement since it made the column compact, but less convenient if a battle was anticipated. Marching in open order with greater distance between the companies would have been a better arrangement if the column had to deploy quickly into a line or even form square against cavalry. That they did not march in open order meant they were expecting no activity from the Americans that would necessitate swift action. Sadly, Tracy knew they were right.

The road ahead of the column was sandy but unimpeded. It galled him that no one had been delegated to fell trees to block the road and slow the British advance. It was an elementary precaution that had been used against the British in the Revolutionary War, particularly at Saratoga, but even that was evidently beyond the ken of the clueless General Winder.

He counted 4 regimental colors. The giant squares of silk drooped listlessly on their long poles; there was not a breath of wind. He nearly dropped his spyglass when he saw something completely unexpected: at least two companies of colored infantry. He found it shocking that the British would employ former slaves, but once he put aside emotion and viewed them with strict military judgment, he saw they held their weapons properly and marched well. It pained him, but they appeared far more military than the Maryland Militia. It remained to be seen how they would fight, but only troops with solid training marched like that, and training was the best guarantee of good conduct on the field of battle.

He wondered why he was surprised. Barney had a number of black sailors with him, and they had done expert work with the cannons. If blacks could handle big guns, why couldn't they handle small arms? The Navy valued competence above all else; at sea in a storm, skin color meant nothing, while competence meant the difference between life and death. He was letting the lessons of his childhood cloud his judgment. Reality was butting heads with Conformity.

The articles of faith of his church and his class, thrust on him as a boy, were firm: blacks were only good for manual labor; they could not be trusted with even simple decisions; they were primitive savages incapable of learning the things a man needed to know. Virginian he might be, but he was a man who delighted in the ideals of the Age of Reason. Montesquieu, Voltaire, and Diderot had all believed slavery had far more drawbacks than virtues. If observation suggested faith had things wrong, he would question that faith and reexamine his values. War had forced him to reconsider quite a number of his beliefs. Still, the prospect of large numbers of blacks with guns greatly unsettled him.

He made his calculations as the column drew near. His original estimate of 5,000 was close; he downgraded it to 4,400. Winder had more than twice the numbers, although nowhere near the quality. The British were formidable, man for man probably the best infantry in the world, but 4,400 was not an overwhelming horde. Numbers eventually beat the Spartans at Thermopylae. Something could definitely be done, if American troops were handled properly. A pitched, formal battle would likely favor the British, but the outcome was not a foregone conclusion.

The meticulously spaced columns moving toward him were impressive, even fearsome, but they betrayed a weakness. Americans faced an infantry army, not a combined arms force. The British had no real field artillery, just Congreves! Tracy had seen them in action numerous times and had schooled his men that fear of them was misplaced. They seldom hit what they were aimed at—unlike artillery manned by experienced gunners.

The Americans had several solid batteries of good artillery, many of them heavy ordinance by army standards. They might not be the great clusters of cannon Napoleon had used to supreme effect at Wagram, but any concentration of well-served artillery was deadly to foot soldiers. The biggest standard land piece was a 12-pounder, but a number of Barney's were long 18s: ship-killers. His men were laboriously moving them toward the Woodyard at this very moment. Loaded with canister, they would be supremely effective man-killers. Barney had plenty of experienced gunners to man them, too.

Tracy looked at the smartly marching infantry and thought of the effect of smashing waves of canister at close quarters. The British were famous for holding their musketry until the range was close and hugely destructive. Marine artillerists could play exactly the same game.

The Americans also had some cavalry, several hundred who actually knew their business. Why weren't they about? They could have slowed and disrupted the British advance, and also sent back a constant stream of reports. Winder was a complete idiot. That was the story of the American war effort: missed opportunities.

The British had a few mounted men, but they looked like infantry seated poorly on a few scavenged horses. He had grown up around horses, so he knew uncomfortable amateurs when he saw them. They would be of little use, scouting or screening. Ross might have slaves feeding him information, but he had no proper scouts. From a military standpoint, he was marching blind. An ambush would have been easy to arrange. Damn Winder!

Tracy caught something out of the corner of his eye—movement in the wood below and to the right of him. He heard rustling noises, saw bushes part and sixteen men emerge into a small clearing. He looked at them closely through his glass. They were not really men; the oldest couldn't be more than seventeen. It looked more like a gang of adolescents out on a lark. The problem was these young fools had guns. They were talking excitedly among themselves, encouraging each other. No, not encouraging each other, *daring* each other. It hit him this was some sort of initiation ritual, a way to prove their manhood. Fire a shot at the British, run for it, then meet back at a barn somewhere to down whiskey of and boast. He looked carefully through his spyglass and saw one held a jug. They had already started drinking.

It was obvious they had no idea what was fast coming toward them. The boys might be foolish adolescents in civilian eyes, but if they opened fire, according to the laws of war they were vigilantes and murderers and enjoyed none of the protections granted members of a legally constituted armed force. The ones who didn't die by British bullets or bayonets would be summarily executed as bushwhackers. Tracy might not like it, but the British would be within their rights.

He should not interfere and risk exposing his position, alerting the British to his presence. If a few stupid boys died that was sad, but war was cruel to the naive and the witless. He could not change that. But... those boys could be turned into marines. They may lack judgment, but they had spirit. It seemed a shame to let recruits perish. Something he had seen earlier popped unbidden into his head, and almost against his will an idea began to form.

CHAPTER ELEVEN

Tracy directed his gaze 500 yards astern and panned his spyglass over the little ship they had passed en route to this lookout. His plan was thin, hastily conceived, and depended on getting that vessel underway quickly. This section of the river was rich in striped bass and summer flounder, superb fishing grounds, but the schooner was clearly not built for fishing. She was moored in a small, heavily wooded cove on one of the many tidal estuaries in the area. The cove lay at the bottom of a small bowl of very low hills, invisible from even half a mile away. A perfect place to shelter, or hide. The tide was at the flood; at ebb, she would be grounded in mudflats.

She was a schooner of 200 tons with two heavily raked masts. The fore and aft rig would make her very maneuverable, but hard to discipline unless conned by an experienced hand. The lines were crisp and sleek; she would be very fast as well. She was a scaled down Baltimore clipper and doubtless a privateer—a coastal raider designed to make dashes to sea to snap up small British transports carrying supplies, dispatches, or payrolls. She could outrun anything large the British sent after her, and her relatively shallow draft made it possible to use obscure spots like the one where she now sheltered. Her crew probably knew the Chesapeake intimately and could take full advantage of the bay's secrets. The little ship was undoubtedly very profitable.

Someone had put considerable thought and care into her design. He just hoped he had enough skill to take full advantage of her assets.

She had probably been secreted away by her owner in light of the British advance; perhaps they hoped to reclaim her later when the British had passed by. There were crates on shore, and he guessed they had brought her this far upriver to make some modifications. He scanned her carefully through his spyglass and found what he had guessed were there. They were concealed under tarpaulins, but from the shapes he knew they were three-pounders, two on each side. They were only pop guns, but effective against unarmed craft. They would also work just fine against men. The name was scuffed but he could make it out: *Lucky Lady*. He laughed. That was exactly what he needed.

He was the only one of them who knew much about sailing, and that was a problem. His four marines understood far more about ships than landsmen did, but were a long way from being sailors. He would have them and sixteen stupid boys for a crew; not promising. At least the marines could work the cannons.

A good wind had sprung up and was fair for speedy departure. If he could get even two sails unfurled and drawing he could make a run for it. He just needed a driver and a jib. They were brailed up; if he simply slashed the grommets holding them with knives they would fall free.

Crude, but it would have to do. The boys could at least sheet the sails home. That only required brute strength.

He wondered if the ship carried ammunition for her guns. Probably; she was in good order and it looked as if the owners had not had time to remove anything of value. The range would be very short. He'd have to bring her broadside to bear quickly, then hightail it out to the river. At least he didn't have to hit anything, just spread a little fear and caution.

Pop, pop, pop. He turned his glass toward the sound and saw what he dreaded. Damn it, the idiot boys had fired. The bullets had gone wide, of course, but the lads shouted with glee, clapping each other on the back. They were having great fun, like merry drunks before the hangover hit. The British light infantry halted and took cover. The boys had gotten their attention. Very bad!

He explained his plan to the marines quickly and they nodded understanding. The schooner lay to the rear of their hill, the boys lay a quarter mile ahead. It would be a mad dash out, and an even madder dash back.

The five marines raced down the low hill with long, almost leaping strides. It was like an athletic competition with no prize at the end save the lives of some foolish boys. He was risking the mission for civilians he did not know; with chagrin he realized he was engaging in exactly the heroics he lectured his men to disdain.

The boys jumped, capered, and continued their pot shots, passing the jug of whiskey down the line so everyone could take a gulp. They showed no awareness of the marines approaching from behind.

"Take that, you limey bastards!" shouted a plump, red-headed boy as he fired his ancient Potsdam musket.

"Kiss my arse, Lobsterback!" yelled a gangly youth nearly, knocked down by the kick of his father's Revolutionary War musket.

The red-coated skirmishers advanced cautiously, but relentlessly. They stopped, fired a volley, reloaded, and plodded forward. The red-headed boy took a ball squarely in the forehead and dropped to the ground. His companion bent down in shock, then realized he could see the oatmeal grey of his friend's brains.

Some of the boys finally understood, as bullets sang past their ears with increasing frequency. Color drained from their faces as the realization dawned this was battle, not a game by a long shot. Two took off running. Two more leveled their pieces and fired at the same soldier. One round succeeded in removing his hat.

The rest crouched down behind the four-foot stone wall. They were terrified, but so drink-addled that they were unable to fight or flee. It was a fear that paralyzed, not energized, at the worst possible moment. Redcoats with fixed bayonets raced towards them from only fifty yards out.

Bill Adams thought of his parents and his brothers. He was only seventeen and didn't want to die without ever having joined with a woman. The death of his red-headed friend drove away the foolish bravado that had got him into this mess. It wasn't supposed to turn out like this! Tears of rage blurred his vision. He reloaded his ancient fowling piece, popped up, braced it on the wall, and fired. One Redcoat went down. Good! They weren't invincible after all.

Bang! Bang! A volley passed over the boy's heads, but it came from behind them—rifles, not muskets. Adams swiveled his head and was astonished to see four United

States Marines reloading their pieces. They were very fast; as he drew a deep breath they discharged a second volley.

"Halt! Dress that line!" called out the grizzled Sergeant Donald Laurie. The bugler echoed Laurie's commands, and the Redcoats stopped their advance. His caution was the product of five years hard service in Spain. The blue of the American Marine uniform was distinctive. Bushwhackers were a nuisance, but marines were regulars like themselves; much more stubborn and steadfast opponents. The red line of skirmishers had become broken by the rough terrain. It was prudent to take an extra minute to straighten it out before advancing further.

Adams felt a sharp pain in his shoulder. A heavily calloused hand yanked him to his feet and a boot thumped into his backside. "Get up, you damned little fool." A very tall, very angry Marine officer grabbed him by the shoulders and shook him. His blue eyes were cold as icicles and bored into his soul. "Listen to me. You're a dead man if you do not do exactly as I say. Run as fast as you can *that* way," he pointed to the rear, "and don't stop until you see the private waiting for you. Follow his instructions. I told him to shoot anyone who hesitates for an instant. Understand?" Adams nodded and took off like a shot.

The other three marines made similar forceful remonstrations to the rest of the foolish little band. Shouts, threats, punches, and kicks catapulted the youthful herd into a fast run that would have done credit to a pack of antelopes. The marines merely had to direct the course of fear and youthful energy.

Tracy brought up the rear, stopping now and then to fire shots at the pursing British. He thought he hit one, but his sole purpose was to keep their heads down and slow their advance. The British were not fools and would soon see how few they faced. His expression was grim; he'd gotten his men into a very bad position for the sake of these boys.

Sergeant Laurie sent a single section of men after them to keep up a loose pursuit. He saw boys running, not soldiers—mad, headlong flight bereft of any discipline. Nothing excited predatory instincts faster than seeing the backsides of fleeing opponents. It would have been the easiest thing in the world to order the entire company to dash after them. Some of Laurie's men threw puzzled glances at him, wondered why they were being restrained. That was the problem. It was a little too easy. With the US Marines involved, mere boys might be a lure. Perhaps a substantial force of marines or militia, or both, lay hidden, ready to spring an ambush. Let the British see amateurs, then hit them with seasoned professionals. Laurie had been warned the Americans would try something and it surprised him they had waited this long. If these boys were indeed a decoy, he would need more men, and Manton's Company would be up presently. Lieutenant Manton was a good and experienced officer. He would take over the pursuit and play it just the way Laurie would if he had enough men, classic stall and hook tactic: one company to pin down the fleeting Americans, fix them in position, while the other swung round and hit them in the rear. He knew Ross was eager for prisoners and needed timely information on the disposition, numbers, and morale of American forces.

Tracy and the marines herded the boys like cattle. He realized they shared many of the characteristics of panicked beasts and the least thing would spook them. "Move, move, move, you little bastards!" bellowed Sergeant Fredericks. The other marines shouted similar harsh encouragements and waved their hands maniacally.

Tracy looked behind him and saw only a few Redcoats in pursuit, but he knew his opponents had not given up; he was being tracked. The Redcoats would follow in greater numbers. He had bought himself a little time—and would need every second of it.

The boys huffed and puffed and slowed their run as some of the adrenaline drained off. Tracy's anger bubbled up. The ship was in sight, this was no time to slow down. He had risked his men for these little idiots. He hit several boys in the backsides with the flat of his sword. They yelped and jumped, and sped up their pace. Spare the rod and spoil the child!

"Go, go, go! Move, move, move!" All of his marines yelled with him. The boys responded, and soon they all reached the edge of the dock. "Halt!" Tracy bellowed in his most threatening voice. They stopped immediately. He had them; good!

The ship was moored close in shore, probably to facilitate the intended modifications. The extended gangplank beckoned at the end of the long dock—a piece of luck, consistent with the ship's name. Ships were usually moored farther out and reached by boat rather than walkway. It would be easy to get everyone aboard. However, the tide had started to ebb; he needed to get underway before long, or they'd be towing the boat.

Fredericks shoved and pushed the boys into something resembling a line. "Ten Hut" he shouted at them. Most of the boys had fathers in the militia. The expectation, at least, was clear. They stiffened their spines, lowered their hands to their sides, and dropped their little fingers close to the seams of their trousers.

Tracy paced slowly down the line, stared ferociously into each pair of frightened eyes, and composed his face into an expression of anger and disgust. He towered over all of the boys, and he knew his exceptional height intimidated even confident adults. He was about to speak when he felt two bursts of air race past his face. Turning his head to look behind, he saw splotches of red moving in the bushes seventy yards away. Just the advance guard; a nuisance, but their friends would arrive soon. He would have to cut his speech short. British potshots would underscore its urgency.

He spun on his heel and faced the thoroughly cowed boys. "I don't like you. My men don't like you. And the British certainly don't like you. But I am stuck with you. Stupid as you are, you are citizens of the country I have sworn to defend with my life. Your parents probably want your worthless hides back in one piece." More bullets passed by, and two of the boys ducked their heads.

"Don't cower, you little nitwits. If a bullet has your name on it, the best cover in the world won't help. You wanted to be real soldiers. Stand tall and face death like men. Like men!" His voice cracked like a whip. "Here's your chance to show the world just what you are made of!"

One fifteen-year-old started to cry. Tracy cuffed him smartly on the cheek. "Shut up with the blubbering, you miserable cur!" Another bullet zipped past. The boy looked shocked, but the tears stopped.

Enough of breaking them down. Time to build them up and get moving. "I don't want to die. I am guessing you don't either. Do exactly what I say, and we all may live to kill more British soldiers another day. We need to get this boat underway before the rest of the British arrive. I can steer and sail her, and my marines can work the cannon. I need you to handle the ropes. When I say pull, or heave, you must do it without hesitation and put every ounce of muscle and heart into it. Your lives depend on you doing precisely what I tell you in the next few minutes. Understand?"

The boys nodded with the unabashed earnestness of youth. They were scared, they had transgressed, but a strong man offered hope and perhaps redemption.

He needed to instill a sense of teamwork and allow them to show some spirit; time for some bravado. "It's do or die; victory or death! Boys, are you with me? Signify by shouting aye at the top of your lungs." He hoped the noise would confuse and unsettle the approaching British.

"Aye!" It boomed forth like the Hallelujah Chorus. The sound was as hearty as it was sincere; pure innocence, pure power. He had lost his innocence about so many things long ago, but he recognized innocence had a force and majesty beyond the normal ken of things, making it a weapon. He hated his cynicism, yet it might just save his life and the lives of everyone involved.

"Time to go! Four of you on each rope; follow orders. The sails won't draw unless those ropes are pulled taut." *Zippt! Zippt!* More bullets whizzed past. "Let's get to it, boys. Sergeant Fredericks, take them to their posts."

"Aye, aye, sir. C'mon, you little buggers, follow me!" bellowed Fredericks, and the boys complied. Their whiskey-reddened faces glowed with excitement, and their fear ebbed because someone was in charge who knew what he was doing. They wanted adventure and they were getting it. Fredericks spaced them evenly on the sheeting ropes and showed them the proper grip.

Tracy raced up the mizzen ratlines, a large hunting knife in his right hand. *Zppt, zppt*—it sounded like a swarm of hornets. He ignored the bullets and focused on the mastcap looming five feet ahead. He hated heights; that was why he was a marine and not a naval officer. He reached the mastcap, flattened himself on his belly, and began crawling along the gaff, cutting the grommets as he slithered along. *Don't look down, don't look down.* Of course, perverse curiosity caused him to look down. The deck appeared very, very tiny. He swallowed hard and willed his tightening neck muscles to relax. Then he took advantage of his precarious position to survey the terrain. A line of red was moving slowly down the hill. He reached the end of the gaff, cut the final grommet, and the sail fell free.

His marines loaded the starboard three-pounders and two stood by with glowing portfires. The ship had plenty of powder and shot, confirming his suspicion that the owners had intended to return after the British marched by. He would get off only one broadside; he had too few men to manage a fast reload under fire.

He crawled back along the gaff, urging his queasy stomach to stay calm, gained the safety of the mastcap, and sped down the ratlines, waving a frantic signal to Fredericks.

"Heave! Heave! Heave!" the sergeant sang out, and the boys put their energy into it. The ropes stretched taught, and the sail sheeted home. The driver filled with wind. "Keep up the pressure, boys!"

Halfway there! They had the driver for power, but needed the flying jib for guidance. Tracy dashed toward the bowsprit, jumped ungracefully onto it, and crawled forward. At least it was low to the surface of the water. Reaching the end, he advanced on to the jib-boom. Once he was sure the flying jib was secure on its rope, he cut the grommets and pulled with all his might until the sail began to slowly slide upwards on the halyard. It was back-breaking labor, but the jib locked into place and began to draw. *Lucky Lady* wanted to go!

He regained the deck and bound the sheets to the bollards with belaying pins, pleased that he still remembered the bowline knot. Once again he heard the noise of angry bees darting past. "Lie down!" he yelled at the boys. No point in unnecessary risk; they had done their jobs.

Lieutenant John Manton watched Tracy through his spyglass. The ship would be underway quickly, but he could catch it before it exited the channel. He was an army officer, but the rules of prize money applied to him and his men just as much as to the navy. *Lucky Lady* would fetch a tidy sum. His Spanish wife Juanita was pregnant with their first child and that money would help purchase a home suitable for his heir. The men, he thought wryly, would probably squander their shares in a drinking and whoring spree.

Manton split his command of two hundred, sent half on a flank march to the left, and kept the remainder deployed in a long skirmish line facing straight ahead. His plan was to approach to point blank range, sweep the decks with musketry, then board. They had to catch her close in; the water was shallow, but few of his men could swim, and they had no grapnels or ropes. The deck however, was low, only a few feet above the water. The channel narrowed a few hundred yards ahead, like the neck of a bottle. Laurie's men on the left would take up position there, making it a choke point. The ones on the right would chivvy the ship, as if she were an animal, cause her to flee one danger while oblivious to another.

Swinging two heaving boarding axes, Tracy and Fredericks finally severed the two anchor cables, and *Lucky Lady* started to move. Tracy took the wheel—it was small enough for one man to handle. She answered easily to his touch, a fine, sensitive helm. He felt a pang of simple pleasure, the joy of a captain conning his ship.

Pop, pop, pop. Manton's men advanced down the hill, small groups stopping to fire every so often. They used rocks, bushes, and declivities for cover so as not to present exposed targets. Most disappeared from view as soon as they fired. Manton had seen the cannon, knew the danger, and warned his men not to present a compact target. He tried to think of a way to provoke the ship into firing too soon, squandering their one resource, making them vulnerable to a rush of boarders.

Tracy saw them, knew he was a prime target. He felt rushes of air, uncomfortably close. Of course they were focusing their fire on him: kill the helmsman, make the ship lose guidance. From their maneuvers it was clear these British had light infantry training; they were not ordinary line troops. It was also clear that Fredericks objected to having his officer the target of their concentrated attention and badly wanted to return fire; nevertheless, Tracy ordered his men to take cover. It would be a waste of ammunition to engage. He had to devise a way to trick the British, draw them in close, make them think he was beaten, about to yield. For a brief second, he flirted with ignoble thought of faking surrender, then giving them a broadside. It might work, but it was an affront to the honor he so prized. If the deception failed, they could expect no quarter. No, a better way would come to him.

The Redcoats were fifty yards out, methodically closing the distance. *Lucky Lady* picked up speed as a welcome breeze tugged at her sails. The dock faded slowly astern, but the channel was constricted and they would be vulnerable until they reached the Patuxent. The area also was replete with oyster beds, which could cause them to suddenly ground. A steady stream of small thuds caught his attention as bullets slammed into the gunwales. He saw Redcoats shoot and duck. It reminded him of a legion of jack-in-the boxes.

One round grazed the arm of Bill Adams, who had foolishly stood up to get a better view of the British. He stared stupidly at the bleeding. Fredericks moved in a crouching run, assessed it, and bound it up with a rag tourniquet. Tracy knew it was nothing, but it would have tremendous significance to the boy, should he survive. He would have a scar to show his suitably awed friends.

Manton rubbed his chin in thought. He had the Americans' attention. They dared not expose themselves, and he had spoiled any clear shots for their cannon. Good. The men downstream were all hidden at a range of only twenty yards. They would rise up and fire upon Sergeant Laurie's command. Laurie himself had orders to kill the helmsman, if he were not already dead by that point. The helmsman looked to be their leader, the only one clearly exposed. Perhaps, Manton reflected, he could be induced to surrender.

Two of his men brought word they had discovered a fishing skiff in the reeds. It was small, but could take six. Manton jogged over and made a fast inspection. With oars and space for muskets, it would suit. Hit them from the rear! Unlike most army officers, he knew something about boats. Years ago he'd been an able seaman, destined to rise no higher than a petty officer by the end of a long career. Then he'd met Captain Pennywhistle, and everything had changed.

The Americans would be looking ahead and to starboard; with a little luck he would be under their lee before anyone noticed. Manton would lead them, and his sergeant could handle things on shore. Good NCOs were a godsend. Properly, his own place was on shore; but he was the only one experienced in boarding actions. It would be the nautical version of a forlorn hope, attacking a fortress. Five men volunteered for the skiff. He promised the first soldier aboard promotion to corporal. God grant, he thought grimly, the man lived to enjoy it. Well, they would have the element of surprise. A quick leap over the stern would be unexpected, especially if ... yes, he needed a distraction. Captain Pennywhistle had taught him the importance of diversion.

Down the broken line of men passed the order: Shout, yell, anything—cheers or curses. They did that, and very loudly; an impressive stream of profanity polluted the humid air.

Tracy altered course slightly, wondered what all the shouting was about. The British soldier was fully as foul-mouthed as his American counterpart, but usually did not give vent in battle. Very peculiar! He wanted to fire one of the cannons, to shake their arrogance and resolve, but it would be like trying to swat a cloud of mosquitoes with a shotgun. He frowned, gauging their numbers; there were fewer soldiers than before. No one had retreated. Ah, so they had split their forces. He spotted the bottleneck fast approaching, guessed their intention, and decided to reserve his fire.

Lucky Lady gathered speed, but the Redcoats kept up a relentless fire as she moved past. Twenty waded into the water up to waist level for better shots. Slivers of wood jumped from the gunwales. Several ropes parted, and a wheel spoke lost a chunk scant inches from Tracy's right hand. One round hit Frederick's musket, smashing the lock-plate and startling the owner badly, but leaving him uninjured.

Manton and his men jumped in the skiff and shoved off. The two rowers put all of their considerable muscle into the stroke, and the skiff sped forward. They were just yards from *Lucky Lady's* stern, but her sails were drawing well and she began to pull away.

Manton's opportunity diminished with each passing second. He desperately cast about for a way to lock onto her stern. The boat contained a few yards of rope and a long stick of stout cedar, smaller than the diameter of a Brown Bess. Attached to a bayonet and impelled by sufficient force, it just might make a crude grappling hook. He had no idea how many extra charges it would take, but thought three sounded likely. That would give the musket a kick like a regiment of mules, but it might drive the bayonet into *Lucky Lady's* stern. It would not penetrate far and would only hold for a minute, but that might be enough.

He grabbed frantically for the cedar staff and jammed the base ring of the socket bayonet hard onto its head. It stuck firmly, almost as good as a weld. He secured the rope round the base of the bayonet, letting a long trail dangle free, pressing down on the end with his boot. Then he loaded the weapon. His men were puzzled by the excess powder, then his intent dawned on them, and they grinned.

Boom! The musket's discharge almost knocked Manton over, and his shoulder would bear the mark for many days, but the bayonet sped true and thudded into *Lucky Lady* just above the pintles. Two men seized the rope before it was pulled into the water, and Manton bound it to the forward thwart with a running knot. The line jerked taut, the little skiff lurched forward and gathered speed as the tow took hold. The Redcoats reeled in the rope, shortening the distance to the *Lady*.

Tracy heard the shot, felt the impact, and looked behind. A little boat was almost under the stern. Very clever! A British lieutenant crouched in the bow, poised to spring, fire in his eyes. Two of the Redcoats raised their muskets and full cocked them. "Not to my ship, you don't!" Tracy bellowed to no one in particular, surprised at his possessiveness. "Fredericks, take the helm! Martin, James, grab your rifles. Stand by to repel boarders. Go for the men; the officer's mine."

The two marines grabbed their rifles, dashed to the taffrail, and leveled their pieces. The British on shore saw the denouement was at hand, rushed forward from cover, and fired a volley that killed Martin and wounded James. A bullet sliced off Tracy's right epaulette and knocked him to the deck. He was dazed from the impact, but his sheer determination kicked in an extra reserve of energy and he staggered to his feet. James looked concerned. Tracy returned the look when he saw blood on James' sleeve.

"Just a scratch, sir," James assured him. "I can fight; time to pay these bastards in their own coin."

Tracy needed help and made his decision. He twisted away from the danger astern and grabbed the speaking trumpet next to the wheel. "Lads, up, on your feet, now! Grab your pieces and get over here on the double! This is your big chance to be heroes." Their desire to be seen as men had gotten them to this situation in the first place, and it was time to exploit it. If some died, so be it; war was cruel, and he hated to lose.

The startled boys jumped up and seized their weapons; the excitement in his voice was infectious.

Manton's two privates fired their muskets, but missed the tall marine at the helm. Manton was now only two feet away from the taffrail. He bound the bottom of his scabbard to his leg with a piece of rope; he needed both hands free to jump aboard and didn't want the sword to impede him.

Private James angrily fired at one of the Redcoats and hit him squarely in the nose. His face exploded. Bits of gore showered everyone in the boat.

Manton wiped grey matter from his face and prepared to jump. "Follow me up as soon as I am on board," he shouted to the surviving four.

A burst of wind hit *Lucky Lady's* sails and she surged forward. The Redcoats who had fired the volley stopped running after her; she was just too fast. They knew their mates would get their chance.

The boys formed up in a ragged line. "Load your damn muskets!" shouted Tracy. Marines would never have to be told, but in his haste he had forgotten new recruits had to be told absolutely everything. He must be getting old! His head throbbed. The boys feverishly did as they were told, some fumbling, some efficiently; finished, they awaited orders. He pointed toward the British who were in the water up to their waists. "Fire!" It was a ragged discharge, hardly a volley, but it shocked the British and made them hesitate.

Manton leaped, his hands locked onto solid wood, and he used his momentum to swing his left leg over the taffrail. He followed with his right and rolled ungracefully onto the deck, directly behind Tracy.

Tracy spun round just as Manton jumped to his feet. They whipped their swords out at the same time, and the blades slammed together so hard that blue sparks flew through the air. Tracy jumped back to gain distance and deliver a more powerful stroke.

Manton drew his blade back to lunge for his opponent's chest, then locked eyes with Tracy. What the ...? My God, it was Pennywhistle! Older, greyer, perhaps, but his spitting image. It could not be; it made no sense. He did what he had never done before. He held his thrust. His brain strove mightily to reconcile violently conflicting thoughts.

The momentary hesitation gave Tracy his opening. He feinted a cut at Manton's head, then lashed out with a violent kick with his left boot. It caught Manton in the thigh and snapped him backwards against the taffrail. The impact knocked the wind out of him, and he lay draped over the side, stunned and exposed. Time for the death stroke.

Tracy raised his cutlass above his head, poised to strike, but then stopped. It was something in the man's eyes; something that for all his combat experience was utterly new. Not pleading, he had seen that plenty of times before. No, it was recognition and surprise. The look you'd flash if suddenly betrayed by a friend. It made no sense. He'd never met the man. It was a mystery, and he hated mystery. It triggered a violent mental thunderstorm and loosed an emotion he thought long dead: mercy.

He decided in a flash. He grabbed the lieutenant by the collar and chucked him overboard to land on top of Redcoats just about to leap onto the *Lucky Lady*. All five collapsed in a tangled heap of limbs and weapons, and Tracy slashed down with his cutlass and severed the rope binding the improvised grappling hook to the stern. *Lucky Lady* ploughed ahead and the skiff rapidly dropped astern.

The boys looked at each other in astonishment and confusion. Why had the officer done that? Marines were tough and ruthless; such men never spared opponents.

No time for reflection, Tracy realized. The bottleneck loomed only yards ahead. He looked at the boys and smiled. They were the perfect lure for what lay ahead, but he would have to time it well or they would probably all die.

"Fredericks, take the helm. Boys, load up, then form up two ranks, nice and neat, facing the shore. Straight backbones, elbow contact with the man on your left, muskets tight at your side and even with your toes. Eyes front and center. C'mon, c'mon, smartly now!" The boys obeyed. The lines were far from good, but they would do. They were sitting ducks.

The Redcoats at the bottleneck wondered about the men formed on deck, but thought them a splendid target just too good to miss. "Hold your fire," said Sergeant Laurie. "Wait for my command." Twenty yards... almost time. "We will wipe the deck as smooth as a newborn's bottom. Pop up when I give the word."

Tracy stretched himself on his belly, slithered forward, and hugged the gunwale. He would be very hard to see from shore. He held a smoldering portfire in his right hand. The timing would have to be exquisite.

He could see little through the open gun port, but it would be enough. The shore drew closer. Time slowed to a snail's pace, everything seemed unnaturally clear, unnaturally vibrant. He noticed the faint scent of cherries and saw a frightened fawn bound up the hill, probably spooked by lurking soldiers.

There it was! One second nothing, the next a solid bulwark of red; at least fifty muskets leveled at the boys standing above and behind him. He was close enough to see faces. Now! He touched the portfire to the cannon's vent hole.

Boom! The little popgun thundered back on its tackles, flame gushed forth, and two hundred musket balls sped directly into startled British faces. It was a giant scythe that cut down twenty men and disoriented the rest. He heard screams, groans, and curses.

He jumped up and touched the glowing portfire to the second cannon. It belched death and smashed ten Redcoats into bloody pulps.

The screams faded as the breeze increased and the ship gained speed. Laurie looked in horror at the carnage, but gamely rallied his men.

Tracy raced back to the helm. He took the wheel and commanded the boys to stand down. They had done their part. He told them to relax for a bit; they could bask in a small ray of glory.

He could see the Patuxent directly ahead. Steady as she goes, just four hundred more yards. It felt good to have the wheel in his hands. She was a fine little ship; a shame he would have to ditch her. The immediate peril was past, but he still had to figure out a course once they gained the main channel. The British would certainly have small craft in the river. At least the wind was strong and fair. His clothing felt very damp. In all of the excitement, he had forgotten the humid, sweltering heat.

The face of the British lieutenant popped unbidden into his head. Who was he? The man's expression said *old friend*. He had been mistaken for someone. It seemed Fate was toying with his sanity. First the *doppelganger*, then this unknown officer. He kicked his speculations to a remote corner of his mind, telling himself he had enough to worry about.

The bow entered the main channel. He took out his spyglass and scanned in all directions. All clear: a welcome and unexpected piece of good fortune. He turned the wheel slowly to port and put her on a course heading north, trying to remember maps he had seen of the area. There was a village five miles ahead. He would have to beach the *Lady* before that and strike overland for the Woodyard. He wondered how many men Winder had assembled there. He hoped the assembly point had not moved.

His men and the boys sat placidly on the deck, eating salt pork and stale bread and washing it down with cider. The ship's hold contained plenty of supplies. Everyone would be fed and rested when they started the hard marching.

He did a cold evaluation of his actions and decided the verdict was not entirely unfavorable. He had saved the boys and probably secured a few new recruits for the Corps. He had disrupted the British at least a little. He had the information he needed. Not a bad day's work.

The sore-backed Lieutenant Manton cursed himself. He had lost good men. He had no prisoners and no ship. He could have had both if he had not hesitated. He'd had the tall marine dead to rights, could have laid him out with one good thrust. He had been a fool, but had never been so startled in his life. The heat punished everyone; he had seen men with heat stroke rave and shout at hallucinations. Maybe he had just experienced a taste of it. It was a poor explanation for his behavior. No, the man had certainly been real. But if he were not Pennywhistle, who the blazes was he? An unasked-for flutter of intuition told him he would soon have his answer.

CHAPTER TWELVE

Pennywhistle had been ordered to take extra pains to make his column's movements conspicuous and unmistakable. It was the opposite of everything his experience had taught him, but it made sense given the circumstances. He and Major Malcolm made sure their seven hundred men kicked up plenty of dust, made lots of noise, and took the most heavily traveled roads. The marine uniforms were similar to the army's, save for their highly distinctive, round coachman's hats. He doubted the Americans cared about the differences; they were all simply "Redcoats".

They relaxed their usual pace, both to conserve energy and to give more time for enemy scouts to spot them. He even encouraged the unthinkable while marching: talking in the ranks. Their fifers and drummers played with gusto. The marines marched with two six-foot-square silk flags on nine-foot poles. The King's Color featured a Union Flag with a small white ship with furled sails in the center. The Marine Color featured a large blue fouled anchor on a white background, surrounded on each side by red roses and green and purple thistles. These flapped proudly in the fitful breeze, when they didn't hang limply in the heavy air. When the wind favored them, it was a brave and inspiring sight to the men, dispiriting to the enemy.

Less inspiring was the smell. The column stank. Each man carried four pounds of very hard salt pork, which wept slightly in the frying heat, giving the column a rank aroma that could be detected for miles.

He and Malcolm rode two fine white horses at the head of the column. He had never particularly liked horses and rode with an inexpert seat, but the white mare named Rossamun did not seem to mind. His newly acquired spurs would probably prove unnecessary, but Malcolm had insisted he wear them. Malcolm worried about enemy snipers targeting them, but Pennywhistle assured him American marksmanship was greatly exaggerated. Some fine shots certainly existed, but any snipers today would be townsmen who hadn't even qualified for the militia. Sure enough, the column had been shot at twice today by vigilantes, but the shooters had been execrable marksmen with inferior weapons.

Even a blind man could not fail to discern the column's presence. Little bands of militia and a few scattered horsemen had made discreet appearances throughout the day. None seemed disposed to approach close enough to provoke a fight; he suspected that had less to do with lack of spirit than a lack of coordination among the higher ups.

He had not been told to avoid a fight, but he did not seek one either. When he, Malcolm and the Marine Brigade had joined Ross, the General had decided to employ the men as a feint. Pennywhistle's column was intended to make the

Americans look toward the Potomac, while Ross approached the capital from the opposite direction. Pennywhistle and Malcolm hoped to convince the Americans that Ross was shifting his axis of attack toward Ft. Washington on the Potomac, seeking to coordinate with the British squadron slowly making its way upriver. Ft. Washington was all that stood between the squadron and the water approaches to the capital; a land assault on it made perfect sense.

Fort Washington was a brick fortress mounting a number of very heavy guns, a mile upriver and on the opposite side of the shore from Mt. Vernon, with a garrison of around a hundred men. The water was shallow in front of it and any ships would have to pass very close to its guns. Even inexperienced artillerists would score a few hits.

His efforts today might actually cause Fort Washington to be reinforced. Not good for the British navy, but very good for the British army, as it would remove American troops from field work.

He and Malcolm planned to make camp as noisily and obviously as possible with the onset of evening. Once it was fully dark, his men would leave the campfires burning and make a night march back to Ross's Army. It would be a real test of endurance and character.

He stopped Rossamun and unfurled his spyglass. He was supposed to meet a small detachment of marines from Commodore Gordon's squadron. He looked forward to seeing his good friend, Peter Spottswood. He and Spottswood had a long history, and the lieutenant had helped him greatly after the death of his beloved Carlotta. More than that, his strategic instincts were first rate.

He panned his spyglass back and forth, but saw only a little knot of American horsemen on a small knoll four hundred yards away. They looked well uniformed, probably a militia unit of propertied gentlemen, to judge by the quality of horses and side arms. They had their spyglasses out, and one of them wrote furiously in a small ledger. Their orders would be to observe and report, exactly what Ross desired. They were obviously counting numbers. He hoped they would take note of the fact the column was on the main road to Ft. Washington, fifteen miles ahead. It was the same little play he had staged several times earlier today. His audiences would report to their commanders.

He wondered who was actually in charge of the Americans. They seemed to have a lot of puffed up militia generals of little or no experience. He had certainly seen some fancy and creative uniforms today, lots of blue and gold.

He opened his Blancpain: five o' clock. Where was Spottswood? He should have arrived hours ago, but he'd probably had to dodge a few patrols. Unlike Pennywhistle, Spottswood was definitely trying not to be conspicuous.

It was time to make camp. The men could snatch a few hours' rest. If they departed the camp by ten, they could probably join up with Ross's men early tomorrow morning. The march back would be fast, quiet, and stealthy; everything the advance had not been.

The column marched light, in the sense they were not accompanied by a baggage train, which meant each man traveled heavily indeed, toting roughly seventy pounds of food and equipment. Each man carried an extra shirt, overalls, and shoes in his knapsack, with a rolled up blanket stowed atop. The twin knapsack straps constricted the chest, which made breathing difficult; Pennywhistle had ordered them loosened. The sagging canvas knapsacks looked much less military, but it eased the strain on the burdened men.

One thing he was truly grateful for were the extra shoes. Well, low boots really, called shoes to distinguish them from cavalry boots. Military issue shoes had a reputation for being cheap, and hard marching wore them out quickly. The Maryland roads abounded in sharp pebbles. He had noticed poorer militia marching in bare feet; that would reduce American ability to move quickly and cause a lot of straggling.

He and Malcolm agreed upon Mt. Prosperity Plantation as the bivouac site. It featured an oak-lined avenue from the entrance gate to the white pillared brick house a quarter mile away. Any attackers would be fully exposed, and there were some small gullies near the main home that would make excellent defensive positions. He would treat himself to one of the beds in the house for a few hours' sleep.

He was anticipating a visit to Morpheus when he heard a sharp crack. He glanced at Malcolm riding next to him. The major pitched forward, a surprised expression on his face. A rivulet of red trickled down his chest. Malcolm touched the hole for a brief second, then slowly toppled from his horse without a sound. The bullet had just placed Pennywhistle in command of 700 men.

He recovered quickly and looked around, spotting a tall oak tree a hundred yards distant. A man crouched on the lowest tree branch. Pennywhistle pointed to the tree and angrily shouted to a squad marching alongside, "Bring that man to me! I want him alive!" Was the man a legitimate soldier, or merely a farmer with a grudge, just another damned Yankee bushwhacker? It would make no difference to Malcolm, but it made a great deal of difference to him. He respected soldiers doing a nasty job even if the results were personally painful, but civilians acting outside of the laws of war excited only his contempt. People who wanted to fight belonged in the army. He hated cowards who hid behind their civilian occupation and only played the soldier at moments of opportunity when they commanded all the advantage. That sort of behavior needed to be suppressed harshly, and he had just been given an opportunity to do so.

The squad surrounded the tree and pointed their muskets up at the sniper. "Get down from there immediately, or we turn you into a sieve," shouted an angry corporal. The man climbed down slowly and reluctantly. He was immediately seized by four none too gentle Redcoats and frog-marched directly to Pennywhistle.

"Let me go, damn you! Let me go!" shouted the sniper.

Pennywhistle looked at the man carefully. His attire was ordinary, but he had a peculiar, slightly satanic-looking face; pinprick eyes with a jutting, misshapen jaw, pointy teeth, and a short triangular beard which obscured his receding chin. When his bulbous lips moved, he gave the impression of a goat chewing his cud. The only thing worthy of note was the fine American Long Rifle he carried. Pennywhistle saw terror in the man's eyes.

Pennywhistle wasted no time. "What is your unit?" The man said nothing; apparently he was tongue-tied with fear.

"What is your unit?" There was no response. "Damn you, sir! What is your unit?"

"I, I ... uh... I don't belong to a unit," the man stammered and stared at his feet. "I am Mt. Prosperity's gamekeeper. I was just trying to defend the plantation since the master is gone. You don't belong here or in this country. I was just doing my part." He looked up sheepishly as if to wheedle some sympathy.

Pennywhistle's eyes flashed fire. A roaring anger burned out any thought of mercy. He did not raise his voice but it dripped with ice-cold menace. "Just doing your part, you say? What part would that be? Skulking in the weeds? Shirking your obligation to stand with the militia? Bushwacking? You, sir, are nothing but a murdering jackal. I care nothing for your motives and do not wish to know your name. You shall forfeit your life as payment for your misdeed."

Sergeant Dale had pounded up to Pennywhistle's side and now spoke up. "I can arrange an immediate firing squad, Captain," said Dale.

"No, firing squads are reserved for soldiers. This coward deserves a criminal's fate. Take a squad and string him up. That oak tree he fired from will serve. Stretch his neck and let him dance the Paddington frisk so that all may see the fate of bushwhackers. Don't bother to take the body down. Let the crows have their portion. It's a damned shame we have no tar; with that, the corpse would last at least a month."

"No, no!" The man screamed in terror. "I at least deserve a trial! I got a wife and five children. Please sir, I beg of you, give me another chance! Don't leave my children orphaned. Please! Please!"

Pennywhistle sneered at the man. "You gave Major Malcolm no trial before you executed him! A wife and five children, you say? If you display the same judgment about family that you do about war, they probably will be glad to be rid of you. At least shut your mouth and try to die a man.

Take him away, Sarn't Dale. This slinking scoundrel has already pushed my patience far beyond its limits."

Dale and a parcel of vexed marines quickly bundled the shrieking man out of Pennywhistle's sight. He had more important matters to worry about. He wanted to give Malcolm a proper military funeral, but the day was hot, and an immediate burial would be necessary. There would be no salutes fired, or the men would think a battle had been joined. The marines tenderly draped Malcolm's body over his horse's saddle.

Evidently, the inhabitants of the plantation had fled at the approach of the British. More precisely, the white inhabitants fled. The slave population remained. Once they saw the soldiers were disciplined and not rowdy marauders, a few came out of hiding, and soon they were talking with the black Colonial Marines. Then they led them to a storehouse of Smithfield hams. The plantation had plenty of chickens, pigs, and cattle as well. The men would eat their fill tonight and march with contented bellies, and even if their packs were no lighter, their provisions would be fresher.

Pennywhistle issued orders, and the men set up their messes and cooking fires. He rode up to the main house, dismounted, tied Rossamun to a hitching post, then went inside. Sergeant MacDonald, with an odd look on his face, met him and the door and told him that a lady of the household, one Amity Parke, desired to speak to him. MacDonald said she was most insistent, would not take no for an answer, and was "a mite long in the tongue and perhaps a bit tetched in the head."

Pennywhistle's anger at the bushwhacker had not abated and he really did not need more complaints about the British running off slaves. He had small patience with wealthy folk decrying the financial inconvenience of war, but this was probably her home, and he felt honor bound to at least hear her out; yet another annoying burden of command. Also, angry civilians often let slip the most useful bits of military information. He affixed his most patient smile, willed his tongue to be diplomatic, and walked calmly into the main parlor.

"I want my money!"

The woman was well into her sixties, tall and stately, with a patrician face that did not match the screech in her voice.

"We sold you food in the past and you paid. Now you think you can just march in here and take what you want? We gave your commissary officer's good quality vittles, and this is how you repay us? Fie, sir, fie, on you and your King! I demand you put things right! And to add to the insult, you brought nigger soldiers with you! Nigger soldiers!"

Most unexpected! A collaborator, feeling ill-treated. How arrogant! For all of their boisterous patriotism, plenty of Americans had been willing to sell the British food. Indeed, Cockburn would have had a hard time maintaining his fleet in the Chesapeake without them. This plantation was distant from the places the British bought food; goods would have to have been transported. That suggested considerable preparation and forethought. She had probably been doing business with the British for some time, and had probably made quite a bit of money from it. Despite all of the people on both sides who thought this a stupid and unnecessary war, she was heavily invested in its continuance. She just did not like the reality descending on her doorstep.

He looked into her eyes. There was none of the fear and grief he had seen far too often in civilians despoiled of their property and possessions by war. That always elicited his sympathy. He saw greed and malice. He saw a hard woman and a hard bargainer—the same in peace as in war. He doubted she cared much about the outcome, as long as she got paid. She was of a breed he hated: those who believed war an opportunity, not an abomination.

Mt. Prosperity was primarily a tobacco plantation, and tobacco wore out the soil quickly. Perhaps the war had actually revived the plantation's fortunes. The house was certainly well maintained and expensively furnished.

She stared at him imperiously. She looked accustomed to compliance and immediate service. She had probably seen the sergeant as an inferior and browbeaten him. No wonder the sergeant thought her a bit off. Pennywhistle said nothing. Let the silence speak. Let her fret. He kept his face bland and expressionless, with just a hint of an enigmatic smile.

He let a full minute pass, let the silence become oppressive. She sought advantage from him, but he could wring something from her.

She struck him as intelligent; clearly she liked to control. She probably knew a lot of things besides provisioning. She could be very useful, if played right. He already knew her patriotism was of the financial kind, so he would not reason with her; he would aim straight for her real heart. Not the one of noble sentiment, but the one fashioned from avarice.

He slowly bowed his head, clasped his hands behind his back, and paced back and forth four times, as if wrestling with great and mighty considerations. He wanted her to believe he took her very seriously. He did, just not in the way she wanted. Finally, he faced her directly.

"Madam," he said in a patient voice that nevertheless scolded like a birch rod on a backside, "the coloreds that march with me are not soldiers but something much finer:

marines. They are far better disciplined than your white militia, who are chiefly renowned for their capacity for drink and fast running. I understand your frustration and have a certain sympathy for your plight, but my options are very limited. My orders are to assume that any plantation deserted by its owners is in that state because they are active members of the militia. As active members of an enemy force, all of their goods and possessions, if captured, are forfeit to the Crown. It is a regrettable but iron law of war. I have spoken to two of your slaves, who have assured me that your son, Colonel Daniel Parke, is the commander of the 7th Maryland Regiment of Militia. I would be within my rights if I simply chose to burn this place to the ground. You are fortunate that I am a man of compassion and reason, far more forgiving than my commander, Admiral Cockburn."

"But, but, we have helped you!" She sputtered in sheer frustration.

"*You* may have, yet your *son* will order his men to kill us if we meet. Very paradoxical, wouldn't you agree?"

She said nothing, and her angry expression changed to one of confusion.

"Still, there might be a way for you to obtain some compensation for your losses. It is not much, but I have a small sum of gold guineas with me, and authority to issue chits redeemable after the war. I have need of certain very trivial pieces of information. Nothing that would compromise your own or your country's honor, nor the war's outcome, I assure you, merely superficial bits of guidance that would make my men's lot easier." He doubted she had any honor to compromise, but it was as well to flatter her.

Her anger vanished in an instant. Her eyes blazed with hope and greed. The penny dropped! She positively cooed, "I am agreeable to hear how I might be of assistance."

He had her! Once he had inveigled her into the first betrayal, each succeeding one would be easier. He would have to be cautious; he would treat her like a pearl diver and persuade her the prize she lusted for lay just a little deeper; make her gradually descend into murkier and murkier moral waters.

Gold held no special fascination for him, but he realized that was not the case with most men. It had a bewitching effect on even the most rational of minds. He remembered the middle-aged fools at the burnt out cabin. The tale of Midas spoke much about human nature. Flash real gold, promise more, and people's scruples disappeared like morning mist at the first hint of sun.

He thrust his fingers into his pocket and produced a stout leather purse, brought it up to waist level, and rattled it significantly. The noise suggested its contents. Her eyes widened evilly, a cobra seeing an easy meal. He had given the predator the scent; time to draw her toward the hunter.

He reached inside the purse and produced a single gold guinea. He moved toward her and held it within a foot of her face, letting the fading sunlight glint off its contours. He moved it back and forth a few times, and she followed it intently. He felt like a stage mesmerist. Her reaction disgusted him nearly as much as it interested him. He hated manipulation, but scruples could never be allowed to supersede his moral obligation to husband his men's lives carefully, to find out any information which could protect them.

"I have five more of these, which can soon be yours. A few simple answers will make this one your own. Are you ready...? Forgive me, madam, we have not been properly introduced. People must have a way to address each other. Let us remedy that situation. I am Captain Pennywhistle; Captain will do. I thought I heard someone address you as Amity. Might I call you that?"

"Yes, my name is Amity." She had gone from imperious to docile in a few sentences; she really wanted the money. He had subtly just lowered her status. Names were the most personal things imaginable, almost mystical. Cultures immersed in magic believed that a name was a sacred and dangerous thing, something to be guarded closely and not easily surrendered. A name conferred the power to summon up the most dangerous of demons to visit his attentions on a person. In a way, he was her demon.

More prosaically, names involved dominance. He would call her by her first name, very personal for a *grande dame*, while she would never know his first name and address him only by rank. He would repeat her first name often to get her used to him using it; this would breed a sense that he knew her very, very closely; not sexually, yet extremely intimately. He would initiate, while she would only respond. He reminded himself to hand her guineas at regular intervals, just like biscuits to a spaniel when you were training her to hunt. In the process, he would bleed her for every last scrap of information.

He saw the eagerness in her eyes and hated himself for what he was about to do. Even a bad old woman deserved the comfort of family in her old age. Sooner or later, the leak would be discovered and retribution would be exacted, probably in the form of shunning. It would be very hard on an old woman to be estranged from her family and her country.

No reason he could not make things a bit easier now. He remembered what he had used to loosen slaves' tongues. He still had some of it left in a bottle in his right saddle bag. It would make betrayal a bit less obvious, and easier. And more excusable.

"Sarn't MacDonald," he called out, "get in here, front and center." MacDonald, a tall, red-haired Highlander who spoke Gaelic as his first tongue, appeared quickly and snapped to attention. "Sir, how may I help you, sir?" His Scots burr was almost impenetrable.

"Sarn't, I have a wee dram of that magic liquid that has made Scotland renowned the world over in my saddlebag. I wonder if you would fetch it and bring it here directly? The lady and I have some congenial conversation ahead, and I feel a spot of Scotland's finest product would make pleasant things even more agreeable." He smiled and held the Sergeant's eye.

"Och, aye, sir, I wull see to it immediately!" MacDonald said sturdily; he knew whiskey in any discussion usually steered it toward a good outcome. He snapped Pennywhistle a crisp salute and departed at a dash.

"Please, Amity, let us sit and talk. If we are to be frank and direct with each other, we must be comfortable." He saw two wing-backed, red leather chairs in the corner. Westering sunlight gave them a mellow glow, and they looked heavily padded for extra support. The Palladian window gave a fine view of the lawn, now festooned with small camp fires and men in red bustling purposefully about. He took her gently by the hand and led her to the chair.

She jumped at the touch of his hand and looked him directly in the eyes with an unquestionably sexual gaze. God, she was excited! The old crone repulsed him, but her state gave him another bit of leverage.

MacDonald appeared with the whiskey and set the bottle gently down on small table next to the chairs. He handled the bottle reverently, as precious cargo, which it was to any Scot. He found two crystal glasses in a tall mahogany cabinet and set them next to the whiskey, then he stood to attention. "Anything else you'll be needing, sir?"

"No, thank you, MacDonald, that will be all."

"Very good, sir." He saluted, pivoted smartly, and departed.

Pennywhistle slowly poured two glasses and handed one to Mrs. Parke. He would nurse his, watching carefully to see how she consumed hers. Her cheeks looked rosy. He wondered if she had a fondness for drink.

He raised his glass. "A toast. To better times!" He kept it matter of fact, sincere, devoid of any suggestion of her reversal of fortune. He wanted to appear civilized and reasonable, a mannerly gentleman under even the most adverse of circumstances. She might mistake it for weakness, which could actually work to his favor if it made her overconfident.

She did not pause to savor the splendid aroma, as he did, but took a deep draught that fell just short of a gulp. Clearly not a regular drinker of fine Scotch. She brightened visibly as the smooth fire coursed down her throat. He took a tiny sip of his and smiled pleasantly at her. The scotch was excellent, but the smile was utterly false. Time for business.

"Amity, please tell me more about your associations with my countrymen. I should like specifics about your plantation's role in supply considerations." He was curious to find out how deeply she was invested in the war, and it was good to get her talking about something familiar and important.

"We have done a tremendous amount for you! Tremendous." She was quite indignant that something patently obvious had gone unrecognized. She launched into a lengthy chronicle, which, while tedious, furnished a wealth of information: dates, quantities, locales. She carelessly dropped the names of other collaborators. Hers was a financial apologia of a sort. It was as he'd inferred: people living beyond their means on a used up farm getting much needed infusions of cash. And he was right about her having a head for detail.

She and her son had indeed supplied the British Navy with everything from fresh water to ham, beef, and fresh grains. Fleet demands were prodigious; one ship of the line alone consumed three tons of water per day and could easily account for 30 bullocks a month. Pennywhistle quickly discovered how war inflated the price of nearly all victuals. She had been very disappointed with the British army—not that they had landed and were marching on her country's capital, but because they appeared to have no further need of her services. He realized with a start that she had stopped talking and expected some sort of response.

"A very exact and complete recapitulation, Amity; you would make a fine commissary officer. We are not without gratitude for our American friends." He fought to keep the irony out of his voice. "I give you this in consideration for past services." He tossed her a guinea, which she caught in midair. Her eyes blazed with delight.

"Now, tell me about your son. What sort of man is he?" He expected she would want to boast. She seemed completely untroubled by the hypocrisy of her son being a militia leader. He saw her glass was only half full, reached over, and topped it off.

"He is a good man, Captain, the best. He is a widower. He provides well for me and for his children. He is a brave man, too. His men love him, will fight hard for him. You would not want to meet him in battle. He would give you a thorough trouncing." She smiled archly, and he smiled inwardly. Like many Americans, she greatly overvalued the fighting prowess of amateurs. Her pride was natural, but he doubted it was justified. He glanced around the parlor. Everything was of the best quality. Good provider indeed --- perhaps too good. No wonder the family scrambled to find other sources to pay expenses.

"Then pray tell, Amity, why did he leave you behind? I should think he would have evacuated all his family."

"I would not allow it!" she said fiercely. "He had his duty and his children to think of, but someone had to stay behind and make sure the British behaved themselves! I knew your people would not molest an old woman who had the courage to defend her hearth and home. You are on the property of people who have done you many good turns. Your men simply ignored me when they first arrived. I hoped to persuade them to leave things be. I failed in that. You have done an excellent job despoiling the plantation!" she said with asperity.

"It is war, Amity, not a *soirée*. Armies are like the locusts of Egypt and destroy a lifetime of labor in the twinkling of an eye. My men have taken only food. They have looted nothing and left your buildings and home untouched. You will have your property back in good condition when we depart. That is more than could be said when your forces burned York to the foundations. But I digress. I should like to know why your son didn't make some sort of a stand here, at least skirmish with our men. We marched in unopposed. The grounds have excellent defensive possibilities."

"Don't think he didn't consider it! I said we should stand, and he thought the same at first. But he listens too much to his second, Major Grimes. Grimes counseled caution. Regroup and attack later, he said." She took another draught from her tumbler, as if she needed reinforcement to embark upon a distasteful course.

"Are all of the local militia in the area alerted and with him?" he interjected casually, almost as an afterthought, even though it was vital information.

"I am sure they are, but allow me to continue about Grimes." He had interrupted the story she wanted to tell, and it annoyed her. She wanted something off her chest.

"Of course, Amity, pray continue."

"Daniel treats everything Grimes says as gospel truth. I hate that man! Daniel simply cannot say no to him. He has guided Daniel down the wrong path more times than I can remember." There was real venom in her voice. "Archibald Grimes is a bad influence, a bad influence. Something about the man just isn't natural. God forgot to put something in, and Satan rushed into the void." Her voice had risen an octave. Grimes clearly was a bad seed in her family garden. It was worth exploring.

"You used the word 'unnatural' about Grimes. What exactly did you mean?" He again topped off her tumbler. The son sounded irresolute. Perhaps the second was the real voice of command.

Her grey eyes clouded, her eyebrows arched, and her lips pursed in disgust. The age lines in her face deepened. "I mean Major Grimes has never married, never courted anyone. He has plenty of property, good looks, he could make a fine match, yet has resisted all our efforts to find him a bride. He is nearly thirty. A man should be wedded. There have been ... rumors. No one knew why he suddenly left his law practice in Washington. I catch him looking at Daniel...." She trailed off, as if she found it too disgusting to continue.

Pennywhistle put the clues together. Here was the peculiar love never spoken of in polite company. Every city had its molly houses—inns which catered to that unusual trade. He did not understand it, but he knew of two high-born officers who enjoyed a discreet connection that mostly went unremarked. It certainly did not affect their soldiering abilities. So Grimes and her son had formed a liaison. No wonder she was bitter.

"You believe Major Grimes has caused your son to make ill-considered decisions? He advised your son not to defend this place? Why? Did he do it to spite you? He must have known you disliked him." Perhaps the rest of his tactics were unnecessary. He had stepped into a family quarrel, and deep waters might be quickly reached.

"That's exactly right! He doesn't care anything about this place or our family, and he hates me because I have constantly warned Daniel what he risked. Sometimes Daniel rides over to the old Waterman place late at night, when everyone is asleep. He thinks no one hears him leave, but I do. I've prayed to God to take this curse from him!" Tears formed in the corners of her eyes. The emotion seemed honest enough, but it was hard to tell with a woman so calculating.

"What exactly is the Waterman Place, Amity?"

"An old farm four miles from here, along Boggy Creek. The family went bankrupt. The land has gone back to seed. The militia usually musters there, first Tuesday of the month. How *can* a good man have such strange, debased longings? Tell me! Tell me! He is an elder in our church!" Her eyes pleaded with him to supply some sort of rational answer. Pennywhistle suddenly had the unpleasant feeling he was a priest in a confessional, expected to dispense some sort of prescription for absolution.

"I am a soldier, Amity, not a philosopher. I have no idea what lies in a man's heart, but sometimes people are driven by forces they do not understand and cannot control. Those forces are powerful and render appeals to morals and reason impotent. I suspect it is that way with your son." He found the son's morals much less significant than his twin allegiances to Mammon and Columbia. Daniel Parke tried to serve two masters, both in love and war. Such men usually came to a hard end.

If the Waterman Place was the site of Daniel's illicit trysts, it would be a place of familiarity and importance to which he might repair in time of peril. The militia held their monthly muster there. It would make sense for the colonel to regroup and reorganize his men on that spot.

He would pay the place a visit after he departed Mt. Prosperity. The slaves would know the location.

He could not afford any militia on his line of march. A strike assault would be the perfect time to test the modified Congreves. Night attacks were always pure confusion, but if the rockets flew accurately they might wipe out the enemy while putting his men at small risk. It could be done quickly, spectacularly, and would definitely send a dramatic message that the British could strike unexpectedly at any time. The slaves would know the location.

He had what he needed. The old woman had fallen silent. She looked deflated, yet relieved. She had told her dread secret to someone. She stared into her drink. There was no reason to be cruel.

"I am not without humanity, madam. You have indeed endured much, and your tale of woe has moved me." Indeed, a slight sympathy for her moved into his breast. Whatever Daniel Parke was as a family man, soldier, or romantic partner, he had a mother who loved him. She bore a huge weight, trying to protect her son from his own desires and shield him from being branded a social outcast. She was certainly corrupt and venal, yet possessed a streak of humanity. It troubled him that he would use that humanity to destroy that which she held most dear.

"I cannot undo what has been done, but I can give you these guineas as slight compensation." He reached into his purse, extracted the coins, and handed them to her. She smiled slightly; it was tinged, not with greed but puzzlement. He realized he had given her something already, something she'd hardly expected—an audience for her pain. "No further damage to your property will occur. For your own safety, I must confine you to your room until we leave. It will only be for a night and a day"—he would not give her accurate information along with the coins. "I wish you and your family well."

He gave her the money to assuage his guilt. He certainly did not owe her a farthing, but it would help him sleep just a bit better. At least it was not thirty pieces of silver. God, he needed rest. That feather bed he had spotted earlier beckoned seductively.

"Sarn't MacDonald!" he called, and MacDonald appeared a few seconds later. "Please escort Mrs. Parke to her room. Make sure she has every comfort and post a guard to make sure she is not disturbed."

"Very good, sir. Captain, Lieutenant Spottswood has arrived. He is very keen to speak with you."

"Thank you, Sarn't." Pennywhistle walked over to Mrs. Parke, extended his hand, and helped her to her feet. "And now, madam, I must take my leave of you and attend to my duties. Please follow Sarn't MacDonald."

"Thank you, thank you, Captain, for your kindness." She squeezed his hand tightly in gratitude. This time there were no sexual undertones. "It is good to know humanity and kindness have not perished entirely. It gives me hope."

"Indeed, madam, in war, more than other times, hope must be held high, lest we allow despair to pull us low. Good night." He watched her leave, and again felt a wave of guilt. She might not have much hope twenty-four hours hence.

"Tom, Tom! How are you?" A deep, cheerful voice boomed across the parlor. He turned to see Peter Spottswood standing in the doorway. It was a great relief to see his friend. Spottswood was hours overdue, and he had feared the worst.

"Peter! Finally! I thought you'd run into an American patrol."

"My men exchanged a few shots with a small group of militia, but we drove them off without much difficulty. Can we sit and talk a bit? We have a great deal to discuss."

"Please forgive my lack of manners. Malcolm's dead, murdered by that fellow dangling from the tree in front. I have command of the entire column now, and I should be glad of your advice. My talk with the lady of the house has unsettled me, yet it has provided information we can use. I have some excellent whiskey left from our chat. Let me get you a glass. The red chair is very comfortable."

Spottswood looked concerned. "Can I be of assistance?"

"Could you take care of Malcolm's funeral, say a few appropriate remarks, perhaps a short homily, and cite some germane portions of scripture?" Pennywhistle paused thoughtfully. "I have not set foot in a church for many years and fear that, as an apostate, I could not conduct a service with the conviction his memory deserves. We don't have a chaplain, and Malcolm was a staunch Presbyterian. You still subscribe to the Christian Faith, do you not?"

"I would be honored to take care of the proprieties. Consider it done. But I would never call you an apostate, Tom."

"I do not believe I am estranged from God, Peter, merely from the Christian God. I am quite convinced of God's reality and have seen clear evidence of His hand in human affairs. I simply do not want any blathering priests, perfumed princes of the church, or canting preachers thundering at me to deny the admonitions of my reason, my heart, and my intuition. All preachers offer a misleading and invidious choice: know God through their words and dogma or know Him not at all. Their works have nothing to do with spirituality but everything to do with earthly dominion over the minds of men, and their purses. Their exhortations have occasioned far too much bloodshed down the centuries. I require no intercessors when I need an immediate and direct audience with God."

"Not all men of the cloth are bad, Tom," said Spottswood soothingly. "I know one or two who do some good and would respect your independency of thought."

Pennywhistle sighed in exasperation. "I refuse to believe their pettifogging twaddle that God is a wrathful, jealous tyrant who condones the slaughter of whole peoples simply because they fail to acknowledge His existence in a certain, very particular fashion. To believe God so petty as to value abject bootlicking and mindless ceremony over noble deeds and kind hearts makes Him seem a foolish and contemptible, rather than an understanding, omniscient deity. I cannot credit that God is beguiled by Sunday words of worship prattled by people who gleefully practice the Seven Deadly Sins the rest of the week. I could never swear fealty to a capricious being who would deny my marines salvation because they failed to attend church, tippled too greatly, or cursed chaplains too fearful to administer last rites under fire."

"What about Jesus, Tom? Do you not find him remarkable?"

"An extraordinary gift to the world, certainly, but mankind has proven deaf to his pleas for compassion and charity. I am certain he would be appalled at the pillage, rapine, and murder carried out in his name. I witnessed so much of it in Spain that I have trouble regarding the Christian Faith benignly. I watched a French officer, rosary beads in hand, calmly order the burning of a town filled only with women and children. I saw two captured French soldiers skinned and boiled alive by Spanish guerillas, led by a priest. I saw a bishop nail the tanned hide of a French soldier to a church door and loudly tell his parishioners Jesus blessed his vengeance. I admire Jesus greatly, but I do not like what the Christians have done with him."

"I think you are being too hard on Christians, but I have as much contempt as you for men who commit evil under the cloak of religion. At any rate, banish any concern about the funeral, you have enough to worry about, I know." Spottswood let out a long sigh. "I believe I will have that drink. I have had a long and tiring journey, but I think a profitable one." He eased himself into the chair and smiled at its luxurious softness. "I confess I am puzzled by the Americans at Fort Washington. We have had patrols watching it for the last two days, and there seems to be very little activity."

Pennywhistle handed Spottswood a tumbler of whiskey. "That does seem strange. I would have expected it to be a hotbed of preparations. Your squadron is a real threat, or at least most reasonable soldiers would see it that way."

"The Americans are disorganized, Tom; no one seems to be in charge. We have seen no artillery drills at all nor any new shipments of powder or weapons. Most importantly, no reinforcements! I have seen no evidence of line infantry. The men are lackluster and ill-disciplined. I watched the place myself for hours through a glass, and I swear the garrison commander was intoxicated. He looked glassy-eyed much of the day. He bustled about to no purpose, barked some orders that were ignored, consulted with a few other officers, then went back into his quarters and never emerged. No patrols were sent out. My men and I were able to move close to the fort undetected. An alert garrison would have detected us."

"What does Commodore Gordon think, Peter?"

Spottswood smiled at the formality. Gordon was Pennywhistle's close friend.

"He thinks we can manage well enough on our own. Our main enemy is the Potomac; it's treacherous water and has slowed our progress greatly. It's studded with all manner of natural obstructions and shoals that go under the collective name of the Kettle Bottom Shoals. We have no reliable local pilots. No warships have ever passed this far upriver. The water levels are low because of the lack of rains, and we repeatedly hit hidden sand bars and oyster beds which ground our ships. We have to put out divers, find the obstruction, remove all of the guns and hoist out stores to lighten the ships, then use kedge anchors to haul our ships free. Then we have to put everything back when we have floated clear, and start over. It's taken us five days to log just a few miles." He grimaced at the memory.

"It's backbreaking in this ridiculous heat. It would be disastrous if the Americans staged even small hit and run attacks. Why has this much vaunted Navy of theirs made no appearance? They observe us from time to time, but do nothing to hinder us. They have missed many opportunities to hurt us. We have scouts on the banks and cutters patrolling in advance of the ships, but mostly nothing stands in front of them. Gordon does not think that will change."

Pennywhistle's eyes assumed a faraway cast that Spottswood knew well. He was analyzing things. He was two feet away physically, a thousand miles mentally. Spottswood knew better than to disturb his cogitations. A full minute passed in silence.

"They made a bet and they lost." Pennywhistle spoke slowly. "They gambled nature was their best defense and deployed their military forces elsewhere. Perhaps it was not unreasonable. No warships ever tried to beat the Kettle Bottom Shoals. The Americans simply assumed it could not be done. They never factored in British doggedness and ingenuity. Perhaps that's why an inept commander is in charge of Fort Washington. They never expected he would have to defend the place. That is why there are no drills, no patrols, and no infantry reinforcements. If Fort Washington is not reinforced, can it be eliminated as a threat once you are close in?"

"Normally, Tom, I'd say we need help. But Gordon thinks we can engage it from the river, then land marines and sailors to take it from the rear. Its defenses are stout on the river side, but I have pinpointed two profitable avenues of approach on the landward front. Once the fort is captured, it's just eight river miles to Washington. Eight miles!

"We took one prisoner today, held him briefly, then released him on parole. He told us the chap in charge of the fort is a Captain Dyson. The Americans have been following the movements of your column closely. Your feint has them flummoxed and they have no idea what to make of it. They only know the British are in motion and active. They are dashing off in all directions.

"I have ten men with me, all stout hearts, and all with light infantry training. Gordon said I was to report to you, but if nothing had changed at the fort, I was to use my discretion and remain with your command rather than return to the squadron."

Pennywhistle smiled broadly. "That is excellent, Peter. Your presence is most welcome, most welcome. From what you have said, I doubt you will see much action with Gordon, but if you stick with me I can positively guarantee it. There is a big battle coming, a veritable showdown with the Americans, I'd say not later than the day after tomorrow. I plan to be in the thick of it. We will be outnumbered and every skilled hand we can muster helps to even the odds.

"You and I have done something even most experienced marines have never done. We have fought in a large scale land battle and know what to expect. What's coming will be small compared to Salamanca, but I believe it will be decisive. General Ross is a very able disciple of the Duke."

"It will be a great pleasure to fight alongside you, Tom, be in on the kill. I owe you so much." Spottswood took a long, thoughtful sip of the whiskey.

"But you won't have to wait until the big battle, Peter. I am contemplating an action this very night and I should like your opinion of my plan."

"I am eager to hear it. Let me propose a toast first," said Spottswood heartily. He raised his glass, as did Pennywhistle. "Success to us, and thunder and confusion to the Americans!" They clinked and drank.

"Now," said Pennywhistle, "let me explain."

CHAPTER THIRTEEN

The army had moved a few miles northwest from the Woodyard, and John Tracy found the main American camp at Oldfields in chaos. It was less a unified camp than a patchwork quilt of militia units. Each unit's garb differed slightly from its neighbors, although most sported vaguely military tailcoats in some shade of blue. Quality of attire varied widely and depended mostly on the wealth of a unit's members. Headgear was eclectic as well. Some had shakos, some slouch hats, some top hats, and a few grandees appeared in outlandish, plumed *chapeau de bras* that defied description.

Most units fielded muskets. The best equipped units had . 69 Springfields, or variants thereof which could use standard cartridges, but a few carried fowling pieces, shotguns, or ancient weapons that belonged in a museum rather than a battlefront. More than one unit had not received any guns at all and carried pikes.

Drill differed from unit to unit, and at least four different drill books were in use. Colonel Alexander's Smyth's manual was officially prescribed, but nonetheless some used Steuben, Dundas, or even the ancient Humphrey Bland. Most officers had no experience coordinating their movements with anything larger than their local company. Many company grade officers owed their positions to election by their men and were careful not to be too harsh in matters of discipline. Even so, many men resented being given orders by officers who were usually just neighbors. Amongst themselves, officers argued about seniority, precedence, and the relation between regular and militia commissions.

There was much bustle and activity, but it appeared to be simply for the sake of doing something, anything, rather than any part of an intelligent design. Troops marched, rehearsed the manual of arms, and made cartridges. Many officers searched earnestly through leather bound military manuals, trying to learn the secrets of command. Drums thundered, bugles blew, and orders were shouted, yet the sense of a guiding hand was absent. A number of men sat idle, waiting for someone to tell them where to go and what to do. The smell of past its prime beef being cooked filled the air as men prepared their evening meals. Many had not eaten at all during the day, as supplies had been late in arriving. Hunger did not improve their morale.

Tracy shook his head in disgust. A line from Hamlet popped into his head unbidden: *'Tis an unweeded garden gone to seed. Things rank and gross do possess it merely.* He had never seen such a lack of professionalism on such a large scale. But professional problems could be solved through careful planning and discipline. He had another problem that was less amenable to direct resolution.

He sat himself down on a canvas camp chair lent him by his friend Captain Miller and took a crumpled letter from his pocket. It was marked with an unusual seal: the Greek letter omega, slightly altered to resemble a golden horse shoe. Omega was appropriate; the plans in the letter could spell the end of the American Experiment. He pored over its traitorous contents for the tenth time, and scowled just as he had nine times before. He could scarcely credit that a prominent gentleman could pen such drivel.

He had been appalled at the first letter from "The Knights of the Golden Horse Shoe". They discreetly sought his help to "save the American people from a tyrannical and poisonous government." He had feigned interest in order discover their full design and identities, expressing a desire for more information and inaugurating a correspondence. He had saved all of the letters in a strongbox; they might be needed as evidence in a court of law. His oath required him to defend the Constitution against all enemies foreign and domestic. The fight against the British was obvious and clear, that against home grown scoundrels much less so.

The first letter had been signed "An Unknown Friend"; several letters later, the writer had revealed his name: Harrison Gray Otis, a prominent Massachusetts Federalist and a member of one of the Bay state's oldest families. Tracy had met Otis once at a reception in Boston and had apparently impressed the man, but Otis had misread his disapproval of plans to invade Canada as a blanket indictment of the war effort in general.

Tracy credited that the Knights represented legitimate regional grievances. The life's blood of New England was international trade, and that had been strangled by the British blockade. Unemployment was at an all time high, as were bank failures. Banks in Boston had suspended payment in specie. Half of Maine was under British control, and His Majesty's government appeared eager to make the occupation permanent. Yet the grievance that had finally pushed the Knights from vocal disgruntlement to stealthy sedition was a domestic threat: conscription. Involuntary military servitude was anathema to all English speaking peoples, but lagging enlistments had compelled Madison to propose it.

Otis was the leader of the Knights and said all of its three-score members were "upstanding, well connected gentlemen of unquestioned integrity" no longer content to remain mere observers while the ship of state foundered on rocky shores. Action was necessary, perhaps violent action. Otis had given code names for his two closest associates: "Castor and Pollux". Tracy penetrated the amateurish veil of secrecy by paying close attention to Otis's descriptions of their activities. The men were almost certainly George Cabot, a prominent Boston merchant, and Caleb Strong, the governor of Massachusetts. The organization was an octopus that had extended its tentacles throughout the highest levels of New England society and government.

Otis had revealed that he and several members of his organization had opened secret negotiations with British commissioners to conclude a separate peace favorable to New England. Likely these commissioners worked for Sir John Sherbrooke, the Lieutenant Governor of Nova Scotia. Sherbrooke wanted to connect New Brunswick and Nova Scotia with Quebec by establishing a linking colony called New Ireland, to be carved out of Eastern Maine. The territory of Maine had been annexed by Massachusetts, but was considered a poor relation. Eastern Maine was a very poor relation, and Easterners had great hostility for their distant overlords in Boston, who evinced little care for their welfare. Tracy guessed Eastern Maine might well be traded away to force the conflict to a speedy conclusion. A separate peace would likely detach New England from the rest of the states, and probably doom the entire Union.

Tracy thought of himself as a Virginian first and an American second. He realized Americans often thought of themselves as citizens of states, rather than citizens of a nation. People said "The United States are..." as if the nation were merely an aggregation of states. People needed to say, "The United States is..." acknowledging it to be a single, indivisible entity. What might be good for a state might not be good for the nation. It was as if the sad legacy of the Articles of Confederation had never quite died.

Otis was too circumspect to state directly why the Knights wanted Tracy's particular support. In flowery prose heavily laced with a practiced salesman's flattery, he poured out his admiration for Tracy's patriotism, probity, and heroic exploits during Captain Bainbridge's cruise with the *U.S.S. Constitution*. Tracy discerned a more sinister intent beneath the patriotic rhetoric. Otis, like the rest of the conspirators, was a civilian. Otis alluded to but did not directly define certain contingencies that might arise where a military man's special "talents and experience" might be needed. Otis harped on Mr. Madison's stubborn refusal to see reality and "end this pernicious conflict at the earliest possible moment." The President might prove a problem requiring a violent solution. In other words, Otis wanted an assassin.

Tracy was disgusted by the war, but he was no murderer. Madison might be inept, but he was elected by the people and was his legally constituted superior in the chain of command. Even a veiled threat against the President's life amounted to treason.

Otis had enclosed an indigo ring emblazoned with a golden omega/horseshoe and had informed Tracy he would be approached by a contact wearing a similar ring and given further instructions. Tracy stared at the ring for a full five minutes before reluctantly putting it on. He disliked wearing any kind of ring, but this was harsh necessity, not vanity.

He had to keep his priorities straight. The upcoming battle needed to be won, and he could not allow even a fraction of his concentration to be diverted from that goal. The longer he looked at the camp, however, the more he despaired of a good outcome. He jammed the letter back in his pocket, hoisted himself to his feet, and set out to find the bumbling author of this military confusion.

He was unable to locate General Winder. The commander was off conferring with Madison and the Cabinet, but Tracy talked to General Stansbury, the man in immediate charge, giving a full report of his reconnaissance. Stansbury, like Winder, was another non-professional, an attorney in private life. Stansbury listened half-heartedly, and Tracy got the feeling that all of his efforts had been to no purpose, that the General's mind was already made up. He did not look like he credited Tracy's estimation of low numbers. The General seemed to want to magnify the danger, perhaps to inflate his sense of self importance—or to justify in advance any failure —rather than reduce it to manageable proportions that could be handled. It was also possible that his hysteria was so deep-rooted no amount of facts could shake it; he was like a diseased man unwilling to take a medication to cure his affliction.

Stansbury did tell him where he could find Barney. The man might be an inept ditherer, but at least he grasped that Barney was a valuable resource. As Tracy walked through the camp, he thought, *Much could be made of these men, if only we had the time to give them proper training.* There was nothing wrong with their hearts or their courage, but both were wasted without drill and good generalship.

The men all looked tired, worn out, thoroughly used up. He stopped and chatted with a few random officers, who acted much more curious about the information he possessed than Stansbury had. At least some of the company grade officers were trying to think. He got an excellent précis of the recent movements of the various units. There had been a great deal of marching and counter-marching throughout the day as conflicting reports of a British advance filtered in.

The high command had reacted with confusion and something approaching madness. The British were here; no, they were there. Ross was at Upper Marlboro; then he was approaching the Potomac. Then a report came in he was in a third place. The British were on the left; no, they were on the right. Horror of horrors, they were to the rear! Every report was investigated, detachments were sent out. In the end, all of the reports proved worse than useless. They squandered precious energy, dispirited the men, and left everyone in a high state of agitation and exhaustion. Many men never even had time to prepare a hot meal.

At the end of the day, all the Americans knew was that the British were out there, somewhere. Tracy and his marines were tired from their long march as well, but they were far more fit and used to hardship. The boys he had rescued had responded surprisingly well and wanted to stay with him. They might be young, but they wanted to fight, so he would see they got the chance.

He would not have time to even teach them the basics of drill, but he would put them to work with the marines and not allow them to be poached by militia units. They could copy the movements of men who knew the manual of arms as well as they knew their own names. Men were imitative creatures. If they were put among brave men, they would act bravely. If they were put among cowards, they would follow suit.

He finally spotted the tall, somewhat portly figure of Commodore Barney. His ruddy face was ordinary and placid, but his lively, perceptive eyes commanded attention. He was in animated conversation with Marine Captain Samuel Miller, who was senior to Tracy on the Navy list. Miller was a good man and a stout fighter. Tracy wished the army was filled with men like Barney and Miller.

"Captain Tracy reporting, Commodore." He snapped to attention and briskly saluted Barney. Barney returned a more relaxed salute.

"Tracy, good to see you! I am eager to hear your observations, get some current, trustworthy information. You would not believe the mad rumors flying about."

It took Tracy an hour to give his report. Barney listened carefully, stopping him now and then to ask questions. Miller inquired about the health of the British. He wanted to know how they were bearing up under the heat.

"I was afraid you wouldn't make the party," said Barney. "I can see I was right to worry, you bent your orders a bit, didn't you? No matter, you were right to do so. You confirm exactly what I suspected: their numbers are greatly exaggerated. We might just be able to beat them."

He smiled briefly, then his expression soured. "I see a lot here I don't like. No, I don't like it at all. My men are the only ones I know will fight. We need to choose a position and prepare it fully. No one seems capable of putting himself in the British commander's position to anticipate his moves. We are only reacting, and doing that badly. You have brought first-rate information, yet it looks like Stansbury is not going to use it. Winder rode off hours ago on another fool's errand."

Tracy realized that Barney was frustrated and wanted to speak to someone he trusted and who appreciated sound military assessment.

"Commodore, what would you do if you were Ross? I am eager to hear your perspective."

Barney pondered for a minute. "We know his objective is Washington. There are three ways he can approach. The southern and eastern routes are the most obvious and quickest, but Ross will choose neither. The Anacostia River blocks each one; he knows we will blow the bridges. The roads from Baltimore and Annapolis all run through Bladensburg, to the north and east of the capital. We can destroy the bridge there, but the river shallows are fordable for determined troops a few hundred yards further on. I am certain that is the spot he will aim for. In a way, it could give us an advantage. We would know where they must cross and subject it to a withering artillery fusillade. Our little army will end up there eventually, but it would be so much better for us if we got there early." He paused, ruminating.

"We have some big pieces, three 18-pounders. They are not very mobile, but hugely destructive. The earlier we arrive and get them properly sited the better. We will need time to dig earthworks. The sailors and marines can anchor the line. Make the enemy come to us. Their infantry will not be able to advance faced with our artillery. If we can pummel them with canister, tear them up, even our novice troops might be able to manage some sort of counter stroke. In a plain, open field slugging match, our prospects are dim. From a prepared position, we have a fighting chance. The trouble is, all of these damned politicians are coming here and making unhelpful suggestions! The generals aren't sure what constitutes advice and what constitutes an order. James Monroe is the worst of them. I know Madison listens to him."

"I have encountered Monroe myself sir," said Tracy with disgust. "No doubt he means well, but I am quite certain his military convictions are as dangerous as they are erroneous. He never commanded anything more than a company, but thinks himself qualified to plan for an entire army. We will be undone if he is listened to."

Barney looked at the boys behind Tracy. "They get younger and younger, don't they? It was good of you to do what you did. If you don't mind, I might have need of them. We have men to serve the guns, but not many boys to support them. We need powder monkeys for the cartridges. It does not require much skill or training, but plenty of pluck and courage. From what you just told me, they have both."

"Your taking them would be a relief, Commodore. I did not know how I could manage their training. I am certain they will be gratified to fight under your command. But I would like to get them fed, sir. They, indeed all of us, have had a long march and are hungry. Have any supplies arrived?"

"Biscuits, beans and bacon, will have to do, I am afraid. My men have just finished eating and there is some left over. It will be the first of several harsh lessons for those boys, the same I learned as a young lad in the Revolution. Eat what you can, when you can. You never know when you will eat again, and the fare next time will probably be worse. We can assign them to gun crews tomorrow at first light. For now, bivouac everyone with Captain Miller's marines. I am certain you two have much to discuss."

"We do, sir."

"Good luck to you, Tracy. I will go and remonstrate," he sighed deeply, "with the esteemed General Winder, if I can find him. I will see if I can convince him to shift our position to Bladensburg. I fear it is a doomed enterprise, but the effort must be made. I will represent your observations to him most forcefully. Perhaps coming from a senior officer they will carry more weight. He apprehends only rank and station, not merit and experience." Barney squared his shoulders, as if confronting an evil and contrary wind, and stomped off in the direction of his horse, which an aide was holding ready. He mounted up gracelessly, far more used to pitching decks than the backs of four-legged beasts.

Miller walked over to Tracy. "I don't envy that man his job. It's enormously frustrating being one of the few professionals in a sea of amateurs. He is respected, but his words go unheeded. At least he believes we can stop them. I don't think most of the militia officers do."

"What do you think of our chances, Sam?"

"Bluntly? Very poor, John. The sailors and marines will fight well, and the militia might put up a decent scrap if we had more time to organize them, but it's a case of too many cooks spoiling the soup. You know what inexperienced men are like, John. Hit them in the right place, break a single unit, and the lot of them will flee like frightened deer." He scowled.

"President Madison was out here the other day, with two large horse-pistols strapped to his coat. He did not look like he had a clue as to how to use them. They dwarfed his small frame and made him appear a figure of fun rather than authority. In his black frock coat, he looked like a wizened old parson down on his luck. I spoke to him. He seemed a decent enough man, but he tends to adopt the opinion of the last cabinet member he spoke to. Armstrong and Jones, the Army and Navy secretaries, were out here, but he listened mostly to Monroe. Strange that a diplomat should have that much influence." Miller shook his head, then continued.

"The oddest thing was that Monroe gave orders to several militia officers about the placement of their men, and he was obeyed. He tried it on me and I told him in no uncertain terms that US Marines took no orders from anyone outside of their chain of command. He looked like I'd hit him with the beam of a house frame. Then he nodded pleasantly and said, 'Very good, Captain,' and he rode away. A peculiar world, indeed!"

Tracy laughed. "Great confidence, good brain, no military acumen; just enough experience to be full of himself, just enough to wildly misread the situation. Would that we could send him back to France!"

Miller burst into deep-throated laughter. "Ironic, isn't it? They laugh at us in times of peace, constantly cut our numbers and funds, yet demand our services when times turn threatening. They hate professional soldiers and loathe anything like a standing military, but a dim part of them understands we may be their salvation. They call us leathernecks, primitives, ridicule our stern discipline, and deride our intelligence, saying we are little better than trained brutes at a circus. But now, with their backs up against the wall, all of our alleged misdeeds and foolishness are suddenly forgiven."

Tracy turned thoughtful. "They need us. We are the last line of defense for the republic. Even if it's the eleventh hour, we still have time to make things right."

"Amen to that, John," said Miller.

CHAPTER FOURTEEN

Under cover of darkness, the marines marched the four miles to the Waterman farm and halted behind a small hill 500 yards from the farm's edge which shielded the brigade from the Americans bivouacked on the other side. The men formed up by company in neat, toy soldier rows. Company officers performed roll calls and were pleased to discover that they had lost no men to straggling.

"Are your men ready, Peter?" asked Pennywhistle. Three hours of sleep in the feather bed had helped tremendously. Most of the costliest mistakes in war were committed by men suffering from too little sleep. His mind felt clear and focused, and he brimmed with optimistic energy. Of course the ambush would succeed!

"They are indeed, Tom. This has the potential to be a very smart little engagement. It's a great pity we don't have time to stick around and follow things up. From what I have seen, I believe we could break them permanently." Spottswood had only been in this theatre a few weeks, but he had already found the Americans far less formidable than the French he had fought in the Adriatic. His attitude stopped short of contempt, but it was certainly dismissive.

"Have you noticed that they know nothing about castrametation?" Pennywhistle replied. "There is no order to the layout of their camp, and the various messes and their fires are badly strewn about with almost no defensive capabilities. Even their pickets all look to be talking to friends, having a good time rather than doing their jobs. They appear to have no captain-of-the-day about. Makes me wonder if they have even given the job to anyone. What do you make of their numbers?"

"I'd say, seven, maybe eight hundred. About what you'd expect for a militia regiment. Strange, since they know a large force has occupied Mt. Prosperity. It seems more of a holiday outing or sporting event for them. I don't understand why they are not marching immediately for the main American encampment. Standing still and doing nothing seems a fool's strategy, but maybe they are not sure quite where to go with threats from east and west. Your column was very bad news for them, Tom, and was definitely unexpected. Perhaps they mean to move at first light."

"I doubt that," said Pennywhistle thoughtfully. "If they did, they'd all be sound asleep by now. It's been full dark for an hour, yet no one has moved to douse the campfires. Men are only retiring by twos and threes. My guess is they will move tomorrow when they damn well feel like it, and that could be anytime until noon. There's independence for you! They might well be stalling until they receive orders from higher authority. From what Mrs. Parke said, her son and his ... ah, friend may have very different ideas about how to proceed. But we will see to it they move smartly, and a great deal earlier than they intended!"

"Too right, Tom!" Spottswood paused, wrinkling his nose in distaste. "That business of the two unnatural gentlemen is very unsettling, but you are right, the concerns of love may be interfering with the business of war. It could account for what we see. Reminds me of a captain I once knew who kept his mistress on his ship, mixed business and pleasure. Compromised his judgment and lost him the respect of his men. Venus and Mars may go together in mythology, but not, it seems to me, in real life."

"Given their position," Pennywhistle gestured towards the camp, "what do you think should be our tactics?"

"I think three volleys delivered in rapid succession. You see that ravine down there?" Pennywhistle nodded. "Their camp is at the bottom of a natural bowl. We are perfectly positioned on its lip. Extraordinary no one gave any thought to holding the higher ground! The ravine is like the spigot on a barrel, and the logical egress point if the Congreves land where you say. The militia will make for that. If I allow a certain interval between volleys, factor in their running speed, I can launch a rolling fusillade which will savage them. Start with the base of the funnel, move toward the middle, and finish at the top."

"If we had more time, we could plug the top of the funnel and compel the surrender of the lot of them," said Pennywhistle. "But we can't afford to be encumbered by prisoners, and it would take hours to sort through the business of parole. And I am not sure these amateurs understand the concept, or would honor their paroles anyway.

"We need to move out as soon as the fireworks and races conclude, as we have a good many miles to cover by dawn. Seven hundred fewer troops to fight will be very welcome news to Ross. You still have your pocket watch? The old J. Bird of Bristol?"

Spottswood smiled, extracted the watch from his pocket, and flipped it open.

"You really should replace it with a more precise one, but it will do." Pennywhistle produced his Blancpain and opened it. He held up a lantern so he could read the face. "Let's make sure our times are synchronized." Even good pocket watches varied in consistency; small wonder battlefield accounts sometimes gave conflicting times for the same event. "Both 10:06, good. Give me ten minutes to get the Congreves ready. I will launch the first at 10:16. I will fire six of them at thirty-second intervals, in a sixty-degree spread. If the Americans have been told the Congreve's are inaccurate, they are in for a surprise. Open fire at your discretion. After the last volley, sound the recall and proceed to the assembly point. I want to be gone from this place within half an hour after the last rocket drops."

"Understood, Tom! My men are most eager, but they are too well trained to let headstrong impulses carry them beyond the scope of their orders. There will be no mad dashes of pursuit."

"Good luck to you, Peter." Pennywhistle clapped him on the shoulder and departed at a brisk, purposeful pace.

Pennywhistle's rocketeers were two hundred yards away, at right angles to the position of Spottswood's men. Using very small lanterns, the Royal Marine Rocket Troop aligned their launch platforms and poles, calculated distance and arcs, and trimmed the fuses. All of the Congreves featured 12-lb warheads. The bursting powder inside would shower the Americans with innumerable tiny shards of metal, officially termed "spherical case shot", but colloquially known as "shrapnel", after the Royal Artillery General who invented the design.

The rocket men went about their business purposefully and quietly. The only noises filling the night air were the mating proclamations of crickets, cicadas, and bullfrogs, punctuated at irregular intervals by the hooting of owls and a yowling wildcat expressing his challenge to a rival in love.

One distinctive cry in the far distance struck Pennywhistle as odd. It was the sound of a peacock, a bird native to Asia, not North America. Likely some local grandee had imported a few to mimic English aristocrats and impress his neighbors. Ah, the pretensions of the nouveau riche!

This would be the first true combat test of the improved weapon. If they worked, the Congreves could move from novelties to true stalwarts in the pantheon of artillery.

Pennywhistle walked slowly up and down the line, speaking words of encouragement to each rocketeer, making sure each rocket was fitted to its ladder-like launcher and the launcher was properly elevated on its triangular struts. He answered questions about flight time and the possible spread of metal fragments from the warheads. He showed each man where he wanted his rocket to land, and how to aim it. His orders were for the first rocket to be fired on his signal, the rest to hold fire until they saw how the first one fared.

He checked his watch. 10:15, almost time. The cloudy, nearly pitch-black night formed a perfect backdrop for the upcoming lurid red rocket bursts. The gnats were active as usual; he idly wondered if the rockets might disperse them. He made one last survey of the burning American campfires through his spyglass. His marines' portfires glowed crimson; they held them close to the fuses and waited for his command. Pennywhistle's watch hands touched 10:16. He raised his sword high, then sliced down decisively.

Woosh! The first rocket zipped into the night. It arced steeply and rose high in the air, gave the fuse time to burn. He willed it to track, not go wild. Then it descended, swiftly and true to its course, to burst three hundred yards distant at an elevation of twenty feet. The bright red blotch lit the night like a grand firework and caused everyone on the British side to let out a long "Ahhh!"

Colonel Daniel Parke heard the huge bang and saw the peculiar red flash through the open flap of his tent. He froze for a half second, threw down the map he had been reviewing, pulled on his boots and paused to tuck the hem of his shirt into his trousers. He grabbed his sword and dashed madly, but clumsily, from the tent. In his haste, he'd put his boots on the wrong feet. He rushed onto the parade ground, searched for officers, and, finding none, began to wave his sword to attract attention. Darting his head left to right, he could find neither drummer nor bugler to sound the assembly.

Pennywhistle saw people suspended in the split second between understanding and action. American statues stared skyward, not sure what had happened. The red glow persisted long enough for him to see perhaps twenty men fall as unseen objects struck them from above. A second after the glimmer faded, the screams started. He had hit their right flank as planned.

Woosh! Woosh! Woosh! Woosh! Woosh! The rockets dashed skyward. *Bam! Bam! Bam! Bam! Bam!* Pressure waves smashed the night air like giant fists. The explosions moved gradually left, like a giant arm sweeping across the land. The barrage lasted two-and-a-half minutes. Pennywhistle watched the spectacle through his glass. Most of the rockets were true to their courses. Two were a bit off. He would adjust the right dorsal fin slightly on future models. Cockburn would be pleased.

The American camp degenerated into madness. Men scattered in every direction, seeking a safe haven that did not exist. The general flow of running was down the ravine—just as Spottswood had predicted.

Parke grabbed running men and shook them. If one man would rally, others would follow. "Stop, damn you, stop!" he shouted repeatedly. "We need to form a line, defend ourselves!" Men looked at him stupidly, then broke free of his grasp. "For God's sake, grab your muskets!" He hit several men with the flat of his sword. "Remember your duty!" They cursed him, but did not stop running. Battle was not supposed to be like this! He was doing what a leader was supposed to do, but it was having no effect. Maybe it was God punishing him for his "affliction". Tears of frustration formed in his eyes.

Rockets burst, men died, and his troops acted as if he did not exist. He had trained these men, given them his best efforts; they were his neighbors and his friends. How could they desert him?

"Amos, Amos! Stop, stand with me." Parke jumped in front of the man and waved his arms. Amos Appleton was his neighbor; maybe a personal, instead of a military, appeal would work.

"To blazes with you, Dan, I have to save my family! Get the hell out of my way or I'll kill you!" Appleton's face was that of a bedlamite. He had always seemed a gentle, reasonable man. Parke got out of the way.

Major Grimes appeared out of the confusion. He had been inspecting defenses on the right when the first Congreve exploded. He had suffered an instant of pure terror: not for himself, but for the man he loved. Forgetting all his customary reserve, he sprinted forward and embraced Parke. "Thank God you are safe, Daniel! I feared the worst." His grip was not that of a brother or comrade.

Parke shoved him away. The men must never know. They had always been discreet. He saw the hurt and fear in Grimes face. "What's happened, Archie? Have you seen where the rockets came from? My God, how could this happen? You said we could regroup here and ambush them later!"

Blood drained from Grimes' face, leaving it a sickly grey in the lurid glow of the camp fires. "I don't know, Dan. This can't be happening, can't be happening! How did they know we were here?" His speech slurred. Parke looked closely and saw a one-inch shard of metal lodged just behind his second's right ear. Small dots of red plopped down his neck, as if from a leaky spigot. Grimes started to sway slightly. Parke grabbed him just as he passed out.

"You are hurt! How badly?" No response. Bracing Grimes' weight, Parke felt his neck. The pulse was strong; good, but he had to get him to safety. Slinging Grimes over his shoulder, he joined the horde of running men headed down the ravine. What little command and semblance of forethought the Americans possessed vanished in that instant.

Spottswood waited until all of the Americans had passed twenty yards ahead of his position. His ten score men lay prone, hidden from view, then rose up quickly when he blew his light infantry whistle. The rear rank stood erect, the front kneeled.

"Fire!" A huge serpent of fire lashed out through the darkness. The force of impact shoved forward those stuck by bullets, pushing them into fleeing companions, who stumbled and fell. A collective, unbelieving gasp coursed through the mob. They had been fired upon from behind! First the rockets, now gunfire from nowhere! Panic set in. Those unhurt jumped up and ran even faster. They gave no thought to their wounded friends. It was every man for himself. No officer even attempted to rally them.

Men dropped on all sides of Colonel Parke, but he kept his footing and his grip on his precious cargo. Someone had once said he was a lucky man; maybe it was true. He had to get clear of this mess. He forgot all about his men and thought only of one man. Battle was strange, confusing. He did not feel fear so much as bewilderment. He could not assemble a coherent picture, merely fleeting impressions: flashes of bright red, loud bangs, stinking smoke. Utter darkness, then waves of crimson light, followed by horrid screams and cries. No pageantry, no flags waved proudly, no heroics, and no one caring a jot for honor.

A fallen, bleeding man clutched his trouser leg and plaintively begged, "Water, water, please, water!" He knew he should help. Instead, he kicked the man in the face and pulled his leg free of the fainting grip. So this was the "baptism" of fire, the indispensable experience, according to the orators. He would have preferred to dispense with this one.

Spottswood's men reloaded methodically. They were grim reapers and ruthlessly efficient. They did not lack hearts, but they were too well schooled in their task to consider paying them any mind. It was hard to see in the darkness, but Spottswood had them aim at a point sixty yards ahead. "Fire!" The second volley crashed out. Animal cries pierced the night. "Reload in quick time!" The marines did just that.

Parke heard the nearly inaudible *click* as the marines full-cocked their pieces, and his latent survival instinct kicked in at just the right moment. He pitched himself down hard on the ground, twisting to cover Grimes' body with his own. As he did, he heard the buzz of bullets pass above him and felt a wave of hot air. He had always told his men to stand tall and never bob and weave; so much for theory.

The carnage was awful. Two thirds of the men who entered the ravine soon lay prone in the heavy grass. Many were alive; writhing, gasping for air that would not come, or moaning in slow agony. Arms, legs, torsos, and unidentifiable body parts dotted the ravine, like human crab grass. It was all so different from the books on war Parke had so diligently digested over the years! He had lived through it, yet he would be hard pressed to reconstruct the events of the last few minutes for a historian. He would never quite trust battle accounts again. Tears flowed freely but brought no relief from the pain in his heart. All he could think of was getting Grimes to a surgeon. There would be time later to think of striking back at his tormentors. He made a solemn vow to do that.

The final volley boomed out thirty seconds later. More cries of pain and despair echoed off the sides of the little ravine. Men on both sides coughed from the roiling clouds of brimstone-laden smoke.

Spottswood's job was done. The remaining Americans would not stop running for a good long time, perhaps not until they reached their homes. At the very least, they would not be doing anything military for the next few days, and that was all of the time that mattered. Mrs. Parke's information had been most useful. He wondered if her son had survived. Considering his sexual proclivities, perhaps it would be merciful if he had not.

"Cease fire! Cease fire! Cease fire!" shouted Spottswood as he made energetic sideways motions with the flat of his hand. "Form up by company. Smartly now!" The men complied quickly and silently. Spottswood noted smiles of satisfaction here and there. "Column, forward, march!"

The assembly point was four hundred yards away. The rest of the Marine Brigade was already formed up and ready to march. Pennywhistle walked up to Spottswood and asked, "How did it go?"

"We did great execution!" said Spottswood brightly. The adrenaline of victory was rushing through his veins. A small triumph at no cost to his men! Then he heard the low moaning in the distance and his voice changed as the momentary elation passed into sadness. It did not take great bravery or skill to shoot unarmed men in the back, even if it made military sense. It was men who were dying in that ravine, not animals. "Those men are out of the war," he said quietly. "I hope it discourages others from joining up."

"It might, or it might inspire them to do so to exact revenge. In any event," said Pennywhistle grimly, "we did our duty. We can be content with our conduct without being proud of it. Most importantly, we demonstrably have real artillery now, which might help to limit the American advantage. We need to move out. I doubt if we will run into any further opposition tonight."

He unfurled a small map next to his lantern and traced a route with his fingers. "We need to be here by 11 a.m. tomorrow." He pointed to a spot eight miles west of Upper Marlboro, five miles east of a little village called Bladensburg. "I regret to say we will need to use the Moore quickstep, for our presence is needed urgently. We want to take advantage of the night, when the temperatures are cooler. We will stop in seven hours, let the men eat a little, and grab two hours sleep. There looks to be a stream here at," he paused and looked closely at the name on the map, "Appleton. Pleasant name, and I gather home to many varieties of the fruit. If the men want to partake of the orchards, let them."

"We are getting mighty close to the capital, Tom. The Americans are not going to surrender it without a fight. It's their pride and joy, their symbol, their shining proof that King George was a complete fool thirty-eight years ago. We can't just walk in and take it, like a small child stealing newly baked biscuits when granny is not looking."

"No, indeed. You are correct, Peter; a battle is shaping up, and a decisive one. I think it just might be tomorrow. That's why we need to push our men hard tonight. We also need to let Cockburn know the results of our test. We still have ten of the new Congreves, and we'll target them at the American Artillery. I so wish we had time to modify the Army specimens! But we need to be content with the achievable, not the ideal."

Sergeant Dale walked over with a horse. "Just what you requested, sir."

"Thought you might want to ride, Peter," said Pennywhistle. "You will need every ounce of strength for battle."

Dale paraded the large, dapple-gray horse in front of Spottswood. "Name's Greystoke, sir, seems agreeable enough. The battle just now bothered him not at all. He just kept chewing grass," said Dale approvingly. "Rounded him up after his master decided to abandon him in the interests of personal safety. Figured the law of salvage applied." Pennywhistle and Spottswood exchanged amused glances at Dale's code words for *looted*. The horse bobbed his head slowly and placidly.

"If you say he is suitable, Sergeant, far be it from me to gainsay your wisdom. Bring him over here, and let's get acquainted." Spottswood walked around the animal, assessing points. He did indeed seem agreeable, and very healthy.

Parke slumped dejectedly on the Marlboro road. He took a sip from his canteen and looked at his timepiece; almost 4 a.m. The first cherry streaks of dawn stretched above the eastern horizon. Archie snored in the grass next to him. Parke breathed in the morning air deeply and batted away some gnats. He needed to rest. He had already trudged three miles with his burden, stopping from time to time to give Archie water and to check his pulse. Archie had not regained consciousness, which Parke thought a blessing. The wound looked painful. He was only a mile from the plantation house; his mother would know what to do. She hated Archie, but she would help a man wounded while fighting for his country. Dr. Crawford could be called and would put things right. He just had to carry Grimes a bit further. He was on the home stretch.

With care, he re-shouldered his precious burden and soldiered on.

He was dreadfully weary, but love gave him the strength to keep going. "Where there's a will, there's a way," he murmured to himself. The adage reminded him that he had first met Archibald Grimes five years ago over the matter of a will. His childless first cousin had left him a substantial estate, but a flawed will drafted by an alcoholic attorney had thrown the matter into probate court. Parke had determined to get the best Georgetown lawyer he could find to untangle the mess, someone who specialized in wills and estates. His family attorney and several wealthy friends all gave him the same name: Archibald Grimes.

Desire had stirred in him even that first time he'd met Grimes, as they shook hands over the lawyer's mahogany desk, neatly adorned with a heavily gilded rococo ink well, well-trimmed quills, and leather-backed blotting paper. This particular longing was a dangerous, unnatural creature he kept safely locked in the dungeons of his soul. His better nature had so far been successful as a prison warden, but the Janus-faced beast pleaded constantly and cleverly for release. The beast whispered an alluring promise that would delight his loins and his heart, yet smiled mockingly at the prospect of his temporal and spiritual ruination. It would have been so much better to kill the beast outright, but this yearning was impervious to even the strongest will.

Grimes proved charming, poised, and thoroughly knowledgeable about his specialty during their initial interview. He was a plainspoken, gregarious gentleman with a brilliant smile, who likely inspired confidence in even the most diffident of clients. His mellifluous voice was perfectly suited to the elegance of his words.

He was not handsome in the conventional sense. His angular face was full of unusual angles and planes, yet the overall effect was to invest it with a distinctiveness that held the eye. He was tall, well proportioned, and moved with an easy grace.

Grimes' courtly manner indicated no interest in him beyond that of an attorney concerned for the welfare of his client. However, occasional, almost imperceptible sparkles in his eyes spoke an entirely different language. It was a language of the heart, needing no words. People without their unusual proclivity would have missed the message entirely.

When the case was successfully concluded, it was the most natural thing in the world to invite Grimes to dinner a week later. A celebration of grand proportions was in order, and the neighbors who had recommended Grimes to Parke wished to congratulate the one for his professional triumph and the other on his good fortune. The coterie of well-wishers made the dinner a public event; a perfect cover for the very private feelings simmering just beneath the surface in the two honorees.

The Lion and Lamb Inn in Alexandria was famous for its foods and wines. Dinner opened with a spicy Maryland terrapin soup, followed by steaming bowls of peas, beans, carrots, and candied yams served *à la française*. The fish course featured fillet of summer flounder sautéed with just the right touch of butter and lemon. The Inn's signature dish, an American version of Yorkshire Christmas pie, constituted the main course. The magnificent thirty-pound pie contained a large turkey, an oversized goose, three ducks, three partridges, and a half dozen pigeons cooked, boned, seasoned, and stuffed one into another. The whole was wrapped in a sweet pastry crust. A case of Beaujolais perfectly complimented the poultry. Hearty toasts were proclaimed frequently, and as soon as a gentleman's glass was emptied, it was refilled by solicitous servers. Peaches, apples, and pears, Brazil nuts and almonds, and Gouda cheese from Curaçao concluded the feast. The meal left everyone with bulging stomachs and smiles of repletion.

After the obligatory after-dinner coffee was consumed, the brandy and cigars came out. Talk turned loud and general among Parke and Grimes' dozen well-wishers, while a private conversation developed between the guests of honor. They shared many interests and views of life. Nothing whatsoever was said about the unseen creatures of lust the two sensed were guiding the conversation; yet four hours after the start of the meal, their souls had forged an understanding, under the very noses of their oblivious friends.

Grimes liked to hunt, and the hunting was splendid at Mount Prosperity. Grimes accepted Parke's formal invitation to visit for a few days as an honored guest and stalk a gigantic, wily stag that had so far eluded every hunter's quest to bag him.

The hunt for the wary beast took the better part of a day and gave the two men plenty of time to talk frankly, away from inquisitive ears. The stalk became more a journey into their own inner natures than the quest for a prize of Nature. They were about to give up when they spotted the beast silhouetted against the dying sun.

Grimes brought the stag down with a single shot to the head. The two men clapped each other on the shoulders and danced and capered with glee. They had achieved the impossible! Emotions were running high and they were alone in the deep forest. A look passed between them that was profound in its implications. Seeing the self-same soul-hunger mirrored in each other's eyes was the key that released their beasts, and in that instant their worlds changed. They grabbed each other with wild abandon. Kisses were exchanged, clothes were shed, and their deepest desires consummated.

Neither had ever trod this road before, but afterwards they knew it was the only one they wanted. What had passed between them was no casual coupling but something extraordinary. There would be no going back to what had been. Their lips dared not speak the word LOVE, but their hearts shouted it. It would be difficult, it would be complicated, and it necessarily would occasion much dissembling. They would make it work because the strength of their bond left them with no choice.

Society said it was wrong. They had positions to maintain; much was expected of them. In the years since that first assignation, Parke's rational mind had repeatedly warned him of the dangers of their connection. He worried about the consequences of discovery, but a life without Archie hardly seemed one worth living. The heart had its own agenda, and that agenda was far stronger than any admonitions of the mind.

But now many of his neighbors were dead, the rest of the militia routed. He could not think how the British had found them. They had to be the same forces that had occupied Mt. Prosperity. Well, that meant they would be gone now. He wondered how much damage they had done.

How could he serve his country *and* his heart? He had children, a mother, and responsibilities. He was a respectable man! After this night's debacle, he might never regain the respect of the men who'd survived. Even worse would be the unspoken recrimination in the eyes of widows, the forlorn misery in the eyes of children whose fathers had died because of his failure of command. How could he put things right? He had no answer. All he did know was that the British had damaged everything he loved. It was far easier to focus anger than confusion. The goddamned Englishman behind the attack would pay dearly!

Chapter Fifteen

It was just after 6 a.m., but the morning was already sultry. The thick humidity made the air more suitable for swimming than breathing. It would soon be scorching hot—a bad day for a big fight. Tracy took off his heavy shako, ran his fingers through his sweat-matted hair, and absent-mindedly wiped the perspiration from his face with a small handkerchief. His blue wool uniform felt like a giant scabbard. He took a sip of his tea, pure heaven. Things were a little better today, but a long way from anything approaching well organized.

At least he and his men were in the right place. No, that wasn't quite true; more like in the correct general area. After much dithering, the main part of Barney's advice had been heeded. The Bladensburg Bridge was the key. The trouble was, they were posted a mile to the rear of it, the third of three lines, and were not in supporting distance of the first two. He had no idea why Winder chose to deploy his men in three lines, but then Winder's entire plan of battle was a complete mystery to everyone.

The camp bustled with activity. It should have heartened him, but failed to make any inroads on his growing pessimism. His own men were well equipped and well fed, but many of the steadily arriving militia looked hungry, having out-paced the lumbering supply wagons. Many of the quartermasters were amateurs and much of the promised food had not arrived. Those lucky enough to receive salt pork or beef boiled their breakfasts over camp fires and talked nervously about what lay ahead. Untrained men advanced untutored opinions about British strategy. Much of the talk questioned the wisdom of the high command marching men aimlessly about and wearing them down right before a battle. Tracy's intuition told him the militia sensed fear on the part of their leaders: the fear of amateurs facing disciplined regulars. Distrust of command was powerfully corrosive to morale.

Assembly sounded in a few units, and raw recruits formed up in lines that were crooked and only vaguely military. Company quartermasters organized the issuance of cartridges. There never seemed to be enough. There was a shortage of flints as well.

Tracy and Barney found a decent spot for their artillery; the best available, considering the ground Winder wanted them to occupy. A mile was about the maximum range for their guns, just about their distance from the bridge. Trouble was, that was for solid shot. Even on a good day, a hit at that distance was problematic. Canister was most effective for close support of troops but worked best at ranges under 400 yards. They were too far back to use it to shore up the front two lines.

Their position occupied a gentle rise of ground with a long ravine in front. Two of the big eighteen-pounders commanded the Washington Turnpike, and three 12-

pounders controlled the ground to the south. If the British wanted to reach Washington, they would have to disable the guns.

Lowndes Hill on the opposite bank might have been a better site, not just for the artillery, but for the army as a whole, but without consulting Winder, Stansbury had decided he did not want to fight with the river blocking his line of retreat. He'd ceded the approaches to the bridge to the British.

There was a shallow brook in front of Barney's position, which would slow the advance of the British and make them easy targets for the big guns. All in all, a fine spot from which to launch a counter attack.

It puzzled Tracy that the Bladensburg Bridge still stood. The bridge should have been destroyed as soon as the army crossed over! It gave quick and easy access to the heart of the American position. Someone must have given the order, but even simple orders were proving problematic. Orders would be issued, but then ignored, forgotten, or flat out disobeyed. Winder and Stansbury communicated poorly and often seemed at cross purposes. Secretary Monroe continued to meddle.

Troops continued to swell the American ranks. A regiment of District militia passed his position, and he carefully observed them. They wore nothing that could be called uniforms; their attire was varied and came in a rainbow of color, most of it unrelated to the preferred blue of the regulars. They marched poorly and looked to be badly winded and out of shape. Not surprising; a day before they had been city folk: clerks, stable-boys, and apprentices. They carried their weapons inexpertly and followed no discernible marching cadence, seeming ignorant of or indifferent to the orders barked at them.

Still, their faces looked cheerful, and they would probably fight given the chance. The key was to demand just enough, yet not too much, to understand their limitations. Never value earnestness over training. Explain clearly and in detail their particular task in the battle plan. Protect them by placing regular units close by, give them something to emulate. Wellington had done exactly that in Spain, placing newly trained Portuguese alongside British regulars. Prepared positions that included cover were best; don't put them out in the open. Don't use them for attack, use them only for counterattack. Place them under an experienced officer who knew his business and what to expect from green troops.

Daniel Morgan had done it exactly right at the Cowpens in the Revolution. He told his first two lines of raw militia they only had to fire three volleys each, then they could retire on the regulars in the third line. The militia only had to stand against the British for a limited time, well within their capabilities. Cowpens had been a smashing victory. He wished today's army had a Daniel Morgan in command.

He took out his spyglass and surveyed the field, trying to get a general idea of numbers. Best he could tell, there were around six thousand men, give or take a few hundred. If things were decided by sheer numbers, the Americans enjoyed a clear advantage. But what really counted was the solid core of regulars and dependable professionals. That number was closer to seven hundred. At least his marines would give a good account of themselves.

The British army was considerably smaller, but contained not a single amateur. All of their men were trained, blooded, accustomed to fighting in coherent units, and knew exactly what to expect once the bullets started to fly and men started to fall. No matter how well the Americans fought today, there would be no wholesale panic on the British side.

He savored the last sip of his tea and wondered if he could scavenge another cup. He noticed Miller walking toward him, a smug expression on his face. He only wore it when he had just conquered some obscure tactical problem. Maybe Miller had seen something he had missed.

"Good morning, John! Splendid summer day for a big, glorious fight!" Tracy shot him a scalded cat glower, then burst into laughter when he saw the mocking smile on Miller's face.

"Well, it could be a lot worse, Sam. It could be raining. At least our powder will stay dry."

"Very true, John. I had a few ideas I wanted to discuss with you. I thought we should have a plan for our little area. The army does not appear to have one. We are so far back that we may be fighting three separate battles today."

"Agreed. I see much ado, but little happening. I heard Stansbury's people have been marching for thirty-six hours straight." He shook his head, half in amusement, half in disgust. "I wonder who is giving the orders."

"I heard Monroe stuck his oar in again," said Miller. "He actually ordered Stansbury to make a night march and ambush Ross. But of course, no one had any solid information on Ross's location, merely wild speculation. No one bothered to tell Winder that. Stansbury panicked, obeyed, and he and his men shambled off to the east before Winder could recall them. That's how the thirty-six hours came in. Can you believe it? Even now, we don't know exactly where Ross is; and if we did, Stansbury is hardly the man to launch a sneak attack. Winder is vexed and issued Stansbury a new set of orders: to post his men one hundred yards to the rear of the bridge. They are to be the lamb staked out to lure the tiger into range. We need every man concentrated near the bridge, so we can hit the British with volleys before they even set foot on our side. We will be all right here if the troops in the orchard hold long enough, much less so if they break and run." Privately, he doubted they'd be able to run, no matter how frightened they became. He had never seen such exhausted, footsore soldiers in his life. He had heard one man mutter to another, "I don't care if I die, so long as I can sleep first."

"Beall's regiment is supposed to join us from Annapolis today, probably coming from the same direction as Ross. I wouldn't be surprised if some of Stansbury's trigger-happy militia mistook Beall for the British."

"Dear God, let that not prove so!" Tracy said feelingly. "But Sam, what about the bridge?"

"Only the Upper Marlboro Bridge has been blown, and Ross is making a small demonstration against the one at Pig Point. Barney told me Winder is still worried that Ross is going to strike south at the last second to move alongside the British squadron moving up the Potomac. Winder does not know which end is up. He is so buffaloed by the British, he thinks they are going to do a double somersault and land direct in our rear. At least we can hold our sector. Maybe even swing round and hit them from behind."

"I gather the hill will be hinge and the marines will be the door," said Tracy.

Miller nodded. "I think the British will come straight at us, form a skirmish line on that flat ground two hundred yard ahead, then advance up the hill. I am going to take as given that our first line won't contain them. You see that small gully on the right? If we let the British advance far enough, we could actually have the advantage of them."

"And hold them off, for how long?" asked Tracy.

"I honestly don't know, John. In a perfect world, with a good plan and good generals, I'd say indefinitely. But Winder is an appallingly bad strategist. He is trying to defend too much ground. We could make this a breakwater to smash their wave. We know where they will come and we could force them to fight our battle: defend, then we counterattack. We might be even able to wreck them thoroughly. You are far too discreet to repeat this, so I will be brutal. As it stands, we will be lucky if we can hold here an hour. It all depends on our support units, and they are all militia. If they hold even briefly, we have a chance. If they break immediately, we..." he smiled ruefully, "are in for a hell of a whipping." He laughed derisively. "On second thought, perhaps you should shout it far and wide among the brass hats. Might shake them up a little, but they are too much the army mules to heed our advice." He sobered and looked at Tracy keenly.

"I don't trust the army, but I do trust you. I'd like to have some advance warning that can be relied upon. You're a good horseman. Why don't you borrow a mount from Barney and go see for yourself? There is nothing more to do here. You know precisely what to look for, exactly what these unschooled militia dolts will miss."

"I would be delighted," said Tracy. "I am sick to death of sitting around waiting for command to come up with ideas I had long ago. If anyone questions me, I will simply say I am acting on Barney's authority. His name and a confident manner on my part will go a long way to answering any fool questions from militia generals. But maybe I am aiming too low. I should proclaim I am sent by James Monroe and act with his majesty and approval."

Both men laughed loudly. They were heartily sick of politicians. Sadly, the heady prospect of battle—waged by others—was attracting these dubious specimens of humanity like flies to carrion.

"Let me gather my maps and glass and I will be off, Sam. I will head down the Upper Marlboro road and watch. That is my best estimate of their avenue of approach."

"I'll see you in a few hours, John. Exercise your customary caution and exquisite good sense."

"You mean like our esteemed commander, General Winder? Of course! Have you even seen him this morning?" To Tracy's way of thinking, a commander should be everywhere and conspicuous, taking care to let his men know he was working tirelessly on their behalf.

"I have not. He's probably jawing with the politicians. I am sure Madison will put in an appearance. Probably wants to be able to tell Dolly whether the dinner party celebrating our glorious victory is on for tonight. Personally, I'd tell her to start packing now. At any rate, you and I both need to get moving. I need to make sure our guns have plenty of canister. We have a surfeit of solid shot, but long range shooting is only going to slow the enemy down. It will be when the Lobsterbacks are close in, almost upon us, that our guns can mow them down like sheaves of wheat and decide the day.

"Oh, and thanks for the youngsters. I assigned them to gun crews at first light this morning. The sergeants are instructing them even now. I heard several boast they beat the enemy once and will do so again. You did something for them, John!"

"Just rescued them from their foolishness. I only hope I did not save them from possible death only to thrust them into a situation where death is practically guaranteed. They really have no idea at all what is coming."

"Can't be helped. They will just have to grow up a little faster. But at least they will fight with US Marines. That will improve their odds greatly. Good luck to you, John. See you in a few hours."

"Thanks, same to you. Let's make a vow to dine together this evening, wherever we may be."

"Done! Let's just hope it won't be in hell."

CHAPTER SIXTEEN

Six hours earlier, Pennywhistle had ridden quietly up and down the long column. "Close up, close up, keep moving," he'd quietly urged the men. He felt crueler than the worst slave overseer, but it was imperative the column reach Ross at the earliest possible moment. Darkness had brought far less of a drop in temperature than he'd expected. The night march pounded the life out of the marines. Hour after hour of three steps at the trot, then three steps at the walk wore down the resolution of even the stoutest of hearts. Mile upon weary mile in eighty-five degree heat caused men to lag behind, become literally stupid, and in a few cases, pass out. When that happened to a man, several of his mates would patiently hoist him to his feet, splash some water on his face, give him some to drink, then urge him on.

He stopped the column for ten minutes each hour, standard march procedure, so the men might rest and fill their canteens. It was important the men not become dehydrated. It was very hard to get them marching again after the each halt. Sergeant Dale had to threaten a few men, a truly rare occurrence. A quiet admonition was usually sufficient.

Pennywhistle rode by one private and noted his odd, shambling marching gait, as if his legs were operating independently of his brain. He halted Rossamun, dismounted, and walked over to the man. The man kept marching. Pennywhistle shook him slightly, and expression popped into the man's eyes. He had been marching sound asleep.

Enough. Pennywhistle called a halt at 3 a.m., instead of 5 a.m. as planned. He told the men the march would resume in three hours.

There was no attempt at making an orderly camp. Most of the men collapsed where they stood and simply went to sleep. They were too drained to even care about eating. A few filled their canteens from a nearby stream, and ten stalwarts turned their attention to a nearby apple tree. No one spoke; that would have required too much energy.

"Shouldn't we post pickets?" inquired a worried Spottswood.

"Let the men sleep, Peter. They marched while we rode. You and I can handle the task. I doubt if there are any Yankees about to cause trouble. I want to discuss a few things with you, anyway."

"Where are we exactly, Tom? I looked at your map earlier, but I confess I have not been keeping careful track of our progress. Truth is, I dozed off in the saddle several times."

"It wasn't just you. I confess I had to fight to stay awake. I am a bit more alert now, as I realize we are close to our goal." He produced a small lantern and lit it with a flint and striker, then unfurled a map. "I am not privy to Ross's plans and I am making an educated guess, but I think he will strike for the Bladensburg Bridge. Based on that assumption and a rate of march similar to ours, I'd say we will encounter his advance patrols about here, five miles east of Bladensburg. I estimate that's a four hour march from our present position. If we resume at six, we should make contact by ten. A little later than I'd like, but given all the men have been through and the weather, I think we have done well. Of course, it's based on a lot of if's, but I do not think I am mistaken."

"I have no reason to doubt you, Tom. I know you; you never just guess. You think things through and consider every possible variation before speaking your mind. But nevertheless, I am concerned about how well the men will fight if we see action today."

"I am a little worried, too. This heat is a wild card, unsettling every expectation. Our men are excellent soldiers, but discipline or no, they have limitations and can only take so much before collapsing. When we make contact with Ross, I will ask that he give them another two hours of rest before sending them into action. I think that, a good meal, and the prospect of finally meeting the Yankees in open battle will summon up their best efforts. Of course, I might be entirely mistaken about their being a fight today, in which case they will get plenty of rest. But my intuition tells me we will see action by the afternoon, and it has never failed me." Pennywhistle took off his round hat and sprinkled a little water from his canteen on his head. Then he brought the canteen up to his lips and drained the rest of its contents.

Spottswood smiled and followed suit. Even a slight relief from the heat was welcome.

Pennywhistle reached into his haversack and produced an elegant silver brandy flask. A look of surprise flitted across Spottswood's face. Pennywhistle was not much of a tippler, unlike many officers.

Pennywhistle was about to drink when he caught Spottswood's expression. He smiled. "Not what you think Peter. Hot chicken soup. It's pleasantly spicy; a Southern recipe courtesy of Mrs. Parke's cook. I commented on how much I enjoyed the bowl she prepared, and she sent some extra along. It was her way of wishing me luck." He took a deep gulp and offered it to Spottswood. "Try some. It's quite good, and so thick it can almost be called a meal."

Spottswood tasted it, somewhat cautiously, then licked his lips. "It's delicious! A sight better than the bland stuff our cook made back in Cork. Maybe the Yankees are actually good at something! I wish I had a hundred gallons for my men."

He and Pennywhistle talked as the sky lightened. At first their conversation was technical, all about possible arrangements in the battle approaching; then it gradually changed to reminiscences of their time together on *HMS Active* in the Adriatic.

Spottswood turned serious. "Do you think of Carlotta often? I think of her sometimes. She was a fine woman, a remarkable woman."

Tears clouded the edges of Pennywhistle's eyes. "Not a day goes by that I don't miss her. I don't blame myself anymore. I finally realized she was a casualty of war, even if an indirect one. I could only have prevented her death if I had the gift of second sight. It took me a year and a half to understand that. You tried so hard to help, to console, to make me see it was not my fault. I shall be forever in your debt. I have not relived the horror of her death in my dreams for fully a year; a good sign, I think.

"I do think often of what might have been. Children, a settled family life, growing old together. I was willing to give up the Service, find a safer occupation where I could spend time with her. It would have been difficult for her, an Italian in England, but she would have won over the hearts of all who met her, as she did everywhere she went. I fear she has spoiled me for other women."

"How are her children doing? It was a very handsome gesture on your part to assume responsibility for their education. I remember them as being very perceptive, very brave lads."

Pennywhistle brightened noticeably. "They were uncertain about leaving Italy at first, but their mother had always told them to trust my judgment, and I knew they liked me. I told them they had a choice, and that I would respect whatever decision they made. They could stay with their aunt, live their lives safely on the island that was familiar to them and grow up to become tradesmen; or they could take a risk, journey into a much bigger world, and become gentlemen. Being adventurous young sparks, they chose to come with me to England. It was hard on them at first, but they proved resilient.

"Nico just turned fourteen. He started Harrow this year. I was dubious about a public school instead of tutoring at home, but my brother assured me it is the future of gentlemanly education. Nico seems to like it. He said some older boys tried to bully him at first, but the instruction I gave him in *Savate* came in very handy, and the boys learned it was unwise to trifle with him. His English is almost flawless now.

"Marko is twelve and still at the old home in Berwick. He has been pestering me by letter to secure him a midshipman's berth, but I really am loath to condemn any young life to the business of war. Gordon would, of course, take him aboard *Seahorse* in an instant."

"You surprise me, Tom. You are the finest soldier I have ever met, yet you seem unwilling to allow another to follow in your path. I thought you believed the profession of arms to be an honorable one."

Pennywhistle sighed pensively. "Somewhere deep inside I still do, but I confess I am tired. I have been fighting twelve years and I am plain sick of death; tired of seeing it, smelling it, living it, inflicting it. Tired of sending promising young men into the meat grinder, filling their heads with patriotic nonsense and words like *duty, honor*, and *country* so that I can spend their lives to secure some cheap, fleeting military advantage.

"I am weary of despoiling in the blink of an eye what it has cost men a lifetime to build. I'd like to build something, create something, maybe even invent something that leaves the world a little better for my having been in it."

He looked thoughtfully into Spottswood's eyes. "My mind tells me I am doing my right and proper duty, but something deeper eats at me. The poets tell us that battle exalts a man, pushes him to the apotheosis of his gifts, and makes him more than he was before. I wonder if they have it all backwards, that battle actually diminishes a man and makes him a slave to the base and primitive. I sometimes feel I am up to my neck in a slimy moral cesspool and each battle pushes me a little deeper into the mud, a little closer to drowning. Sometimes, the mud clogs my gullet and chokes my sense of right and wrong. It's like never being allowed to bathe, even though you devoutly wish it.

"It gets worse as the years go by, not better. I used to be able to recall the faces of all of the men I had killed. Now what I see in nightmares is an blurred whirlpool of angry, pleading, and sad men all shouting the same question: *Why, why?* I want to believe I can return home and be the good squire, the respectable local magistrate, the kind country gentleman who helps his tenants. Yet I fear I have wallowed in violent solutions far too long for that to be possible."

Spottswood looked puzzled, then concerned. "You have done what you had to do. More times than I can recall, you have taken certain death and turned it into a mighty grab at life. You have never taken life lightly or profligately. Our profession requires that some men die that others might be saved. Many, like me, are alive today only because they have had the great good fortune to come under your command."

Pennywhistle looked up and smiled. It was a smile devoid of mirth, one of utter resignation; the look of a man who knew his fate and accepted it. "Thank you for that. At any rate, I am too well trained in my duties to permit harm to come to you and my men. My responsibilities to you, my friend, and to the men sleeping over there, far outweigh any delicate moral conflicts pummeling my sensibilities inside of my own odd head. I want to see this business through to—" He stopped in mid sentence. Something was wrong. His senses snapped to full alert. What was it?

It hit him in an instant. The birds had stopped chattering. His peripheral vision detected a hint of movement in the woods a hundred yards away. It was a flash of brown, definitely human. He leaned forward and turned his head toward the forest.

Bang! The top of his left epaulette flew off. Damn it! He was going through uniforms like a monkey went through bananas! Sniper! Good shot; not inexperienced. Intended as a head shot; bullet just a bit too low. Hunter; but not used to human quarry.

"Damn bushwhacker!" shouted Spottswood. His eyes blazed with rage. "He's mine!"

"No, Peter, let me." Pennywhistle dashed off in the direction of the shot, glad of physical exertion to purge the morbid thoughts he had just expressed. His long legs covered the one hundred yards of open ground in a bit over fifteen seconds, and then he plunged deep into the wood. He saw a figure running, perhaps twenty yards ahead. He put on a burst of speed and closed the distance.

Strange how the onset of danger banished fatigue. The loping figure ahead was tall and agile. His mind grew cold, calculating. *Control the anger, don't kill him; find out what he knows and if he has passed the information to others. Almost there, get ready. The range is just over a yard. Now!*

He launched himself into space, open hands outstretched. His hands landed square on the back of the man's shoulders and his one hundred eighty pounds crashed down like a giant brickbat. There was an *ooomph* as the breath departed the man's lungs and he slammed into the ground. Pennywhistle raised his right fist to strike, even as he flipped the prostrate person over and shifted his full weight to pin his prisoner to the ground.

What the hell?

It was not a man, but a woman, and a beautiful one at that. The face was grimy from the fall and the clothing was worn, but any man with a normal sexual appetite would instantly see beyond that. To his surprise he saw no fear in the deep-set eyes, only defiance. The tumble had knocked off her wide-brimmed slouch hat to reveal honey blonde hair very sensibly bound up in a bun. She was dressed in a man's bib and brace overalls and a rough wool shirt, but they did not entirely disguise her womanly curves.

She had a sculpted, oblong face; a superb jaw line; high cheekbones; and intelligent, cornflower-blue eyes. A slightly aquiline nose forestalled complete perfection, but added character. Cleaned up, and in proper woman's clothing, she would be a classic beauty. His loins tingled against his will, while some ineffable sense of danger warned him to proceed with caution. An image of the Manchineel tree in Spain flashed into his mind. It was beautiful: its leaves and fruit resembled an apple tree's, but it was so toxic that merely standing next to its burning bark could cause blindness.

Why was she out alone, shooting at British officers?

"Who the hell are you, girl? I demand your name! You have just earned yourself summary execution!" He glowered down at her and hoped the whip in his voice would induce an outpouring of honesty, but there was no response. "Speak up! Speak up! I need a name." He lowered his voice and relaxed his imperious tone ever so slightly, "Speak frankly, and I may spare your life." She contemptuously turned her head away.

"God's blood," he said in exasperation. "Are you waiting for me to give you my card on a silver salver that we may have a proper introduction? I find a speeding lead ball a very formal invitation." She rolled her head and looked him directly in the eye. God, she was beautiful.

She laughed loudly and fully for a few seconds. "I guess it was kind of a calling card. My friends call me Sammie Jo, Sammie Jo Matthews." Her lips compressed into a sneer as her insolence returned. "But you ain't none of my friends."

What the devil kind of name was Sammie Jo for a beautiful woman? It sounded a sick joke, but then he remembered Americans liked short versions of proper names. "Samantha Josephine would be your formal, your Christian name?" It sounded a hopelessly ornate name, completely at odds with the body beneath his.

"Ain't nobody hereabouts calls me that, but I guess that's the name in the family bible." There were no tears, no pleading, and no entreaties to be released, just a simmering anger.

He was certainly not her friend, but felt that repeated use of her informal name would give him more control. He rose to his feet. "Get up, Sammie Jo. No tricks, no false moves." He drew his cutlass and motioned for her to rise. "Try anything and I will not hesitate to use this."

"Don't aim to be tricky. I ain't stupid." She spoke with an ugly country twang that was at odds with the pleasing music of her voice. She rose slowly, as if to make sure she was uninjured, brushed herself off, and breathed deeply. She had recovered quickly from the tackle; very resilient. She moved with the lithe grace of the natural athlete. She turned to face him. Her eyes blazed and her lovely mouth contorted in contempt; here was another one of those Americans with a pathological hatred of the British. Reason alone would make few dents in her convictions.

He told himself she was merely an annoying pest, and pests were best dealt with by summary extermination. Another part of him argued she could be part of a larger pattern. He should find out what she knew first.

But there was something more. She piqued his curiosity. Was she the Manchineel tree, a lovely, alluring poison, or an uncut frontier diamond? He wanted discover more about her; not as prisoner, would-be assassin, or illegitimate combatant, but simply as a woman. There was something strangely compelling about her, as if he knew her from long ago. He looked at her closely and he realized she was an American incarnation of Diana, Goddess of the Hunt: fierce, independent, in need of no man to protect her. Like Diana, quite capable of violent and dangerous action. In myth, Diana destroyed Actaeon, the mortal who caught her bathing in the woods. He had been luckier than Actaeon, although if her shot had been an inch lower he would not be standing here now.

He never took his eyes off her, lest she bolt, but bent down and picked up her weapon. It was a perfect specimen of an American long rifle: tiger stripe maple stock, octagonal swamped barrel, beautifully filigreed brass patch box. He held it easily in his left palm. Very well balanced: .44 caliber, 60 inches, nine pounds. In skilled hands, it was an elegant weapon, if slow to load. Its like had done great execution among British officers in the two wars they had fought with the Americans. Had she borrowed it, or was it her own?

Her piece was the favored weapon of long hunters in the deep woods. Her clothing was weathered and practical. She must have been following them for some time, stalking them the way a hunter stalked game.

He sheathed the cutlass, walked over to her and relieved her of her powder horn and possibles bag containing balls and greased leather patches. She sensibly did not move when she saw the determination in his eyes, but he was close enough to smell her. Despite the dirt and mud on her from the fall, she smelled wonderfully fresh. He tried to block the delightful womanly scent, but succeeded only partly. His nether regions proclaimed their interest. He had been too long devoid of feminine companionship and it was unbalancing his judgment. He reminded himself beauty in the forest was often a tool used to blind the unwary to real danger.

"Very fine weapon, Sammie Jo. Where did you get it?" He tried to sound calm, detached, and merely inquisitive. He loaded the weapon carefully, while he waited for an answer. She looked him up and down, her expression flitting between approval and disdain. She said nothing. He decided she had not yet made up her mind whether continued defiance would be to her benefit.

"Come now, Sammie Jo, I have spared your life. Surely you can favor me with a brief answer to a direct question." He pointed the weapon in her direction, although he was careful not to aim at her. "I am impressed; this piece has a double set, single lever trigger for precision. Is it a hair trigger? I have been informed many American rifles feature them."

"Yuh got a name, Redcoat?" Impudent question, but at least he had her talking. It might help her to see him as human, rather than a mere son of perfidious Albion. A small gesture, yet a beginning.

"My name is Captain Pennywhistle of the Royal Marines. I wish I could say it was a great pleasure to make your acquaintance, but I find it hard to feel joy when someone has just tried to murder me. Still, it wasn't a bad shot, although a torso shot is always wiser than one aimed at the head. I think you forgot to factor in the wind."

She looked puzzled for a split second, then laughed. His response had caught her off guard. She clearly did not expect detached analysis of her shot. It was, after all, praise of a kind. "I would have had you too, but you bent forward jest as I fired. I don't miss very often. And the piece belonged to my father. He left it to *me* when he died, rather than my brothers. He always said I was the best shot in the family. I've been hunting almost since I could walk." Her defiance vanished as she spoke, replaced by pride. He had an opening. Now he knew how to proceed.

"Let's get moving, Sammie Jo. You will march with us. I cannot release you until we are well away from this place and your tongue can do no damage. We can talk on the way. I have some questions for you." He gestured with the weapon toward the marines in the distance, prompting her to move. He walked slightly behind her as a precaution. "What's the finest shot you ever managed with this piece?"

"I once shot a running deer at dusk, nigh onto two hundred fifty yards, and I weren't more'n ten. That's when Pa knew I was a real hunter. When I got a little older, he let me do most of the huntin' for the family. Always brought back a bigger bag of game than my brothers."

Good, keep her talking, find out the small things, then move on to more important ones. Everything she said made sense and configured with her appearance and actions.

"How long ago did your father pass?"

"Five years ago. My brothers and I kept the farm running. Ain't much, jest a small spread. We make enough to get by. I'm alone now; they done run off and joined the army. I would have gone too, but girls ain't welcome. Pa fought in the first war against you people; always told us the British were trouble and could never be trusted. I thought maybe I'd do my bit to help, since yu'uns is right in my backyard. Pa said when he fought with Morgan's Rifles he always aimed for the officers and never wasted his time on the men. You had the biggest epaulettes. Figured you were a good choice." She seemed unconcerned she was talking freely.

He made an educated guess. "You have been following us for many hours, I'll be bound. How did you find us? I'll wager you weren't looking for us."

"I wasn't. Out huntin'. Found a big stag at dusk. Stalked him for hours. He ran right across the road a few hundred yards from the rear of your men. They didn't see him, but he alerted me to you. I followed you, figured I'd try a shot about dawn. If y'all had just stayed put, I woulda had you. Damn, Pa woulda been proud of me if I'd drilled ya." She actually smiled. It dazzled, but vanished in an instant. Her face assumed its previous sullen, defiant expression.

"So you are unconnected with any militia group then? This was purely a foolish stunt?"

"Ain't foolish if you are doin' somethin' right for your country, just foolish if you miss. Ain't no militia round about here, anyway."

Useful information, and probably true. If she wanted to fox him, she would have claimed scores of militia swarmed the area. Captured Americans had tried that gambit on him many times. The column was safe, then. She had told no one, had no one to tell. She was just a civilian with a gun, with more patriotism than good sense. She had acted on an impulse, but tracked them with real skill. Her action was foolhardy, but undeniably brave.

Spottswood walked toward them, his eyes filled with puzzlement. "You are joking. *This* is the sniper?"

"Indeed it is. Allow me to present Sammie Jo Matthews; a local hunter who decided stalking British bucks was more challenging than pursuing ones of the animal variety. Hawkeye here," he inclined his head in her direction, "is a dangerous bird of prey who has just had her wings clipped, so watch out for her talons."

Spottswood's angry eyes swept over her like a lighthouse beacon sweeping a murky sea. Her beauty caused them to brighten for a brief second, but they quickly darkened to unforgiving contempt and disgust. This damned forest vixen had come within a hair's breadth of killing his friend, and looked eager for repeat action. "Tom, I hate to say this, but she deserves a dangle and a fatal bout of hempen fever. Her sex is irrelevant; she is a bushwhacker outside the laws of war. We should do it now. Quick and simple: tree, rope, two men to run her up. I will take care of it."

"No, wait, Peter. She knows nothing. She is here purely on her own hook. Not even Yankee militia use women to fight their battles. She is a stupid girl who acted hastily, without judgment. It hardly seems fair she should die for it. Anyway, a summary execution of a woman would not sit well with our men. They are tired, their emotions are ragged, and violence against women smacks of a wild barbarian horde rather than the modern, disciplined unit of which they are proud. Let's give her a taste of what we have endured. Make her march with us. When we meet up with Ross we will let her go. She knows the area. She might be of some marginal value to us."

Spottswood knitted his eyebrows together in surprise and pursed his lips into a disapproving O, as if he had just bitten down on a sour grape. "I would never fail to execute an order from you, Tom, you know that; but I must ask you, why are you sparing this vicious woodland urchin? Are you truly deciding things according to the logic you prize? Or are you letting a pretty face unbalance your reason? Do not allow this ill-bred creature to stir memories of the good woman you lost! Save your mercy for the worthy and the weak; this woman is neither. You gave the last vigilante exactly what he deserved. You told me each rope collar slapped on a bushwhacker sends a message to the Yankees. Here is your chance to show you make no exceptions for anyone. I know I am being impertinent, but you always taught me the good subordinate asks questions to help his commander make the best possible decision. How did you put it on *Active*? 'I want thoughtful subordinates, not supine lackeys.'"

Pennywhistle was about to shoot an angry retort, but stopped himself as the lieutenant's words hit home. The lieutenant was doing his duty, exactly as Pennywhistle had taught him when they first met four years ago. Spottswood was right. Loins were shouting down logic, and the rational voice in his head was no longer icy cold. A dutiful soldier would execute her without hesitation, and not lose a moment's sleep over it. He was a sentimental fool, and he had to admit her unaffected beauty made him think her passion might not just be confined to shooting; an idle thought, but a distracting, dangerous one.

"You are right to ask the question," he replied carefully, "but I am still convinced we gain nothing by ending her life, and might profit by the saving of it. At the very least, it will show the Americans we practice mercy, even if undeserved, toward women. She may still despise us after release, but her tale will spread. It is an inconsequential matter alone, but might convince a few we are not monstrous, freakish spawns of the dread serpent Cockburn. This war will be over soon enough, and we will resume our former very healthy trade with the Americans. There is no reason to make our legacy here darker than it need be."

Sammie Jo listened to all this; yet, as before, did not plead, beg, or remonstrate. Two marines had quietly moved forward and leveled their muskets at her, but she appeared to pay them no heed. She radiated contempt, displayed no fear. Pennywhistle guessed she was frightened, but would not allow him the satisfaction of seeing it. Her watchful eyes showed energized intelligence, and her darting glances in various directions reminded him of a trapped animal plotting an escape. He caught her eyes and she returned his gaze steadfastly. He thought he caught a gleam of approval. In a flash he knew: she felt the illogical attraction as well.

"Peter, it's almost six, time to sound the assembly. If it will quiet your mind, I will put Sammie Jo in Dale's charge. And we will put more flankers as we advance. The closer we get to Ross, the more danger that we will encounter bushwhackers, and others will be acting with more preparation."

"Fair enough, Tom, but let's have Dale and the girl march close to and ahead of us. I'd still like to keep a weather eye on her. There is always the possibility someone with a gun will come looking for her." He looked at Pennywhistle with an expression of resigned exasperation. "She is a very dangerous burden and will cause us far more consternation than she is worth." He shot her a haughty glance of aristocratic disdain. "My horse is better bred than she is."

Sammie Jo scowled back with the look of a peasant who had just told her fellow serfs to torch their lord's chateau. She looked Spottswood up and down and laughed—not a polite, lady-like titter, but a countryman's guffaw. She spoke slowly in a twangy, backwoods voice that was as confident as it was disrespectful. "Sure is a real knee-slapper when a jackass talks about a horse's breeding. I know lots about horses, but I doubt you do, 'ceptin' maybe the brown stuff that drops from their rumps; same stuff as comes out whenever you flap your jaws. Not a big surprise, since your whole personality puts me in mind of a horse's rump."

The marines covering her blinked in surprise. No one spoke to an officer like that!

Spottswood let out a shocked bellow of wounded dignity. "You impudent guttersnipe! How dare you speak to a king's officer with such unmitigated arrogance! You should be on bended knees in thankfulness that your betters have condescended to spare your worthless hide. You should be offering up your highest hosannas!"

Sammie Jo smiled inwardly. *The little turd swallowed the bait*, she thought. She wanted to stir things up, foment anger. Angry men were careless men—perhaps careless enough to give a girl a chance for escape—so she shook her head scornfully. "Looks like I aimed at the wrong Redcoat. I would have done folks a powerful service if I'd shot off a spiteful tongue; must be hung in the center and clacking at both ends."

"Curse you, madam!" Spottswood fumed, scarcely able to credit backtalk from a bumpkin. "All of you ignorant Yankee trash are as far below English ladies as foul rags are beneath linen. You have the mouth of a fishwife, and I am certain a heart as black as the hands of a chimneysweep. You clearly require a swift and immediate lesson in manners! By God, a stout horsewhipping will make you sing a different tune! Ten lashes and you'll be the most docile creature in creation."

Spottswood's eyes blazed with fury and he turned toward the columns' pack horses, wondering if one of their saddles contained a horsewhip. If not, a cat-o-nine tails would do.

"Big man with a horsewhip, ain't ya, Mr. Redcoat!" Sammie Jo shot back, smiling evilly. She knew just how to provoke a pompous man: threaten his masculinity, his status, or his pride. "Without it, I bet you're a just lily-livered, no 'count, groveling weasel; a piss ant with a pedigree. I ain't of a mind to jaw with you; never thought I could learn much from a fool's ravings, but damned if your words don't make me bust a gut laughing." She let out another guffaw that was pure malice. "See, I ain't the kind of mousy little woman that your sort of high and mighty gentleman is used to, the kind you can beat on or scream at to make y'all feel strong. I ain't afraid of your threats, and I'd just like to see you try and teach me some manners with your bare fists. I'm half polecat and half bear, and I can outwrestle the meanest gator. Whuppin' a jumped-up little pipsqueak like you don't present no particular hardship."

"How dare you! You... you... you..." Spotswood sputtered as he struggled to find the appropriate insult.

She put her hands on her hips and braced her feet wide apart; the stance of a predator calmly sizing up its prey and determining how best to bring it down. She slowly surveyed Spottswood from head to toe, in the manner of a wildcat appraising a stag. He looked strong enough, but she saw doubt and hesitation in his eyes—exploitable weaknesses.

Her tongue might be inclined to hyperbole, but her body argued her challenge should be taken seriously. She glowed with health and was formidably built: long, sturdy legs, broad shoulders, and toned arms. She was graceful in the manner of a jungle cat rather than a lady, and exuded a physicality completely out of place in a drawing room but very much at home in the forest. She was probably two inches taller than Spottswood.

When she spoke again her voice oozed ridicule. She wanted to goad the Englishman. She hated being a prisoner and the feeling of subservience it provoked. Knocking the stuffing out of one of her captors felt very satisfying just now. "You're right on one thing, Mr. Lobster. I ain't no English lady, so I don't think and act like one. You won't never catch me sayin', oh so polite-like, *please noble sir, forgive all my transgressions and vouchsafe me an ounce of your most tender mercy.* You stiff-arsed, scarlet scoundrel, put away your highfalutin' words and show me if you got any manly spirit 'neath your fancy uniform." The British officer's face was exactly the picture of shocked puzzlement she'd hoped to provoke. She was certain he had never met a woman with her spunk and sass.

"Don't tell me a real gent like you is afraid of a mere... girl!" She crossed her hands over her heart, pretended the start of a swoon, and smiled mockingly. "Tarnation! If I ain't as shocked as a virgin finding out she's pregnant! What's this here world comin' to if there ain't no more Galahads?"

She laughed yet again, her cruel eyes conveying her real meaning. But the laughter ceased abruptly and her mouth became a determined slit. Her heart beat rapidly, but it was in the rhythms of an experienced athlete, not a frightened cur. Her pupils dilated in feral eagerness, her nostrils flared and her breaths turned long and deep. The tanned skin on her high cheekbones stretched taut and her leg muscles tensed like those a panther poised to strike. Her fists rose in a flash and she held them like an experienced boxer. Her voice was low, husky, and rippled with the excitement of the hunt. "Go on, try your luck; put your fists where your big mouth is. Remember you won't be swingin' at no lady. I dare you to fight... coward."

The marines within earshot stared at each other in astonishment and disbelief. Questioning a man's courage was the ultimate insult to a serving officer, and had it come from a gentleman, it would have provoked an immediate duel. Coming from a low class Yankee bitch it seemed extraordinarily strange; gentlemen never challenged rabble, and girls were beyond the pale. America was a very odd place!

An alarmed Pennywhistle realized that what had begun as farcical exchange was moving toward a violent showdown. Spottswood was determined to act, and so was the woman. She had confounded all expectations by reacting with aggression rather than fear, preferring escalation to conciliation. Any sensible person seeing the inferno in Spottswood's eyes would have understood that provocation was a dangerous course and would have backed away, but this girl seemed to court danger. Her expression was one of a dragon-slayer about to act. She might lack judgment, but there was a devil-may-care bravery about her he could not help but admire. A woman challenging a King's officer to a fist fight was an extraordinary thing, particularly since both parties were sober. Instead of intervening as his duty demanded, he watched in stunned fascination, overwhelmed with a curiosity to see what happened next.

Spottswood was in an impossible position. If he employed violence, he would appear a ruffian and a bully, certainly no gentleman. If he did not, he would look like he was scared of a Yankee witch and possibly forfeit the respect of the men. He hesitated for a second, then took several slow, belligerent steps toward Sammie Jo, basic animal posturing, hoping she would back away in response.

She instead stood rock steady. He instinctively raised his fists, but checked himself and realized he needed to discredit her, show her challenge was beneath his gentlemanly contempt. Derisive words were his best weapons. "I shall never debase myself by laying even a finger upon you, a female. As woodland Public Ledger I imagine quite a few men have laid fingers upon you and writ their signatures large all over your body."

Sammie Jo bristled and growled. "I ain't no whore, you mincing Bloodyback, but you're about to find out that I am the orneriest she-devil in creation!"

"A whip is all you deserve, you bumpkin. It should prove a fitting schoolmaster to train a hayseed hoyden. If ten lashes are not lesson enough, then we will try twenty, trollop!"

"Better bring an army to help, hatchet-face!"

"Forty lashes, jackwhore!

"You'll need Dutch Courage, cod's head!"

"Sixty lashes, harpy!"

"Better call your butt boy to hold your hand, back door usher!"

"Eighty lashes, Medusa!"

The air crackled with incipient violence. A score of marines attracted by the tumult watched from ten yards away and began to quietly make bets on the outcome of the fight. 19 wagered on their officer, but all were impressed by Sammie Jo's size and fierceness. None of the marines had ever seen her like. One man simply said, "She'll win; I see it in her eyes." He put two shillings down to back his words.

Sammie Jo advanced carefully toward Spottswood, body turned sideways to present the smallest target. At three feet she began to slowly circle the surprised officer, like a hawk closing on a pigeon, looking for an opening. Spottswood put up his guard, but it was clear from his face that he still could not credit that the girl would actually fight.

"Stop! Now! Both of you!" Pennywhistle's voice roared, commanding absolute obedience. He was appalled he had let this run on so long and had allowed his fascination with an odd woman to unbalance his reason and make him forget his duty. Their invective was preposterous, yet badly injurious to good discipline. Now both combatants looked as if they had been physically slapped, and they lapsed into a stunned, surly silence. The score of marines sheepishly melted away.

Sergeant Dale walked up slowly and with great dignity; exactly the right man arriving at the right time in the right way. His impassive demeanor was a welcome contrast to the superheated local atmosphere rippling with menace. He read the situation perfectly and briefly looked Sammie Jo up and down. His eyes betrayed just a hint of disapproval, but his voice remained steady and calm. "Might I be of assistance, Captain?"

"Ah, Sarn't Dale, just the man I wanted to see. We have a prisoner, Sammie Jo Matthews. I am putting her in your charge. Bind her hands. She will march with us, and I want you to make sure she causes no trouble." *Time to sow a little fear*, thought Pennywhistle. "If she causes the slightest difficulty or lags behind, deal with her severely. If she bolts...." The implication was clear, and Dale noted that he did not address her as Miss.

"Aye, aye, sir!" Dale saluted crisply, his expression matter-of-fact. He stared Sammie Jo sternly in the eye for a few seconds, although he had to look up to do so, and pointed his Baker Rifle at her. "Let's go, missy. No tricks. Move along smartly, now."

She complied quietly, but not before her eyes shot one last salvo of stilettos at Spottswood. Pennywhistle expected she would not resist overwhelming force intelligently applied. Dale looked hard and fit, probably the kind of soldier her father must have been. She would have no doubts he would shoot her at the slightest provocation without compunction. Still, she was a very swift runner, knew the local forest far better than he, and probably possessed a number of forest hides. She would run, given the slightest opening.

The long marine column marched twenty minutes later. Most men managed to wolf down some hard biscuits first, and many took a quick run at the apple trees before falling into line. The rest had done wonders for the men, although fatigue was still noticeable in the drawn faces and hollow eyes. Pennywhistle relaxed the pace from the Moore Quickstep to the standard marching speed of two miles an hour. The men marched for fifty minutes each hour, then rested in place for ten. He wanted to husband their strength for the battle that he felt certain lay directly ahead.

He watched Sammie Jo carefully. She kept the pace seemingly without effort. She had as remarkable reserves of strength as she had of foolhardy courage; even Dale seemed astonished at her stamina. She said nothing, made no complaint, did not even breathe heavily. Her calculating eyes gleamed with the alertness of a scout and swept the ground ahead. Her nostrils flared from time to time, apparently detecting scents that his nose was too civilized to detect. She moved with the economy and the fluidity of a prowling panther. It was mesmerizing to watch the rocking of her hips and the rotation of her superbly muscled backside. Rousseau spoke of the natural man. Perhaps Sammie Jo was his distaff counterpart.

She might be ignorant about polite talk, fine manners, and fashionable attire, but there was an earthy energy radiating from her that made the fortune-hunting beauties trolling the Pump Room in Bath seem lifeless husks by comparison. Her tongue was unguarded and direct; her meaning plain, untainted by any hints of drawing room guile. The Bath beauties' sham smiles, scheming eyes, and mirthless laughter reminded him of witches employing glamours to beguile unwary mortals. Years of carefully dodging their spells had enabled him see them for what they really were.

He glanced frequently at Sammie Jo as he rode, and his tired mind began to idly compare her to the women in England who had sought his attention. The artist in him saw the Bath women in pale pastels, Sammie Jo in bold primary colors.

The gold-digging nymphs of Bath walked with graceful poise, curtsied elegantly, and danced with smooth, flowing steps. They spoke softly and mellifluously, always careful to fully articulate their vowels and let everyone know they possessed an accent reflective of a genteel upbringing. They displayed bird-like appetites, ate daintily, and always avoided the punchbowl, lest even a hint of silly spontaneity mar their well bred personas. The sum total of their studied refinements caused him to see each of them as less a woman than a mantrap, set by a designing mother usually lurking nearby.

Dance innocently with a painted enchantress more than twice, offer some polite compliments, speak briefly about some bland subject, and you could well cross an invisible line. Soon afterwards, her overjoyed father might initiate a detailed inquiry into your financials and lineage, preparatory to negotiating a detailed prenuptial contract. With luck, you might be allowed a kiss or the use of her first name to seal the unsought engagement.

The greatest aphrodisiac to a husband-seeking siren was not a man's youth, handsome face, or gracefully rounded calves, but the size, firmness, and prosperity of his rent rolls. A big manor house wanting a woman's touch had sex appeal that compensated age, pot bellies, or spindly legs. A man was not just a man but an income, an identity, and a station in life.

Turning marriage into a Smithfield Bargain bothered him; it made a man little better than a prize bull purchased at London's chief meat market for stud service. He understood and accepted that heirs and property mattered, but surely physical passion and romantic desire deserved better than being rendered silent backbenchers in the parliament of love.

The prevailing expectation was that love would eventually sprout and grow between two partners matched by class, backgrounds, and outlooks, carefully yoked together. Love started as a seed that, once planted, might be watered with affection, consideration, and care. With luck, that seed would grow into a shade tree of love that would spread its branches far and wide. Passion might eventually supplant mere rutting.

He didn't buy that high-minded twaddle for an instant. He had experienced true love with Carlotta and knew there was nothing else like it in the universe. The difference between the real article and an imitation was the difference between a bonfire and an ember. The sexual unions that flowed from it eclipsed ordinary coitus as naturally as the sun outshone the moon. Love was a marvelous, ineffable, transformative thing that could not be conjured into existence simply because one wished it. It either existed or it did not; there was no middle ground. A quick extinction by a bullet was preferable to a slow, wasting death as the life-long partner of a woman for whom your heart had no affinity.

The flapping wings of a bald eagle caught his peripheral vision and ended his reflections on love and lust. The eagle swooped low, fast and graceful, chasing some prey and passing a foot over Sammie Jo's head. She glanced up and smiled briefly, almost as if she were directing it—not just Diana, but a female embodiment of the Yankee Republic.

The hours passed, the angry sun scorched the skin, and the dusty road insulted the lungs. The prospect of danger, the air of expectancy, the heightened senses all agreed with the primal intuition screaming that death loomed closer with every passing mile. He could not say he enjoyed the feelings, but they certainly made him feel fully alive.

When they were three miles from the anticipated destination, he called a thirty-minute halt for the men to refill their canteens and snatch a few quick bites of food. He also sent Spottswood ahead to try to establish early contact with Ross's patrols. There was always the danger of an isolated horseman being ambushed and captured, but Spottswood had volunteered, and the sooner the column joined with the main army the better for all.

He was also relieved Spottswood would no longer be in close proximity to Sammie Jo. He had made no further verbal protests, but the tension in his body shouted his mistrust and his wary eyes rarely left her. He shot scowls at her every few minutes, as if his eyes could cast a curse.

Spottswood was right about her lack of breeding, but missed the essential point. Unburdened by the deadweight of genteel pedigree and its attendant manners, her tough and combative character rose naturally to the surface, perfectly suiting her to the rough life she had chosen.

He walked Rossamun toward a small brook and let her drink. Then he summoned Dale and a very suspicious Sammie Jo.

"I can untie your hands, Sammie Jo, if you promise not to run. I am not without compassion and presume you would like some food and drink. Have I your solemn word that you will remain in my custody until I release you?

She looked him directly in the eye. Her expression was subdued but in no way submissive. "I'll stay put for the time being. I'm hot and thirsty and need some grub and water. Not going to bite the hand that aims to give me somethin' I want."

"Good. Extend your arms, please." She flexed and raised her arms behind her. He undid her bonds, and she rotated her arms in large circles several times and brought them above her head. She locked her fingers, stood on her toes and gave a mighty stretch. Then she let out a long sigh, brought her arms to her sides, and swiveled to face him, simple pleasure in her eyes. She again reminded him of a jungle cat; a picture of relaxed muscular poise, yet alert and ready to strike without a second's warning. "Thanks, that feels a heap better." She smiled at him for a split second. "All right, Pennywhistle, what you got in that there haversack that's good to eat."

So she remembered his name! She had refrained from addressing him by any name or title before. Certainly calling him by his name was better than the insults she had heaped upon Spottswood. She looked truly hungry. He had something reserved for a special occasion, a delicacy. No reason to open it now, yet it felt right. The girl was getting to him. He reached inside his haversack and produced a brightly colored tin.

She looked puzzled. "What's that? Don't look like no food I ever seen."

"You haven't seen it before because it's very new, something unknown in America. It's Donkin's Best Tinned Pork. I met Brian Donkin, a confident, enterprising chap before shipping out. I liked his pitch and the science behind it seemed brilliant. The cooked meat is packed in a can, tightly sealed with tin, and stays fresh until it's opened. The meat is far better than old salt pork. It's a revolutionary idea. I regret we won't have time to heat it, but it's still quite good served cold. Let me open it, then take a whiff and tell me you don't want some." He took out his dirk from his boot, thrust it into the top of the tin, and rotated it clockwise as he cut. The girl watched with curiosity.

When the top came off, he smiled and inhaled deeply. He realized he was hungry himself and could have devoured it all in short order. Instead, he handed it to her, along with a spoon.

She took it tentatively, as if someone had handed her something dangerous. She sniffed warily, then broke into a broad smile. "Say, that smells right good. D'yall mind if I pitch into it directly?" She seemed to be asking permission. Courtesy? Unexpected.

"Be my guest, Sammie Jo, eat as much as you want." He helped himself to some ship's biscuit and old Stilton cheese.

"Thanks, don't mind if I do." She ate slowly, but with great concentration, seeming to savor every mouthful. She looked up at him once, smiled, and said, "Ain't never had vittles this good."

Strangely, her comment pleased him. He poured some water from his canteen into a tin cup and handed it to her. She drank it thirstily, and handed it back to him for a refill. He obliged. She drank the second cup more slowly, almost thoughtfully, and then looked up at him.

"I don't get you, mister. I tried to kill you, still might, and here you are treating me like I been invited to some fancy court dinner. Y'ain't even tried to get inside my britches;

most men would have. Pa always told me a man don't do you a good turn lessen he wants something from you. So, Englishman, what do you want?"

"Your good behavior, for a start. I'd certainly take it as a favor if you'd at least postpone killing me until we have finished our meal and talked a bit."

She laughed. "I can do that!"

"I confess I am curious about you and your people. I have never encountered a forest huntress. There is much about you I don't understand. I wish we had met under more favorable circumstances and that I had more time to hear your story. I fear our association will be brief, but it need not be entirely unpleasant. I have no wish to harm you. I merely want to make certain you cause no damage to my people. You Americans may find it hard to credit, but we English can be quite forgiving and civilized." He smiled gently, hoping he might temporarily overcome her cynicism and convince her at least one Englishman was benign.

A surprised look crossed her face. "Are ya sayin' ya don't want me? I figured maybe ya spared me jest so you could have me. Pa said I had to be real careful, learn how to take care of myself when a man came sniffin' around. Y'ain't one of them back door ushers, are ya? Pa told me some Englishmen be funny about women."

What bold cheek! He laughed loudly as a spiral of merriment soared up from the bottom of his toes to the last follicle on his head. His gentlemanly reserve had been misconstrued entirely. He had restrained his lust a little too well.

He looked at her crestfallen face. Her pupils dilated, her nostrils flared, and her tanned skin flushed. Was she offering herself to him? She seemed unacquainted with the restraints of civilization; perhaps this extended to the sexual realm as well. He had heard tales that people of the backwoods sometimes formed alliances quite casually and troubled themselves with marriage only after a pregnancy occurred. The way she spoke made him doubt she was unacquainted with the act of love. But it could be a trick. The girl was resourceful and might figure her best chance for escape would be when they were private—and intimate. He struggled to compose himself and frame a reply.

He chased away the longing in his trousers and summoned up stern rationality, analysing the look in her wide blue eyes coldly and carefully. He saw excitement, but caught a hint of something else. It flitted across her iris for only a fraction of a second: calculation. The sad look on her face was designed to command attention through an appeal to sympathy. She had targeted a perceived weakness. She might be uneducated in the ways of civilization, but she had a doctoral degree in assessing raw emotion. She correctly gauged her own beauty, knew it a valuable commodity, and understood its uses for a variety of barter arrangements. His reply to her question would tell her how vulnerable he was to its blandishments. It could all be genuine, since danger was sometimes a great spur to passion. He did not doubt she would follow through if given the right signal.

He wanted her, but he was not a fool. This was hardly the time or the place, and he did not for a second forget his duty. She was trapped, and her instinct of survival overrode every other consideration. It was also quite possible she had some of the female praying mantis about her. The male of that species lost his head, literally, after joining.

He realized she had been watching him very, very carefully. He had seen the look before; a cat tracking a mouse with its eyes. He needed to unsettle her, keep the initiative.

"I assure you, Sammie Jo, I am not one of those unnatural gentlemen. My desires are healthy, robust, and I fully appreciate the charms of the fairer sex. Yours are certainly considerable. I confess I am unaccustomed to such frankness in a woman. I am learning much in my sojourn in America. Allow me to return your candor with some of my own.

"Bluntly, it would please me greatly to explore matters of passion with you. I like you, you intrigue me, but I do not trust you, and I would never be so foolish as to be near you without a weapon handy. Do not for an instant forget our countries are at war. I spared you in a moment of misplaced reflection. I am not prepared to surrender either my duty or my life in service of simple desire. You are my prisoner, and I cannot allow anything to obscure that. March with us a few more hours, behave yourself, and you will be released unharmed. Please finish your meal. We need to resume our progress within the quarter hour."

She looked disappointed for a second, then smiled. The gambit had been tried and had failed. No harm, no offense taken. "You're sure different from the men I know. Guess they were boys; never met a real gentleman before. Most men can't resist a chance to be with a woman: anytime, anywhere. They'll do anything, give up anything, to hoist a woman's skirts up above her head. Course, I don't wear skirts very often." She laughed heartily with unaffected naturalness, nothing prim or delicate about it.

He smiled back at her in spite of himself. Her humor was infectious. "Remember, Sammie Jo, war changes circumstances, and it changes people. We would never have met without it, and I doubt you would behave as you are doing if we had met in the usual course of events. We are two ships that have passed within hailing distance because of unexpected storms. I don't believe we are destined to scrape hulls."

"Scrape hulls?" She laughed. "That's real funny. Don't be too sure, though. Got to admit, y'ain't what I thought an English officer would be. Y'ain't cruel, ya treats me like a lady, and—" she paused as if thinking deeply, "—ya sure run fast and ya sure know your weapons. Might be fun to see if you can shoot better'n me. I saw ya had some kind of rifle in your saddlebag. Ain't never seen a shootin' iron like that."

"It's called a Ferguson Rifle. It's a breech loader; very few specimens exist. It would be capital sport indeed to test my skill against yours." He paused briefly and a haunted look slithered down his face as if a mask were being peeled off. His eyes locked onto hers. His voice became eerily calm and oddly distant; that of a man recalling deeds done long ago and far away. "But shooting animals is quite different from shooting people. You missed me because you don't know much about killing men.

"I have no doubt you are a skilled marksman. It is a fine thing to execute a superior shot against a stationary target in broad daylight. It's even more impressive to hit a running beast at a distance in twilight. But both are vastly different from shooting one person on a battlefield choked with smoke, fire, and noise; especially when regiments of trained and disciplined soldiers are trying their best to kill you." His emerald eyes narrowed and she saw flickers of a disturbing inner fire. "Trust me, Sammie Jo, battle is different from anything your mind can conceive; the reality is far worse than the most sinister imaginings."

His voice dropped an octave and came out as an ominous, husky whisper. All traces of politeness bled out and his speech became grave and darkly hypnotic.

"Perhaps you imagine yourself an avenging angel, a wrathful goddess, or a warrior princess, but I see only a foolish girl standing on the edge of a bleak precipice."

She blinked hard at the stark change in his manner. The humid air seemed to sizzle with some kind of weird, unnatural, electric charge. His eyes burned and his face flushed a deep crimson straight out of the Nether Regions. A chill raced up her spine.

"Forget all the stories, tales, and odes to glorious battle you have heard. They are the words of tricksters, military carnival barkers; lies designed to ensnare the unwary. Truth is the first casualty of war. There is no poetry in battle, and those who proclaim it so have never been in one. It is just brimstone, thunder, horror, stench, and confusion. Count yourself blessed you have never seen the Gorgon face of war. To look upon it turns your heart and sensibilities to stone. War alters you in terrible ways, hollows you out and makes you a stranger to your former self. It is a dark bridge over a black river; you can never return the way you came." He looked down at his right hand, regarded it gravely, and was relieved there were no tremors today. They were becoming more pronounced and frequent. He compulsively clenched and unclenched his fist several times before continuing. His expression was funereal when he looked up again.

"You think yourself tough, prepared for anything. You can probably lick most of the local bucks in a fight. You possess physical courage, I give you that." He paused for a few seconds, staring off into space. He refocused his eyes on her; they bored into her soul. His voice took on an acid edge. "But you are an innocent, a child who toys with fire. You have wandered from a haven of safe routine into a domain of tigers. These two-footed tigers do not kill out of the necessity of filling an empty belly, as the beasts you hunt. They kill for all manner of reasons and causes, many distressingly trivial and specious. Their organized bloodshed is more destructive and efficient than anything in the animal kingdom, but it is apparently Nature's plan to keep the numbers of the human species in check.

"I have come to regard horror as the more honest face of Nature. In battle she fills the world with despicable objects and occurrences that both tempt and repel me. I have seen and done things that would make the worst demons in hell run screaming mad with terror. I have lost count of the deaths I have inflicted and of the trusty comrades who have perished at my side; one minute men, the next, shards of bone and scraps of bloody gristle."

She winced as his rage and conviction slammed against her like physical blows. Her mouth froze in surprise and her eyes widened with fear. Yet she could neither look away nor resist the baleful spell he was casting.

He shuddered involuntarily. Regret was the enemy of the professional soldier, and if indulged at all was far better left unspoken. Yet here he was babbling like a magpie and showering a perfect stranger with the toxins of his soul! But perhaps it was exactly because she was a stranger. He was not likely to ever see her again, and so she posed no threat to his reputation or his conscience. What remained of his gentlemanly propriety demanded he stop now, but the unruly child inside in his head shouted he was not yet finished. It also occurred to him that lancing his spiritual boils might warn another away from danger even as it diminished his own burden.

The fire in his eyes abated and his tone changed to one of resignation. "Most of the carnage just blurs together, but some deaths you never forget, though you would give a

King's ransom to do so. Those particular extinctions mark you with the Grim Reaper's inexpugnable brand. You become chained to his herd for as long as you walk this darkling plane.

"Four deaths are forever seared into my consciousness and form the cross of my soul's burden: a man, a boy, a cat, and a girl. I was in earnest conversation with my best friend at Trafalgar when a blast of canister carried away his entire lower jaw in mid sentence. Bone, teeth, and a fragment of tongue fused together in what remained of his face, and the sickening parody of a man still attempting to speak. The transformation from man to ghoul took only a second, but it took him a week to die.

"Peppito, a Portugee powder monkey I had befriended, was mashed into pulp by a cannonball. One second there was an eight-year-old boy with a sparkling smile, and the next a bloody ball of fleshy twine.

"Screwloose was a giant tabby cat and a fierce mouser, but a gentle friend to the entire crew of *Bellerophon*, a ship on which I was proud to serve. He was put into the launch and towed astern when the ship was cleared for action at Trafalgar. That launch was smashed to kindling. Quite a number of shellbacks wept.

"Molly died a few days ago." He looked at Sammie Jo with eyes begging forgiveness. "She looked much like what I would imagine you looked like as a child. If I had not tried to be clever, she would still be alive today. Damn, damn...." His voice trailed off and his eyes welled up.

He cleared his throat. He wiped his eyes dismissively and they turned hard again. "You are an imprudent ingénue living in a world of make believe." His low voice rumbled with contempt. "You think you can play the part of a combat tourist and merely dabble in battle. Dip your toe in the whirlpool of war and not have your soul sucked into the maelstrom. Well, it doesn't work that way; go in for a penny and you are soon in for a pound.

"You think because you have outwitted beasts in the woods, you can outwit the God of Battles; that you are too clever to ever be killed in some nameless, pointless skirmish. You know nothing! Nothing, I tell you!" He hurled the last words with real venom. He took a deep breath and closed his eyes for a second. When he opened them, he spoke tenderly, compassion returning. "Yet I would rather have you a live fool, than die a battlefield savant."

He said nothing for a full minute. His melancholy mask gradually reformed itself into something human.

Sammie Jo simply started at him, astonished he had confided in her as a man might confide in a priest. She knew herself to be unsentimental, yet she was moved by his words. She wished she had the power to grant him absolution from his imagined sins. His warnings clearly sprang from an unexpected concern for her welfare; gentlemen did not usually trouble themselves about no account crackers they had only just met.

Reason returned to Pennywhistle with a pain like a migraine's lance. He had spoken as if in a trance. He had lost control, something an officer must never surrender. His pining over a lost innocence made him no better than a child weeping over a broken toy. He saw apprehension in the girl's eyes; she had likely concluded he was a very dangerous man. Yet a second later, her expression changed again, to one of curiosity. She apparently wanted to know more. Best he should redirect her attention.

"You are perhaps two and twenty years of age; let not war steal your youth and laughter. You have a long life ahead of you, a future with a husband and children. When I release you, have the good sense to walk away from this madness and never look back." His voice caressed and his eyes became beacons of kind light. "I pray to God this is my last war. I promised myself this time I would be careful to spare any lives I could. Strike a blow for life, not just death. You just happen to be the beneficiary of that promise. I could not save Molly, but perhaps I can spare you."

The solicitude in his face and the sincerity in his voice pushed hard against her disdain of all things British. She was amazed that he considered her worth saving; no one had ever spoken so in her presence. The Englishman was a thoughtful man, by no means a bad one.

"I will not cause you any trouble. I give you my word," she said solemnly.

A promise was something he hardly expected. She sounded sincere, yet it might be a ruse. A careful survey of her earnest face told him she spoke honest words. He heard a slight cough. He turned and saw Dale standing close. He did not know how much Dale had heard, but he knew it would not go any further.

"What is it, Sarn't?" he inquired blandly.

"The men are formed up, ready to march, sir. You said you wanted to be informed."

"Very good, Sarn't Dale. Please bind the prisoner and take charge of her."

"Aye aye, Captain. Here, missy, get up, get up." He pointed his Baker at her.

It was an abrupt end to the audience.

Pennywhistle mounted Rossamun, surveyed the column, and issued a string of orders to several subalterns. He favored Sammie Jo with a quick glance, then dismissed her from his mind. The column began to trudge forward. The weariness of his soul had allowed despair to gain temporary dominance; that must never happen again. He needed rest badly; it would be the easiest thing in the world to find a shady tree and drift off to sleep on the grass beneath; so wonderful to succumb to a few glorious hours without care and responsibility. Yet he knew that would not happen, because the unforgiving bugle call of duty overpowered the siren song of fatigue.

Sammie Jo marched ahead of Pennywhistle and said nothing. She had seen briefly into his soul, something she never expected, never sought. She was not a sensitive person, nor accustomed to introspection, but that he had revealed the depths of his being was obvious, even to her. Layers of pain, sadness, and remorse folded over a solid core of steel: the ruthless and merciful mixed in odd proportions and undergirded with an unshakable confidence of self.

He was still an enemy, but he was a man too, and a handsome one at that. A few minutes before, he had merely been an obstacle. He bore closer investigation. She not only would not run, she would stick around as long as possible. It occurred to her that action followed this man as a hound followed a fox. She had come looking for a fight, to contribute to the cause. If she shadowed him, she would surely find an occasion. No one ever mistook her for a helpless woman, and with a rifle in her hand she was more than the equal of any man.

CHAPTER SEVENTEEN

Five miles ahead of Pennywhistle, Lieutenant John Manton of the 4th Regiment of Foot spotted the first American scouts. They stood exposed, blocking the main road to Bladensburg. Their uniforms were blue and well cut, indicating these were probably gentleman volunteers from Baltimore. Two under strength companies, maybe 150 men. They were crowded too close together for a skirmish line and spaced too far apart for a regular one. It was as if they had not quite decided and had settled for the worst of both worlds. Clearly, amateurs commanded here. They yielded no ground on his approach, apparently seeking to discover the seriousness of British intentions.

The light company of the 4th could handle them. He had only been in command in the four weeks since Captain Hines died after a long bout with malaria, but the company had responded well to him. He wondered if the American line shielded a large force to their immediate rear, if they were in advance of the main force, acting as scouts or a screen. There were several houses on either side of the road ahead. He saw faces in the upper floor windows: riflemen seeking commissioned targets. They demanded his immediate attention.

There was a long, low ditch ahead; it appeared to be a partly dug canal. It afforded good cover only fifty yards from the Americans. Better still, it was at nearly right angles to their line, perfect for enfilade fire. Amazing the Yankees had not noticed, had not recognized the tactical edge they'd yielded. He dispatched two sections under the senior sergeant and junior lieutenant. They advanced in short rushes, and were to open fire on the Americans as soon they reached the ditch. That should keep the militia occupied.

He retained the remaining two sections under his command. One went with him and jogged straight for the two-story brick Federalist home. The other, under Sergeant Bates, forked left and quick-stepped toward the blue clapboard saltbox. Both groups methodically spread themselves out. Running men in a close group are far easier to hit than running men with wide gaps in between. Experience had taught him to scoff at American marksmanship, but it was as well to be prudent.

Shots kicked up dirt near his men, but it was nothing they had not endured before. They knew what he wanted and had been drilled in how to carry it out. Orders were transmitted by hand signals. No one stopped or hesitated; theirs were well ordered footsteps in a dance of death. When they got within twenty yards of the home, half of the soldiers fired their muskets at targets on the upper floors. It was not generalized volley fire, but carefully aimed, individual shots. The other half smashed in the front doors and dashed through with fixed bayonets. Despite all the flying lead, no one was hit. The startled Americans on the second floor fired too high and the British on the lawn below had trouble making shots tell because the solid pine window lintels provided good protection. But the defenders were kept busy, their attention completely focused on the men on the lawn.

Manton formed the men single file in the hall and told them to regroup on the second floor landing. He gave the signal and they pounded remorselessly up the stairs. No talking, no extraneous movement, just brutal efficiency. The Redcoats burst through the second floor door of the drawing room, locked eyes with six terrified Americans, and rushed straight at them. Two put up a suitably heroic struggle, but lacking bayonets, they were no match. The Redcoats gutted all but one in under a minute. The last man threw himself on the floor and begged for mercy. Manton had no time for prisoners, so a Redcoat merely clubbed the survivor into unconsciousness and left him behind. Everyone assembled on the lawn ten minutes later. Not a man injured; a small victory of training and experience.

Bates' section charged up presently. They had secured the second house. With all snipers eliminated, it was time to drive in the main line of enemy pickets.

Manton unfurled his spyglass and slowly surveyed the American position. His mentor, Captain Pennywhistle, had taught him thorough preparation was the key to success. The American fire against the men in the ditch was spotty and so far had injured none. The men in the ditch felled an American from time to time. They wisely conserved their ammunition and fired just enough shots to occupy American attention. The defenders waited for the attackers to make the decisive move. Always a bad thing to surrender the initiative, but Manton was glad to face a timid commander.

He heard someone shout his name and saw a horseman galloping toward him. When he recognized Lieutenant

Spottswood, he smiled. Presumably, Captain Pennywhistle could not be far off. He had not seen Pennywhistle since his arrival from France; he had simply been too busy with his duties, and the captain had been carrying out long range reconnaissance.

"John, how are you?" asked Spottswood, as he dismounted. He handled horses well, unlike Pennywhistle. He extended his hand to Manton, who shook it enthusiastically.

"Just rooted out some Americans from those houses, operation straight out of the Shorncliffe drill book, so I am feeling very well indeed. What brings you here?"

"I need to find Ross and Cockburn. The marine column is just a few miles behind me. I figured a fight lies ahead, and from your actions just now, I trust I am not mistaken. The marines naturally want to be in the thick of the action, so I was sent to find out where Ross needs us."

"Last I saw, Ross and Cockburn they were chatting on horseback near that red barn." Manton pointed southwest, towards the structure half a mile away. "When I passed them, Cockburn was thundering away with his usual enthusiasm. Ross mostly listened, while several aides wrote furiously. Cockburn urged an immediate attack in no uncertain terms. 'What will they think of us back home if we hesitate now?' he said.

"I think my men just ploughed the road for a local advance. We are all headed for the Bladensburg Bridge. It is incomprehensible that the Americans have not destroyed it, but our scouts report it still stands. Either the orders were not issued, that fits with what we know of their command, or they have not be carried out, which fits with what we know of their discipline."

"I concur, John; a terrible lack of professionalism. We can't give them a chance to make a stand, to dig in. We have to make it a war of movement. Hit them fast, hard, and never stop advancing. I need to be off. I wish you luck." He mounted up.

"Give my regards to Tom when you see him. Let's all meet for a drink in the President's House when this is over."

"Splendid idea!" Spottswood put the spurs to his horse and departed in a cloud of roiled dust.

John Tracy watched Spottswood depart. He sat atop a docile black mare four hundred yards away and followed him through his telescope. He did not know Spottswood, but recognized the officer he had been speaking with. It was the same one who had led the boarding attempt on the *Lucky Lady*.

Tracy saw that the militia commander failed to appreciate the danger to his flank and appeared completely focused on the Redcoats in the ditch. Tracy was here to reconnoiter, not lead, but he could not allow Americans to be slaughtered because of abject stupidity. He spurred his horse to a gallop and sped straight toward the major in command. A man on horseback with a plan, experience, and determination could put fire into even the most lukewarm troops. Green troops wanted decisive leadership most of all. The Major ranked him, but regulars could usually impress militia officers who were uncomfortable with responsibility. Daniel Morgan's Cowpens design popped into his head. At least a part of it could work here. Give the British exactly what they expected, but use it against them.

"Good morning, Major!" he boomed with great confidence and good cheer. "You're doing a splendid job holding the Redcoats, but if you'd permit me, we can do more. John Tracy, Captain, United States Marine Corps, at your service, sir." He almost neglected to add the 'sir' at the end, but he knew militia types could be punctilious about honors rendered, even if they hardly merited them.

"Good to know you, Captain," the officer replied. "I'm John Boatman, Fifth Baltimore City Regiment. The British are proving less aggressive then I feared. I told my men to expect a charge, but none has been forthcoming." He looked thoughtful. "Course, I am a cotton broker by trade, can't say I have any experience with either battle or Redcoats. I am right proud of my men, though. This is their first fight and they are doing well. They've been steadfast and stout-hearted. We've lost a few, but not a one has run. We have pinned down the British for the past quarter hour. Truth be told, I'd like your professional assessment. I feel we could do much more today, just as you say, but I am strictly a book learned soldier."

Tracy sighed with relief. A militia officer asking for advice! The man sounded and looked terribly, terribly earnest. He was probably right about the men. They just needed better guidance.

"Glad to oblige, Major. The British are going to go round your left, attempt to take you in the rear. The line in front of you will advance in a minute to keep your attention. It will be the unforeseen assault that does you in. I counsel an immediate withdrawal."

"Withdrawal?" Boatman barked with surprise. "I hardly expected that from a Marine!"

"You misunderstand me, sir. Withdraw in orderly fashion, lure them in, then execute a quick about face and smash them in the teeth with a determined volley at close range."

"A much better design, Captain, much better!"

"Can you keep your men in good order, Major? This will be a very delicate business. Once novices withdraw, it can be difficult to arrest their flight. This all depends on absolute obedience to orders. Can they manage two fast volleys?" Morgan had ordered his men to deliver three, but the Major was not the inspirational leader Morgan had been, and Tracy thought two more reasonable. "Two fast volleys, then they may retire, pleased they have done their duty and acquitted themselves with honor."

Boatman smiled. "I am quite certain they can. We may not be experienced, but we want to fight. If you could explain to them exactly what you have in mind, we can do this, I am confident."

"Would you be offended if I temporarily took command, Major?"

"Not at all, Captain. I and my men would very much welcome a regular officer."

Tracy noted smiles on the faces of the men. They desperately wanted a blooded officer they could trust to direct them, and he would not disappoint.

The Redcoats in the ditch fixed bayonets, rose up as a mass, and formed up on the lip of the gully. The sergeants checked the alignment. They walked slowly, menacingly, forward, 75 paces per minute. It was not a fast battle step, but one designed to give their opponents plenty of time to contemplate the dreadful power inexorably headed their way. It had repeatedly proven its worth against untested troops. With their weapons loaded and leveled at waist level, each man maintained a two foot interval from his companion, both to spread the line wider for envelopment and to present a less compact target.

Two hundred yards north, Manton used the saltbox farm house as a shield for the remainder of his troops. Unlike the first group of Redcoats, when the advance was sounded, they would advance at the run. It was a matter of rhythm, of pacing, a way to confuse opponents. The enemy would brace themselves for the methodical onslaught of one group of hostiles and think themselves blessed with time to prepare. When another group appeared from nowhere and made a mad, fearless dash at them, they would realize in a split second all time was gone. Attack from one direction might be fended off, but attack from two would be utterly beyond their ability to cope.

Tracy had just finished explaining things to his new-found command when he spotted the Redcoats moving out of the ditch. He glanced to the left, looked for the flanking movement, but discerned nothing. No, the Redcoats were out there. Of course, they were lurking behind the farmhouse. Solid tactics; don't show yourself until the last possible second. It protected the men as well as increased the shock value of their appearance by making it sudden and unexpected.

Tracy was out of time. Things would happen very quickly, but it was his turn to shock the Redcoats. "Ten hut!" he bellowed to the men from Baltimore. "Dress ranks. Shoulder arms." Their execution fell short of regular standards, but considering the situation and their training, their evolutions were commendably done. The Redcoats, relying on the bayonet, had not yet opened fire. He counted on that. "About face. Forward march at the quick step."

This was the critical moment, and it came down to the sheer force of Tracy's personality and will. This was not just a test of the men, it was personal. If they trusted him, did exactly what he said, they could pull this off, but the whole business could just as easily turn into a rout. They were violating the first rule of safety from an animal standpoint: never turn your back on a hungry predator unless you could confidently outrun him. With troops, however, running was invariably a bad thing, unless it was in the advance. In the retreat, it was far too easy to yield to flat out panic; discipline vanished and every man thought only of his own safety.

He decided it was the sheer confidence in his voice that did it. The men executed the about face handsomely, at least for militia, and began to move steadily towards Bladensburg and safety. There was no talking or grumbling, only the startled cries of three gophers flushed from their lairs by the advancing line. No one glanced over his shoulder, even though it would have been understandable, given the advancing line of red. He had their trust, they had their instructions; now it was up to him to time things exactly right.

The retrograde movement stunned Manton. It seemed too orderly, too disciplined for militia. The maneuver might have been a bit slow for regulars, but it was well done, and a sensible course of action. Still, it might just have been luck; even novices with minimal training sometimes got things right by accident.

He could just let them go. They were merely a detached arm of the main American force. It made sense to conserve his strength for the big battle ahead, wait until the rest of the army came up before continuing the advance.

But the temptation was simply too great. His blood was up and he wanted to drive them off the battlefield in abject terror. With luck they would be finished as a fighting force, at least for today. His plan was sound; he would stay with it. He would wait just a bit longer, give the enemy a chance to think they would get clean away. Build up their hope, let their confidence flourish, then yank it away, to be replaced by abject terror.

He unfurled his glass and took a closer look. He wanted to see the officer in charge. The major he had seen giving orders earlier had appeared unsure and cautious; this new conduct seemed at variance. *What the hell!* It was that damned marine officer, the one who was almost Pennywhistle's twin. What was he doing here? That made things at once more dangerous and more exciting. The military situation might be different from his first assessment, but now he had a chance for a measure of personal revenge. A cautious voice whispered that everything was just a little bit too easy and that the man he faced was a consummate professional. The marine understood the British; he was the only American commander he had encountered who seemed completely un-awed by them. Pennywhistle had always told him to keep things impersonal, detached, and never let hot blood outweigh cold logic. Was he doing that now?

Perhaps he was too keen for action, but the men in the gully were striding boldly forward, confident of the result, and he would not sound the recall. It was better to back a flawed plan than hesitate, stop, and seek to implement a new and better one. He would just have to trust his men's superior experience to extricate them from any trap the American might have devised.

Tracy felt the pressure building. He risked everything presenting exposed backsides to a skilled enemy. He summoned up every ounce of will to continue on the present course. He had to trust his ears and his intuition in a test of nerves and faith; his nerves, and the men's faith. He had won their trust, now he must push them right to the edge.

At least the British weren't firing. He felt no rushes of air, heard no musket reports. They had dispensed with bugles; the silence made the advance more menacing. Tracy deduced they would wait until they were very, very close to fire; they might even rely entirely on the bayonet. He banked on their curiosity, the momentum of their discipline, and on the sheer shock value of his move. Even the best troops experience a split second of indecision when confronted with the unanticipated.

Tramp, tramp, tramp. The men marched steadily, purposefully. Most kept their eyes front, but a few shot him quick glances. Not even disciplined troops could keep this up for long. He had to be careful, not demand too much. Keep them moving, following commands, under control. Do not give them time to think.

Tracy paid close attention to his peripheral vision. The real threat would come from the flank, and would appear suddenly, like a goshawk summoned from a falconer's distant perch. He could feel the men's mounting unease, but he had seen something in the distance through his glass that had informed his calculations. He had gambled that his deduction was correct, about both the commander and the unit. Not everyone in the American army feared initiative like Winder and Stansbury.

Tracy felt a pressure wave behind, although it might just have been intuition. No, it was definitely pressure. The humid atmosphere was so clogged with moisture that when large bodies of moving men displaced big volumes of air, it could actually be felt in almost the same in the same way as an incoming ocean tide.

"Boys, let's make this short and fast," said Manton. "That militia aims to volley on our men over yonder. We need to stop that. When I give the command, run at them as fast as you can and give them cold steel. Our boys from the ditch will see you, speed up their advance, and give them the same. The Yankees are behaving better than usual, but you know as well as I that their greatest skill lies in running." Manton's men all smiled. "Don't forget to yell for all you're worth! We'll show the Jonathans the price of trifling with real soldiers!"

Tracy caught a quick flash of red on the left. He swiveled his head slightly, to see just what he had expected. The Redcoats emerged rapidly from behind the house and swiftly formed a proper line. He had less than a minute until the flank charge struck, but the flank could wait; he had to take care of the immediate threat. "Halt! About face." The men did as ordered. He saw pure, naked terror in their eyes. The British marched confidently toward them at thirty yards distance, weapons leveled for blood. Their arrogance was almost palpable.

He forced every ounce of defiant ferocity he could muster into his voice. "Just two volleys! You can do this! Make ready." The men brought their muskets to a vertical point and full cocked them. "Aim!" His confidence overmastered their fear and they promptly leveled their pieces at the British. "Keep it low! Fire at the kneecaps! Steady, steady, wait for it." The British were twenty yards out. He could see their faces clearly. "Fire!" An impressive sheet of flame darted out from one hundred fifty muskets.

Because they aimed low, many of the bullets found a home in flesh. The volley slammed into the British like a titan's fist and laid low half their number. The British were stunned at the Yankee discipline but recovered quickly. Being light troops, they did as they were trained. They took cover and sought to reevaluate the situation.

Tracy had no time to rejoice; this had only bought a moment's respite. He prayed his men were up to a pivot. "Shoulder arms! By the left wheel!" he bellowed. "March!" The line swung slowly round, like a gate on a hinge. Impressive for amateurs; give him three months and he would make real marines of them. "Halt." They were at a ninety-degree angle to their former position. He was about to say load in quick time, when he checked himself. He needed to be sure, control their fear, guide their actions with his voice. He called out loudly every discrete command of the reloading procedure.

The Redcoats broke into a run when they saw the Yankees swing round to face them.

"Huzzaaaaaaaaahhhhhhhhhhhhhhhh!" fifty men shouted. They knew they enjoyed a huge advantage if they could get close enough. Only about half the militia had bayonets for their muskets, and they'd have to reload before they could fire again. The British intended to impale the militia men on their cold steel before that could happen.

Manton ran yards in advance of his men; his sword aloft, his expression fierce, his determination unshakable. He knew he was an obvious target, but the madness of the berserker was upon him and he thought it important to demonstrate to his men his contempt for Yankee marksmanship. Pennywhistle had taught him years ago that men are only as brave as their commander.

Tracy waited. If the British got too close, his men were finished. He figured he could coax one more volley out of them after the initial one, before they broke and ran. He saw movement out of the corner of his eye at two hundred yards' distance. Yes! The plumes on their red-crested brass helmets were distinctive. Dragoons: likely John Maxwell's boys. He had shared good times with Maxwell at the College of New Jersey years before.

Tracy switched off anything resembling human emotion. It was always thus in moments of extreme stress. He became a steam engine of rational calculation. He measured distance, rate of closure, expected reload time, before he chose the precise moment to open fire. It all became a question of abstract mathematics, and the professors had always told him he excelled at that. They had to squeeze in one more volley and hope that Maxwell could be relied upon.

At forty yards, Tracy yelled, "Fire!" The volley was solid, hitting the British hard, knocking down many of their number. Even so, it failed to arrest the momentum of their charge. "Reload in quick time," bellowed Tracy. If half the men could get off another shot before British steel crashed into them, he would count it a signal achievement. He just hoped it would be enough.

A trumpet sounded, making his heart leap. It was quick trilling of the advance, and it meant the thing that infantry in the open fear most: cavalry! A Troop, 1st US Dragoons, Captain Richard Maxwell commanding; fifty men, which meant the troop was under-strength. They spread themselves out and drew sabers, advancing at their mounts' brisk walk.

The British were twenty yards out; they would surely recognize the threat behind the trilling trumpet. A lot of Tracy's men had not finished reloading, but he dared not wait any longer. "Fire!" A ragged volley lashed out. Several British soldiers fell, but their advance continued. A number of his men looked about to break and run. "Steady, men!" A few more muskets fired, as the slower men obeyed his order.

The ragged volley savaged the British, but missed Manton. Worse than the musket fire, seconds before the crashing din, he had heard the dread sound of a cavalry trumpet. Manton stopped dead in his tracks. As the roiling cloud of gun smoke cleared, he heard the trilling again and locked onto its source. He saw the advancing cavalry, and all of his fury and bravado evaporated in an instant. Training took over.

He might be close to smashing the American infantry, but fighting dragoons in the open was a fatally losing proposition. Mounted men slashing down hard with razor-edged sabers against madly running men was a cavalryman's ideal, a soldier's nightmare. He had far too few men to form square.

There was the possibility that British skill and courage could somehow change the odds, offset the hard logic of overmastering force at point of contact. But that was the voice of the British press, sheer propaganda, hardly good military logic. Americans on horseback might be amateurs, but even amateurs could do great damage.

Manton discarded every notion save survival and commanded the bugler to sound the recall. He had to get his men out of the open and back to cover. "Rally back at the house!" he shouted. The men responded without hesitation. The red tide ebbed.

The blue horsemen quickened their pace to a brisk trot. The horses moved well, seeming to understand more than basic battlefield equitation. The men looked healthy and fit, fully capable of sabering down a fleeing Redcoat. The crested helmets struck Manton as oddly ornate and beyond the budget for a militia unit. Cavalry helmets were costly japanned leather, which afforded protection from saber cuts, and were usually tailored to a single individual rather than a product of mass production. But he had been told the American regular cavalry would not put in an appearance, because they lacked mounts!

No, the scouts had gotten things wrong. The horsemen had to be regulars, probably the 1st Light Dragoons.

Manton heard another bugle call. The horsemen brought their sabers to a point, arms thrust boldly forward, wrists angled slightly downward. A charge was imminent. He waved his hands frantically at his soldiers and pointed his sword toward the farmhouse. It could be turned into an improvised Gibraltar.

Withdrawal was inglorious, hurtful to morale, and a cut to his command judgment, but it was the correct thing to do.

In war, it was always advisable to take the long term view, ignore small reverses in the interest of larger success later. He had at least discovered one thing. Backed with a proper commander, the Americans would fight—and they had at least one competent commander in the field.

Pennywhistle's father had battled them in the first American War. Pennywhistle had told Manton his father repeated the same observation time and again. "Underestimate American resolve and courage at your own peril. They may lack skill, but they do not give up easily."

They were only a hundred and fifty yards away when the horsemen broke into a full gallop. Manton was almost out of time.

"Run!" Manton shouted. "Head for the farmhouse!" The company bugler again blasted the recall. The men dashed toward the farmhouse. It was a deadly, converging race between them and the horsemen.

He could hardly credit that he was running, and it made him damn angry. Twice he had been outfoxed by the American Marine! There would not be a third time. He told himself to be patient, reminded himself revenge was expensive and frequently involved more harm to the seeker than the object of his vengeance. This debacle proved the truth of that; had he listened to the warning voice of reason, half his men would not now be lying in American dirt, dead or dying.

His lungs burned, his skin heated, and his heart thundered. He cursed himself as he ran, wishing he could do more to protect his men, but all his thoughts were drowning in the raw instinct of survival. He waved his sword as he rushed forward and bellowed like a town crier, "The farmhouse! C'mon, c'mon! You can make it!" But not all of them would.

As he ran, Manton noted the horsemen did something only professionals did. Instead of slicing at the back of the neck, which was protected by a high stiff collar and tall shako, most raced just slightly ahead of the infantrymen they targeted and slashed backwards at the unprotected face and throat. He glanced back and saw an American cut at Johnston, the slowest of his men. The back-slashing saber dug a huge trench from forehead to chin and he fell without a sound. It took the greatest determination, not to stop, sprint back, and revenge himself upon the killer. There was nothing he could do for Johnston, but a great deal he could do for the rest of his men.

He continued racing forward, yelling "Move, move, move!" He stopped for few seconds to suck in some deep breaths, faced about, and vigorously flourished his sword in the direction of the farmhouse. Soldiers ran past him, blurs of wind and red motion. The most advanced were just entering the farmhouse. A trooper, not more than thirty yards away, dug his spurs into his charger and galloped straight at him. Manton turned and ran without dignity.

He caught sight of Jackson, his head nearly cut in two by a horizontal slash just below his nose. Stevenson turned to face his attacker and took a sword through the throat. A trooper slammed his sword down on the back of White's skull, crushing it like a cheap tin cup. Manton heard a horse's labored breath very close and guessed what was about to happen.

He acted on instinct, sensing the horse was directly behind him. He spun round, darting left, away from the trooper's right hand, already starting its downward motion.

Manton's quickness and dexterity saved him. The trooper missed, and his own sword thrust took the horse in the left eye—always wiser to aim for horse rather than rider. The beast screamed in pain, reared up, and rolled over, pinning his rider. Another horseman barreled toward him. He had been lucky once, he did not think he would be a second time. Most of the men were inside the farmhouse.

Only ten yards. He sprinted as fast as he ever had and remembered to weave. Weaving men were much harder targets. His breath came in labored gasps. A saber flashed by, so close he felt the rush of air. His men shouted at him from the farmhouse. He saw the open door. Shots came from the window and one killed the trooper who had cut at him. Some instinct caused him to duck. Another saber missed.

He leaped onto the veranda. Two men grabbed him and yanked him inside the house. "Thanks," he said breathlessly. He was safe on an island as a sea of horsemen raced harmlessly by. The advantage shifted.

The range was close, the troopers large targets, and the Redcoats were firing from fixed positions. Most of them used window lintels to steady their muskets. *Pop, pop, pop.* The Redcoats opened up a steady stream of well aimed shots. Manton saw two troopers fall, then a trumpet sounded the recall. The enemy commander was no fool; he clearly saw it was pointless to continue the contest. The horsemen sped off as quickly as they had come.

Manton relaxed a little and ordered his men to stand down. He hoped some of the men in the ditch had held out. Such as were left would report to the farmhouse. Now he had to just wait.

The men drank from their canteens and chomped hungrily on ship's biscuits and a poor local cheese that was supposed to be cheddar. He felt as he always did after a fight, glad to be alive, but this time displeased by his own lack of foresight. He removed his shako and absent-mindedly ran his hands through his hair, almost as if to make sure his head was still attached. He looked at his black shako and noticed the top half its green plume was missing. There was also deep cleft in the crown. In all of the excitement, he had not even felt the impact of the glancing blow.

He felt exhausted and inadequate. Part of him said he had done everything he could; no commander could be expected to foresee every possibility. Still, maybe there was something to all the talk of breeding.

His mentor Pennywhistle was a gentleman by birth, lineage, and training. Manton had grown up a street urchin in the Shoreditch slums, his early training in the hard school of the gutter. He was a rarity among rarities in the army: a commissioned officer who had started Service life as a lowly press-ganged sailor in the navy. Every day, it amazed him men saluted him and addressed him respectfully as mister or lieutenant. To them, he was a subaltern.

He knew the speech, manners, and talk of the gentleman; he'd learned much in his years as Pennywhistle's manservant. He had always been a fast study, a good mimic, and completely convincing as an actor. His commission proclaimed him a gentleman, King George had signed it; but it did not make him any less an imposter in his own mind. He was here because of skill, luck, and the great kindness and vision of Thomas Pennywhistle. What would Pennywhistle tell him to do under these circumstances?

He needed to calm down and allow the forces of reason to come back into play. He decided he was being weak, allowing himself the dangerous luxury of regret. He had been told no cavalry was about, so he had acted on flawed and imperfect information. His men had not panicked when the cavalry attacked. They had fled on his orders to the place directed; they had not scattered and been run down like frightened game. They were still a fighting force in play, and as such represented a kind of defeat for the cavalry.

He had suffered a reverse, taken casualties, so what? That happened in war. The men's spirits were good; they were far from beaten. He heard them talking among themselves: they were pleased they had seen the cavalry off. In a few minutes, he would assemble them, do a roll call, form them up, and march on. He took a sip from his canteen and speculated about the pestiferous American Marine.

A very pleased Captain Maxwell cantered up to Captain Tracy. "Good to see you again, John. I saw some soldiers in a pickle, decided it was a good time for my boys to help. They've been itching for action ever since the new mounts arrived. I had no idea you were in charge. You handled your people right well. How did you come to command militia?"

"Thanks, Richard, this is strictly a temporary command. It's good to see you, as well. Let me return the compliment. That was a fine bit of soldiering just now; you saved our necks. I have been out here reconnoitering. I am guessing your troop was doing the same. It's definitely the main body of the enemy in front of us. I think a battle is just hours away."

"I agree, John. I will be glad to give your men an escort back to our main position. It worries me that things are so chaotic. I got tired of waiting around for someone to give me orders, came out here on my own hook. I wanted to see things for myself. I don't think Winder has any kind of a real plan. His dispositions are atrocious. Apparently, no one taught him the principle of concentration of force. It's up to us to provide backbone. I hope it will be enough."

Major Boatman walked up, and Tracy made the introductions. "Thank you, both of you," the major said. "I am so grateful for your assistance. My men are bursting with pride! They have seen the elephant and they didn't flinch. With such men as you on our side, I believe we may actually prevail today."

Maxwell and Tracy exchanged skeptical glances that the joyful Boatman missed. They hoped fervently they were wrong, but were much less sanguine about the battle ahead.

"Major," said Tracy, "let me return your command. I have other duties to attend to. If you will follow Captain Maxwell, he will get your men back to the main lines. I wish you great success today!"

Amidst a flurry of salutes and cheerful words, Boatman and Maxwell departed, leaving Tracy alone with his thoughts. He mounted his horse and slowly trotted back towards the main position.

The thing that weighed on his mind was the lack of bayonets. If Maxwell had not come along, British bayonets would have decided the issue. Every enemy soldier had them; perhaps three quarters of the Americans did. The British knew how to use them, but most Americans had only the vaguest idea. That difference could prove disastrous, and decisive, in battle.

His marines had thrown up makeshift fortifications this morning, but no other forces had done so. The army had had plenty of time to prepare positions, yet they had squandered it. He shook his head in frustration. He pushed the horse to a loping gallop, decided there was no time to lose.

CHAPTER EIGHTEEN

Colonel Parke angrily put the spurs to Saracen. He was not exactly sure where the main American forces lay, but he guessed they would be close to Bladensburg. He had taken the fastest mount from his stable and knew if he pushed him hard, he might just make it to the big fight he knew was shaping up.

Archibald Grimes had regained consciousness at Mt. Prosperity, spoken lucidly, then gently slid into a deep sleep. The doctor had removed the metal shard from Archie's head and had assured him Major Grimes would make a full recovery. There was nothing more to be done at home. His mother disliked Archie, but she'd agreed to care for him because he had made clear his ire would be great if she did not.

His command was destroyed. He was ashamed, but determined to reclaim at least some part of his lost honor. Perhaps he was not fitted for command, but he could at least volunteer his services, even if it was as a lowly private soldier.

It troubled him that what had happened might be some sort of divine retribution for his tainted appetites; "navigator of the windward passage" was the derisive term his neighbors would fling at him if they knew. He had fought against his feelings for years and begged God for release from this cruel character test on a nightly basis, but when he'd met Archie he'd realized he lacked the moral strength to struggle any longer. He'd thought his secret safe, but after last night, he was no longer sure. It would ruin him if it leaked, but in the wake of his military disgrace perhaps it did not matter. Even if he survived, nothing would ever be the same again. Death on the battlefield did not frighten him. Rather the reverse; it seemed alluring, promising honorable release. He was a man on the edge, a man with nothing left to lose save his miserable life.

Sammie Jo's feet ached and the soles of her shoes were almost gone. The hard marching on the rough road was draining her reserves of strength, but her face looked alert and determined. She had been soldiering along steadily for a good three hours but disdaining the marine's cadence, and she was damned if she would let the Englishmen see that she was wearing out. She pursed her lips, held her head up, and trudged onward.

She watched Pennywhistle closely. The man seemed indefatigable and insufferably calm. He barely seemed to sweat. Was he even human? A few riders came and went. He conferred with them, wrote something on paper each time, then they dashed off. She gathered they were close to their destination and she would be released soon. She had no doubt the Englishman would honor his promise. He had old fashioned, quaint notions about the honor of a gentleman. Her backwoods friends would have laughed at his fancy, high flown words, but they would have respected the sentiments behind them. He might talk like a dilettante—she had heard that term somewhere—but she instinctively felt the steel in his words.

She hoped he would return her rifle when he released her. It was her most prized possession and she felt naked without it. With a rifle she reckoned herself a significant if hidden asset to the American forces. It briefly crossed her mind to shadow the British and shoot Pennywhistle at the earliest opportunity. It made military sense to kill the commanding officer of an enemy column, but he had spared her when most would not, and she was not without an innate sense of gratitude. Promises aside, a second shot at the English marine officer would guarantee her death. She was brave, but not stupid. She was a survivor.

There was always the possibility that if she stayed in his vicinity a truly high ranking officer might present himself, maybe even the ogre Cockburn. She would love to draw a bead on him! His loss would weaken the British, and everyone would lionize her for his death.

Captain Pennywhistle surprised her; he was both more than and different from what met the eye at first acquaintance. He spoke in a modulated voice that he used almost as an orchestral instrument; it could be commanding as a trumpet or soothing as a flute. His refined accent was that of a swell, yet he disdained florid speech and spoke with directness.

Wear on his uniform proclaimed he was a combat officer, not a bandbox soldier, yet his uniform was so well tailored that it would have done credit to the greatest lord. He wore his hair short in the fashionable Roman way, and his long, sandy-red sideburns were exquisitely trimmed. He shaved so closely that he looked as if he had just stepped from a barber's chair.

Yet the cultured surface veiled something deeper, similar to the way the coat of a crouching wildcat blended seamlessly with a coniferous forest. What he had confided to her about his past confirmed the dark judgment of her intuition. Beneath the tall Englishman's polished exterior lurked a very driven, very hard man.

His handsome face was unscarred, but the same could not be said of the inner man. She had seen the devil's eyes in him. He had spoken with a furious energy that reminded her of Moses berating idolaters. Yet such was his intensity that Moses was a brook to his waterfall. Twice she had detected a very faint tremor in his right index finger. That likely went unnoticed by ordinary people, but years spent in the forest had schooled her to spot even tiny signs of weakness or injury in game she stalked. He was highly strung for all of his surface gentility.

Her father had always told her she was a headstrong girl, far too prone to yield to impulsive actions. She knew he was right, but today she would be patient and work hard to restrain her nature. She would not try to push events, but wait to see how things unfolded.

Many of the local gentry considered her an annoying, unruly presence, but that had changed when folks found out how well she could shoot. She had entered five turkey shoots and won them all. Her triumphs embarrassed the local young bucks, but brought her the admiration of the crowd.

Part of her devoutly wished she could be a fine lady. She had carefully observed the refined women of Baltimore when she had accompanied her father there on his twice-yearly supply trips. Women of quality looked disdainfully on her and her father as hayseeds, but she was awed by their polished manners and clothing. She remembered one woman in particular emerging from an Assembly Room. She was about her own age, clad in a splendid, high-waisted Empire dress of silken ivory and gold, decorated with Spanish lace and Greek pearls. Sammie Jo wished she owned such a dress, but even if she owned one her lack of deportment would make clear that the woman wearing it was merely impersonating a lady. She had but to open her mouth to destroy any illusions of gentility.

She'd always wished she could attend a place like Mrs. Fletcher's Finishing School for Ladies in Baltimore. She knew she was a poor ornament for a gentleman seeking a good marriage alliance: she possessed little skill at embroidery, played no musical instrument, and was an indifferent singer. She knew nothing of reciting poetry, sketching flowers, or foreign languages. She ventured opinions on matters that interested her, never deferred to anyone if she thought them wrong, and thought nothing of striking up a conversation with a man to whom she had not been formally introduced.

While quality women were not supposed to trouble themselves with commerce, she was a sharp bargainer when it came to selling the hides and pelts from her forest ventures. She possessed a quick mind for arithmetic, which came in very handy dealing with shady traders who tried to trick her with long columns of figures.

Growing up, she had been feared by boys and girls alike. Both had attacked her as odd and freakish. She was just too darned tall. She'd never backed away from a fight and found she could beat them all at wrestling. The forest became her friend, because it brought her peace from taunts and jeers. She learned to keep silent and be alert to its wisdom. Her eyesight was acute, and when mated to a rifle she was a force to be reckoned with.

Her pa, a widower with little experience with women, had been ashamed of her. Even when he found his tall, gangly daughter could shoot better than his sons, things had improved only slightly. He'd always treated her like a changeling, even though her resemblance to him left no doubt as to her parentage. She was just not obedient like the Good Book said women should be. He had not really accepted her until he lay dying, and even then she thought it had been less about love than trying to beguile the Creator with false repentance.

Because of her countrified speech, many people assumed she was illiterate, but she had been reared on the Bible, and her strict Calvinist father had made sure she could read it just fine. She liked to learn—her brothers found that odd— and she treasured the few books that crossed her path. She'd once traded a bundle of fine deer hides to a sea captain for a book titled *Sense and Sensibility*. Its author was "A Lady", and that interested her. Just think, a book written by a lady! She did not much understand the world the book spoke of, but it let her discover something of how women of the better classes lived. She liked the heroine's frankness and intelligence, but seriously questioned whether men like Colonel Brandon really existed.

When she went into the village of Crofton to buy salt, the women of the town either pointedly ignored her or shot her prim, pursed-lip looks of disapproval. Men's eyes often lingered in appreciation. She knew exactly what their staring meant and why their women sometimes cuffed them on the head.

The English officer was the first man to ever treat her like a woman of breeding and refinement, as if she belonged in *Sense and Sensibility*. He acted as if it speaking to her was pleasant, and there was not a hint of condescension. He spoke a courtly language that was alien to her, yet he just assumed she had the innate intelligence to understand. There was none of the leering that she had grown used to.

Most of all, he conveyed a sense of dependability and purpose she had never felt from any man. He did not boast, swear, or shout, but spoke quietly and modestly. Yet something in his carriage and manner said he was used to being obeyed. She'd caught a look in his eye that boded ill for any man who chose to try physical conclusions with him.

She regarded men with deep suspicion and had become expert in gauging their vulnerabilities. The only weakness she could find in him was that he was a man of serious mien who never did anything for impulsive reasons, quite unlike herself. His word was gold, and he clearly expected others to honor their promises. Normally a foolish conceit, but something in his speech and bearing demanded that those around him live up to their highest character, and even the lowliest would feel honor bound not to disappoint.

She instinctively trusted him. Most men she encountered had characters of straw and were easily set afire. The marine was a rock, impervious to the heat of ordinary temptation.

Pennywhistle called a halt, and the column came to a full stop a few seconds later. He took out his spyglass and examined the ground directly in front. Ross's army should be half a mile ahead. He caught sight of some red splotches of color in the woods: flankers, moving slowly and methodically forward; they guarded the army's edges against any stray

American woodsmen with dreams of glory. A horseman was galloping down the road toward him, probably carrying orders in response to Pennywhistle's request that the men be allowed at least two hours of rest. He decided even if the request was disavowed he would rest them anyway. They had earned it.

The horse slowed to a walk and moved alongside. The rider saluted.

"Lieutenant Buxton, sir. General Ross sends his compliments. Your men will take position at the right rear of the army, to be held in reserve. Your request for a two-hour rest is approved. It will be my honor to guide you to a site that should suit, with shade, fruit trees, and good water. It's half a mile ahead, a small field on the right. Your services, however, and those of your modified rockets, will be needed much sooner. I fear you personally will get no rest. If you will follow me, sir."

"Very good, Lieutenant." He returned the lieutenant's salute, then motioned for Sergeant Dale, who came alongside promptly. "Pass the word down the column. Two-hour halt, half a mile ahead. Food, water, and rest." Dale smiled, as did Pennywhistle. "Very good, sir. This will have the best possible effect on the men."

Smiles blossomed down the column as the word spread. The men advanced, renewed spring in their steps. Once halted, most of them would simply drop to sleep where they had fallen and sleep the sleep of the dead until drums and bugles heralded their resurrections.

Marching in the terrible heat had tested the strength of even the most stalwart among them, and they were at the extreme limit of physical endurance. Quite a number of men in his immediate view showed signs of heat exhaustion. He noted the pale, clammy skin, facial expressions of nausea, occasional outright vomiting. Two men had beet-red faces, which betokened the next stage, heat stroke, possibly not far short of a fatal event. Shade, water, and rest were not luxuries now, but military necessities. Pennywhistle called over Crouchback, who wore his customary sour expression, and quietly gave him instructions. The Cockney private eyed the two men Pennywhistle indicated, nodded, and jogged over to them. Sure enough, their canteens were empty; Crouchback handed over his own canteen and made sure each man drank and poured some water over his head. It emptied Crouchback's canteen, but he would be able to refill it when they stopped. Following the rest of Pennywhistle's orders, he continued along the line, exhorting the marching men to finish what water they had, and to share if necessary.

Despite the privations, Pennywhistle mused, when the time came to fight, he knew every man would reach down deep inside, dig beneath the empty pit of weakness, fatigue, and despair, and dredge up reserves of strength, steadfastness, and determination that were invaluable in battle. He could never decide whether training and experience created their remarkable character, or merely liberated and guided something already present, but he did know it was an extraordinary thing to witness. He was greatly humbled to command such men. It made him all the more determined never to hazard their lives recklessly.

Miles away, Colonel Parke reined Saracen to a halt. The horse was badly blown and sweat darkened his glistening hide; the last few miles had been at the full gallop. Had the ride been longer, it might have proved fatal. He was fond of horses and this was his best, but frankly he did not care anything about equine welfare today. He had reached the headquarters of the 5th Maryland Regiment and he thanked God he was not too late. The battle had not yet begun. He could still redeem himself.

He dismounted in front of a small group of officers and recognized Lieutenant Colonel Sterrett, the commanding officer. They had had business dealings over the years, although they had not socialized much. While he could not precisely call him a friend, he certainly knew him to be a man of character, someone you would instinctively trust in a dangerous situation. He was deeply embarrassed by what he must reveal, but he hoped Sterrett would appreciate his determination to set things right in some small way.

Sterrett spotted him, waved, excused himself from his fellow officers, and walked briskly toward Parke with his hand extended. "Parke, Parke, my good man! A great pleasure to see you. A most unexpected pleasure! I should have thought you would be with your regiment. I am honored you have taken the time to pay a social call! Or is it business that brings you here?"

Parke tried to manage a smile, but it came out more of a baring of the teeth than anything resembling an expression of joy. His face was deathly pale and his palms sweated heavily. He shook Sterrett's hand with less than his usual strength.

Sterrett's face registered the changes in Parke and his expression immediately became serious. "What's happened, Dan? I can't tell whether you have seen a ghost or lost your closest relative. You look like you could use a friend."

Parke barely restrained tears. "Steven, something very bad has happened. I could certainly use a friend just now, but more than that I wish to presume upon your good offices as a soldier. Could we go someplace and talk? I know you are a busy man, but I need your help."

"Certainly, certainly, Dan. I will be happy to assist you if it is within my power. We can talk over there." He pointed to a large apple tree. He reached inside his pocket and produced a small silver brandy flask. "Have a few sips. You look like you could use something to steady you."

Parke took the flask from Sterrett as they walked. His hand shook slightly. He drained the flask desperately, not even bothering to savor the fine aroma first. When they reached the tree, Sterrett spoke quietly, with great kindness. "Tell me what oppresses your mind. Surely it cannot be as hopeless as your face suggests? Every problem has a solution."

Amidst tears of anger, perplexity, and self recrimination, Parke poured his heart out for the next ten minutes. Most of it, anyway; he said nothing about his relationship with Archie. He spoke breathlessly, as if he had to get every word out before some disgraced part of his mind forbade speech entirely. He realized he was attempting to justify his actions.

Sterrett listened with patience, nodded from time to time, kept his face relaxed and impassive. He waited a full minute after Parke had stopped before replying.

"Dan, what happened to you was terrible, I will not deny that. I feel great sympathy for you and your men, but I think the disgrace lies not in you, but elsewhere. You were surprised by bloody-minded veterans for whom your men were hardly a match; and forgive me, but I think your second-in-command let you down rather badly. You gave him specific instructions about posting pickets and instructed him to send out patrols, but he failed to do so. You did the right thing, issued the proper commands, but I think, no, I *know* his actions constitute a serious dereliction of duty. You did what you could to rally your men. I think your actions reflect credit on you, as does your wishing to serve with me as a gentleman volunteer. I will of course, be happy to honor your request. We need every man we can get. I know Archibald Grimes is your friend, but he served you very ill yesterday. I will say no more of that, for I know he nearly paid the ultimate price for his mistakes. Please take heart. Yesterday was but a prelude; the real contest is today!"

Parke realized his love for Archie had blinded him. Archie was a wonderful man, but not a very good soldier. His mother had warned him about Archie's want of judgment on many matters, but he had refused to listen.

Sterrett was right. Yesterday could be expunged if the Americans carried the day in the next few hours. Victory always erased the stain of an early defeat. He was ashamed of his actions, but he would make sure he took an exposed position in the fight ahead and proved to one and all that his courage was genuine. The sadness faded, and a small glimmer of hopeful resolve flickered to life in his heart. He wanted revenge on the red-coated bastards who had caused the whole mess, and he could hardly do that if he was locked in a straight-jacket of despair. No, he would fight!

The marines continued their marching, and Pennywhistle was pleased that no one straggled, despite the oppressive heat. He again glanced at Sammie Jo striding steadily along. She wore an expression of bulldog determination, as if she had just decided to leap a ten-foot wide canyon and was about to lean into her runner's stride. The swagger in her long, loping steps shouted her contempt for close order military discipline and for authority in general. He doubted she would be so fiercely independent had she been brought up in more genteel circumstances. But perhaps her independence was her charm.

He had met plenty of women who behaved with a perfect correctness that turned them into scheming predators. His brother had frequently said it was time for him to find a wife. As a captain, he had the rank where marriage might benefit his career. His brother had directed a stream of candidates his way during his last leave, all of them suitable from a conventional point of view. Trouble was, conventional women thinking conventional thoughts seeking a conventional life bored him.

Yet not every maiden schemed. He recalled an independent-minded gentlewoman he had met five years earlier who had, much to his surprise, agreed with some of his views of marriage. He generally avoided discussing the subject, but fatigue, pain from recent injuries, and a few glasses of claret conspired on one occasion to loosen his normally cautious tongue. The lateness of the hour and the intelligent patience of his listener accomplished the final demolition of his gentlemanly reserve. He spoke to her fully and freely, well into the long watches of the night, as if she were a friend of long acquaintance, though he had known her only a few days. She had responded with the same kindness and insight she showed her brothers.

She'd had a soothing, honey-sweet voice that was as refreshing as a draught from a cool mountain spring on a hot day. She was tall: thin and willowy. She had an amiable face that stopped just short of pretty. Far more importantly, she possessed an able intellect, an observant eye, and a singular wit. Her name was Jane.

He had been a bleeding wreck when her brother, Captain Francis Austen, late of HMS *St Alban*, had chanced upon him in a backstreet in Portsmouth. Austen later said he had looked a candidate for a dissection table: his face grey, his left eye swollen shut, and blood trickling from his mouth. His right hand had seemed welded to the hilt of a bloody cutlass, and he'd been bleeding profusely from a bullet wound on his upper left arm. When Captain Austen found him, he'd barely been able to gasp his name. Four men lay dead at his feet, and most of the cobblestones nearby were bathed in blood.

An exhausted but nonetheless voluble Sergeant Dale had explained to the impeccably dressed naval officer that a party of killers disguised as a press gang had fallen upon the marine captain for reasons unknown. The officer had been overwhelmed by sheer numbers. Dale had been returning from leave, had seen a superior in dire straits, and "could not resist a good scrape." Together, they had dispatched four villains and put the remaining four to flight just before the captain arrived on the scene.

Austen then gave Pennywhistle a shot of French brandy from a hip flask while Dale employed his sergeant's sash as an improvised tourniquet. He and Austen then hoisted the marine to his feet. Pennywhistle's hands braced on their shoulders, they helped him hobble two blocks to the safety of the Crown and Anchor Inn. Austen then commanded the innkeeper to prepare a room and summon a surgeon, in a booming voice that brooked no disagreement.

Pennywhistle had rallied enough in the twenty minutes it took the surgeon to arrive to explain matters to Austen and earn his lasting respect and admiration. The brigands outfitted as sailors worked for the Duke of Argyll—a rich, vindictive old peer who blamed the marine for his grandson's death, even though everything had been done in strict accord with the *Code Duello.*

There had been a previous attack, but it had been made by inexpert individuals who had easily been dispatched. "I was careless," he told Austen. "I should have known a man like that would never give up." The Duke's new policy looked to be that of weight of numbers; if enough men attacked Pennywhistle in a tight corner, someone's blow was bound to prove fatal.

The surgeon had pronounced Pennywhistle "a tough bird" and said the wounds might have dispatched a man less fit. A small tot of rum helped the marine endure an hour of probing, cutting, stitching, and bandaging. The bullet had missed bone and came out intact, enclosed in clothing fibers. Pennywhistle adamantly refused the surgeon's offer of a good bleed and a stiff purge, but listened carefully when he said the marine needed a month-long convalescence to recover his health. "A quiet lodge in the country would do nicely; with lots of fresh air, sunshine, surrounded by pleasant folk."

"I know just the place," Captain Austen had said. "Just the place" turned out to be Chawton Cottage, home to his unmarried sisters, Cassandra and Jane. Both proved to be superb nurses, but he took a special liking to Jane. Her sparkling intellect proved a far better medication than the nostrums prescribed by the surgeon. Good minds were as rare as pearls in oysters, and he came to realize that Jane craved stimulating conversation just as much as he did.

In his long talks with her, he came to understand why women sometimes became so anxious to find a husband that they turned courtship into an almost military campaign. Many were so desperate that they stooped to any ruse, stratagem, or artifice, no matter how devious or base. An unmarried woman's wealth was controlled by her father or brothers, and all of that passed to her husband upon marriage, save what might be specifically reserved for her in the prenuptial contract. The only financial control she could exercise over her husband had to come from her wit and wiles. Learning how to manipulate the future husband in the courtship phase might appear unseemly and opposed to romance, but it was sound practice if she wished to exercise any financial power and independence during the marriage.

Jane was of gentle birth, but as the daughter of a country parson she came from modest means. When her father died, she would have to leave the parsonage and live in greatly reduced circumstances. She depended for everything upon the good will of her brothers. She had no dowry to offer, and at 33 was considered a confirmed spinster. She had never possessed striking good looks, and her intelligence sometimes intimidated men. She'd had one serious proposal from a perfectly respectable gentleman years ago, but she had turned it down for the simple reason she felt she would never love the man.

Pennywhistle respected her immensely for following her heart, considering the hard lot it had brought her in life. It reassured him that not all well-born women were avaricious scalp-hunters; some actually thought romantic attachment trumped all other concerns. Jane's sterling character and gentle heart outshone the painted faces and elaborate coiffures of the harpies of Bath.

She had come to trust him, to regard him almost as a fifth brother. She shared with him something she had only shown her family: her writing. He'd deemed the manuscript for *Sense and Sensibility* clever, insightful, and inspired at presenting a woman's perspective; it respected manners and etiquette, but gently satirized the restrictions they imposed on people. He encouraged her to find a publisher and felt certain it would enjoy a wide audience. She was pleased at his approval and said he would make a good physical model for a character in a planned second book, a certain Mr. Wickham. "But he will be a charming rogue, with none of your stalwart nature and steadfast moral fiber." He'd laughed and said she was being far too generous about his character.

Returning from his musings to the present, Pennywhistle observed Sammie Jo once more and decided she had one thing in common with Jane Austen: honesty. Sammie Jo was blunt where Jane was tactful, and but they both spoke what they believed the truth in plain language that could not be misunderstood. Such honesty was rare; perhaps if the politicians on both sides had spoken as the two women, this disagreeable war might never have started.

The tired marines reached the bivouac site and promptly sought water, then shade, ate a bit of biscuit and whatever meat they carried, and plopped down into deep sleep. He was relieved he had not lost any casualties to heat stroke. He had heard reports that at least twenty men had perished from it in Ross's main column. He could allow the Royal Marine Rocket Troop only an hour of rest, as he and they were needed at headquarters with the modified Congreves. However, he had one more duty to discharge before he reported in.

Sammie Jo stood before him, wearing a defiant expression. She looked slightly ragged around the edges, but he had to admit she appeared less fatigued than many of his marines. Her tanned face showed no signs of heat exhaustion. A tan was disdained by the polite classes as evidence of base origins and outdoor manual labor, but it struck him as very comely on her.

She stood erect in a pose that would have done credit to any marine, although her bosom made the silhouette somewhat different. He had earlier estimated her height at five ten, but his passion for exactitude now decided it was closer to five eleven.

He thought he detected a wistful expression on her face for a fraction of a second, but decided it was probably his imagination, a projection of his own mixed feelings. He would be glad to be shed of her, for she was a combustible substance with a sizzling fuse. Let her plague her own people. He could not afford to divert even a fragment of his mind from the fight ahead.

Manners maketh man was the motto beneath the Pennywhistle arms, and looking at her, he realized she had none in the conventional sense. She was rough in speech and blunt to the point of rudeness. She appeared to have been dressed by a hurricane flinging old clothes around. She displayed no visible acquaintance with the arts of hearth and home, but considerable acquaintance with the ways of predatory beasts. She likely had no knowledge of crafts but plenty of craftiness.

He had spoken to her about trifles during two of the ten-minute halts. Sheer curiosity had overwhelmed his determination to remain aloof, and she had responded in a surprisingly pleasant fashion. Her voice had a musical lilt, yet she spoke with a peculiar twang that reminded him of guitar strings pulled taut and suddenly released. She drawled her words so slowly it seemed as if she stopped off for a nap between words.

He had a good ear for languages, but her dialect was a challenge to follow. Words with one vowel frequently became words with two. Four became "fo-war", foot became "foo-at" and calm became "cah-alm". Occasionally one vowel became three: short turned into "showahat", glass turned into "glayus", and laugh became " layuf". She said she loved eating "nice white rice", but it came out as "nahce wahte rahce". She dropped r's, turned others in y's and made oy's into ohs. Birds were "buhds", hair was "hayah", and boys were "bohs". She said "dudden", "wudden", and "iden" where he would say "does not", "would not", "is not".

Yet he found her rough-hewn manner and lack of artifice refreshing. It was a relief not to have to dance a conversational minuet with her as he did with women of rank; there was no need for courtly circumlocution to avoid offending delicate sensibilities. He surmised forbidden topics did not exist for her.

She had no carefully cultivated feminine reserve. You might not like what she said, but she left you in no doubt where you stood. Her naturalness served to highlight her stunning inherent beauty as well as let her every emotion stand out in bold relief. He saw sparks of goodness in her, but was not so foolish as to believe her heart was gentle. It was like a rose, girdled by dangerous thorns. Beautiful, tempting, but to be approached only with great caution and deliberation.

He remembered the myth of Pygmalion. Was he regarding her as marble, on which a lonely man could carve an Enlightenment ideal of femininity? She was a long way from perfect; she would need a lot of fixing. But a part of him screamed nothing should be fixed. Her societal naiveté was part of her beauty. There was an old saying: "You can't put in what God's left out." God had been exceedingly generous with the raw materials, but they had been configured in a way that was suited to the vibrant rawness of the New World, not the sedate, restrictive pathways of the Old.

Bucks and beaus in England would covet her as a mistress, yet never consider her for a wife. He sensed she was clever about looking after her own interests and would be a hard bargainer in the commerce of love. She might well demand a trip down the aisle as the price of a permanent relationship.

He let his imagination ponder her fate in England. With the right guidance, a proper sponsor, and a little mystification about her background, she would be a sensation in Bath. If she visited Brighton, The Prince Regent would be entranced with her, and likely would extend an invitation that she be received formally at Carleton House in London.

She would probably be married off to a high born suitor in short order. She might lack a dowry, but her great beauty would render that inconsequential. Rationality vanished when men's lusts were in command. Bess of Hardwick in Elizabethan times had started life as the daughter of a gentleman of obscure lineage and no fortune, but through three clever marriages ended up the second richest woman in England. More recently, Admiral Nelson's infamous lover, the extraordinary Lady Hamilton, had been born in a humble Cheshire cottage, the daughter of a blacksmith. Sammie Jo had the intelligence to be anything she wanted, but he doubted she had any interest in being a painted-up snob fretting over pedigree and protocol. Europe would be not her salvation, but her destruction.

She exuded a musky, simmering sexuality that she made no effort to suppress. In that arena she was far more dangerous than the sexually inert beauties of Bath. She had tried to kill him once, and he could not be completely sure she would not try again. Oddly, he found he could not hold it against her. She probably would give fair warning of a second try. She was brutally frank that way.

He was about to do something he seldom did: take a leap of faith. He would give her back her rifle, send her on her way, and trust to luck that he would never see her again. He took a last look at her rifle. It truly was a superb piece of craftsmanship. Somehow, it suited her. It belonged beside her as much as fine French linens belonged next to a high-born lady.

He walked briskly over to Sammie Jo. He hoped the grim look on his face would reinforce the stern message he intended to speak.

"Sammie Jo, it is time for us to part ways. I will have two men escort you to the edge of the woods, then trust you will have the sense to comply with my most solemn advice to make your way back home as expeditiously as possible. It has been most interesting to make your acquaintance. As I said earlier, I have never encountered a woman like you. You are a remarkable, if dangerous creature.

"But heed well my gravest warning. If we meet again, I shall be an unforgiving, utterly implacable enemy of mercy. If I even catch a glimpse of you lurking nearby, I will have you shot. Or I will do it myself. I trust I make myself clear?" He could not sustain his stern expression and a hint of a smile crept to his lips. "I should regret very much playing a part in your demise. I honestly wish you a long and happy life."

She took the gun from his hand and set it carefully against a tree. She looked him directly in the eye in a challenging manner totally at variance from the way the fairer sex was supposed to glance coyly at men. She was not in the least intimidated by his little speech.

"Thanks, Cap'n. Right kind of you to give me back my piece. Obliged to you for sparin' my life and all. I ain't afixin' to kill ya no more. I give ya my word on that. One good turn deserves another, my Pa always said. I guess Pa weren't right about everything, though. He held your lot was evil. I'm powerful sure you're a good man, and I can read people real well. Bet you could talk a cat out of a tree. Too bad there is a war on. Be fun to see if you kiss as well as you fight."

She removed her slouch hat, reached behind, and unbound her hair. She shook her head slightly and a lovely blonde mane cascaded alluringly to her shoulders. She smiled brightly at him, without a hint of coquettishness. No stately polonaise of courtship and polite talk.

He laughed as he had done the first time she spoke so forthrightly. No woman he had ever known had been so consistently, so artlessly, so shamelessly direct. It both shocked and pleased him. He thought to frame a suitably gallant response of demurral, but her manner said unadorned honesty demanded the same. "I like you too, Sammie Jo. I believe I said that earlier, and that has not changed. If circumstances were different, I would find it most pleasant to join you in an extended excursion into the realms of love and passion. I—"

He cut himself off. He felt his heart race. He had been on the verge of saying he wanted her, immediately. He did. He felt madness in his veins, and his trousers suddenly seemed entirely too restrictive. He thought of her backed hard against the closest tree and his own passionate thrusts. He thought of his hands, her delicious breasts, and her cries of passion. Damn, he was tired and out of control. "But it looks like that journey will have to remain in the purview of the imagination. I have a job to do. I—"

It happened in a flash. She strode quickly forward, clasped her hands behind his neck and pulled him to her. She kissed him hard, wildly. Her lips were full and soft and he felt the firm muscles of her body press against his. Her breasts assaulted his chest, her calf muscles pressed hard against his thighs, and her feet locked behind his shins. Her delightfully wicked tongue flicked briefly into his mouth. His lower body responded strongly in the predictable way. The kiss probably lasted less than 20 seconds, but seemed a lifetime.

She let go abruptly and stepped back, leaving him with a startled expression. She laughed merrily, enjoying the fact she had shaken his aristocratic equanimity.

His stunned brain momentarily lost its ability to readily translate her dialect into the King's English and his ears heard her speech as a foreign tongue.

"Nahwah yah cayin't foahget me! I declayah, yah keyus lahk wahn mixed with fiah! Blayess yoah' haht, sugah plum, yoah ah prahm piece, ah reeahl fahn man 'neath all yoah hah fahlutin' tawahk and fa-ancy ayahs. Weeyush yah could stick ahrayownd, but ah gas yah got to do the bidness yoah bosses tayull yah. Wayone layast thing, Payunnywhissel, yah gaht ah fust nayum?"

"Sugar Plum?" He repeated it several times, in amused surprise. As his equanimity returned, he laughed heartily. He had been called many things in his time, chiefly relating to his mother's state of matrimony or beings from the nether regions, but had never been compared to an especially choice fruit. "It's Tom." He was not even so formal as to say

Thomas. Formality just seemed out of place with this mistress of the woods. "I will miss you, Sammie Jo, but you best be on your way."

She nodded at him and smiled briefly, then matter-of-factly shouldered her weapon. Two marine escorts stepped forward. They both smiled broadly, barely able to contain their laughter at seeing a human side to their captain's character. They knew women liked the captain, but they had never actually seen one storm his works. But then that was typical of Yankees; they never followed the rules. "Let's go!" she said brusquely. She glanced at them dismissively, then stalked in front of them toward the woods.

Just before she reached the tree line she turned and shouted merrily, "Y'all take care, Tom. Maybe I'll see you again after the war."

Or maybe a whole lot sooner, she thought. A man who kissed like that was as rare as spotting a wolverine in the open on a hot summer's day. She should head for home, but an inner voice told her it might be good to finish what they had started. Most men's passions were like firecrackers; easily given and quickly spent in one outburst of no particular significance. She sensed the Englishman's fire was of a different nature; difficult to ignite, but once kindled, one that burned with an enduring flame.

He watched as she disappeared into the woods. Her leonine walk pleased him greatly. Her buttocks swayed with a sensual grace that outshone the mincing movements of debutantes. He shook his head. He needed to banish the thought of her and resume his duties. And here came Dale with a marvelous prize procured from God knows where: a very large pitcher of fresh lemonade! There was no more welcome beverage on a hot summer's day.

"Found it all cold and ready to go on a farmhouse table," said Dale, forestalling any accusation. "Family probably left a few minutes before. We got here sooner than expected, and folk had to flee. I gather they used up their last supply of ice, rather than let us have it. But looks like the joke's on them."

Dale produced a large tumbler from his haversack and filled the glass. "Don't worry about me, sir. I had the other pitcher."

Pennywhistle gratefully drained most of the glass in a series of gulps. It tasted marvelously tart and cold, more exquisite than the best champagne. The ice probably had been brought from Maine the previous winter and been carefully stored in sawdust, since it was worth its weight in gold during high summer. He held his glass out for a refill, which Dale poured. The beverage rapidly cooled not only the heat of the day but the heat from Sammie Jo. He took a long gulp and brushed the cool glass slowly across his forehead.

CHAPTER NINETEEN

Ross and Cockburn both panned their glasses over the road into Bladensburg. It was empty of American defenders. The British columns had halted and were resting in such shade as they could find, awaiting the marching orders that would likely take them into battle. The two commanders furled their telescopes and looked at each other in wonderment.

"I don't understand it, Admiral," said Ross. "Bladensburg itself is largely deserted. Reconnaissance patrols report there are plenty of homes near the bridge that could be used to shelter snipers, to make our approach very hot, but not a one is occupied."

"I count it our good fortune that they have no one of Francis Marion's calibre today directing their actions. But what do you make of the bridge and how it is defended?"

"The bridge span looks to be about 120 feet. If we can push troops across quickly, we might be able to keep casualties to a minimum. It all depends on how aggressively the Americans defend their side. The water surrounding it is shallow enough that some men can wade across on either side of the span. Its marshy ground on the other side, and the terrain slopes gradually uphill."

"What about their artillery?" inquired Cockburn.

"They have four six-pounders covering the bridge, positioned on a rise of ground fifty yards back from the American side of the river. The rest of their guns are posted well to the rear. Once those six-pounders are dealt with, we should be able to advance. The American position is a giant triangle, with the apex of it pointed at the Bridge. The base is anchored on the Washington Turnpike. It looks to me as though the second and third lines are out of supporting distance from the first. If the American commander is not directly behind the first line, I doubt he will have much control over it. The fight at the river's edge will be almost a separate battle from what comes later."

"I wish we had some way to transport shipboard artillery to eliminate our disadvantage. It puts such a burden on the infantry," rumbled Cockburn. "Yet I am in high hopes Captain Pennywhistle might be able to provide some relief on that score. I am also sanguine about the results of the fight ahead. The best explanation I can devise for the American foolishness is the perils of divided command. Our intelligence people report every general on their side is a law unto himself. They scarcely communicate, let alone coordinate their plans. A problem we do not have, thanks to your modesty and generous nature."

Ross acknowledged the compliment with a nod. "I believe you are right about our prospects, Admiral. At any rate, here come Captain Smith and Colonel Thornton. Their reports are critical, although they often disagree."

Captain Harry Smith was not pleased. He had argued the whole way to headquarters with Lieutenant Colonel Thornton. They had both seen the same thing, but had drawn very different conclusions. Both were experienced veterans of the Peninsular War, but whereas Smith believed in thorough preparation and careful maneuver; Thornton was inclined to go straight at them, trusting to shock and élan. Smith was inclined to wait a bit and see; Thornton usually favored immediate and forceful action. Each believed in the innate superiority of his own approach and would argue passionately for it. Smith expected a heated discussion ahead, but he knew Thornton respected Ross; no good soldier could fail to, and both of them would abide by their commander's decision.

Both men stood smartly to attention upon reaching Ross and gave crisp salutes. He returned them. They favored Cockburn with a respectful bobbing of heads.

"Good morning, gentlemen. The Admiral and I should like to hear your reports. Colonel Thornton, as you are senior, you will go first. Please begin. You have our undivided attention."

"Thank you, sir. We can carry the bridge without difficulty. It would be my honor to be the first across. Their six-pounders could be a problem; their fire should be able to sweep the bridge, but I think they built the barbettes incorrectly. The earthworks are just a tad too high for the barrels. They are going to have to adjust the quoins to elevate the barrels and I think it will send the rounds high. The earthworks will also retard their ability to reposition their pieces once we are across. One of my officers reported something odd about the American ammunition. It all looked to be round shot, not very good against soldiers on a bridge. I suspect a battery well to the rear received their consignment of canister.

"The danger to us is more imaginary than real. It might be different if we were facing the French, but the Americans don't look like much. Their dispositions are unsound, and I don't think their morale is good. We can chop them up piecemeal. There are some houses on our side that our men could use as shelters to furnish covering fire to the men on the bridge. The ground on their side is low and marshy, no obstacle to an advance. An orchard lies a few hundred yards ahead. After the first line is broken we could regroup at the orchard, where we would be shielded from the rest of their forces. We could advance from there against the remaining lines. I think the fugitives from the first line will do a lot to help us. Their retreat will panic the remaining troops. It's just a matter of the hounds staying locked on the hares."

"What about our numbers, Colonel? The rest of our troops have not fully arrived, and only your brigade is ready for immediate attack."

"Against experienced troops sir, I'd say that would be a valid concern, but the Americans are just as hot and tired as we are, a sight worse led, and inexperienced to boot. Our scouts report more men are arriving from Washington by the hour, so every minute we delay means greater numbers arrayed against us. They expect time to rest and regroup, and I think it important we not give them that luxury. What we would gain with additional troops is outweighed by the shock value of a well designed immediate attack. Our numbers may improve with passing hours, but their will too, and the Americans are off balance right now, so I think it the moment most propitious for attack."

Ross nodded and turned to Smith. "Colonel Thornton has made some meritorious arguments, but I should like to hear your take on the matter. From you expression, I gather you disagree with him?"

Smith spoke with quiet conviction. "I agree with the Colonel on certain particulars, but I think it is a mistake to go into battle with one boot off. Even with all of our men present, they outnumber us more than two to one. We should wait until all of our forces have arrived. It is possible Colonel Thornton is right, but if we are patient we can still achieve victory, and at smaller cost. His approach makes victory far more problematic than mine." He pointedly ignored the glare Thornton shot at him.

"I don't like to risk everything on one throw of the dice. I also like to make sure I know exactly what game I am entering into. We need to scout the bridge area far more thoroughly than we have. I know it will alert the Americans to our intentions, but I am sure Colonel Thornton will allow that even the Americans can discern we must attack somewhere in the vicinity.

"We believe the water is fordable on either side of the bridge, but we must be sure, not trust to allegedly informed speculation.

"We also need some kind of diversionary attack, one that will take the pressure and attention off Colonel Thornton. I would suggest it be to the north of his thrust, aimed at the American flank on the Washington Turnpike. We need to make it strong enough to be convincing and close enough to be turned into the main attack if the colonel runs into trouble. We could use some of Colonel Brooke's brigade.

"Above all, we must think of the men. I have lost five men to sunstroke and I am certain Colonel Thornton has lost men as well. There is only so much men can take, no matter how gallant their hearts. We need some time, even a little, to halt and compose ourselves. I counsel rest for the troops on the field while we await the remainder on the march. We must take our time and get things right. Surely, a few hours delay cannot be of much account when measured against the welfare of our men."

Ross was lost in thought, his left hand slowly massaging his chin as he weighed a variety of considerations. "Gentlemen, I thank you for your impressions and counsel. Both are valuable. However, I lack one piece of vital information which I believe one of Admiral Cockburn's officers will soon supply. I can make no decision until he gives his report. He should be along in the next few minutes. Until then, the admiral and I will need some privacy to discuss all that you have told us. I will send for you just as soon as I have made my decision. Until then, gentlemen, I bid you good day."

Smith and Thornton saluted Ross and departed. Ross missed the brief glare the two men exchanged; if they had been younger and less civilized, they would have kicked each other.

"What do you think, Admiral?"

"I tend to agree with Colonel Thornton, but you are quite correct, you need Mr. Pennywhistle's report. Ah, he has a superior sense of timing; here he is approaching." Cockburn walked toward Pennywhistle and favored him with a genuine smile. He shook his hand heartily, even before the marine had a chance to salute.

"I am delighted to see you again, Captain," said Ross. "We met briefly a few days ago, but you are a difficult man to forget. I gather you have been quite busy the past few days. I should like to hear an account of your adventures, but time grows short and I would hope you could avoid prolixity. Please begin your report."

Pennywhistle was tired and a concise rendering of his travels was all he could manage anyway. He knew he was not here for a commendation, but only because of his experience with the rockets. He explained the particulars of his assault on the militia regiment matter-of-factly and added, "We aimed the Congreves carefully and their flight parabolas were as I'd predicted. If I had time, I would make a trifling adjustment on the dorsal fins, but as they are, they should function well, and their flight pattern will be reflective of the exactitude of aim of their operators. "With the addition of fins, not only can they be fired accurately, their range is increased by a fourth beyond their usual outside range of 3,000 yards. I gather, however, most of your needs will be for ranges under a mile, no greater than that of a conventional 12-pounder. Am I correct in my assumption, General?"

"You are indeed, Captain. The American third line is just under a mile from the first. But mostly the rockets will be needed for two decisive salvos on the American first line; that range will likely be around three hundred yards. How will these contraptions work against a battery of artillery?"

"A mile is easy enough with the new fins, and three hundred yards is child's play against a packed body of men. Hitting a fixed target such as a gun battery should present no problems. Indeed, the increased accuracy of these modified rockets furnishes you a choice, General. We can certainly destroy or disable the guns, but it occurs to me you may want to capture rather than wreck them, then train their muzzles on their former owners. If that is the case, we can cut the fuses a bit shorter to have them detonate above the gunners to kill the men and spare the cannon. We only need instructions about your preferences.

"The only problem I foresee is limited numbers. We have only ten altered rockets left, and there will not be time to modify any more of them."

Ross's thoughtful face had brightened as he listened. "Excellent, Mr. Pennywhistle, excellent! That is precisely what I wanted to hear. I should like you and the Rocket Troop to report to Colonel Thornton at the earliest possible moment and place yourself under his command. Tell him he will receive detailed instructions within the hour. I will dispatch Major George to take over the Marine Brigade."

"Thank you, sir. I will do just that. I appreciate the confidence you repose in me and my contrivances, and neither I nor they will disappoint." He saluted crisply and departed at a brisk, purposeful walk.

"He seems very sure of himself and his invention," commented Ross. "I like him, but sometimes enthusiastic officers exaggerate. It is a natural enough failing when they present something they have themselves devised. They are not dishonest, they simply get carried away. Dare I trust him, Admiral?"

"If Captain Pennywhistle says something is true, you may absolutely rely on it. He never advances an idea until he has thought it through and considered its permutations from a variety of perspectives. When he first mentioned the modifications to me I was most encouraged, but he warned me that they needed a field test. He gave them one in short order and reported the results. He is a thoroughly ingenious officer but he is also a very careful one. He is not like some clever men, bursting with strange ideas, but without the resolve or method to test them to see if they bear practical fruit.

"It also occurs to me that his modified rockets may confer an additional advantage. The Americans believe they understand the Congreves, and to an extent they do. Experienced officers have probably told their men of their inaccuracy. When raw troops discover that at least some of the Congreves are indeed accurate, it will greatly undermine the faith they have placed in their officers. Better yet, they may imagine them not to be Congreves at all, but some newly created infernal weapon of terror. Either alternative will work to our benefit."

"Thank you for that testimonial, Admiral. I think we may have just remedied our defect of artillery."

CHAPTER TWENTY

John Tracy kept his voice crisp and authoritative. His assembled marines had heard this talk before, but repetition of home truths reassured men under stress and kept important details fresh in their minds. He was careful to use phrases that were easily remembered. Battle was sheer chaos, an unrelenting assault on the ears, mind, and soul. Men did little thinking; they performed rote actions based on instinct sharpened by training.

He walked down the line as he spoke and made eye contact with every man, the gaze letting each marine know his commander reposed special trust in his conduct in the battle ahead. Men assured of their commander's confidence would go to superhuman lengths never to disappoint that man.

"Marines, check your flints. Make sure the edge is sharp, true, and uniform. Let's keep misfires to a minimum. Have two spares ready for immediate use. Never expect more than twenty shots from even a Brandon." The men smiled; English flints came from one small town; they were the best in the world, but a great luxury a marine was unlikely to enjoy. "You are going to be doing a lot of firing today; every man with sixty rounds, twenty-eight in the top tray. Keep checking your cartouches, signal when you run low.

"Squad replenishment men: cast a weather eye on the reserve ammunition carts every few minutes. Make sure your powder monkeys maintain a steady supply of cartridges coming forward.

"We're using buck and ball to give us extra punch today. Each cartridge has 125 grains, not the usual 100. Be prepared for the extra kick and make sure your piece is seated firmly against your shoulder.

"Do things the right way, as you were trained. No shortcuts. No dropping balls down the barrel; make sure your ball and shot are wrapped in the cartridge husk and fit snugly against the sides of the barrel. We don't want balls bouncing randomly and going God knows where. Ram your charge home hard, and make certain it is firmly seated atop the powder. No standing ramrods in the dirt between shots; if we shift quickly you will lose them. Use your vent picks after every tenth round, and keep your touch hole clear.

"Don't fire until you can see the warts on their faces, but don't aim at them. Shoot for the kneecaps, so your rounds will take the bloodybacks in their chests. If the barrel gets too hot to handle, wrap your cleaning rag around your hand or piss down the barrel to cool it off. We don't want our fire to slacken.

"Front rank will kneel with the first two volleys. After that, everyone fires upright in case we have the chance to advance with the bayonet. At 'Lock On' open a firing space to the right for the man standing behind you and give him plenty of room. Ignore the wounded; leave them to the stretcher bearers. Step over them if you have to; make room for the file closers. We don't want any gaps in our line.

"Make sure your bayonets are sharp, not just the point but the edges. If you can't draw blood with a touch of your finger on the tip, see the armorer and have him run it over the whetstone wheel a few more times.

"Battle is a hot and thirsty business. Drink lots of water; it will help stop your lips from cracking and bleeding after biting a score of cartridges. No man will wear his stock today. Splash a little water on your neck from time to time.

"Sergeants, keep the lines as straight as you can and close any gaps quickly. Keep the men in the gully; it gives some protection from enemy fire. Make sure every marine has adequate space to fire; I want no accidental deaths from our own volleys. Shoot any man who runs. Wait; belay that order. There is not a man before me today who will give way even under the hottest fire. Place your chosen men with rifles on the flanks. Have them aim for the reflected sunlight on the officers' gorgets.

"Corporals: Heatstroke will be a problem today; make sure the water butts to your rear are filled to the brim. Tell your designated powder monkeys to be alert when a man signals his canteen is empty. Keep them constantly filling canteens and shuttling them forward.

"Bandsmen: music inspires men to great deeds, so play as loud as you can for as long as you can. Remember your motto. *Nulli secundi*: marine bandsmen are second to none, and I want the enemy to know that! When you can no longer be heard, stow your instruments and report to the rear as stretcher bearers.

"Followers: you women should not be anywhere near battle, but I have too much respect for your honest hearts and steady courage to order you away from those you hold dear. I do ask you to stay out of the line of fire. Keep making bandages and patch up the walking wounded as best you can. Help the more severely wounded to the surgeon. Assist the bandsman as stretcher bearers.

"Finally, all marines must answer the summons of nature before the battle; clear your bladders and your bowels in the latrine over yonder. If you piss yourself in battle, forget about it and keep on shooting! Better yet, piss down your barrel and clear the fouling."

A few men grinned at that, and one elbowed a neighbor who had embarrassed himself wetly the first time he'd been shot at.

Business was done, and the marines looked resolute and ready, but Tracy could not resist adding a final flourish.

"Our cause is just, our training sound, our courage unmatched. Our honor is unblemished, our spirits unbowed, and our duty clear. We will never kneel before a foreign oppressor, and woe betide an army that tries to make us do so. Few on our side today have your discipline and experience: Our Capital and the Republic itself are depending on you for their salvation. Many generations of posterity will remember your conduct with pride. I consider myself a lucky man to command such stalwart hearts."

"Huzzah for the Captain and the Corps!" One marine shouted, and a second later the entire line roared its approval. "Hip hip huzzah! Hip hip huzzah! Hip hip huzzah!" The marines cheered heartily, but when the cheering stopped their faces became the indomitable masks of avenging angels.

"Make the lobsters pay for what they done to my Molly!" shouted a young woman made old by grief.

Tracy's 200 men were ready. He had received a few last minute reinforcements from the Naval Yard, courtesy of his friend Captain Tingey, and they were positioned to protect Barney's big guns and launch at least a limited counter-stroke. If the enemy tried moving around the American left, they were in for a hot reception. The militia units on his left and right appeared somewhat more disciplined than expected. At least they were eager. There was really nothing more to do.

Confident as he was about what to do in the fight ahead, he was much less so about his conduct earlier in the morning. A well-manicured man in a finely tailored black frock coat had approached him just after reveille. He had greeted Tracy by name and discreetly flashed a ring with the omega symbol. Tracy had put his own alongside as the countersign.

The well-manicured man had asked Tracy to call him Polydectes—the Knights had a penchant for Greek mythology —and inquired if there was someplace they could speak privately. Polydectes proved a perfect name for the man, considering what he asked of Tracy. He wanted Tracy to slay a metaphorical Gorgon, or at least be prepared to do so should certain circumstances occur. That Gorgon was the President himself.

Polydectes had tried to make the unthinkable sound reasonable. He'd explained that if the upcoming battle went against the Americans, Washington would likely fall, and the government might well collapse. The Knights had made preparations for such an eventuality, but the President might prove an obstacle. With Madison dead, the country in crisis, and the American People clamoring for leadership, Great Men of Affairs would step forward to fill the void. They could force this ill conceived and pernicious war to a speedy conclusion.

Given Madison's penchant for inserting himself and his cabinet personally into military matters, it was quite likely he would be present upon the field today. With hails of bullets flying it was easy for an unlucky bystander to catch a bullet in the head; the source of that bullet would remain forever unknown.

If Americans looked likely to win the day, Tracy was to do nothing. If things were going badly, Tracy was to act. The Knights trusted his military acumen to determine the course and select the method and moment of the President's demise.

Tracy had been shocked to his very core by the proposal but summoned all of his willpower and kept his face bland and unreadable. This was treason, pure and simple, no matter what artful words the conspirators used to legitimize their treachery. Their design was a betrayal of everything his oath stood for and the entire glorious experiment that was the Republic.

Nevertheless, he'd played along and given his assent, stipulating two conditions to which the Knight's representative readily agreed: he wanted to meet with the group at the earliest possible moment, and with Polydectes in Washington City on the morrow.

He had realized that if he had said no, the conspirators likely had a substitute killer in mind. To baffle their design, he simply had to do nothing. If his side lost today, he would simply claim he had had no opportunities and would maintain contact with the group. He was determined to discover the name of every one of these lurking vipers and see that they were publicly exposed as traitors.

The conspiracy and conspirators would have to wait for now. He had a battle to fight and marines to lead. Besides, a victory today might well prevent the Knight's engine of destruction from even starting up.

After his meeting with the well-manicured man, it had taken Tracy an hour to find Stansbury and give his reconnaissance report. The general had listened half-heartedly, and Tracy had realized his careful observations were wasted on the man; nevertheless, the general had said he would pass them on to Winder. Winder seemed a ghost; haunting every officer's talk, but seen nowhere. Open-minded militia officers welcomed up-to-date information, but both Stansbury and Winder seemed beguiled by the hare-brained observations of Madison's cabinet, particularly the esteemed James Monroe.

He cursed both generals under his breath, feeling that he and his men were lions led by donkeys. Stansbury had ignored his tactful suggestions of blowing the bridge, anchoring the front line under cover of the orchard, and compressing the three lines into two within supporting distance of the other. His observation that the six-pounders covering the bridge needed to trust to mobility rather than earthen protection for safety had been met with a raised eyebrows and a long, exasperated sigh of condescension: how dare a junior officer correct the great man!

He wanted no part in killing the President, but a puckish voice suggested the greatest service he could render the American cause would be shooting James Monroe. He amused himself thinking of ways that it might be accomplished, but with luck the man would get himself killed through his own military stupidity. What truly bothered him was the mentality that pervaded the American command. Save for himself, Miller, and Barney, no one seemed to have any plan for victory; everything was predicated on merely avoiding defeat. No one thought to form a reserve for a counter attack, because none was contemplated. The whole American design could be summed up succinctly: "Hold your ground and hope for the best."

Music brought Tracy back to the present moment. The wind shifted slightly, carrying the sounds of fife and drums to his ears. He heard "British Grenadiers" distinctly. A second later the sound swelled as a small band equipped with bassoons, clarinets, and horns joined in. He unshipped his glass and saw neatly spaced red ranks and flapping silk regimental banners. The carefully cadenced pounding of the drums and the disciplined tramp of thousands of feet impressed him in spite of himself. The Redcoats might have been drained by the heat, but their step was disciplined. Officers marched alongside, although a few were mounted.

They marched in three distinct columns at the quarter distance, each column containing one brigade. The front of each column was sixty feet across, with fifteen feet separating each company from the next. Each column extended 150 feet from front to rear. It was a common arrangement used going into battle, although Tracy seldom used it, since his marines were usually deployed in small detachments on shipboard.

The Redcoats carried their muskets in the support arms position, their bayonets already fixed. The sunlight glinted off the cold steel in quick, bright flashes, which gave the effect of a canopy of dancing fireflies. He recognized the column contained a lot of light infantry and assumed they would deploy into a much looser order quite soon.

The column was chiefly useful for moving large bodies of troops from place to place swiftly, but he knew it would transform into an extended line once battle was joined. The column had great shock value, but the line allowed far more firepower. Nobody in America used columns for battle. That happened only in Europe where there was more open terrain. The broken terrain of America was more congenial to small groups of infantry advancing in loose order.

Artillery was not usually a large factor in battles in America, but could be today if only the Americans had the wit to use their superiority properly. Tracy wished he could repose the same confidence in the militia that he had in the Marine and Navy gunners.

Now came the hardest part of battle: the waiting; standing ready and eager to act, but not permitted to do so until the proper orders came through. With the elusive Winder in charge, those orders might be a long time in coming. The man seemed to change his mind with the speed of a weathervane in a high wind.

Tracy felt the usual symptoms. Adrenaline shot through his veins, galvanized his body for action, but since action was forbidden, it resulted in a heavy, unpleasant feeling akin to hangover nausea. Sweaty palms, parched lips, pounding temples, and arid nostrils plagued him. His eyeballs felt like grapes in a wine press and his joints ached, almost as if under attack by arthritis. Fingers and toes burned with tingling sensations. His skin felt dry and itched. White-hot heat added to the misery. Finally being allowed to fire, run, slash, or take any physical action would bring blessed relief.

He enjoyed one advantage over his men. They had to stand fast, but he was able to pace back and forth and burn off some of the excess energy. He reviewed his preparations and searched his mind to see if he had forgotten anything.

He did not think he had. In frustration, he sat down with a whet stone and began methodically running his sword back and forth over its surface. The blade already had a good edge, but the rhythmic motions served to calm his mind and focus his attentions on the task ahead.

Sammie Jo walked briskly out of the forest and onto a prosperous farm. The fields were neat and well tended, the large barn recently painted, and the ox-blood-red saltbox home sported a brand new roof. She could do with a drink and thought the farm's owners might supply her with one, since she had news about the invaders.

She found the front door ajar. She knocked, then hailed the occupants. When no one answered, she cautiously entered. The furniture was sturdy but plain. Everything was supremely clean and orderly. All in all, she guessed the owners were Mennonites, commonly called Amish. She inventoried the contents of the place for several minutes, realized the owners were teetotalers, then left and walked over to the barn. She made a thorough inspection and found it contained a black, drearily featureless buggy that confirmed her suspicions. Anyone driving it would be pegged as Amish.

She walked around the barnyard and noted the animals had been recently fed. The owners must have departed only a few hours earlier. It made sense. The Mennonites were pacifists and every bit as opposed to war as the Quakers. She had just been given a remarkable opportunity.

Her father had told her she had a contrarian streak and she realized it was never on better display than at the present moment. She should do as the Englishman asked and walk away from the war, but the Englishman's remarks had excited her ingenuity rather than her caution. She would honor her pledge to spare Pennywhistle's life; her father had impressed upon her the sanctity of a man's word. Besides, she found him exciting.

However, that promise did not extend to other British officers. The lessons of the forest could be made to serve the considerations of civilization. She needed to be a chameleon, adopt protective cover, fire from concealment. She must blend in with her surroundings and excite neither curiosity nor interest.

She knew her beauty sometimes struck men and they felt moved to misbehave, so she had to appear as dull and unremarkable as possible. She also needed a way to hide her weapon. She re-entered the home and rifled through the drawers of the chest in the main bedroom until she found what she wanted: a severe, high-collared dress several sizes too big for her, if not quite long enough, in a very unattractive shade of matte black. It had an ample belly. Perfect. She also found a black bonnet that was as unfashionable as it was ugly.

The British found the Amish exotic and strange and gave them a wide berth. The locals tended to grant them wide leeway as well, since they kept to themselves, made no objections to slavery, and paid their taxes punctually. Tensions might be heightened and nerves frayed by war, but there was sufficient chivalry on both sides to allow a pregnant Amish woman to pass unmolested.

Fifteen minutes after her decision, she finished her final preparations. She used straw to stuff the dress, then found some brown bits of old grease in an iron spider near the main hearth and dabbed them carefully under her eyes and cheeks. They would simulate age lines aggravated by hard work. She scooped up some soot from the fireplace and ran her fingers through her blonde hair. The streaks of grey would complement the haggard face nicely. She looked in a small cracked mirror and laughed.

She harnessed an old, sway-backed, brown nag to the small buggy, then made sure the requisite black blinders were in place near his eyes. It was not like the horse was going to make a mad dash to freedom; those days must have passed when the Old Testament was young, but it was important to keep up appearances as a conservative Mennonite. She stowed her rifle and possibles bag carefully beneath her seat.

She knew the roads in the area and decided not to seek the byways, but the main road. She had heard that pipsqueak Spottswood mention Bladensburg; she would make for that town. She would do the opposite of hiding. Rather, she would hide in plain sight! It would give her a good opportunity to observe the military situation first hand. She might even find Pennywhistle. That made her smile. He certainly would never look twice at a pregnant, prematurely aged Amish woman!

"Hyaah! Hyaah!" she yelled and slapped the small whip forward with a light but decisive touch. The horse jerked for a second, then broke into a walking pace. The buggy gained the main road.

Ten minutes later, she pulled abreast of the red-coated column, now bivouacked under pine trees with most of the men fast asleep. She felt an unexpected pang of sympathy for their weariness. She saw Pennywhistle walking along the edge of the improvised camp and talking to an NCO. Good God, did the man ever sleep?

She barely suppressed a guffaw when she passed him and he touched his hat in deference. She bowed her head, as if she were a timid Mennonite, and applied the whip. Five minutes later, she passed another group of Redcoats, then found herself entering an eerily deserted Bladensburg.

She had never cottoned much to the Bible despite her father's best efforts, but she remembered the story of Sodom and Gomorrah and decided Bladensburg resembled them in a way. No salt pillars presented themselves, but it was as if some divine hand had intervened to wipe the place of noise and life. Of course it was just people acting sensibly and fleeing a storm. She halted the buggy.

She looked around carefully for a perch. She decided a home on the edge of town was better than a home in the center. She needed a clear field of fire and plenty of time to observe the approaching columns and line up her shot. The leaders would be on horseback; outsized and inviting targets.

She had made two mistakes earlier. She had been beguiled by an enemy officer and it angered her, although a recollection of his face brought warmth to her loins. But she had been completely wrong in choosing him as a target. She wanted high stakes, not middling ones. She was just one woman with a gun, but if that gun were pointed at the right man, that woman could make a big difference. And right now the American Army needed all the help it could get.

Armies were like the packs of wild dogs she had encountered on occasion in the woods. Each one had a leader. It made sense to kill the top dog, not a mere follower. The army's top dog was Ross, but the real driving force behind the invasion was that devil Cockburn. It would be quite a feather in her cap if she killed the most hated man in America. She had no idea what he looked like, but guessed his uniform would be elaborate and easy to identify. She certainly knew Pennywhistle, and she thought it likely he would meet with Cockburn in the very near future. She could use him as a lure.

She selected an abandoned two-story red brick residence half a mile from the bridge. She tied horse and buggy to a hitching post in the rear, making note of a road that led out of town. Once inside, she found a large bay window on the second floor that gave a clear view of the main road and settled in behind it. She shed her Amish guise and donned her brown woolen shirt and bib and brace overalls. She felt much more comfortable dressed thusly than as a shy, retiring pacifist. She laid out her gear, then tested the window lintel as a firing stand. She could probably only manage one shot, although it was faintly possible she could get off a second. She would take Pennywhistle's advice and go for the torso shot rather than the more spectacular head shot. She smiled.

She heard fifes and drums and looked up to see Redcoats marching purposefully toward her. The first company of them would trudge past her perch in just a few minutes. She wormed out her rifle's touch-hole, inserted a new flint, and loaded her weapon with loving care. She had not long to wait. Cockburn had not long to live.

CHAPTER TWENTY-ONE

The entire war had resolved itself down into one small nexus; an unremarkable bridge spanning a shallow, muddy river. War had an odd way of immortalizing obscure places as it transformed them into sites of strategic moment. The destiny of the capital rested on the fate of the Bladensburg Bridge over the Anacostia. It was only one hundred and twenty-one feet in length, but it bridged the last natural barrier to an advance on Washington. If the Americans controlled it, it was a shield; if the British, a sword.

"Damn it! Why is the President out here exposing himself to risk?" demanded a choleric Barney. "He isn't inspiring anyone. He's a distraction; making us worry about him when all we should be concerned with is licking the Redcoats. I wish he would leave fighting to fighting men and stick to governing. Writing a constitution is not the same thing as writing battle orders." Barney's voice fluctuated between concern and contempt. "I see Monroe is with him today. That's very bad for us. Probably means some more last minute shifts of our positions."

President Madison was on horseback several hundred yards behind Barney's guns and in animated discussion with Monroe and Secretary of War Armstrong. Monroe pointed toward the Bladensburg Bridge.

"That's the whole problem with this War, Commodore," said Miller glumly. "Amateurs led by amateurs; civilians playing soldier and looking for glory without work or risk. We professionals are always the last to be consulted. Have you seen Winder in the last few hours?"

"No, I haven't," replied Barney with asperity. "He's probably out on some exceptionally important errand that will turn out to be of trifling importance. You'd think even an idiot like Winder would realize that with battle imminent, his place is here with his men. Still, his absence might not be a bad thing. At least he can't issue any more stupid orders."

"The burden is on us, Commodore. With no strength or wit at the top, we will have to supply firmness and resolution. Did you have any luck speaking to Stansbury about my idea of a counterstroke?"

"None at all," said Barney in exasperation. "That man may not be a fool like Winder, but he is the soul of timidity. He is far more concerned with not losing a battle than he is with winning one. All he could say was, 'We must stand firm.' I told him twice yesterday and once today, for God's sake, at least blow the bridge. Make it easier for us to defend our ground." Barney pointed to the bridge. "Obviously, I had no success."

Miller's eyes brightened. "Perhaps, Commodore, even at this late hour, we might be able to remedy that defect of action. There is not time to blow the bridge, but there might still be time to hobble the British. Some marines with boarding axes could do real damage to the planking."

"That's a splendid idea, Miller. One advantage of having no real guiding hand is that it makes it easier for underlings to act. Pick your men, sir, and send them on their way!"

Spottswood carried out a brief inspection of Pennywhistle's company, now his. The men appeared cheerful and expectant, despite the heat. He checked weapons and bayonets, and talked briefly with senior NCOs. His men were to be held in close reserve, to exploit any breakthroughs. He formed the men into column and they trotted forward using the Moore quickstep. The need for haste was paramount. Advance elements of the army had just made contact with the enemy. They joined the rest of the Marine Brigade and marched directly astern of Brooke's Brigade.

Tracy watched the President through his glass and wished the man had had the good sense to stay in Washington. As he panned his glass he noticed a marine officer on horseback several hundred yards astern of Madison. He got a good look at the man's face but did not recognize it. That bothered him. The Corps was small enough that he knew virtually all of its officers. Why would someone impersonate a marine?

He puzzled over it for a minute, then a dark expression crossed his face. The Knights of The Golden Horse Shoe were hedging their bet. They had put a second assassin in place in case Tracy failed to act. Damn those fools!

He would not only have to lead his men today but ensure Madison survived the battle. As if he didn't have enough to worry about!

He had a strong feeling he would face his nemesis Pennywhistle today. A man like that would find a way to be in the forefront of battle. He looked forward to it. He had reasoned out who he was. He disliked the conclusion, but it was the only one that explained his adoptive parent's reticence to discuss his paternal background.

Manton had the light company of the 4th ready to launch. They would be inserted as close support after the first wave had attacked. His stomach lurched and his heart beat far too fast, yet rather than frightening him, the signs reassured him. You had to be fully alive and alert to have such reactions. He had survived Salamanca and fought his way through Spain and France because fear kept a man alive. His heartbeat steadied and his outward commands issued crisp and clear. He saw confidence in the man's faces and knew that his manner had reassured them. The contents of his stomach no longer seemed in need of immediate discharge. His facade was pure play acting, but he had learned from a master.

Bill Adams had been assigned as a powder monkey to one of the big eighteen-pounders protecting Barney's flank. For the third time today, he carefully checked all of his cartridge boxes to make sure they were full. He would not have any one say that he had been less than diligent. He was only seventeen, but after the fight on the *Lucky Lady* he considered himself a veteran. He fingered the bandage covering his slight wound of two days before. He felt pain but also satisfaction that he had a souvenir of facing down the hated British. He had never been so scared as he was now, but he had never been so proud either. He was fighting with the best, with US Marines, defending the Capital itself. He wished his folks could see him. He wanted them to know he was no longer a boy, but a man. More than that, a man who did not flinch under fire. He could hear British bandsmen in the distance and knew the opening round of the big battle would come very soon.

"I ain't never been so proud," said Isaac to Gabriel. "First time I get to wear the red suit and I aim to make the most of it." He spoke his words without a hint of the stutter that had plagued him all of his life. Being free of the stress of slavery had unexpected benefits. Isaac and Gabriel both wore uniforms and marched alongside Manton's men as guides, since they knew all of the local roads and possible places where the Americans might spring an ambush.

"I told you the cap'n would come through for us," said Gabriel. " It's up to us to prove he wasn't wrong about us. We finally got a chance to show that today it's us who hold the whip hand. Let's be heroes today!" He reached inside his coat pocket and extracted a deck of cards. He dropped them onto the road. A hero had to get right with the Lord, and cards and gambling were the devil's tools.

O'Laughlin nervously patted Blarney on the head. Blarney responded with vigorous tail wagging. In the short time the dog had been in his care, the animal had become his best friend. The beast was loyal, smart, and brave. O'Laughlin had a strong presentiment of his own death in the battle ahead. He accepted it with the fatalism of the career soldier, yet he was deeply worried that there would be no one to care for this fine animal when he was gone. Perhaps Crouchback might stand in for him. The choleric

Cockney had shown affection for the dog that he had never shown for people. He would speak to the fellow in the next few minutes.

Dale patiently watched the bridge, hidden in a small copse of elm trees two hundred yards from its east end. His task was to see the bridge remained intact until the first British forces arrived. He'd brought plenty of ammunition to stop anyone from laying charges. "Hold until relieved," Pennywhistle had instructed him.

He was taking a risk wearing civilian clothes. He was very mindful of the fate Chalmers almost met, but it was the only way he could reach this vantage point without being identified as an enemy by the American army arrayed on the other side. However, once in position he donned a very odd looking piece of attire that rendered him nearly invisible.

It was a ghillie suit. Essentially a net covering the entire body, made of burlap, cloth, and twine and covered with leaves and foliage, it was designed to make the wearer indistinguishable from the terrain. Ghillie suits originally had been developed by gamekeepers in Scotland as portable hides for stalking deer. Pennywhistle was familiar with them from his boyhood, and he had helped Dale construct one upon his arrival in the Chesapeake. He had told Dale he was certain it would come in handy in the heavily wooded terrain.

Dale could hear the distant music of approaching British bandsmen and knew he had not long to wait. To his great surprise, no one on the American side had bothered to lay any charges. A group of twenty or so militia had made a half-hearted attempt to demolish the bridge with axes an hour ago, but he had put them to flight after killing three of their number. Ill-disciplined amateurs were easily terrified by random death dispatched from an unidentified source.

He found it very peculiar that the Americans had not undertaken a far more systematic attempt at demolition hours before. Their army across the river looked ready for battle, but why had they not positioned themselves on the high ground on his side of the river? That was what Mr. Pennywhistle would have done.

He had done his job, but something ate at him. An Amish woman dressed in black driving an old buggy had passed him as he walked through a town emptied of its 1,500 inhabitants. Why would a member of a sect of pacifists be heading *into* a battle zone instead of fleeing it? It made no sense. And there was something familiar about the woman. She was fat with child, but exceptionally tall. She had whipped the horse forward with an experienced hand, and there was something in the graceful movement of the long arm he had seen before. He struggled to place it.

No, it could not be! And after the captain had spared her life! That nasty woodland witch had donned a disguise and was back to cause mischief. She was bold as a bordello madam and deadly as a viper. She would not be hunting small stuff. My God! Sammie Jo was going for Ross or Cockburn! He had to warn them!

Just then he caught sight of a small column of blue approaching the bridge—US Marines with axes. Damn, they would be much harder to frighten off. He had to stay put and complete his mission. His captain said every problem had a solution, but Dale could not see how he could be in two places at once. One thing at a time; something would come to him. He sighted his Baker on the man leading the column and fired.

A scout breathlessly reported in to Ross. "Bridge still stands, sir."

Ross was dumbfounded. "I cannot believe this stroke of luck, or that even Americans would be this stupid. An avenue of advance into the heart of their country left wide open. A dagger if you will, we have but to push!"

"You must not expect luck if you are not bold, and we have certainly been that," answered Cockburn. "Let us finish this business and make their capital ours!"

Drummers and buglers sounded the advance.

The Royal Marine Rocket Troop entered the outskirts of Bladensburg. They advanced in proud confidence, knowing they had a surprise for the Americans. Pennywhistle smiled with satisfaction; his modifications would make a real difference today. But a second later he frowned as his right index finger twitched slightly. Damn, that had never happened *before* a battle! He clamped his left hand over it in frustration. For some reason Sammie Jo's face slipped into his mind and the twitching stopped. He told himself thoughts of coitus were natural before battle; better to dream of an act which created life than worry about the acts ahead which extinguished it.

He hoped Sammie Jo had had the good sense to heed his warning and return home. But she was headstrong and might not act according to the logic he prized. She might be like one of the boomerangs from the Botany Bay colony which came back at you after being tossed away. He wondered why he was so concerned for the fate of a bumpkin girl he hardly knew. He wanted to put it down to simple lust; he had not been with a woman for some time. But something beyond lust stirred when he recalled the nickname she had given him, Sugar Plum. It was charming, endearing even. "Sugar Plum, sugar plum," he murmured idly as pleasant visions danced in his head. Then he scowled. "Humbug, nothing but humbug." He had been spinning himself a dangerous fantasy. He had no future with such a woman and was glad he likely would never meet her again.

Sammie Jo could see Cockburn clearly now. His black and gold uniform was distinctive. She could do this. It would be her crowning achievement as a long hunter and sharp-shooter. She would bask in glory and might even harvest his head to claim the reward. And yet, an insistent voice in her head, one that she did not want to hear, keened: *What would Pennywhistle think? What would Pennywhistle think?* She hesitated as she saw his face in her mind and cursed herself for her weakness. He had told her battle was a soul-destroying experience to be avoided, that once you passed through its madness you would be forever changed. Had he been exaggerating, trying to frighten her off? Or had he been telling the truth?

The British fifes and drums grew louder, and she knew she was about to find out for herself.

THE END

The end of "Blue Water, Scarlet Tide" but Tom Pennywhistle will return in "Capital's Punishment."

AUTHOR'S NOTES

The United States was never so badly prepared and unready for a war as she was for the War of 1812. When America declared war, the Navy numbered 20 ships and the Army's actual present-for-duty strength was under 10,000 men. The Navy was professional, with a solid cadre of talented officers, but the Army was amateurish, poorly officered, and the victim of years of neglect. The United States faced an opponent with the largest Navy in the world, more than 700 ships, and a trained Army with more than 100,000 effective fighting men. The US Navy had experience from the Barbary Wars, but the last major conflict the US Army had fought was the Revolutionary War. Britain had been fighting around the globe almost continuously since 1793. The United States was the equivalent of a boastful farm boy from a teetotaler household strutting into a bar and loudly challenging its most experienced habitué to a drinking contest.

The causes of the war stemmed from Britain's fight with Napoleon and America's land hunger.

The Royal Navy needed men to crew its ships and did not hesitate to kidnap American sailors on the high seas. They claimed those seized were deserters, or British citizens pretending to be American. They occasionally advanced the claim that people born in America before the Declaration of Independence must still be British citizens.

Britain's naval blockade of Napoleon's Europe adversely affected the finances of the neutral trader with the largest merchant marine: the United States. American ships that traded directly with Napoleon were seized and their cargos impounded. At the same time, American grain was feeding Wellington's Army in Spain. In October of 1811, a British officer counted 200 vessels in Lisbon harbor flying the Stars and Stripes.

Napoleon responded to British efforts to choke off trade with the Continent by seizing American vessels that had first called at British ports. Thus, Americans were caught in the middle of a vast conflict.

Americans in the West had long cast covetous eyes on Canada. It had a population of only 500,000 with plenty of unsettled land. Americans were hungry for land, any land, and saw no reason why all of the continent north of Mexico should not be American. Moreover, they blamed British traders based there for arming the Indians and fomenting trouble along the western frontier. With Britain distracted fighting Napoleon, Canada defended by only 8,000 regulars and possessing a large French speaking population of uncertain loyalty, many Americans felt Canada ripe for easy conquest.

By the time *Blue Water, Scarlet Tide* takes place the war no longer made much sense. Napoleon was beaten and every American effort to take Canada had ended in failure.

Negotiations had begun in earnest in Ghent, but both sides sought last minute military advantage to improve their bargaining positions. The Peace Treaty was signed on Christmas Eve, 1814, but the news took time to cross the Atlantic. The biggest battle of the War, New Orleans, was fought three weeks after the peace had been concluded.

The Treaty of Ghent restored the border between Canada and the United States exactly as it had been before the war. The conflict was merely an annoyance to Great Britain, a sideshow of the Napoleonic Wars. Its chief results were to give the United States a national anthem and make Andrew Jackson a national hero for his victory at New Orleans. The war had a much more significant impact on Canada. It forged a national identity as Canadians united to repel invasions from the US.

Blue Water, Scarlet Tide is a work of fiction, but the portrayal of British strategic and tactical actions is accurate. General Ross and Admiral Cockburn are rendered as they were in real life. As E.L. Doctorow said, "The job of the historian is to tell what happened. The job of the novelist is to tell how it felt."

In the interest of drama I have taken considerable liberties with the American movements in the Washington campaign, but the general portrayal of American actions as inept and uncoordinated is correct. The British did almost everything right; the Americans almost everything wrong.

Barney destroyed his flotilla rather than let it fall into enemy hands. The landing of the British at Benedict was completely unopposed. There was no one like John Tracy to mount anything like a counterstroke. Daniel Parke is a creature of my imagination, and no regiment of American militia was wiped out by a combination of Congreves and musket fire. There were skirmishes before the Battle of Bladensburg, but nothing like the fight between Tracy's Baltimore Militia and Manton's men of the 4th Regiment.

The sailors and marines of Barney's flotilla fought honorably and well at the Battle of Bladensburg. Both Ross and Cockburn were most impressed by their bravery.

Congreves figured prominently in this campaign and later would achieve immortality during the attack on Baltimore, furnishing "the rockets' red glare" of the future national anthem. No one, however, thought to fix the guidance problem with the addition of fins.

The British did grant freedom to slaves who made it to their lines. More than 1,000 chose that option. This caused the Americans no end of worry and greatly disrupted the Chesapeake economy. The thing that Southerners feared most, former slaves armed with guns, came to pass when the British created the Colonial Marines and welcomed runaways into their ranks. The colonial marines fought well in a number of engagements. The British promised them land in what is now Venezuela upon the completion of their service. The British were as good as their word, and their descendants live there to this day.

The war hurt the American economy badly and played havoc with American shipping, particularly in New England. The Knights of the Golden Horse existed, but they were a Copperhead Group in the Civil War, not the War of 1812. However, there actually was a serious underground movement in New England that was exploring secession. It culminated in the Hartford Convention in December, 1814. Moderates prevailed and talk of secession ceased.

The information about ballooning in the book, fantastic as it may sound, is correct. Ballooning did not catch on in the

United States until the mid-nineteenth century, but in France it enjoyed a huge popularity that began in the late eighteenth. A shy, retiring woman on the ground, Sophie Blanchard was the consummate artiste and aeronaut when aloft. Her air shows attracted thousands of Parisians and she became a celebrity. She went aloft in a gondola of very small size and shot off fireworks and star shells before making a parachute jump. Napoleon himself was so impressed that he gave her a special decoration. She died in 1819 when the hydrogen in her balloon caught fire.

The French continued to experiment with balloons throughout the nineteenth century. In 1858, George Nadar took the first aerial photographs of Paris. *Five Weeks in a Balloon*, Jules Verne's first best seller, was inspired by balloon ascents he had witnessed in Paris. 700 people escaped the German siege of Paris in 1871 via balloons.

Balloons were featured in celebrations staged by the Prince Regent after the Battle of Waterloo. "Balloon carnivals," the forerunner of today's balloon fiestas, were staged in London in the 1820's. Charles Green, the great English balloonist, made more than 500 ascents in his lifetime. His three-day journey from London to Northern Germany in 1836 was fortified by two friends, one dog, and three cases of champagne. Charles Dickens was greatly intrigued by balloons and wrote about launches he witnessed from Vauxhall gardens. In 1862, James Glaisher, equipped with an extensive package of scientific instrumentation, reached a height of 30,000 feet and experienced the first European-recorded instance of hypoxia—oxygen deprivation.

Jo-Jo the Dog-Faced Boy, The Fireproof Lady, and Toby the Learned Pig were all actual circus performers. Crespo, Bepo, Miss Columbia, and Miss Angela are fictional characters but do represent types of performers often found in 19th century variety shows.

Thomas Pennywhistle is loosely based on a real-life 19th century Scots officer: Royal Marine Captain Thomas Inch.

Pennywhistle's breech-loading Ferguson Rifle was a real weapon, years ahead of its time. Only about 100 specimens were made, and the few left are found chiefly in museums. A Ferguson in good condition coming on the market today would cause a sensation and likely command a high six figures at auction. The best extant example is in the American History Museum of Smithsonian Institution in Washington, D.C.

For those wishing to learn more about the history of ballooning, I direct everyone to the delightful book *Falling Upwards* by Richard Holmes.

For those wanting to explore the Washington Campaign in depth, I have three recommendations. The best general history, written with a journalist's eye for important details, is *Through The Perilous Fight: Six Weeks That Saved The Nation* by Steve Vogel. *The Burning of Washington: The British Invasion of 1814* by Anthony Pitch is a more anecdotal but exceedingly readable interpretation of events by one of Washington's most experienced tour guides. *When Britain Burned the White House: the 1814 Invasion of Washington* by British TV documentary host Peter Snow is highly entertaining and written with great verve, but should be approached with caution. The author sometimes plays loose with fact in the interests of telling a good story.

The best single volume comprehensive history of the war is Donald Hickey's *The War of 1812: A Forgotten Conflict*. For an insightful, opinionated, and clever interpretation of the War from an American point of view, I recommend

Amateurs to Arms! A Military History of the War of 1812 by John Elting. For a detailed analysis of some of the subtle, non-military points of the conflict, particularly the relationship between Canada and the United States, I recommend *The Civil War of 1812: American Citizens, British Subjects, Irish Rebels, and Indian Allies* by Pulitzer Prize winner Alan Taylor.

ABOUT THE AUTHOR

JOHN M. DANIELSKI

John Danielski believes you learn best by doing and actually carried out many of the ordinary tasks Tom Pennywhistle performs in *The King's Scarlet*. He worked his way through university as a living history interpreter at historic Fort Snelling, the birthplace of Minnesota. For four summers, he played a US soldier of 1827; he wore the uniform, performed the drills, demonstrated the volley fire with other interpreters, and even ate the food. A heavy blue wool tailcoat and black shako look smart and snappy, but are pure torture to wear on a boiling summer day.

He has a practical, rather than theoretical, perspective on the weapons of the time. He has fired either replicas or originals of all of the weapons mentioned in his works with live rounds, six- and twelve-pound cannon included. The effect of a 12-pound cannonball on an old Chevy four door must be seen to be believed.

He has a number of marginally useful University degrees, including a magna cum laude degree in history from the

University of Minnesota. He is a Phi Beta Kappa and holds a black belt in Tae-Kwon-do. He has taught history at both the secondary and university levels and also worked as a newspaper editor.

His literary mentors were C. S. Forester, Bruce Catton, and Shelby Foote.

He lives quietly in the Twin Cities suburbs with his faithful companion: Sparkle, the wonder cat.

IF YOU ENJOYED THIS BOOK
Please write a review.
This is important to the author and helps to get the
word out to others
Visit

PENMORE PRESS
www.penmorepress.com

All Penmore Press books are available directly through our website, amazon.com, Barnes and Noble and Nook, Sony Reader, Apple iTunes, Kobo books and via leading bookshops across the United States, Canada, the UK, Australia and Europe.

KING'S SCARLET

BY

JOHN DANIELSKI

Chivalry comes naturally to Royal Marine captain Thomas Pennywhistle, but in the savage Peninsular War, it's a luxury he can ill afford. Trapped behind enemy lines with vital dispatches for Lord Wellington, Pennywhistle violates orders when he saves a beautiful stranger, setting off a sequence of events that jeopardize his mission. The French launch a massive manhunt to capture him. His Spanish allies prove less than reliable. The woman he rescued has an agenda of her own that might help him along, if it doesn't get them all killed.

A time will come when, outmaneuvered, captured, and stripped of everything, he must stand alone before his enemies. But Pennywhistle is a hard man to kill and too bloody obstinate to concede defeat.

PENMORE PRESS
www.penmorepress.com

The Lockwoods

of Clonakilty

by

Mark Bois

Lieutenant James Lockwood of the Inniskilling Regiment has returned to family, home and hearth after being wounded, almost fatally, at the Battle of Waterloo, where his regiment was decisive in securing Wellington's victory and bringing the Napoleonic Wars to an end. But home is not the refuge and haven he hoped to find. Irish uprisings polarize the citizens, and violence against English landholders – including James' father and brother – is bringing down wrath and retribution from England. More than one member of the household sympathizes with the desire for Irish independence, and Cassie, the Lockwood's spirited daughter, plays an active part in the rebellion.

Estranged from his English family for the "crime" of marrying a Irish Catholic woman, James Lockwood must take difficult and desperate steps to preserve his family. If his injuries don't kill him, or his addiction to laudanum, he just might live long enough to confront his nemesis. For Captain Charles Barr, maddened by syphilis and no longer restrained by the bounds of honor, sets out to utterly destroy the Lockwood family, from James' patriarchal father to the youngest child, and nothing but death with stop him – his own, or James Lockwood's.

PENMORE PRESS
www.penmorepress.com

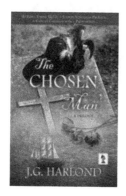

The Chosen Man

by

J. G Harlond

From the bulb of a rare flower bloom ambition and scandal

Rome, 1635: As Flanders braces for another long year of war, a Spanish count presents the Vatican with a means of disrupting the Dutch rebels' booming economy. His plan is brilliant. They just need the right man to implement it.

They choose Ludovico da Portovenere, a charismatic spice and silk merchant. Intrigued by the Vatican's proposal—and hungry for profit—Ludo sets off for Amsterdam to sow greed and venture capitalism for a disastrous harvest, hampered by a timid English priest sent from Rome, accompanied by a quick-witted young admirer he will use as a spy, and bothered by the memory of the beautiful young lady he refused to take with him.

Set in a world of international politics and domestic intrigue, *The Chosen Man* spins an engrossing tale about the Dutch financial scandal known as tulip mania—and how decisions made in high places can have terrible repercussions on innocent lives.

PENMORE PRESS
www.penmorepress.com

Fortune's Whelp
by
Benerson Little

Privateer, Swordsman, and Rake:

Set in the 17th century during the heyday of privateering and the decline of buccaneering, *Fortune's Whelp* is a brash, swords-out sea-going adventure. Scotsman Edward MacNaughton, a former privateer captain, twice accused and acquitted of piracy and currently seeking a commission, is ensnared in the intrigue associated with the attempt to assassinate King William III in 1696. Who plots to kill the king, who will rise in rebellion—and which of three women in his life, the dangerous smuggler, the wealthy widow with a dark past, or the former lover seeking independence—might kill to further political ends? Variously wooing and defying Fortune, Captain MacNaughton approaches life in the same way he wields a sword or commands a fighting ship: with the heart of a lion and the craft of a fox.

PENMORE PRESS
www.penmorepress.com

Penmore Press

Challenging, Intriguing, Adventurous, Historical and Imaginative

www.penmorepress.com

CPSIA information can be obtained
at www.ICGtesting.com
Printed in the USA
BVHW01s0220030218
506823BV00001B/100/P